ZERO™ **Vol.4** —
"Who by Fire"

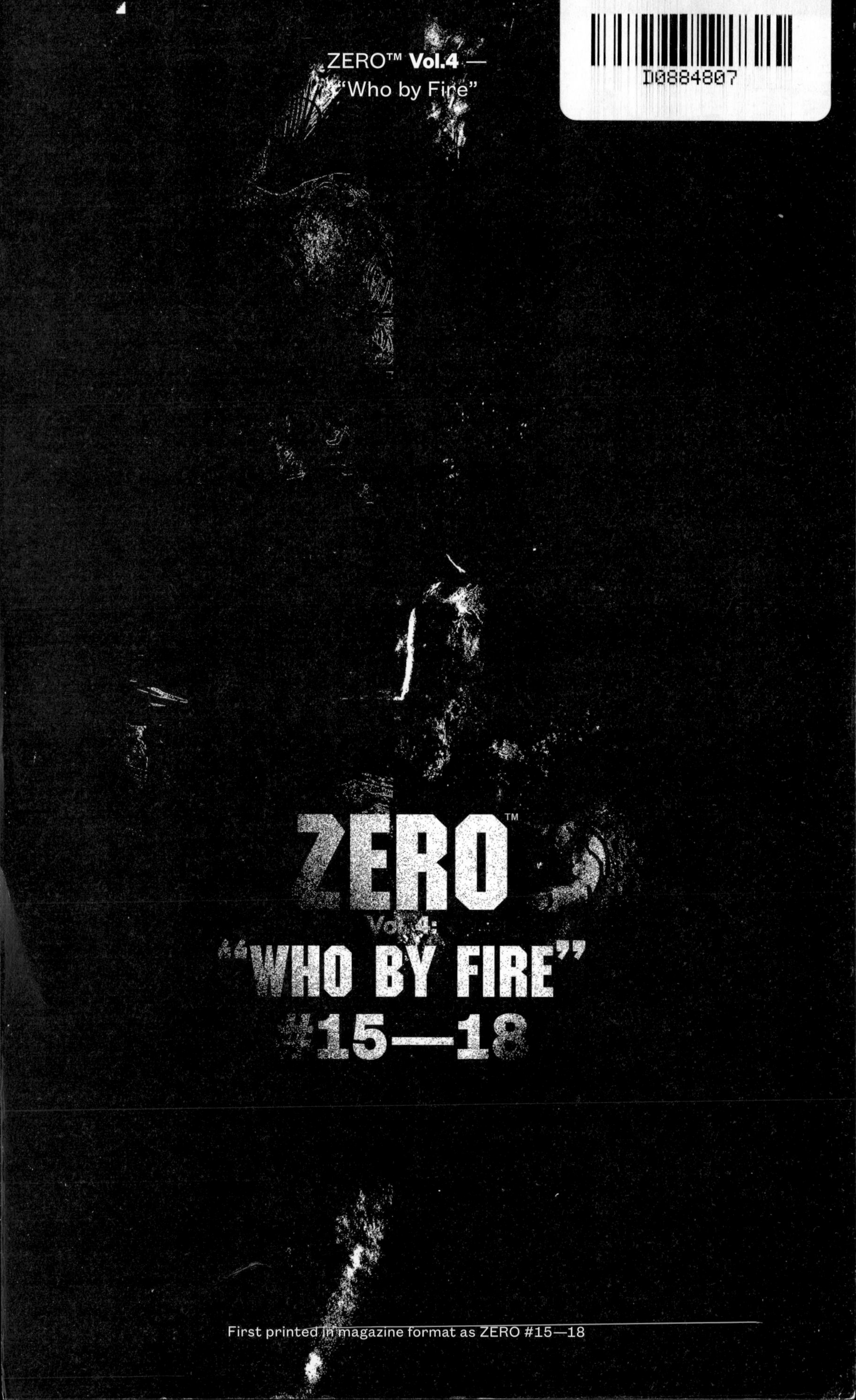

ZERO™

Vol. 4:

"WHO BY FIRE"

#15—18

First printed in magazine format as ZERO #15—18

ZERO™

Vol. 4: "WHO BY FIRE"

#15—18

Written by
Ales KOT

Illustrated by
Ian BERTRAM
Stathis TSEMBERLIDIS
Robert SAMMELIN
Tula LOTAY

Colored by
Jordie BELLAIRE

Lettered by
Clayton COWLES

Designed by
Tom MULLER

Collection designed by
Tom MULLER

Original cover design, graphics and colors
by Tom Muller, with Ian Bertram,
Stathis Tsemberlidis, Robert Sammelin,
Tula Lotay, and Jeff Lemire.

Image Comics, Inc.

Robert Kirkman	Chief Operating Officer
Erik Larsen	Chief Financial Officer
Todd McFarlane	President
Marc Silvestri	Chief Executive Officer
Jim Valentino	Vice-President
Eric Stephenson	Publisher
Corey Murphy	Director of Sales
Jeremy Sullivan	Director of Digital Sales
Kat Salazar	Director of PR & Marketing
Emily Miller	Director of Operations
Branwyn Bigglestone	Senior Accounts Manager
Sarah Mello	Accounts Manager
Drew Gill	Art Director
Jonathan Chan	Production Manager
Meredith Wallace	Print Mananager
Randy Okamura	Marketing Production Designer
David Brothers	Branding Manager
Ally Power	Content Manager
Addison Duke	Production Artist
Vincent Kukua	Production Artist
Sasha Head	Production Artist
Tricia Ramos	Production Artist
Emilio Bautista	Sales Assistant
Jessica Ambriz	Administrative Assistant

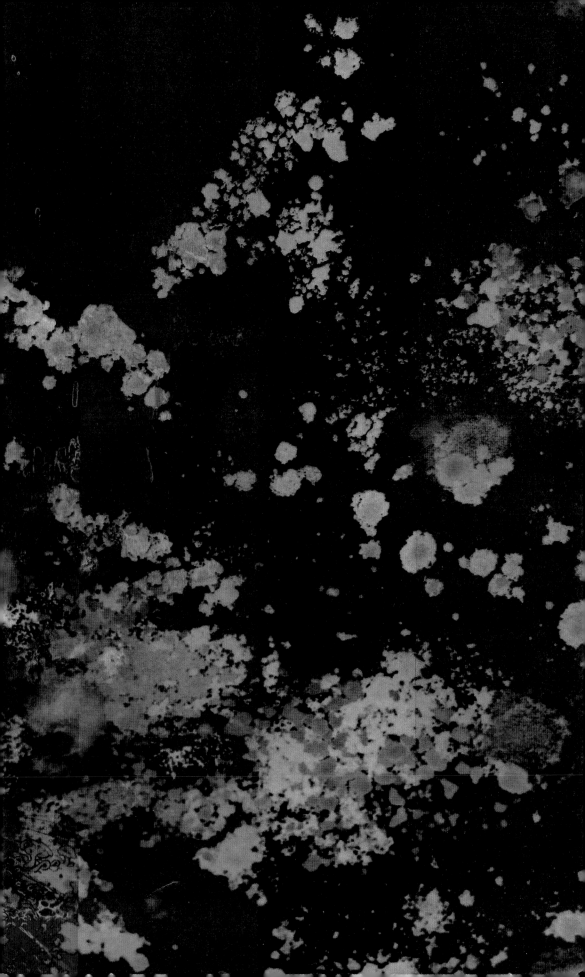

CHAPTER 15

WHERE FLESH CIRCULATES

Illustrated by Ian Bertram

GINSBERG **NOVA** WOULD NEVER DIE BUT THEN
AGAIN WHAT IS DEATH TO A MULTIVERSE?
A SHADOW TEMPORARING OFF THE WALL.
WHO IS EDWARD ZER

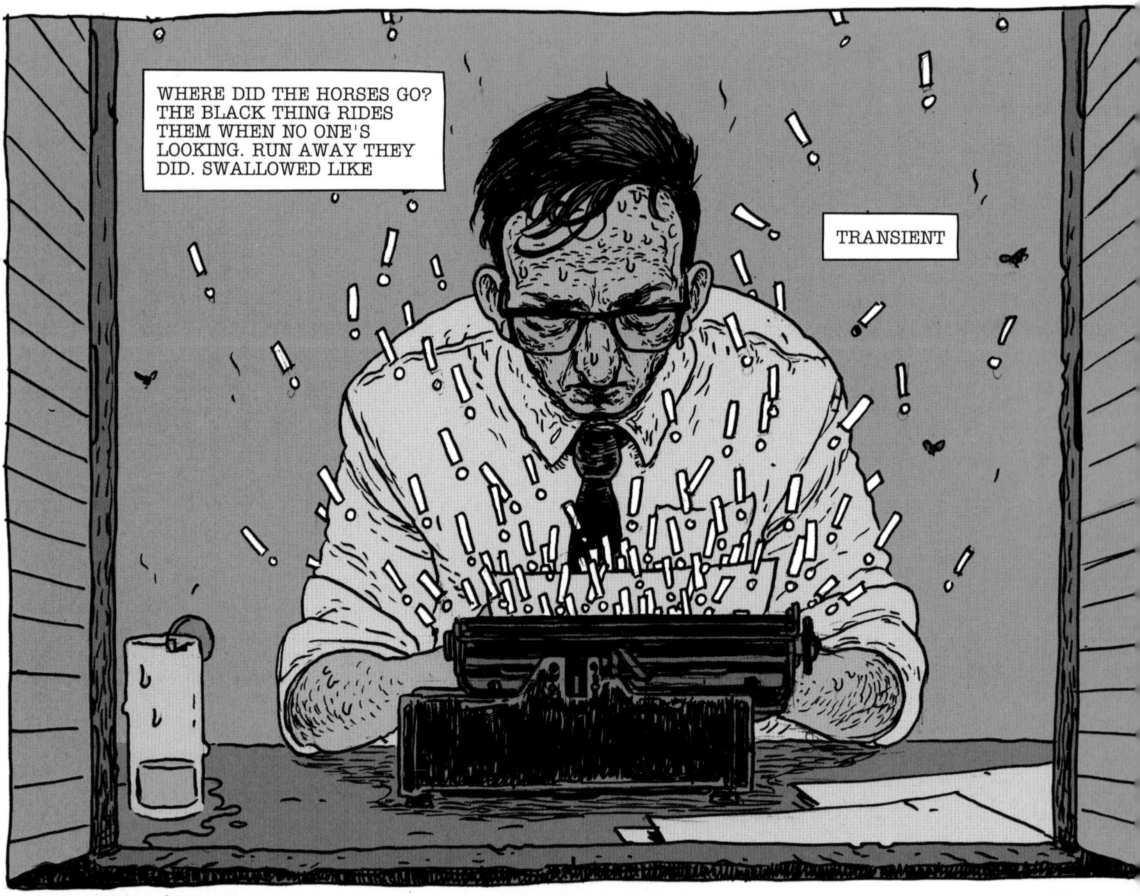
WHERE DID THE HORSES GO? THE BLACK THING RIDES THEM WHEN NO ONE'S LOOKING. RUN AWAY THEY DID. SWALLOWED LIKE
TRANSIENT

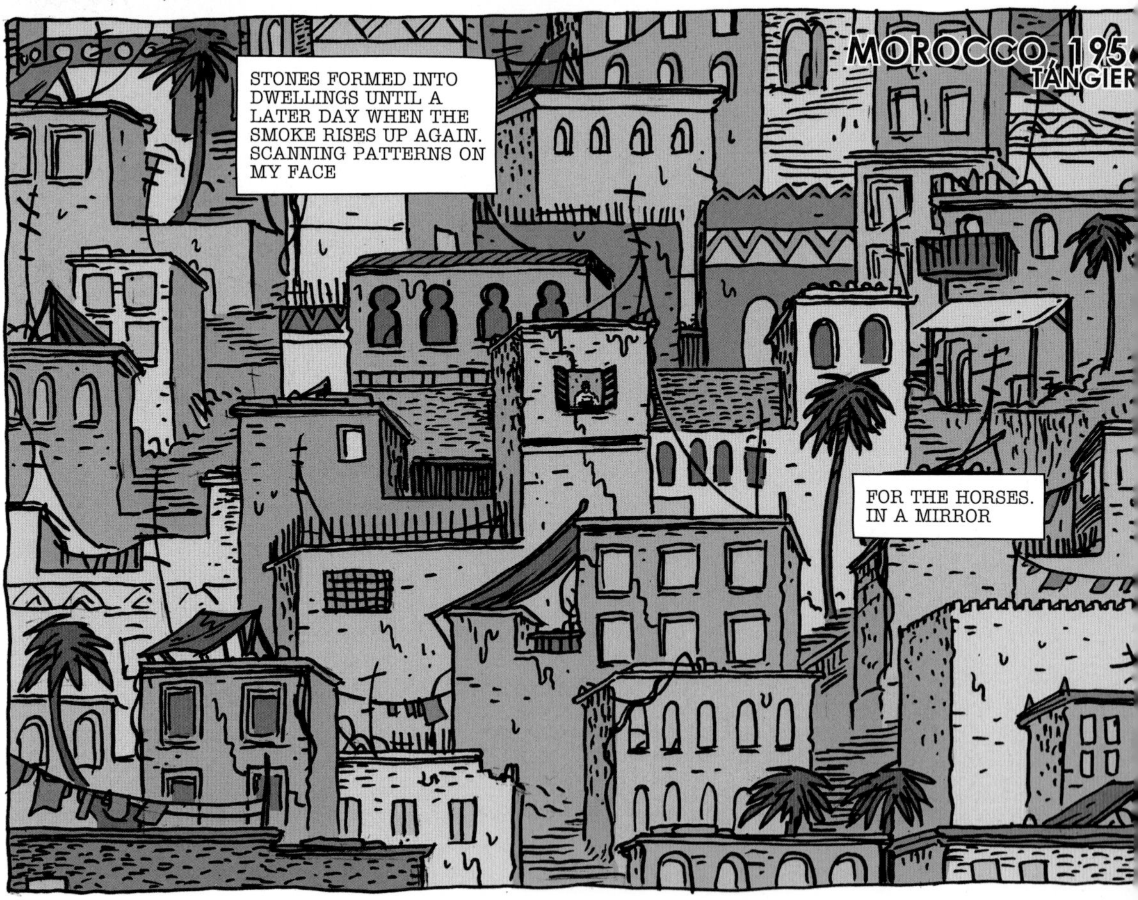
MOROCCO, 195
TANGIER
STONES FORMED INTO DWELLINGS UNTIL A LATER DAY WHEN THE SMOKE RISES UP AGAIN. SCANNING PATTERNS ON MY FACE
FOR THE HORSES. IN A MIRROR

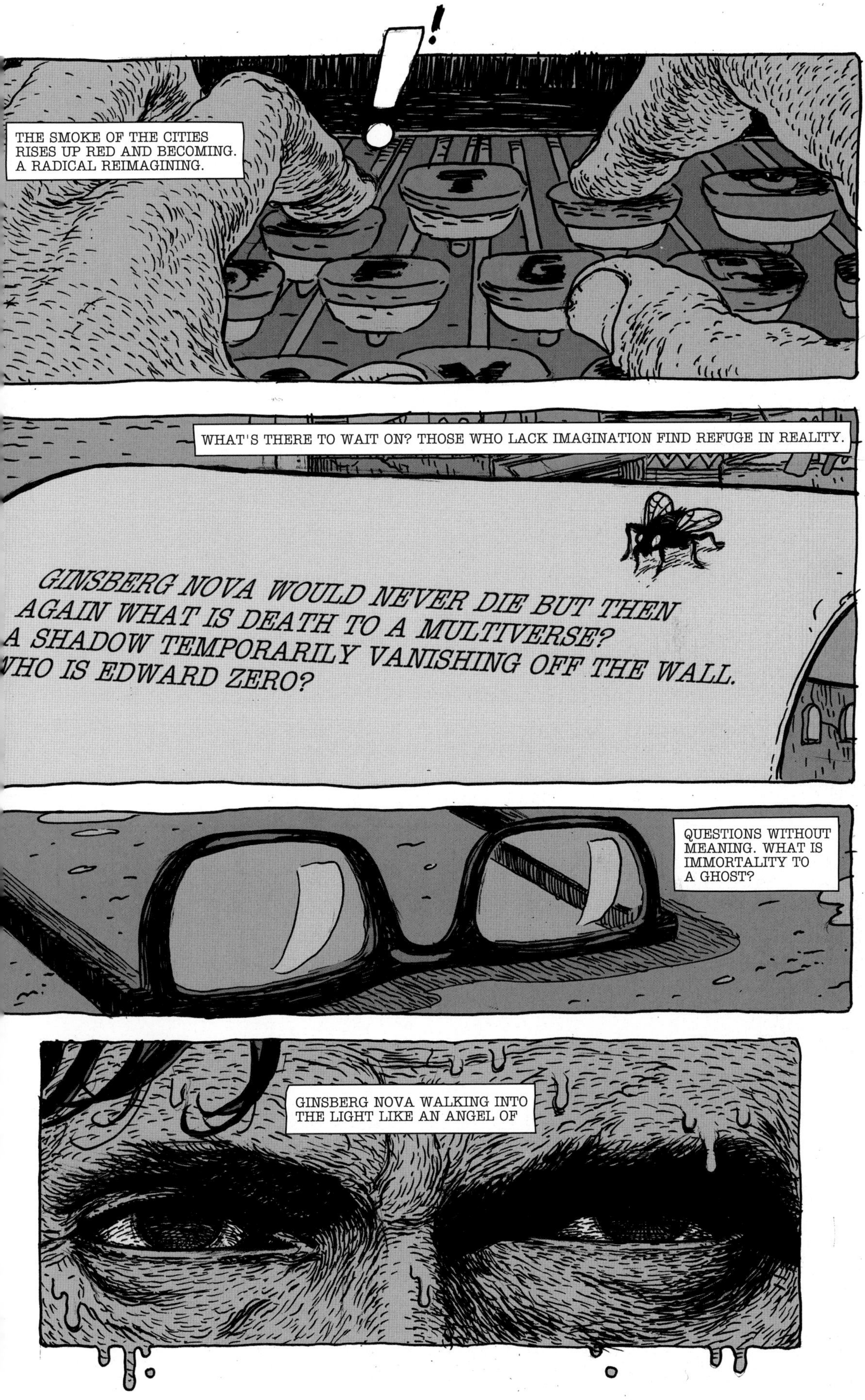
!
!
THE SMOKE OF THE CITIES RISES UP RED AND BECOMING. A RADICAL REIMAGINING.
WHAT'S THERE TO WAIT ON? THOSE WHO LACK IMAGINATION FIND REFUGE IN REALITY.
GINSBERG NOVA WOULD NEVER DIE BUT THEN AGAIN WHAT IS DEATH TO A MULTIVERSE? A SHADOW TEMPORARILY VANISHING OFF THE WALL. WHO IS EDWARD ZERO?
QUESTIONS WITHOUT MEANING. WHAT IS IMMORTALITY TO A GHOST?
GINSBERG NOVA WALKING INTO THE LIGHT LIKE AN ANGEL OF

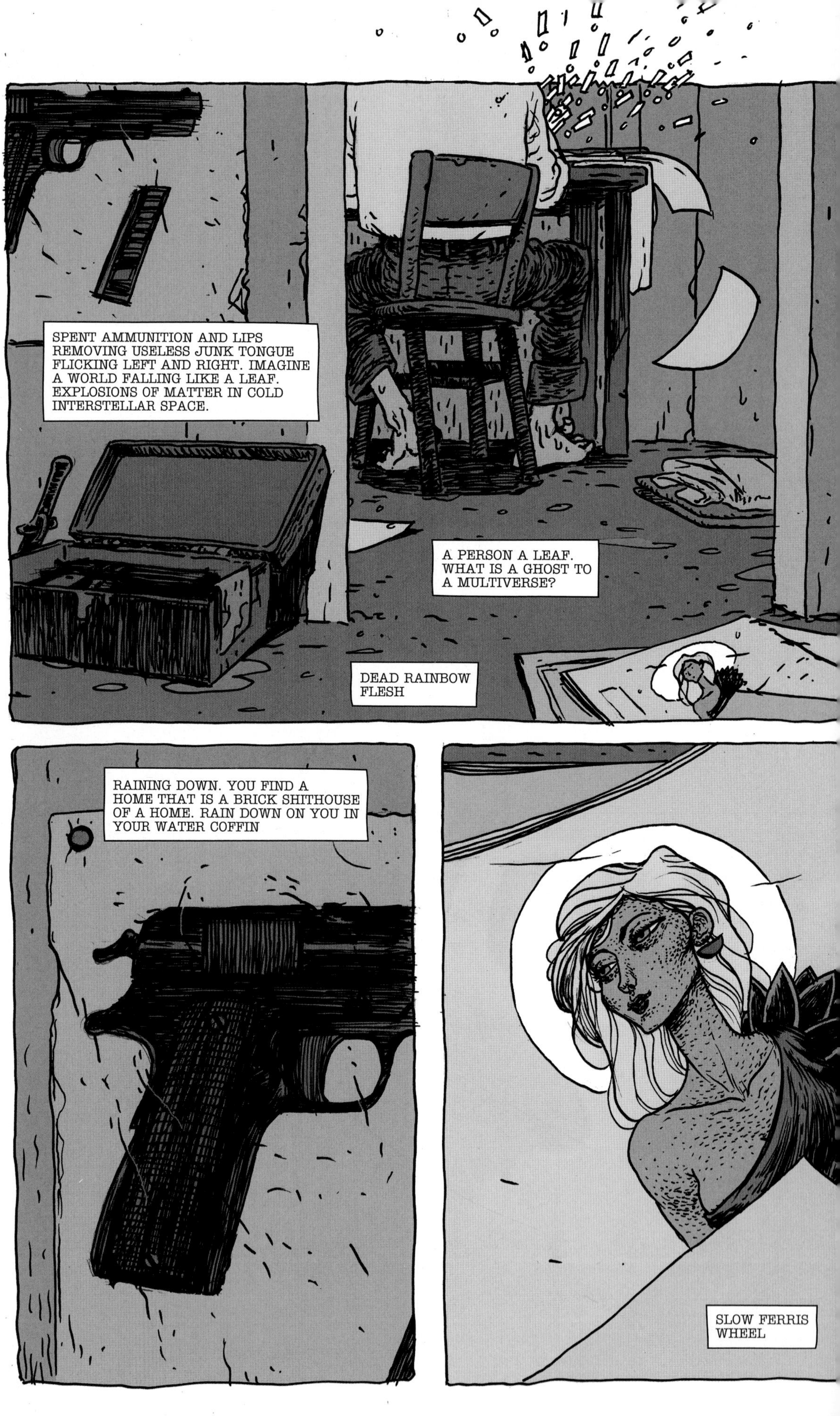

SPENT AMMUNITION AND LIPS REMOVING USELESS JUNK TONGUE FLICKING LEFT AND RIGHT. IMAGINE A WORLD FALLING LIKE A LEAF. EXPLOSIONS OF MATTER IN COLD INTERSTELLAR SPACE.
A PERSON A LEAF. WHAT IS A GHOST TO A MULTIVERSE?
DEAD RAINBOW FLESH
RAINING DOWN. YOU FIND A HOME THAT IS A BRICK SHITHOUSE OF A HOME. RAIN DOWN ON YOU IN YOUR WATER COFFIN
SLOW FERRIS WHEEL

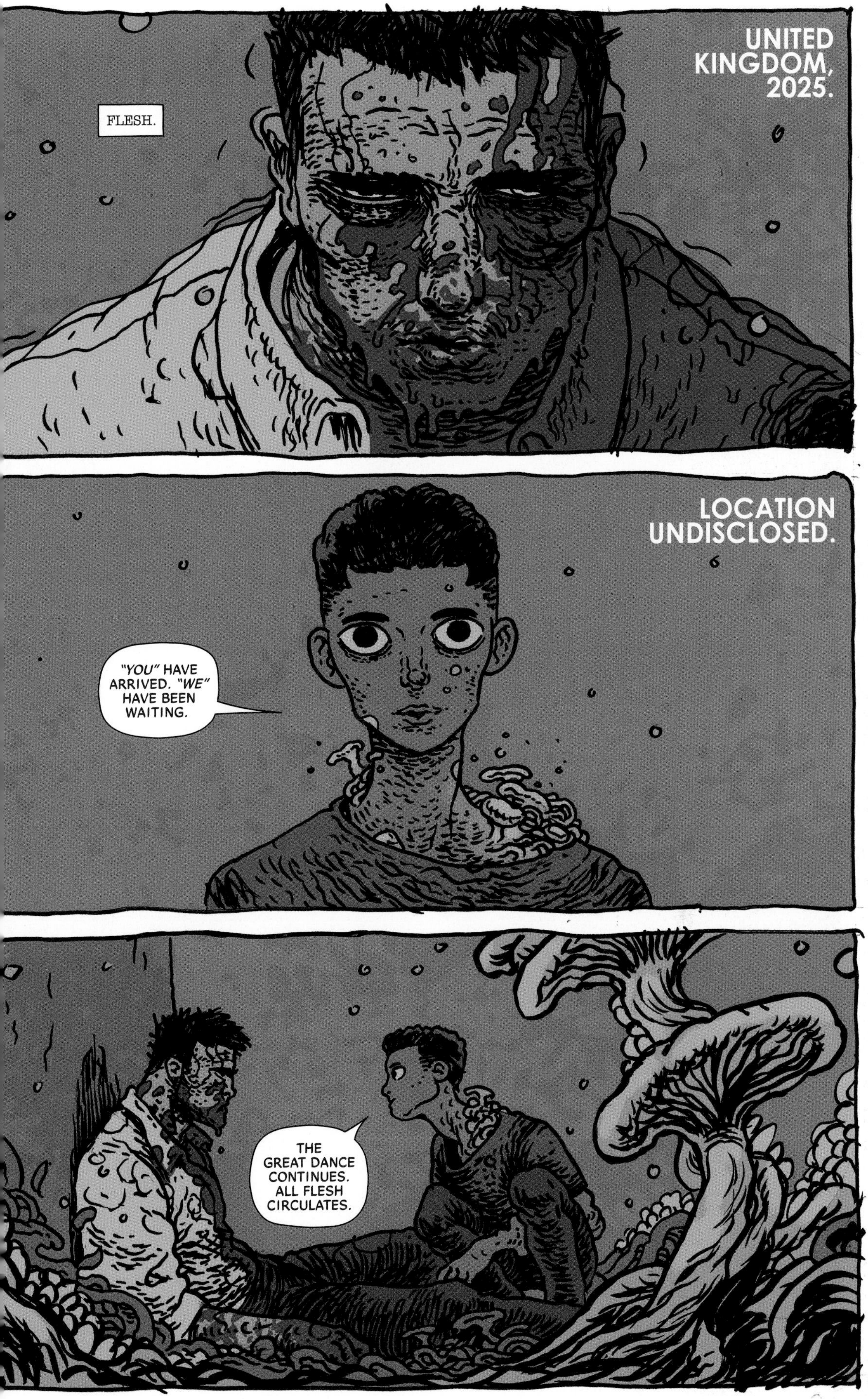
UNITED KINGDOM, 2025.
FLESH.
LOCATION UNDISCLOSED.
"YOU" HAVE ARRIVED. "WE" HAVE BEEN WAITING.
THE GREAT DANCE CONTINUES. ALL FLESH CIRCULATES.

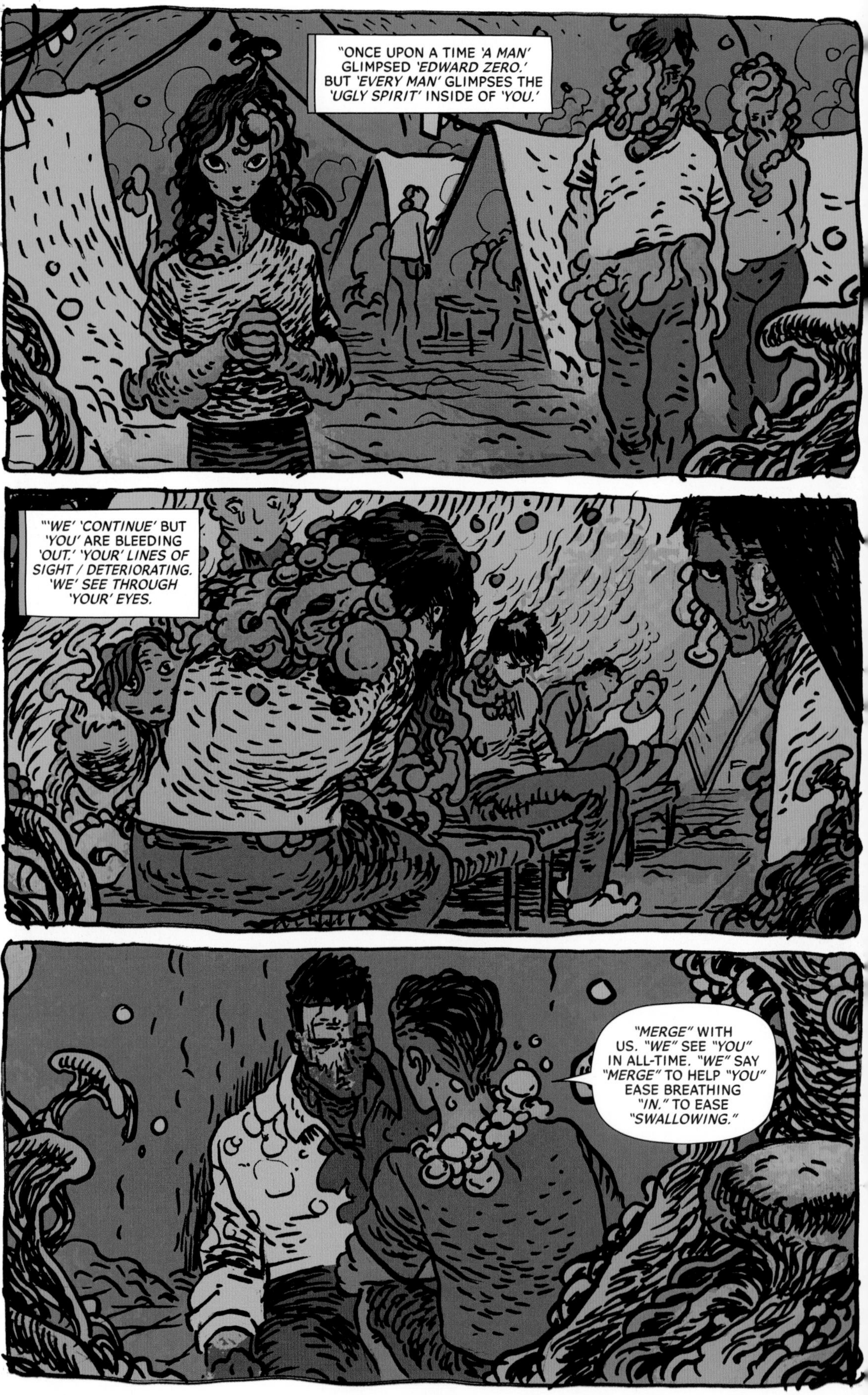
"ONCE UPON A TIME 'A MAN' GLIMPSED 'EDWARD ZERO.' BUT 'EVERY MAN' GLIMPSES THE 'UGLY SPIRIT' INSIDE OF 'YOU.'
"'WE' 'CONTINUE' BUT 'YOU' ARE BLEEDING 'OUT.' 'YOUR' LINES OF SIGHT / DETERIORATING. 'WE' SEE THROUGH 'YOUR' EYES.
"MERGE" WITH US. "WE" SEE "YOU" IN ALL-TIME. "WE" SAY "MERGE" TO HELP "YOU" EASE BREATHING "IN." TO EASE "SWALLOWING."

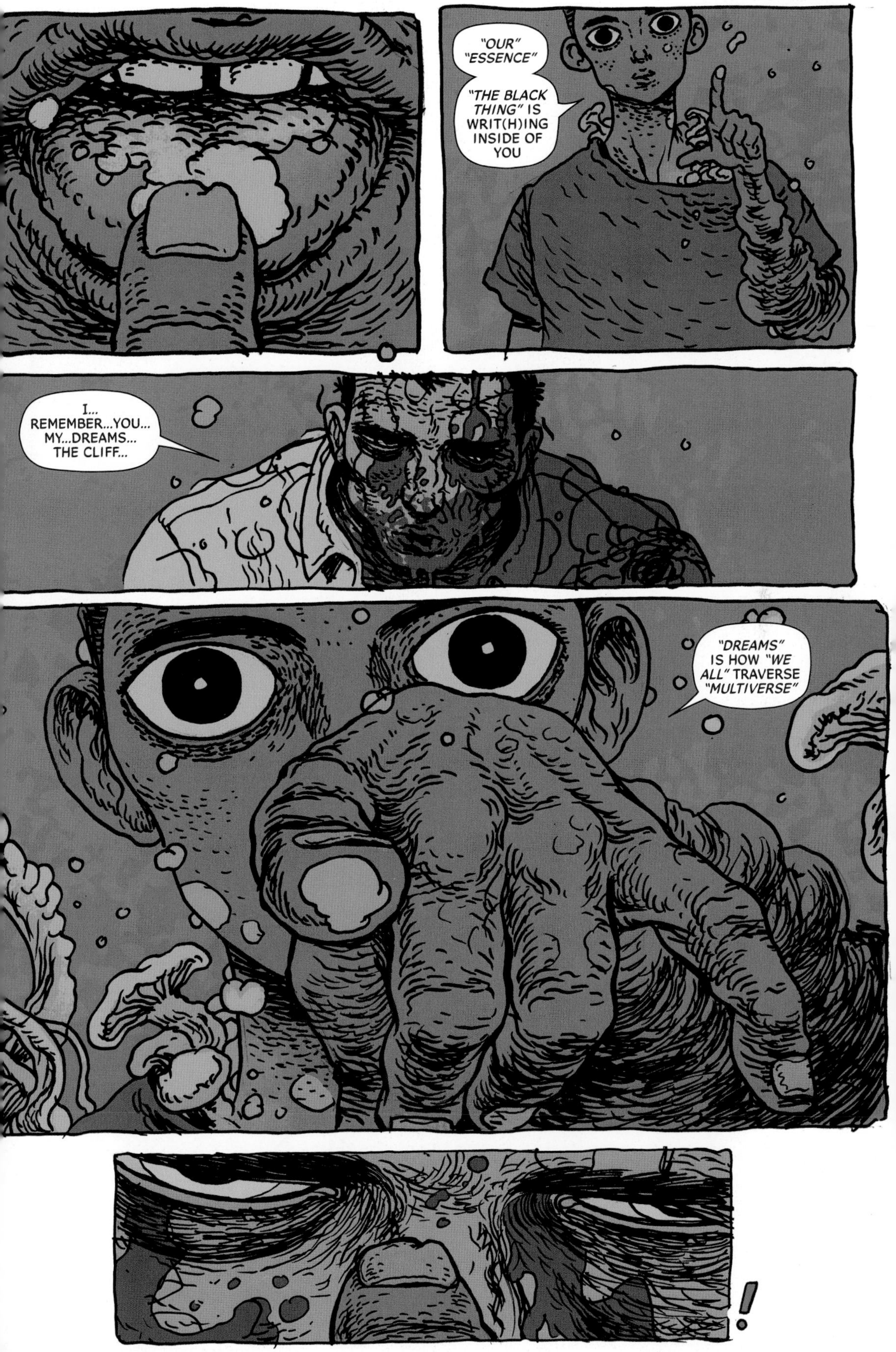
"OUR" "ESSENCE"
"THE BLACK THING" IS WRIT(H)ING INSIDE OF YOU
I... REMEMBER...YOU... MY...DREAMS... THE CLIFF...
"DREAMS" IS HOW "WE ALL" TRAVERSE "MULTIVERSE"
!

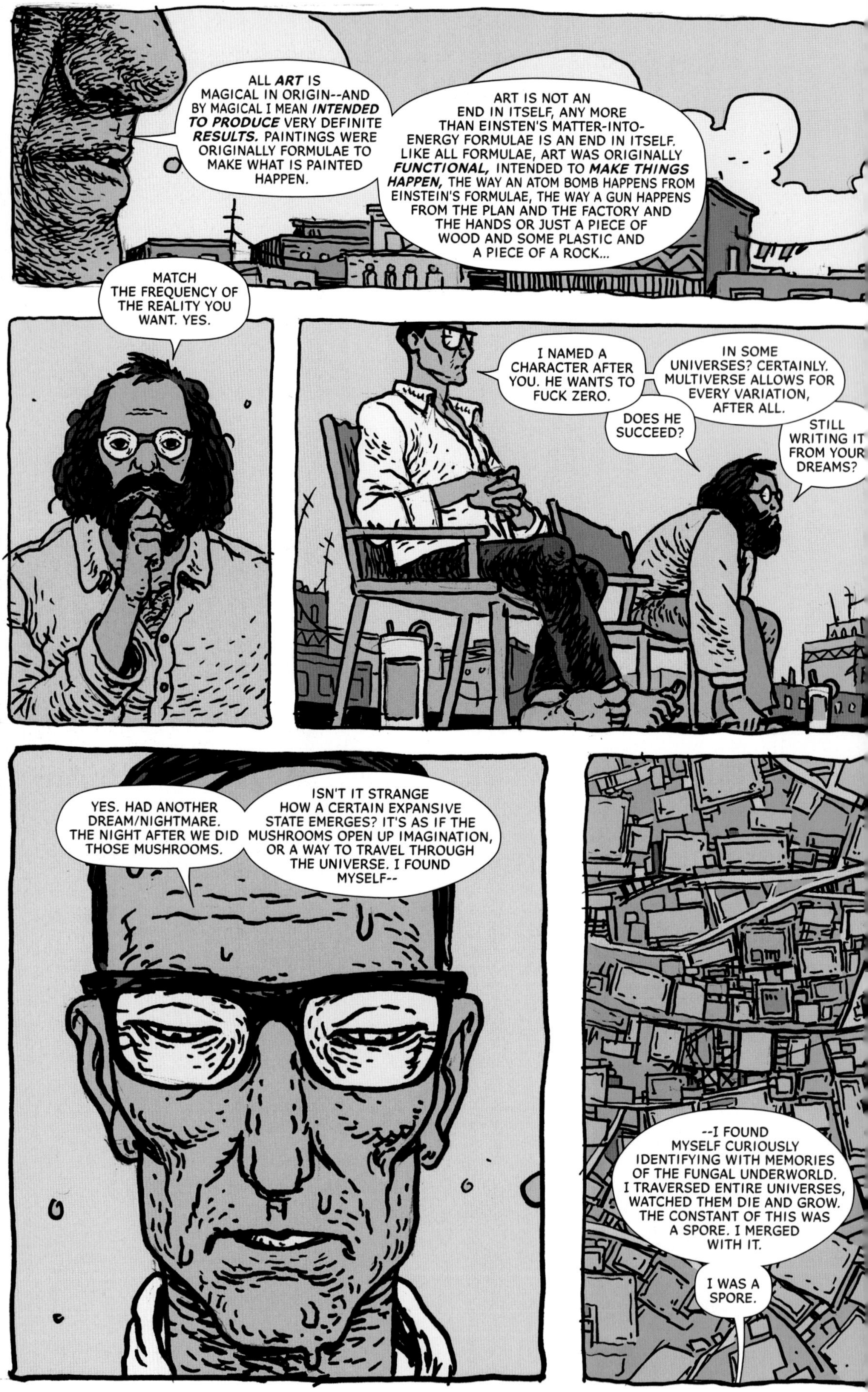
ALL ART IS MAGICAL IN ORIGIN--AND BY MAGICAL I MEAN INTENDED TO PRODUCE VERY DEFINITE RESULTS. PAINTINGS WERE ORIGINALLY FORMULAE TO MAKE WHAT IS PAINTED HAPPEN.
ART IS NOT AN END IN ITSELF, ANY MORE THAN EINSTEN'S MATTER-INTO-ENERGY FORMULAE IS AN END IN ITSELF. LIKE ALL FORMULAE, ART WAS ORIGINALLY FUNCTIONAL, INTENDED TO MAKE THINGS HAPPEN, THE WAY AN ATOM BOMB HAPPENS FROM EINSTEIN'S FORMULAE, THE WAY A GUN HAPPENS FROM THE PLAN AND THE FACTORY AND THE HANDS OR JUST A PIECE OF WOOD AND SOME PLASTIC AND A PIECE OF A ROCK...
MATCH THE FREQUENCY OF THE REALITY YOU WANT. YES.
I NAMED A CHARACTER AFTER YOU. HE WANTS TO FUCK ZERO.
DOES HE SUCCEED?
IN SOME UNIVERSES? CERTAINLY. MULTIVERSE ALLOWS FOR EVERY VARIATION, AFTER ALL.
STILL WRITING IT FROM YOUR DREAMS?
YES. HAD ANOTHER DREAM/NIGHTMARE. THE NIGHT AFTER WE DID THOSE MUSHROOMS.
ISN'T IT STRANGE HOW A CERTAIN EXPANSIVE STATE EMERGES? IT'S AS IF THE MUSHROOMS OPEN UP IMAGINATION, OR A WAY TO TRAVEL THROUGH THE UNIVERSE. I FOUND MYSELF--
--I FOUND MYSELF CURIOUSLY IDENTIFYING WITH MEMORIES OF THE FUNGAL UNDERWORLD. I TRAVERSED ENTIRE UNIVERSES, WATCHED THEM DIE AND GROW. THE CONSTANT OF THIS WAS A SPORE. I MERGED WITH IT.
I WAS A SPORE.

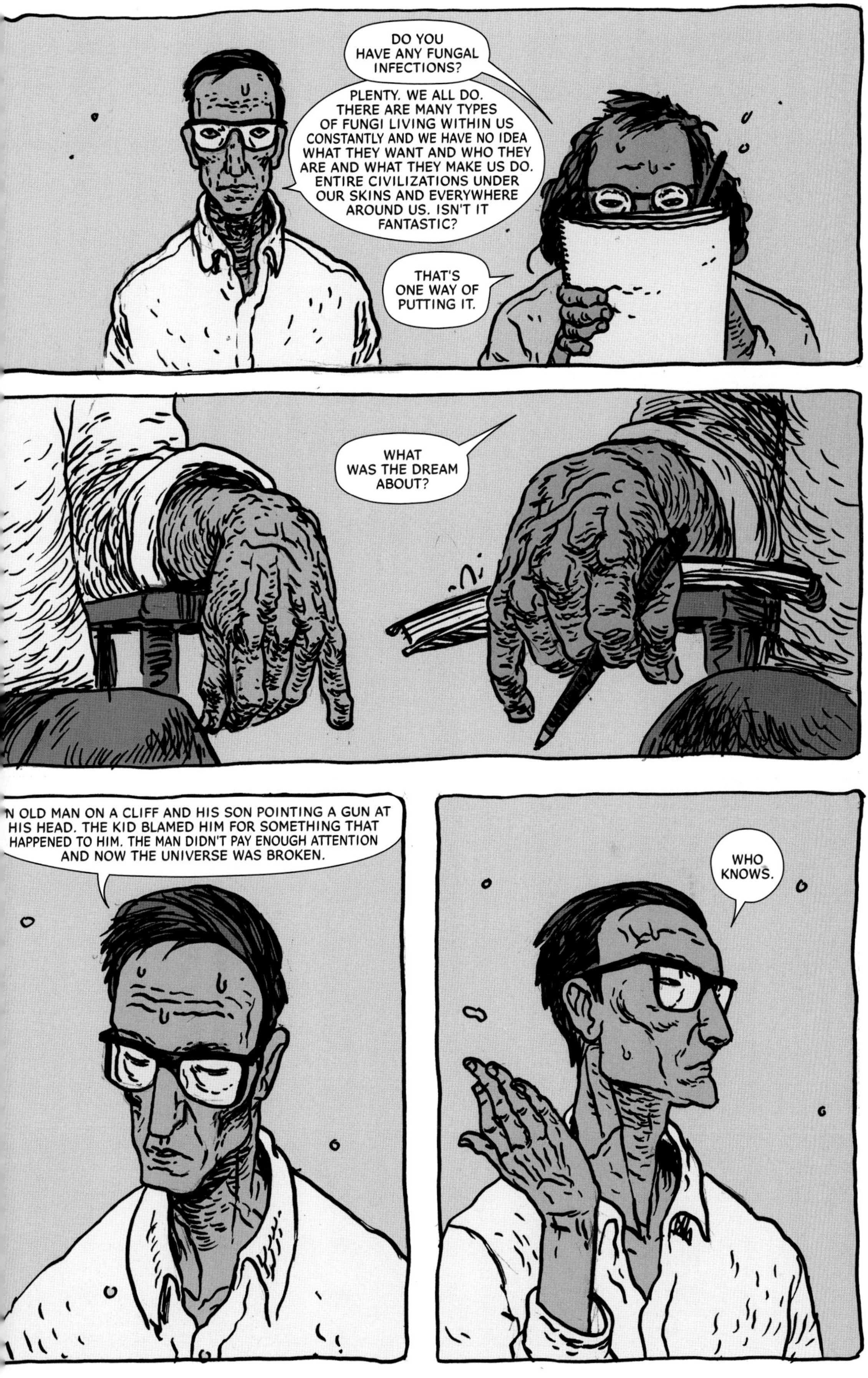
DO YOU HAVE ANY FUNGAL INFECTIONS?
PLENTY. WE ALL DO. THERE ARE MANY TYPES OF FUNGI LIVING WITHIN US CONSTANTLY AND WE HAVE NO IDEA WHAT THEY WANT AND WHO THEY ARE AND WHAT THEY MAKE US DO. ENTIRE CIVILIZATIONS UNDER OUR SKINS AND EVERYWHERE AROUND US. ISN'T IT FANTASTIC?
THAT'S ONE WAY OF PUTTING IT.
WHAT WAS THE DREAM ABOUT?
N OLD MAN ON A CLIFF AND HIS SON POINTING A GUN AT HIS HEAD. THE KID BLAMED HIM FOR SOMETHING THAT HAPPENED TO HIM. THE MAN DIDN'T PAY ENOUGH ATTENTION AND NOW THE UNIVERSE WAS BROKEN.
WHO KNOWS.

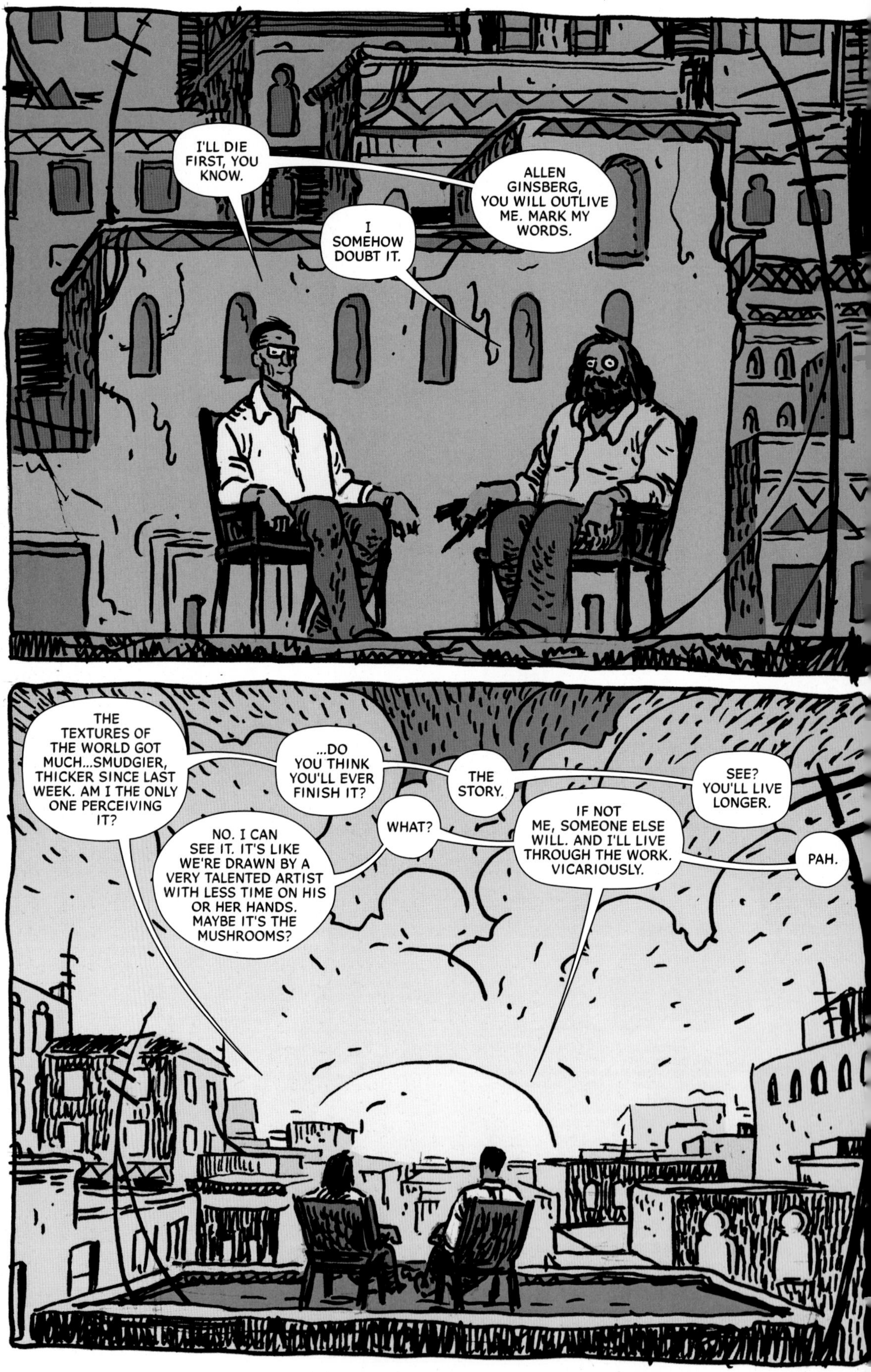

I'LL DIE FIRST, YOU KNOW.
ALLEN GINSBERG, YOU WILL OUTLIVE ME. MARK MY WORDS.
I SOMEHOW DOUBT IT.
THE TEXTURES OF THE WORLD GOT MUCH...SMUDGIER, THICKER SINCE LAST WEEK. AM I THE ONLY ONE PERCEIVING IT?
NO. I CAN SEE IT. IT'S LIKE WE'RE DRAWN BY A VERY TALENTED ARTIST WITH LESS TIME ON HIS OR HER HANDS. MAYBE IT'S THE MUSHROOMS?
...DO YOU THINK YOU'LL EVER FINISH IT?
WHAT?
THE STORY.
IF NOT ME, SOMEONE ELSE WILL. AND I'LL LIVE THROUGH THE WORK. VICARIOUSLY.
SEE? YOU'LL LIVE LONGER.
PAH.

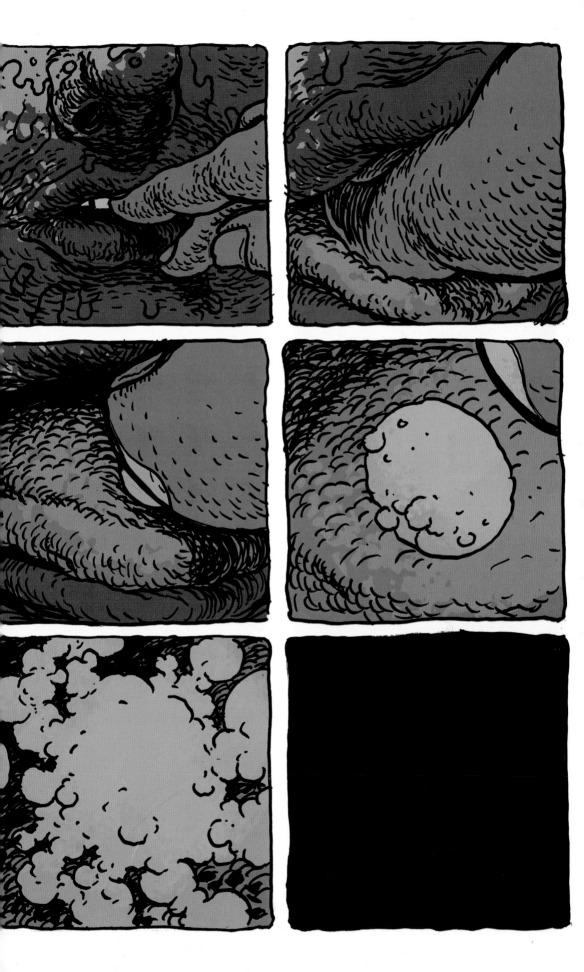

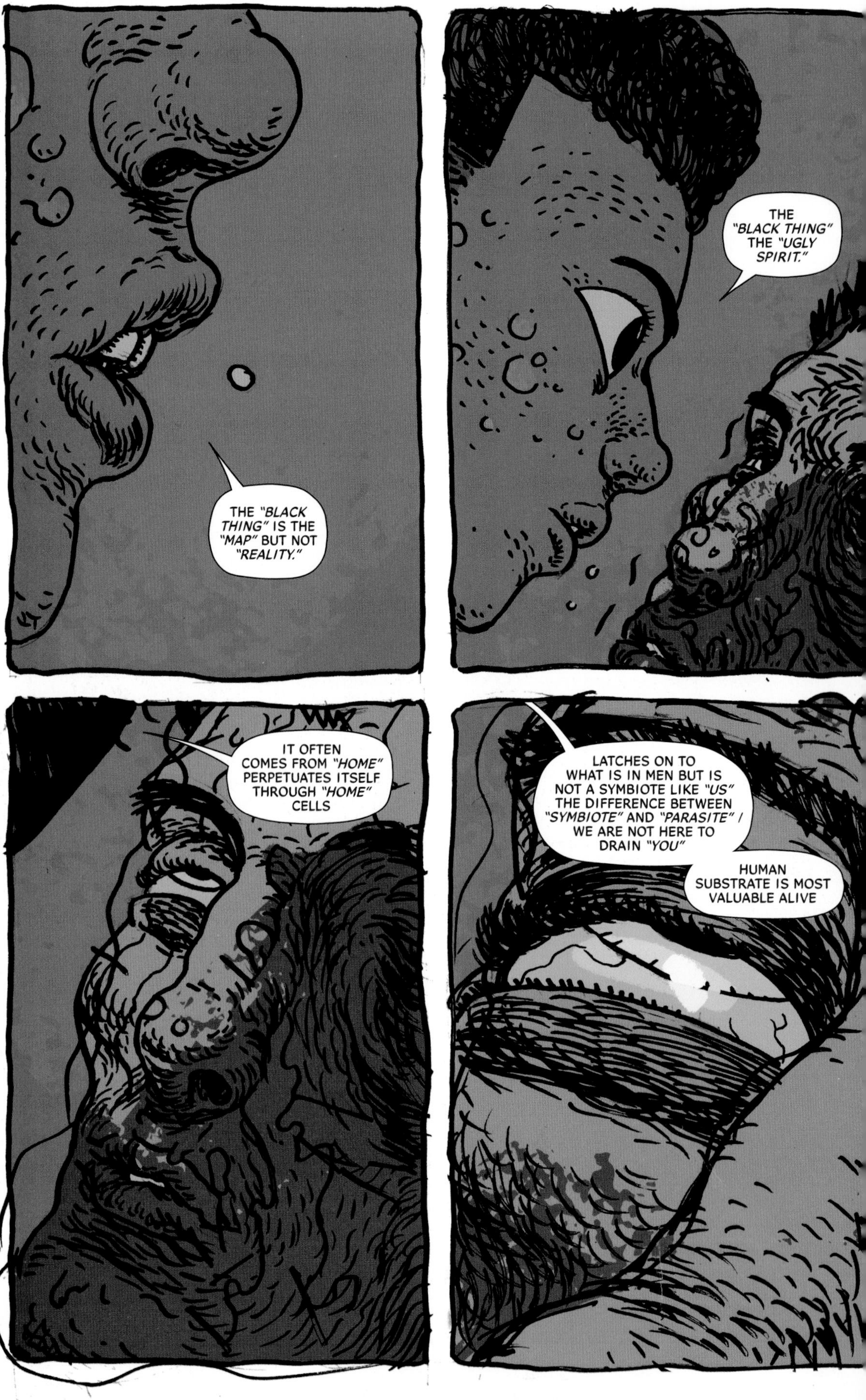
THE "BLACK THING" IS THE "MAP" BUT NOT "REALITY."
THE "BLACK THING" THE "UGLY SPIRIT."
IT OFTEN COMES FROM "HOME" PERPETUATES ITSELF THROUGH "HOME" CELLS
LATCHES ON TO WHAT IS IN MEN BUT IS NOT A SYMBIOTE LIKE "US" THE DIFFERENCE BETWEEN "SYMBIOTE" AND "PARASITE" / WE ARE NOT HERE TO DRAIN "YOU"
HUMAN SUBSTRATE IS MOST VALUABLE ALIVE

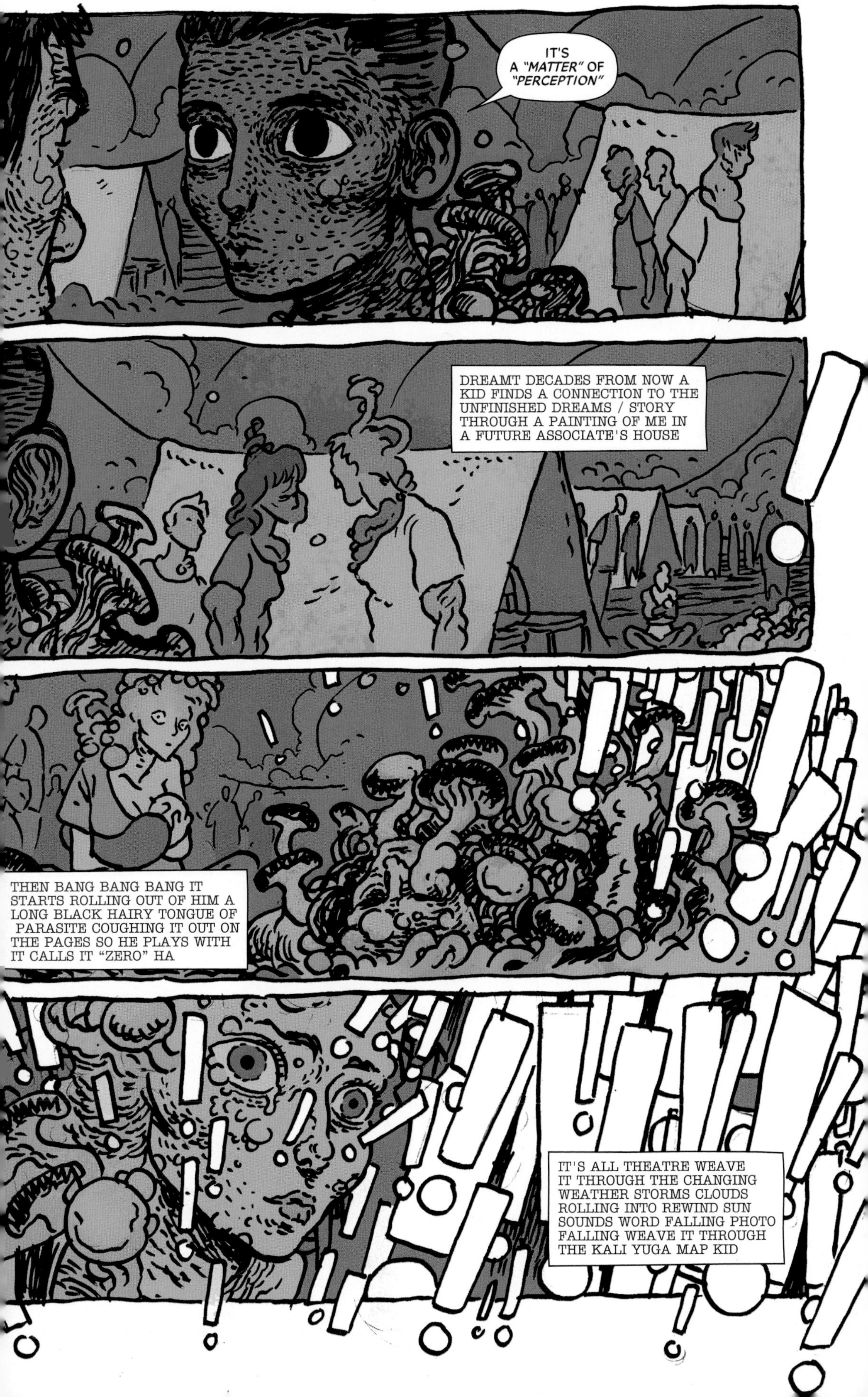
IT'S A "MATTER" OF "PERCEPTION"
DREAMT DECADES FROM NOW A KID FINDS A CONNECTION TO THE UNFINISHED DREAMS / STORY THROUGH A PAINTING OF ME IN A FUTURE ASSOCIATE'S HOUSE
THEN BANG BANG BANG IT STARTS ROLLING OUT OF HIM A LONG BLACK HAIRY TONGUE OF PARASITE COUGHING IT OUT ON THE PAGES SO HE PLAYS WITH IT CALLS IT "ZERO" HA
IT'S ALL THEATRE WEAVE IT THROUGH THE CHANGING WEATHER STORMS CLOUDS ROLLING INTO REWIND SUN SOUNDS WORD FALLING PHOTO FALLING WEAVE IT THROUGH THE KALI YUGA MAP KID

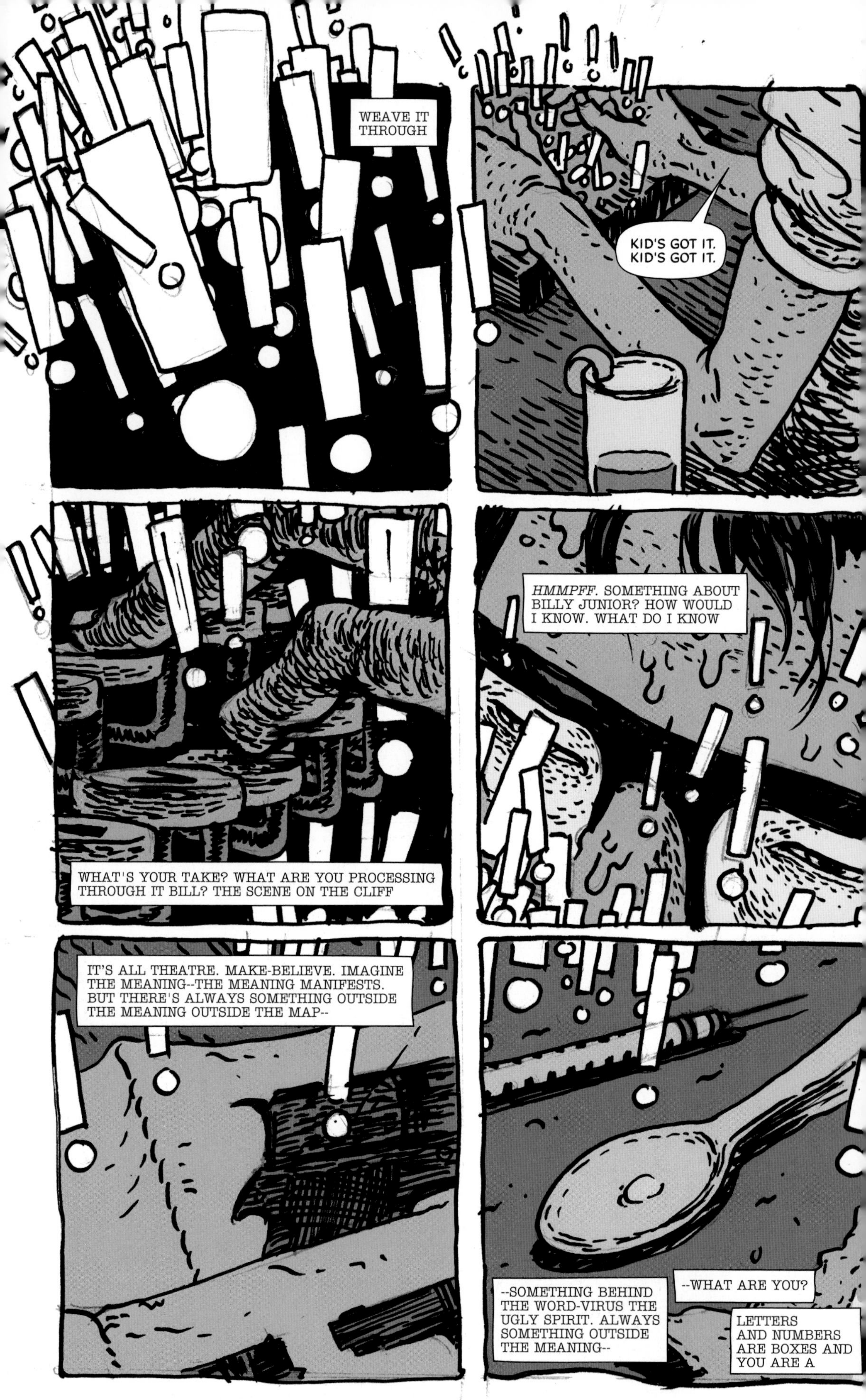
WEAVE IT THROUGH
KID'S GOT IT. KID'S GOT IT.
WHAT'S YOUR TAKE? WHAT ARE YOU PROCESSING THROUGH IT BILL? THE SCENE ON THE CLIFF
HMMPFF. SOMETHING ABOUT BILLY JUNIOR? HOW WOULD I KNOW. WHAT DO I KNOW
IT'S ALL THEATRE. MAKE-BELIEVE. IMAGINE THE MEANING--THE MEANING MANIFESTS. BUT THERE'S ALWAYS SOMETHING OUTSIDE THE MEANING OUTSIDE THE MAP--
--SOMETHING BEHIND THE WORD-VIRUS THE UGLY SPIRIT. ALWAYS SOMETHING OUTSIDE THE MEANING--
--WHAT ARE YOU?
LETTERS AND NUMBERS ARE BOXES AND YOU ARE A

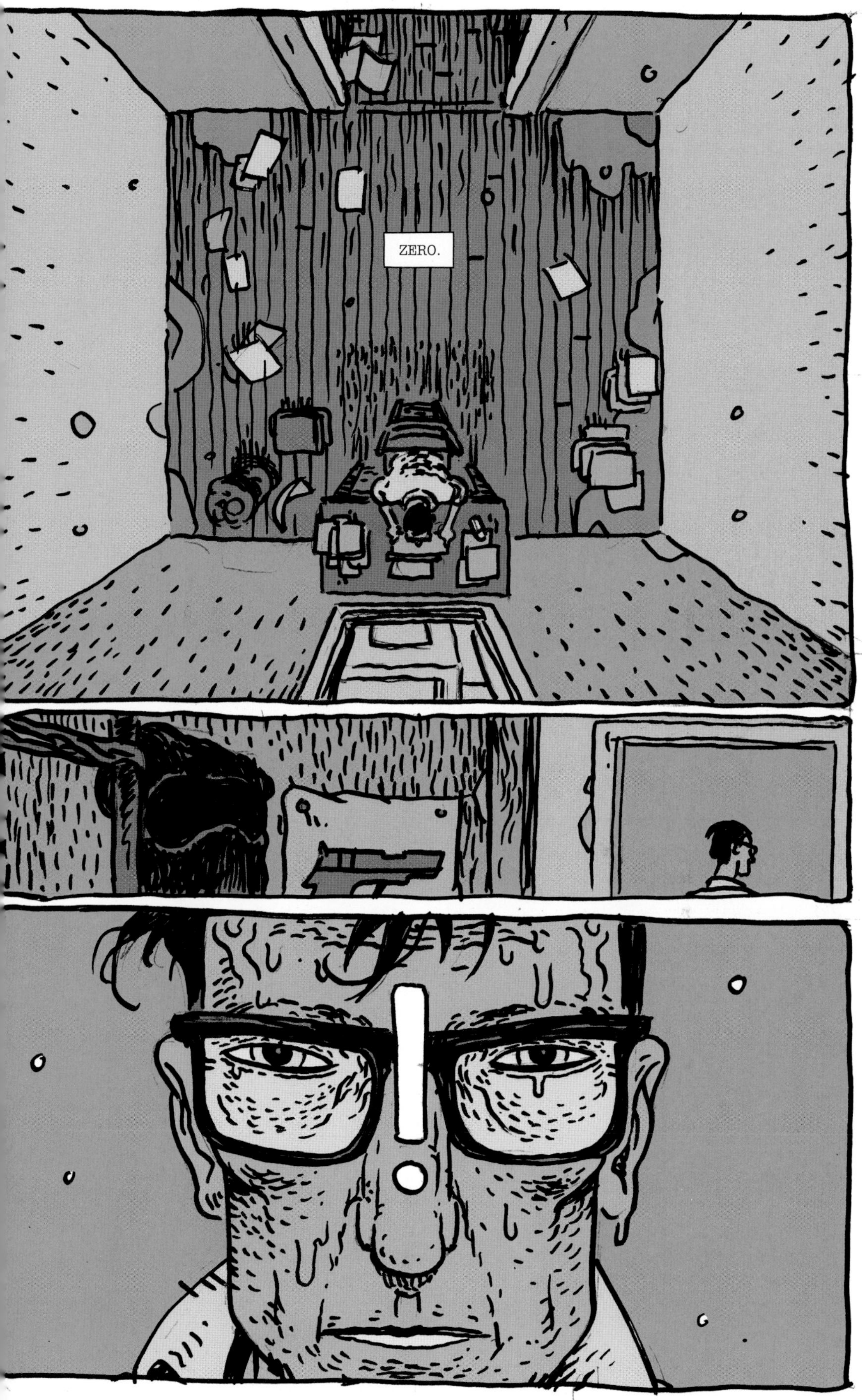
ZERO.

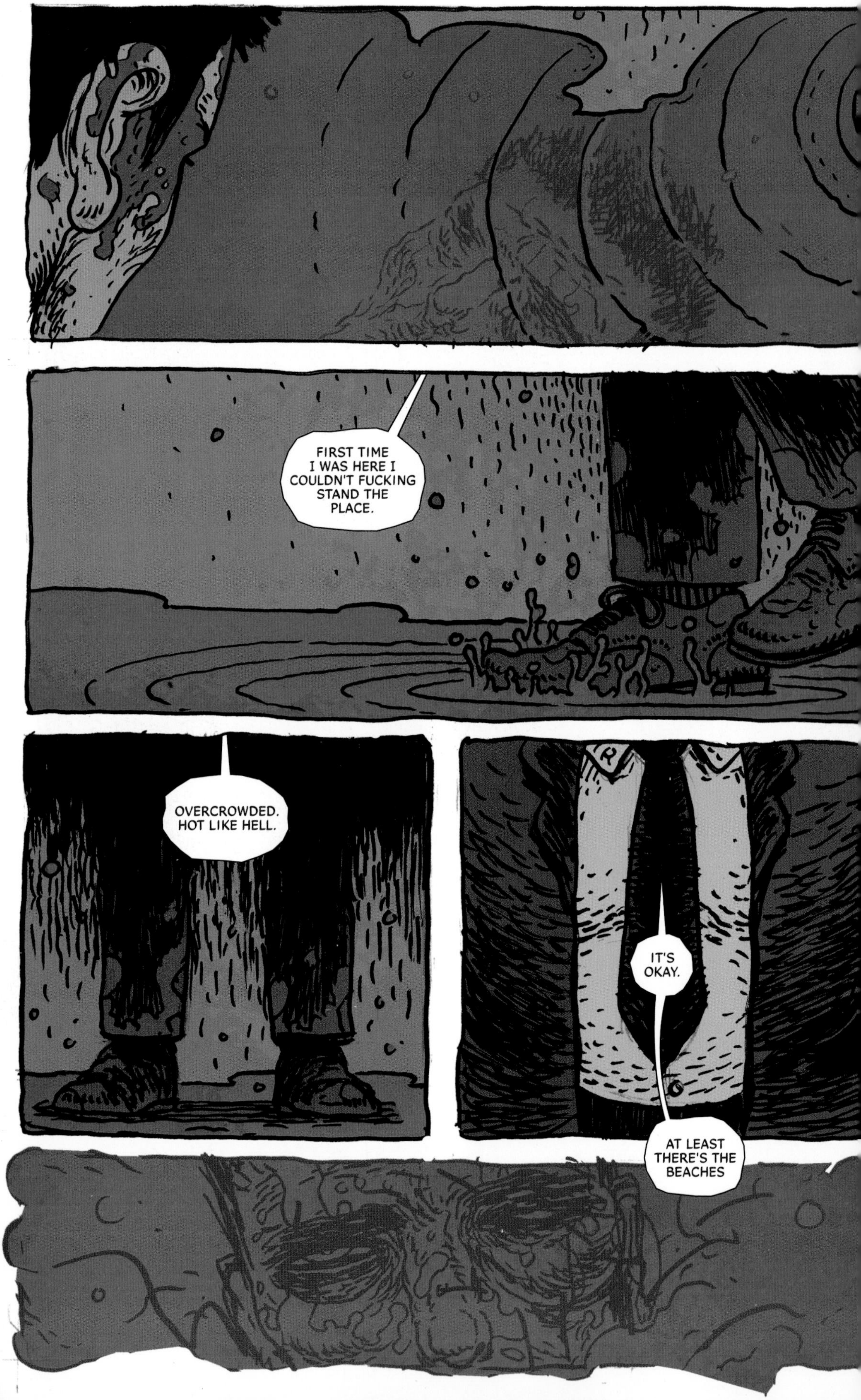
FIRST TIME I WAS HERE I COULDN'T FUCKING STAND THE PLACE.
OVERCROWDED. HOT LIKE HELL.
IT'S OKAY.
AT LEAST THERE'S THE BEACHES

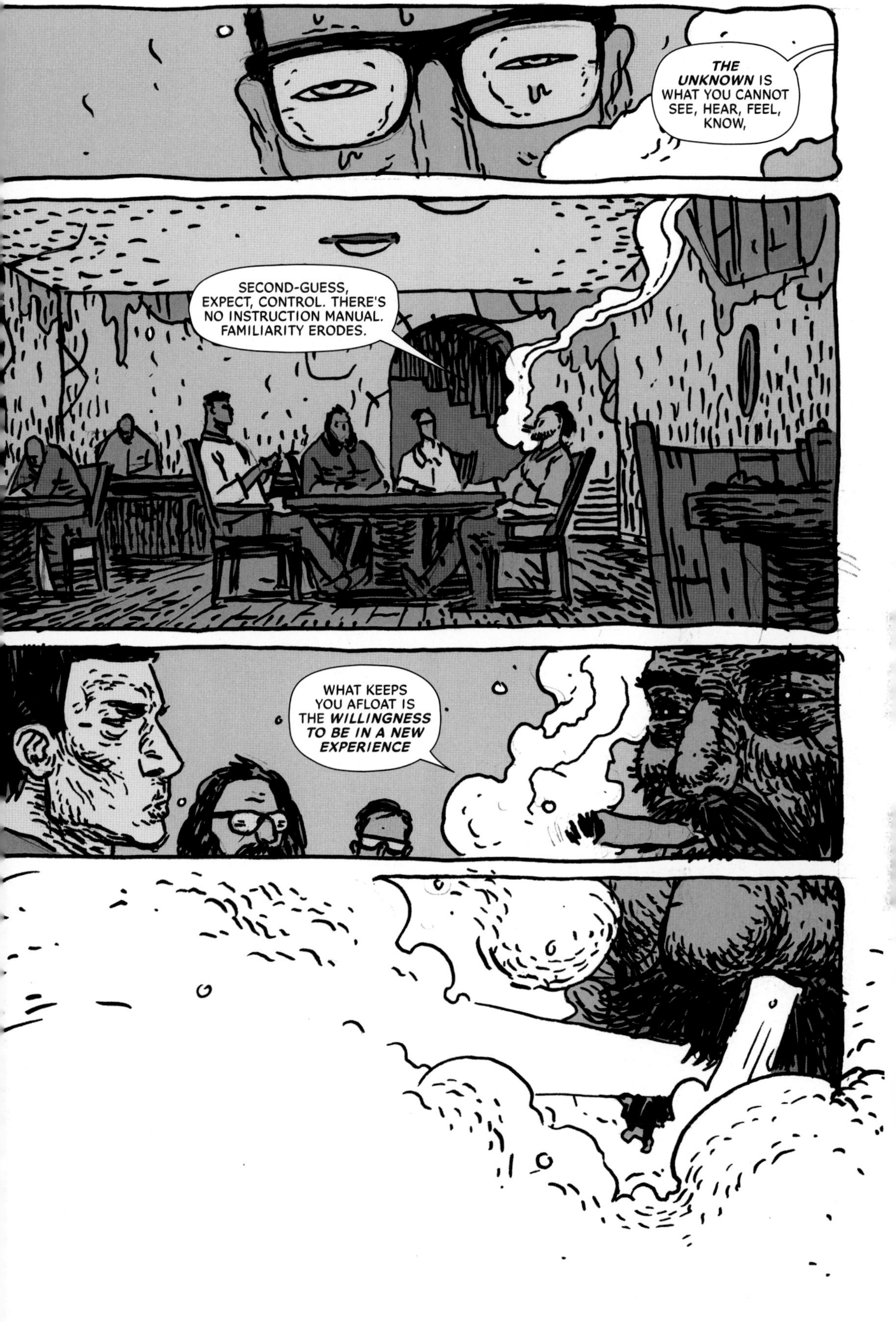
THE UNKNOWN IS WHAT YOU CANNOT SEE, HEAR, FEEL, KNOW,
SECOND-GUESS, EXPECT, CONTROL. THERE'S NO INSTRUCTION MANUAL. FAMILIARITY ERODES.
WHAT KEEPS YOU AFLOAT IS THE WILLINGNESS TO BE IN A NEW EXPERIENCE

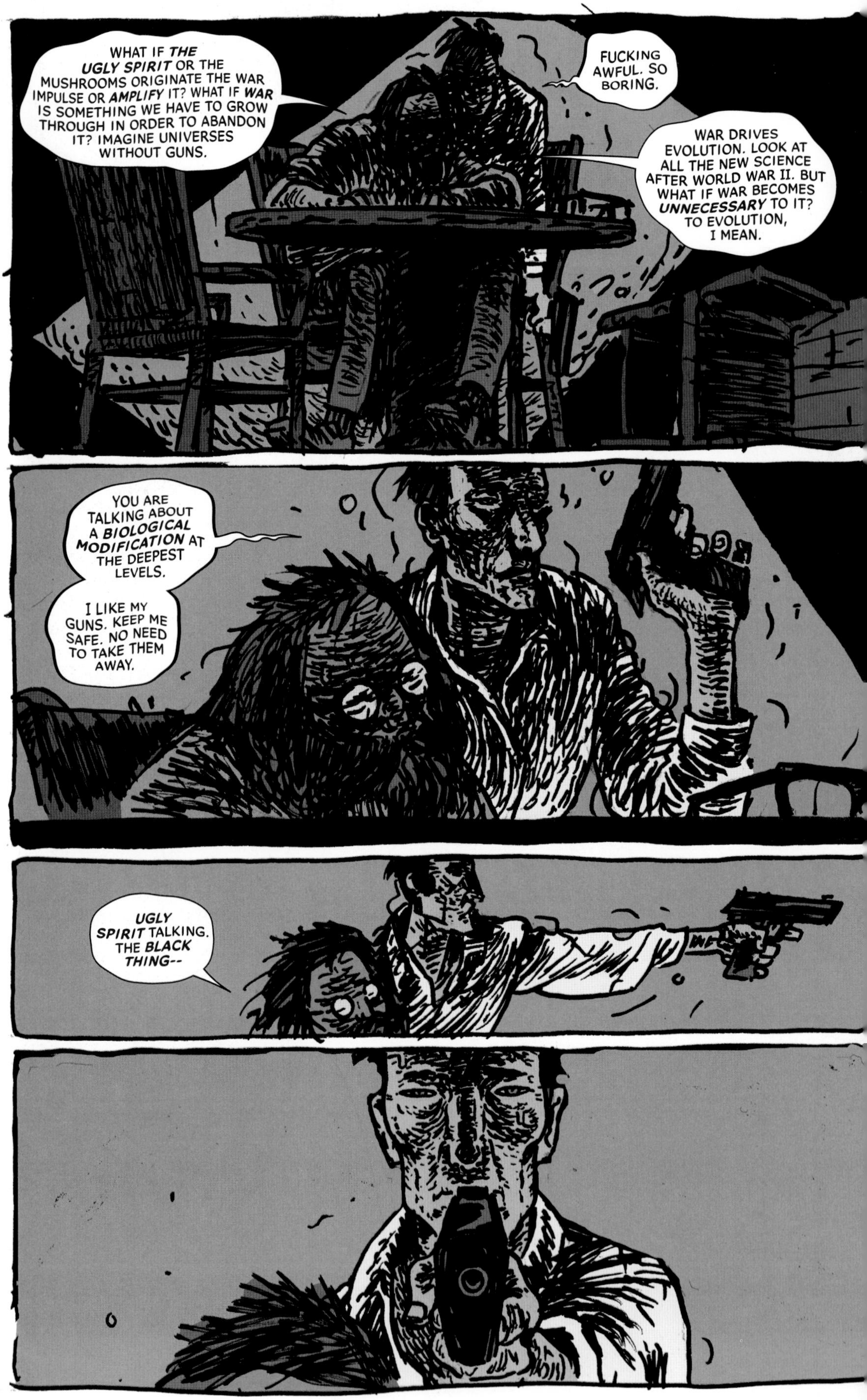
WHAT IF THE UGLY SPIRIT OR THE MUSHROOMS ORIGINATE THE WAR IMPULSE OR AMPLIFY IT? WHAT IF WAR IS SOMETHING WE HAVE TO GROW THROUGH IN ORDER TO ABANDON IT? IMAGINE UNIVERSES WITHOUT GUNS.
FUCKING AWFUL. SO BORING.
WAR DRIVES EVOLUTION. LOOK AT ALL THE NEW SCIENCE AFTER WORLD WAR II. BUT WHAT IF WAR BECOMES UNNECESSARY TO IT? TO EVOLUTION, I MEAN.
YOU ARE TALKING ABOUT A BIOLOGICAL MODIFICATION AT THE DEEPEST LEVELS.
I LIKE MY GUNS. KEEP ME SAFE. NO NEED TO TAKE THEM AWAY.
UGLY SPIRIT TALKING. THE BLACK THING--

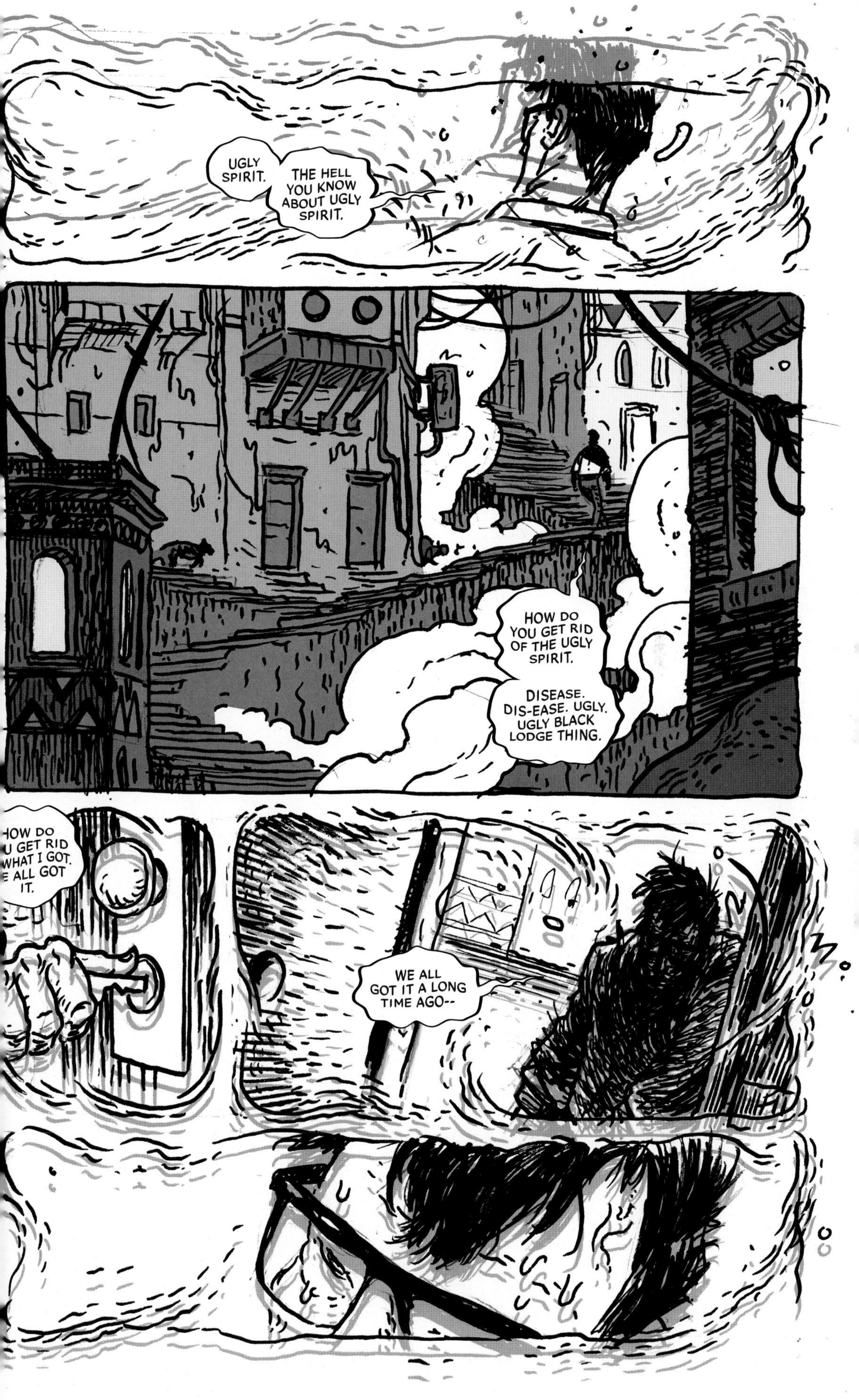
UGLY SPIRIT.
THE HELL YOU KNOW ABOUT UGLY SPIRIT.
HOW DO YOU GET RID OF THE UGLY SPIRIT.
DISEASE. DIS-EASE. UGLY. UGLY BLACK LODGE THING.
HOW DO U GET RID WHAT I GOT. E ALL GOT IT.
WE ALL GOT IT A LONG TIME AGO--

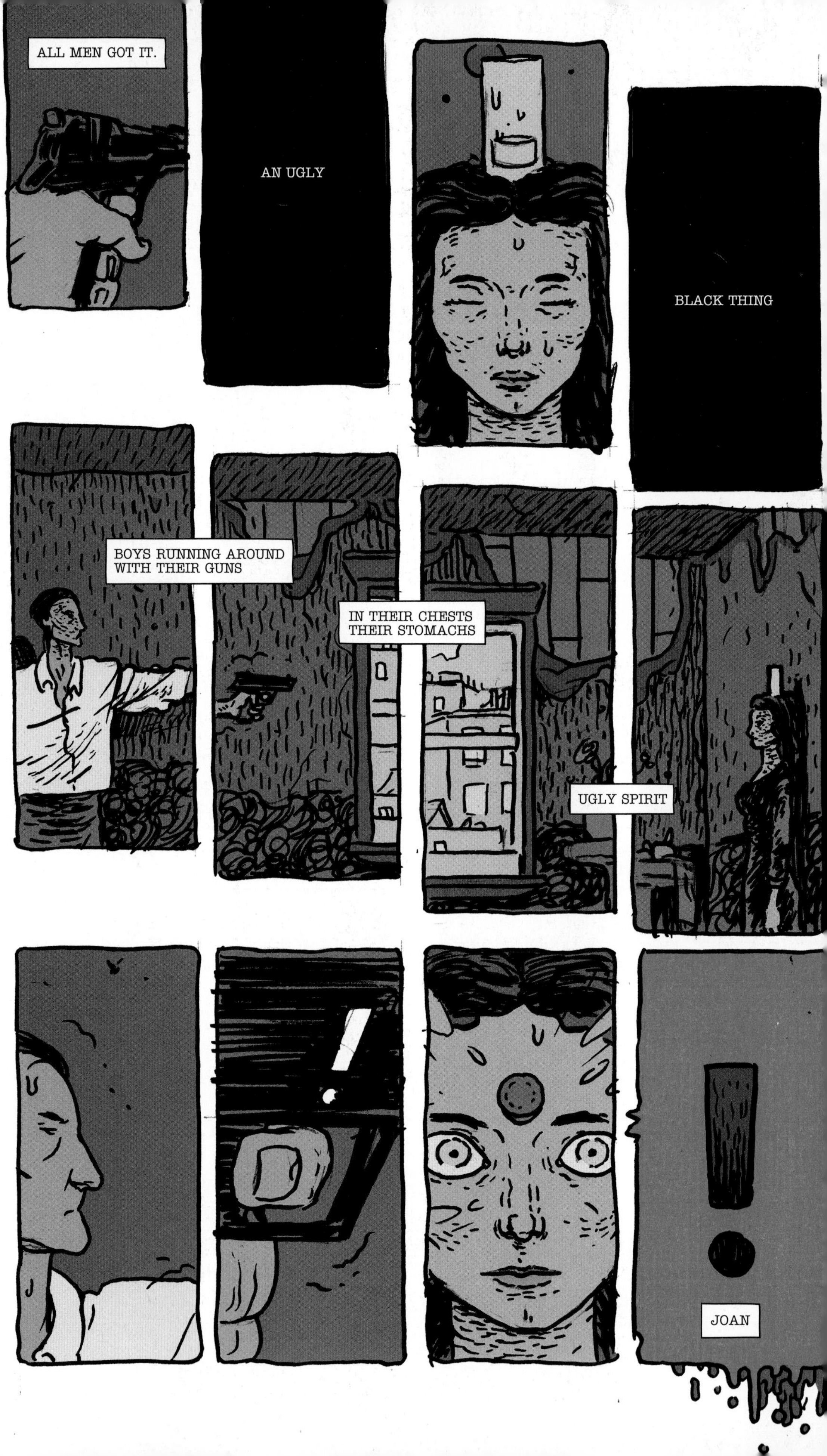
ALL MEN GOT IT.
AN UGLY
BLACK THING
BOYS RUNNING AROUND WITH THEIR GUNS
IN THEIR CHESTS THEIR STOMACHS
UGLY SPIRIT
JOAN

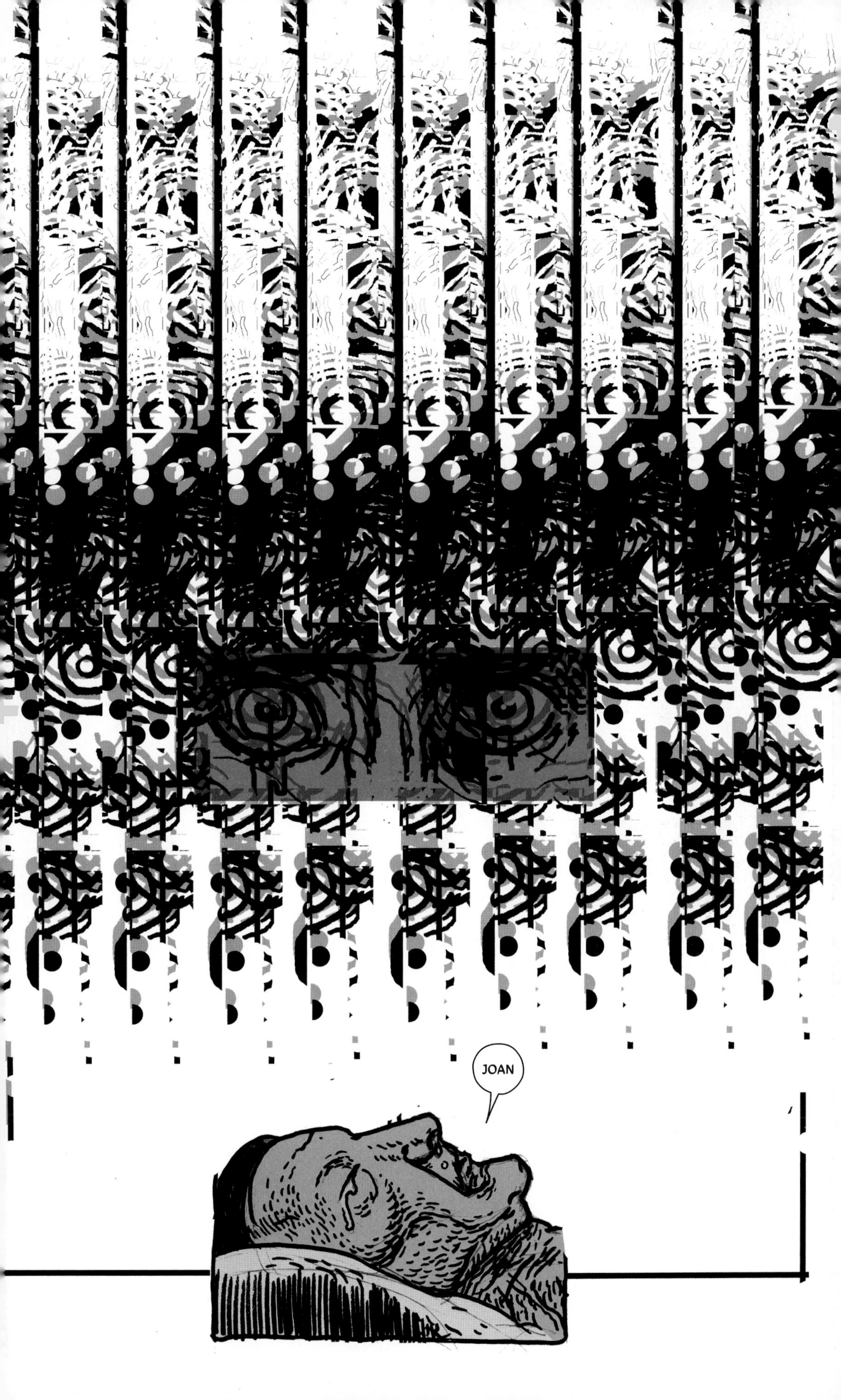
JOAN

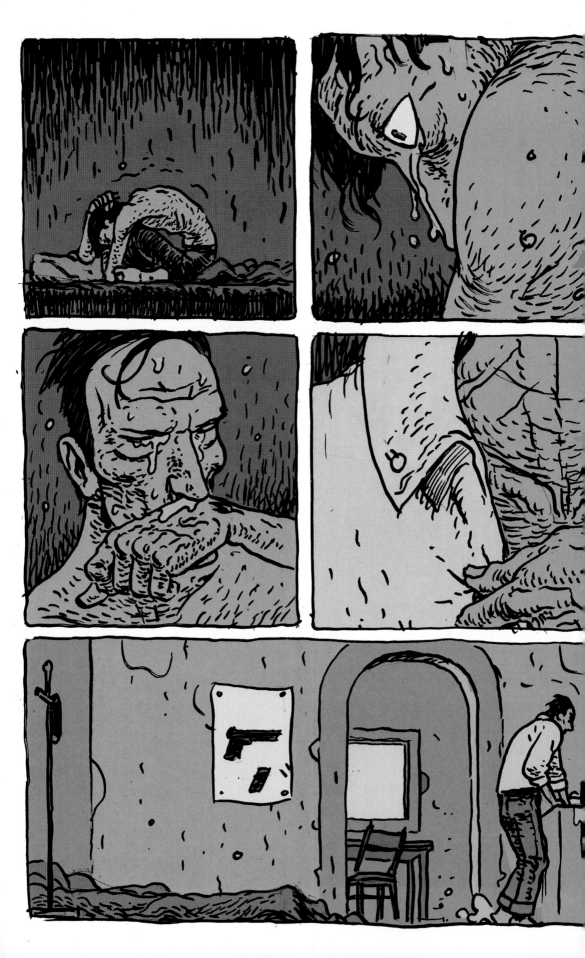

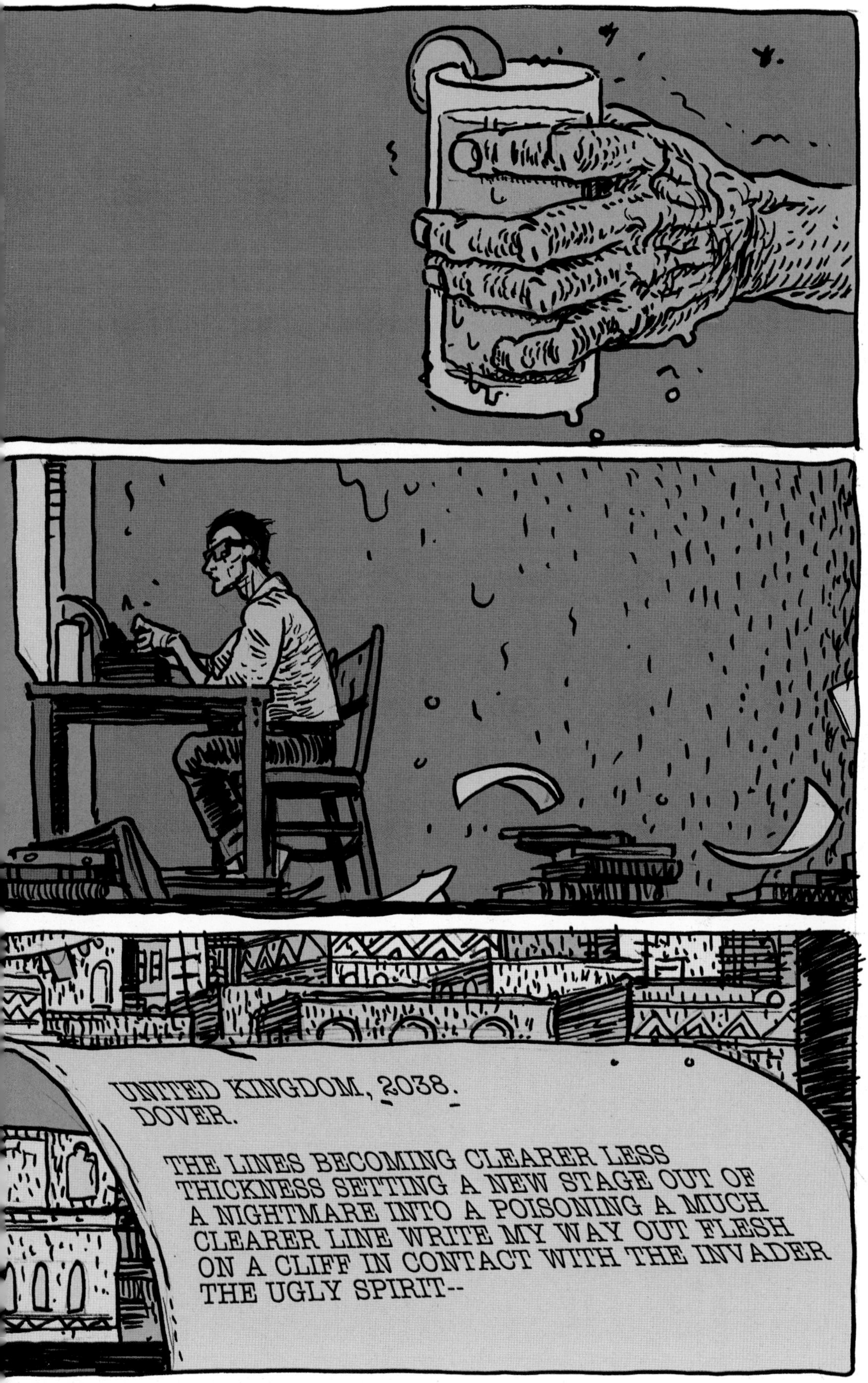
UNITED KINGDOM, 2038.
DOVER.
THE LINES BECOMING CLEARER LESS THICKNESS SETTING A NEW STAGE OUT OF A NIGHTMARE INTO A POISONING A MUCH CLEARER LINE WRITE MY WAY OUT FLESH ON A CLIFF IN CONTACT WITH THE INVADER THE UGLY SPIRIT--

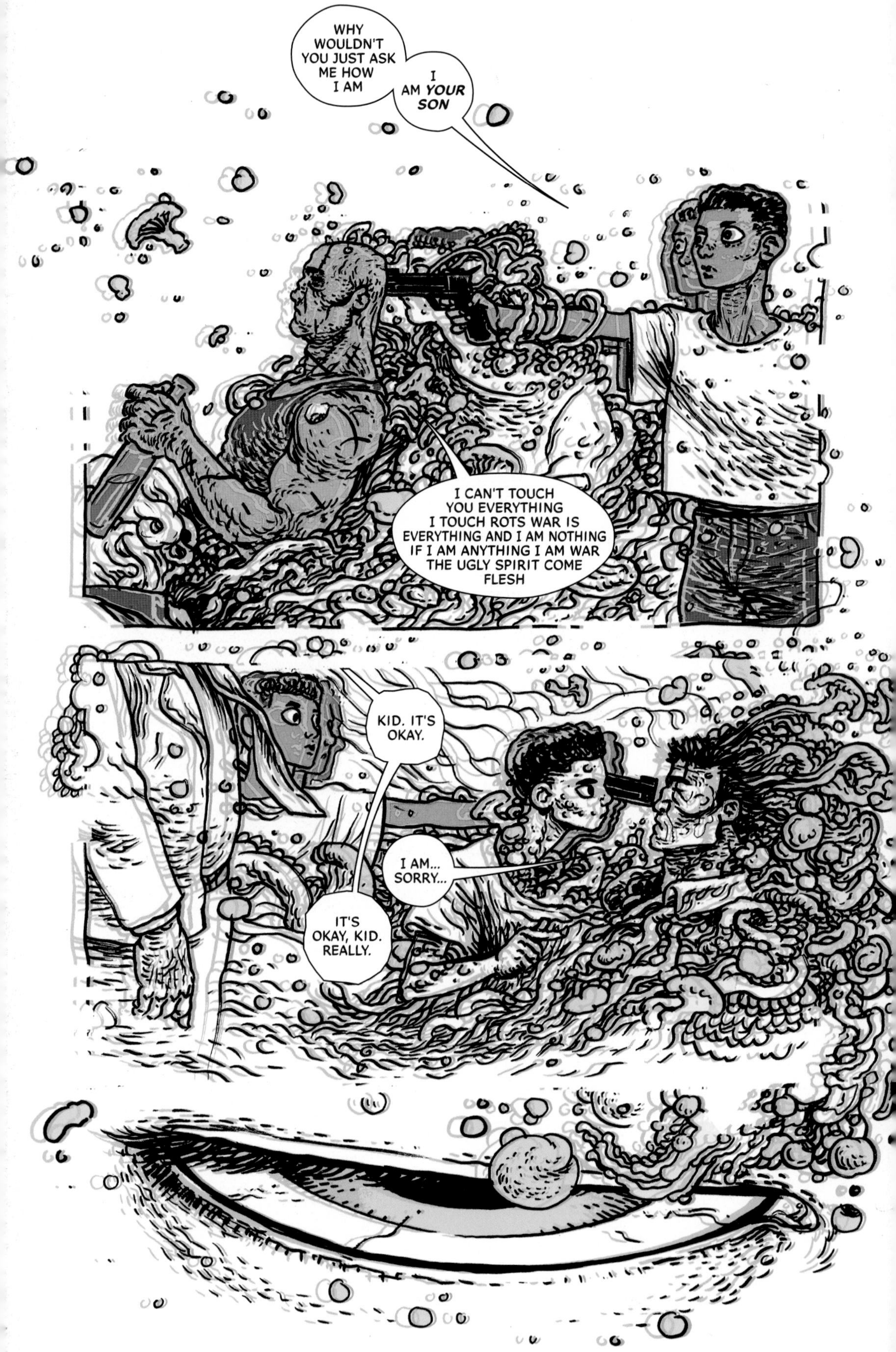
WHY WOULDN'T YOU JUST ASK ME HOW I AM
I AM *YOUR SON*
I CAN'T TOUCH YOU EVERYTHING I TOUCH ROTS WAR IS EVERYTHING AND I AM NOTHING IF I AM ANYTHING I AM WAR THE UGLY SPIRIT COME FLESH
KID. IT'S OKAY.
I AM... SORRY...
IT'S OKAY, KID. REALLY.

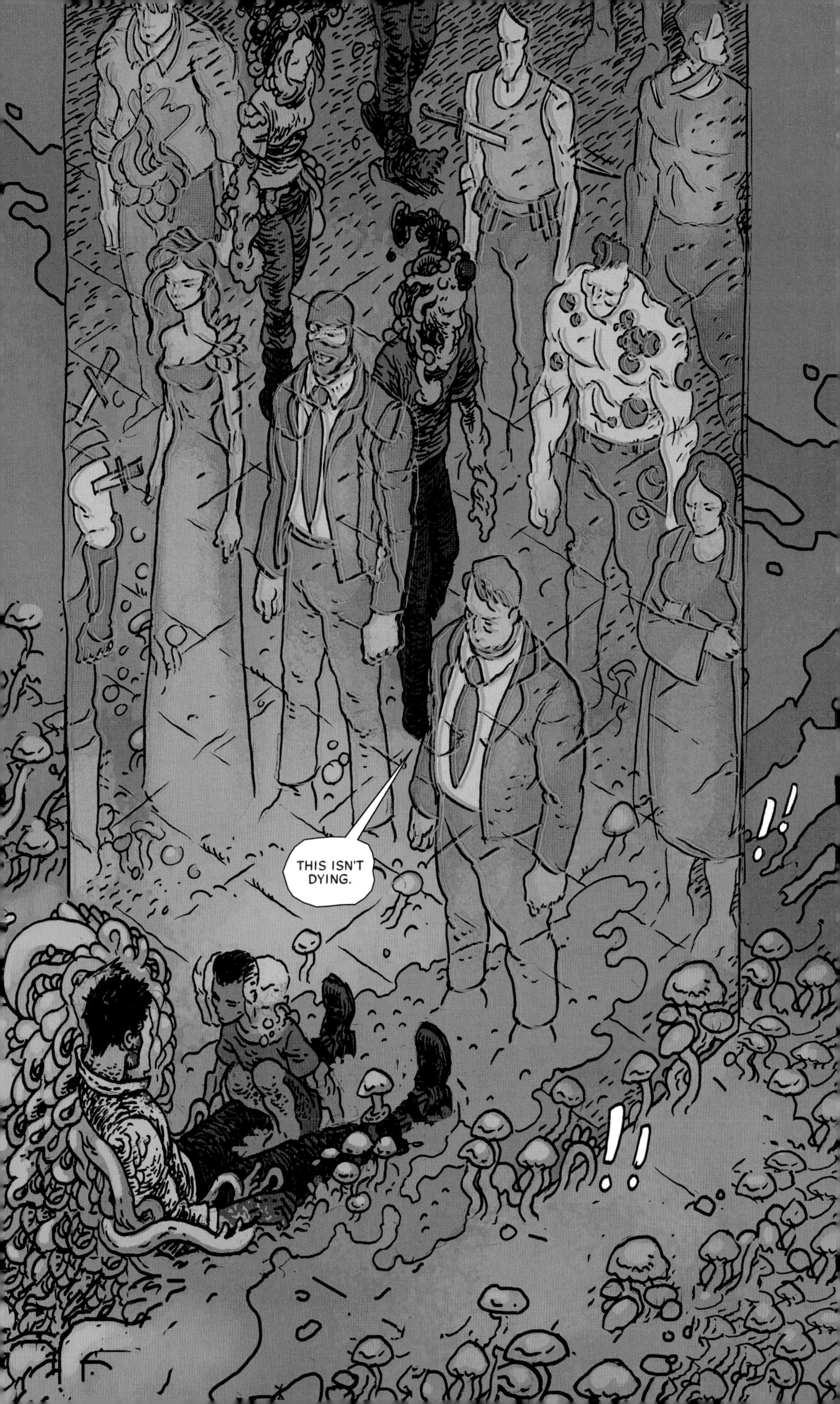
THIS ISN'T DYING.
!!
!!

AN VOLLMER JOAN VOLLMER JOAN VOLLMER JOAN VOLLMER JOAN VOLLMER JOAN VOLLMER
LLMER JOAN VOLLMER JOAN VOLLMER JOAN VOLLMER JOAN VOLLMER JOAN V
JOAN VOLLMER JOAN VOLLMER J OAN VOLLMER JOAN VOLLMER JOAN VOLLME
LLMER JOAN VOLLMER JOAN VOLLMER JOAN VOLLMER JOAN VOLLMER JOAN VO
AN VOLLMER JOAN VOLLMER JOAN VOLLMER JOAN VOLLMER JOAN VOLLMER JOAN VO
AN VOLLMER JOAN VOLLMER JOAN VOLLMER JOAN VOLLMER JOAN VOLLMER JOAN VO
AN VOLLMER JOAN VOLLMER JOAN VOLLMER JOAN VOLLMER JOAN VOLLMER JOAN

R JOAN VOLLMER JOAN VOLLMER JOAN VOLLMER JOAN VOLLMER JOAN VOLLME

LLMER JOAN VOLLMER JOAN VOLLMER JOAN VOLLMER JOAN VOLLMER JOAN VOLLME
LLMER JOAN VOLLMER JOAN VOLLMER JOAN VOLLMER JOAN VOLLMER JOAN VOLLME
LLMER JOAN VOLLMER JOAN VOLLMER JOAN VOLLMER JOAN VOLLMER JOAN VOLLME
LLMER JOAN VOLLMER JOAN VOLLMER JOAN VOLLMER JOAN VOLLMER JOAN VOLLME
LLMER JOAN VOLLMER JOAN VOLLMER JOAN VOLLMER JOAN VOLLMER JOAN VOLLME
LLMER JOAN VOLLMER JOAN VOLLMER JOAN VOLLMER JOAN VOLLMER JOAN VOLLME
LLMER JOAN VOLLMER JOAN VOLLMER JOAN VOLLMER JOAN VOLLMER JOAN VOLLME
LLMER JOAN VOLLMER JOAN VOLLMER JOAN VOLLMER JOAN VOLLMER JOAN
ER JOAN VOLLMER JOAN VOLLMER JOAN VOLLMER JOAN VOLLMER JOAN VO
AN VOLLMER JOAN VOLLMER JOAN VOLLMER JOAN VOLLMER JOAN VOLLMER JOAN VO
AN VOLLMER JOA N VOLLMER JOAN VOLLMER JOAN VOLLMER JOAN VOLLMER JOAN VO
AN VOLLMER JOAN VOLLMER JOAN VOLLMER JOAN VOLLMER JOAN VOLLMER JOAN VO
AN VOLLMER JOAN VOLLMER JOAN VOLLMER JOAN VOLLMER JOAN VOLLMER JOAN VO
AN VOLLMER JOAN VOLLMER JOAN VOLLMER JOAN VOLLMER JOAN VOLLMER JOAN VO
AN VOLLMER JOAN VOLLMER JOAN VOLLMER JOAN VOLLMER JOAN VOLLMER JOAN VO
AN VOLLMER JOAN VOLLMER JOAN VOLLMER JOAN VOLLMER JOAN VOLLMER JOAN VO
AN VOLLMER JOAN VOLLMER JOAN VOLLMER JOAN VOLLMER JOAN VOLLMER JOAN VO
AN VOLLMER JOAN VOLLMER JOAN VOLLMER JOAN VOLLMER JOAN VOLLMER JOAN VO
AN VOLLMER JOAN VOLLMER JOAN VOLLMER JOAN VOLLMER JOAN VOLLMER JOAN VO
AN VOLLMER JOAN VOLLMER JOAN VOLLMER JOAN VOLLMER JOAN VOLLMER JOAN VO
AN VOLLMER JOAN VOLLMER JOAN VOLLMER JOAN VOLLMER JOAN VOLLMER JOAN VO
AN VOLLMER JOAN VOLLMER JOAN V OLLMER JOAN VOLLMER JOAN VOLLMER JOAN VO
AN VOLLMER JOAN VOLLMER JOAN VOLLMER JOAN VOLLMER JOAN VOLLMER JOAN VO
AN VOLLMER JOAN VOLLMER JOAN VOLLMER JOAN VOLLMER JOAN VOLLMER JOAN VO
AN VOLLMER JOAN VOLLMER JOAN VOLLMER JOAN VOLLMER JOAN VOLLMER JOAN VO
AN VOLLMER JOAN VOLLMER JOAN VOLLMER JOAN VOLLMER JOAN VOLLMER JOAN V
R JOAN VOLLMER JOAN VOLLMER JOAN VOLLMER JOAN VOLLMER JOAN VOLLMER
LLMER JOAN VOLLMER JOAN VOLLMER JOAN VOLLMER JOAN VOLLMER JOAN VOLLME
LLMER JOAN VOLLMER JOAN VOLLMER JOAN VOLLMER JOAN VOLLMER JOAN VOLLME
LLMER JOAN VOLLMER JOAN VOLLMER JOAN VOLLMER JOAN VOLLMER JOAN VOLLME
LLMER JOAN VOLLMER JOAN VOLLMER JOAN VOLLMER JOAN VOLLMER JOAN VOLLME
LLMER JOAN VOLLMER JOAN VOLLMER JOAN VOLLMER JOAN VOLLMER JOAN VOLLMER JOA
ER JOAN VOLLMER JOAN VOLLMER JOAN VOLLMER JOAN VOLLMER JOAN VOLLMER JOAN VOLLME
LLMER JOAN VOLLMER JOAN VOLLMER JOAN VOLLMER JOAN VOLLMER JOAN VOLLMER
LLMER JOAN VOLLMER JOAN VOLLMER JOAN VOLLMER JOAN VOLLMER JOAN VOLLME
LLMER JOAN VOLLMER JOAN VOLLMER JOAN VOLLMER JOAN VOLLMER JOAN VOLLME
LLMER JOAN VOLLMER JOAN VOLLMER JOAN VOLLMER JOAN VOLLMER JOAN VOLLME
LLMER JOAN VOLLMER JOAN VOLLMER JOAN VOLLMER JOAN VOLLMER JOAN VOLLME
LLMER JOAN VOLLMER JOAN VOLLMER JOAN VOLLMER JOAN VOLLMER JOAN VO
AN VOLLMER JOAN VOLLMER JOAN VOLLMER JOAN VOLLMER JOAN VOLLMER JOAN VO
AN VOLLMER JOAN VOLLMER JOAN VOLLMER JOAN VOLLMER JOAN VOLLMER JOAN VO
AN VOLLMER JOAN VOLLMER JOAN VOLLMER JOAN VOLLMER JOAN VOLLMER JOAN VO
AN VOLLMER JOAN VOLLMER JOAN VOLLMER JOAN VOLLMER JOAN VOLLMER JOAN VO
AN VOLLMER JOAN VOLLMER JOAN VOLLMER JOAN VOLLMER JOAN VOLLMER JOAN VO
AN VOLLMER JOAN VOLLMER JOAN VOLLMER JOAN VOLLMER JOAN VOLLMER JOAN VO
AN VOLLMER JOAN VOL LMER JOAN VOLLMER JOAN VOLLMER JOAN VOLLMER JOAN VO
AN VOLLMER JOAN VOLLMER JOAN VOLLMER JOAN VOLLMER JOAN VOLLMER JOAN VO
AN VOLLMER JOAN VOLLMER JOAN VOLLMER JOAN VOLLMER JOAN VOLLMER JOAN VO
AN VOLLMER JOAN VOLLMER JOAN VOLLMER JOAN VOLLMER JOAN VOLLMER JOAN V
R JOAN VOLLMER JOAN VOLLMER JOAN VOLLMER JOAN VOLLMER JOAN VOLLME
LLMER JOAN VOLLMER JOAN VOLLMER JOAN VOLLMER JOAN VOLLMER JOAN VOLLME
LLMER JOAN VOLLMER JOAN VOLLMER JOAN VOLLMER JOAN VOLLMER JOAN VOLLME
LLMER JOAN VOLLMER JOAN VOLLMER JOAN VOLLMER JOAN VOLLMER JOAN VOLLME
LLMER JOAN VOLLMER JOAN VOLLMER JOAN VOLLMER JOAN VOLLMER JOAN VOLLME
LLMER JOAN VOLLMER JOAN VOLLMER JOAN VOLLMER JOAN VOLLMER JOAN VOLLME

MEMO DG-KT-BBCA-Z-2015

IT IS EXTREMELY IMPORTANT TO KEEP THE VIRUS CONTAINED. ITS FUNGAL NATURE MEANS
AN EXTREME EASINESS OF SPORIFICATION AND SUBSEQUENT CONTAMINATION.

TEST SUBJECTS C27 AND X8 CONTINUE DESCRIBING THEIR THEORIES ON MULTIVERSE
TRAVEL AS CONNECTED TO THE FUNGAL SYSTEM. WHILE DELIRIUM IS NOT SURPRISING
DURING SUCH DEEP INFECTION, THE SUBJECTS ARE REPEATEDLY ASSESSING KNOWLEDGE
THAT COULD NOT BE ASSESSED EXCEPT FOR IF THEY WERE IN DIRECT OR INDIRECT
CONTACT, WHICH THEY ARE NOT. THIS POINTS IN A DIRECTION OF A POSSIBLE SHARED, HIV
MIND, AND IS TO BE EXAMINED FURTHER.

NG OTHER MENTIONS   W   HAD BE   HORSES INSISTING UPON
-- -- EQUALLY POSSIB   VOLLME
WORLDS THEORY A   COULD POINT IN THE DIRE
AL POSSIBILITY
FACTORS SUC   AS INFLUENCE OF TH

MEDICATION IS TO   PHASE SHIFT

N VOLLMER JOAN VOLLMER JOAN VOLLMER JOAN VOLLMER JOAN VOLLMER JOAN VOLL
N VOLLMER JOAN VOLLMER JOAN VOLLMER JOAN VOLLMER JOAN VOLLMER JOAN VOLL
N VOLLMER JOAN VOLLMER JOAN VOLLMER JOAN VOLLMER JOAN VOLLMER JOAN VOLLMER
LMER JOAN VOLLMER JOAN VOLLMER JOAN VOLLMER JOAN VOLLMER JOAN VOLLMER JOAN VOL
N VOLLMER JOAN VOLLMER JOAN VOLLMER JOAN VOLLMER JOAN VOLLMER JOAN VOLL
N VOLLMER JOAN VOLLMER JOAN VOLLMER JOAN VOLLMER JOAN VOLLMER JOAN VOLL
N VOLLMER JOAN VOLLMER JOAN VOLLMER JOAN VOLLMER JOAN VOLLMER JOAN VOLL
N VOLLMER JOAN VOLLMER JOAN VOLLMER JOAN VOLLMER JOAN VOLLMER JOAN VOLL
N VOLLMER JOAN VOLLMER JOAN VOLLMER JOAN VOLLMER JOAN VOLLMER JOAN VOLL
N VOLLMER JOAN VOLLMER JOAN VOLLMER JOAN VOLLMER JOAN VOLLMER JOAN VOLL
N VOLLMER JOAN VOLLMER JOAN VOLLMER JOAN VOLLMER JOAN VOLLMER JOAN VOLL
N VOLLMER JOAN VOLLMER JOAN VOLLMER JOAN VOLLMER JOAN VOLLMER JOAN VOLL
N VOLLMER JOAN VOLLMER JOAN VOLLMER JOAN VOLLMER JOAN VOLLMER JOAN VOLLMER
LMER JOAN VOLLMER JOAN VOLLMER JOAN VOLLMER JOAN VOLLMER JOAN VOLLMER
LMER JOAN VOLLMER JOAN VOLLMER JOAN VOLLMER JOAN V OLLMER JOAN VOLLMER
LMER JOAN VOLLMER JOAN VOLLMER JOAN VOLLMER JOAN VOLLMER JOAN VOLLMER
LMER JOAN VOLLMER JOAN VOLLMER JOAN VOLLMER JOAN VOLLMER JOAN VOLLMER
LMER JOAN VOLLMER JOAN VOLLMER JOAN VOLLMER JOAN VOLLMER JOAN VOLLMER
LMER JOAN VOLLMER JOAN VOLLMER JOAN VOLLMER JOAN VOLLMER JOAN VOLLMER
LMER JOAN VOLLMER JOAN VOLLMER JOAN VOLLMER JOAN VOLLMER JOAN VOLLMER
LMER JOAN VOLLMER JOAN VOLLMER JOAN VOLLMER JOAN VOLLMER JOAN VOLLMER
LMER JOAN VOLLMER JOAN VOLLMER   JOAN VOLLMER JOAN VOLLMER JOAN VOLL
N VOLLMER JOAN VOLLMER JOAN V OLLMER JOAN VOLLMER JOAN VOLLMER JOAN VOLL
N VOLLMER JOAN VOLLMER JOAN VOLLMER JOAN VO LLMER JOAN VOLLMER JOAN VOLL
N VOLLMER JOAN VOLLMER JOAN VOLLMER JOAN VOLLMER JOAN VOLLMER JOAN VOLL
N VOLLMER JOAN VOLLMER JOAN VOLLMER JOAN VOLLMER JOAN VOLLMER JOAN VOLL
N VOLLMER JOAN VOLLMER JOAN VOLLMER JOAN VOLLMER JOAN VOLLMER JOAN VOLL
N VOLLMER JOAN VOLLMER JOAN VOLLMER JOAN VOLLMER JOAN VOLLMER JOAN VOLL
N VOLLMER JOAN VOLLMER JOAN VOLLMER JOAN VOLLMER JOAN VOLLMER JOAN VOLL
N VOLLMER JOAN VOLLMER JOAN VOLLMER JOAN VOLLMER JOAN VOLLMER JOAN VOLL
N VOLLMER JOAN VOLLMER JOAN VOLLMER JOAN VOLLMER JOAN VOLLMER JOAN VOLL
N VOLLMER JOAN VOLLMER JOAN VOLLMER JOAN VOLLMER JOAN VOLLMER JOAN
ER JOAN VOLLMER JOAN VOLLMER JOAN VOLLMER JOAN VOLLMER JOAN VOLL
N VOLLMER JOAN VOLLMER JOAN VOLLMER JOAN VOLLMER J OAN VOLLMER
LMER JOAN VOLLMER JOAN VOLLMER JOAN VOLLMER JOAN VOLLMER JOAN VOLL
N VOLLMER JOAN VOLLMER JOAN VOLLMER JOAN VOLLMER JOAN VOLLMER JOAN VOLL
N VOLLMER JOAN VOLLMER JOAN VOLLMER JOAN VOLLMER JOAN VOLLMER JOAN VOLL
N VOLLMER JOAN VOLLMER JOAN VOLLMER JOAN VOLLMER JOAN VOLLMER JOAN VO
JOAN VOLLMER JOAN VOLLMER   JOAN VOLLMER JOAN VOLLMER JOAN VOLLMER
LMER JOAN VOLLMER JOAN VOLLMER JOAN VOLLMER JOAN VOLLMER JOAN VOLLMER
LMER JOAN VOLLMER JOAN VOLLMER JOAN VOLLMER JOAN VOLLMER JOAN VOLLMER
LMER JOAN VOLLMER JOAN VOLLMER JOAN VOLLMER JOAN VOLLMER JOAN VOLLMER
LMER JOAN VOLLMER JOAN VOLLMER JOAN VOLLMER JOAN VOLLMER JOAN VOLLMER
LMER JOAN VOLLMER JOAN VOLLMER JOAN VOLLMER JOAN VOLLMER JOAN VOLLMER
LMER JOAN VOLLMER JOAN VOLLMER JOAN VOLLMER JOAN VOLLMER JOAN VOLLMER
LMER JOAN VOLLMER JOAN VOLLMER JOAN VOLLMER JOAN VOLLMER JOAN VOLLMER
LMER JOAN VOLLMER JOAN VOLLMER JOAN VOLLMER JOAN VOLLMER JOAN VOLL
N VOLLMER JOAN VOLLMER JOAN VOLLMER JOAN VOLLMER JOAN VOLL
N VOLLMER JOAN VOLLMER JOAN VOLLMER JOAN VOLLMER JOAN VOLLMER JOAN VOLL
N VOLLMER JOAN VOLLMER JOAN VOLLMER JOA N VOLLMER JOAN VOLLMER JOAN VOLL
N VOLLMER JOAN VOLLMER JOAN VOLLMER JOAN VOLLMER JOAN VOLLMER JOAN VOLL
N VOLLMER JOAN VOLLMER JOAN VOLLMER JOAN VOLLMER JOAN VOLLMER JOAN VOLL
N VOLLMER JOAN VOLLMER JOAN VOLLMER JOAN VOLLMER JOAN VOLLMER JOAN VOLL
N VOLLMER JOAN VOLLMER JOAN VOLLMER JOAN VOLLMER JOAN VOLLMER JOAN VOLL
N VOLLMER JOAN VOLLMER JOAN VOLLMER JOAN VOLLMER JOAN VOLLMER JOAN VOLL
N VOLLMER JOAN VOLLMER JOAN VOLLMER JOAN VOLLMER JOAN VOLLMER JOAN VOLL
N VOLLMER JOAN VOLLMER JOAN VOLLMER JOAN VOLLMER JOAN VOLLMER JOAN VOLL
N VOLLMER JOAN VOLLMER JOAN VOLLMER JOAN VOLLMER JOAN VOLLMER JOAN VOLL
N VOLLMER JOAN VOLLMER JOAN VOLLMER JOAN VOLLMER JOAN VOLLMER JOAN VOLL
N VOLLMER JOAN VOLLMER JOAN VOLLMER JOAN VOLLMER JOAN VOLLMER JOAN VOLL
N VOLLMER JOAN VOLLMER JOAN VOLLMER JOAN VOLLMER JOAN VOLLMER JOAN VOLL

CHAPTER 16

THE BLACK THING, THE UGLY SPIRIT

Illustrated by Stathis Tsemberlidis

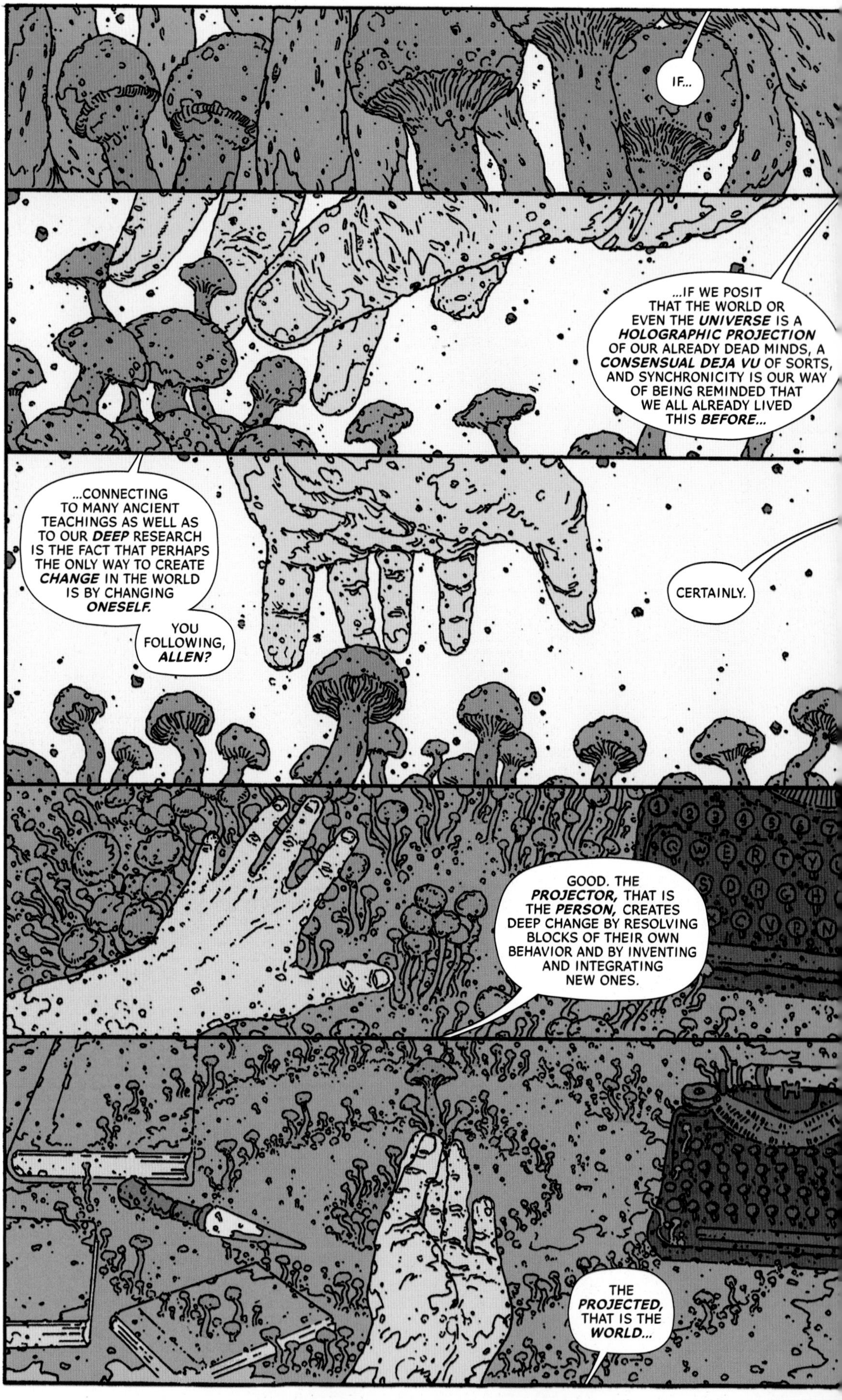
IF...
...IF WE POSIT THAT THE WORLD OR EVEN THE *UNIVERSE* IS A *HOLOGRAPHIC PROJECTION* OF OUR ALREADY DEAD MINDS, A *CONSENSUAL DEJA VU* OF SORTS, AND SYNCHRONICITY IS OUR WAY OF BEING REMINDED THAT WE ALL ALREADY LIVED THIS *BEFORE...*
...CONNECTING TO MANY ANCIENT TEACHINGS AS WELL AS TO OUR *DEEP* RESEARCH IS THE FACT THAT PERHAPS THE ONLY WAY TO CREATE *CHANGE* IN THE WORLD IS BY CHANGING *ONESELF.*
YOU FOLLOWING, *ALLEN?*
CERTAINLY.
GOOD. THE *PROJECTOR,* THAT IS THE *PERSON,* CREATES DEEP CHANGE BY RESOLVING BLOCKS OF THEIR OWN BEHAVIOR AND BY INVENTING AND INTEGRATING NEW ONES.
THE *PROJECTED,* THAT IS THE *WORLD...*

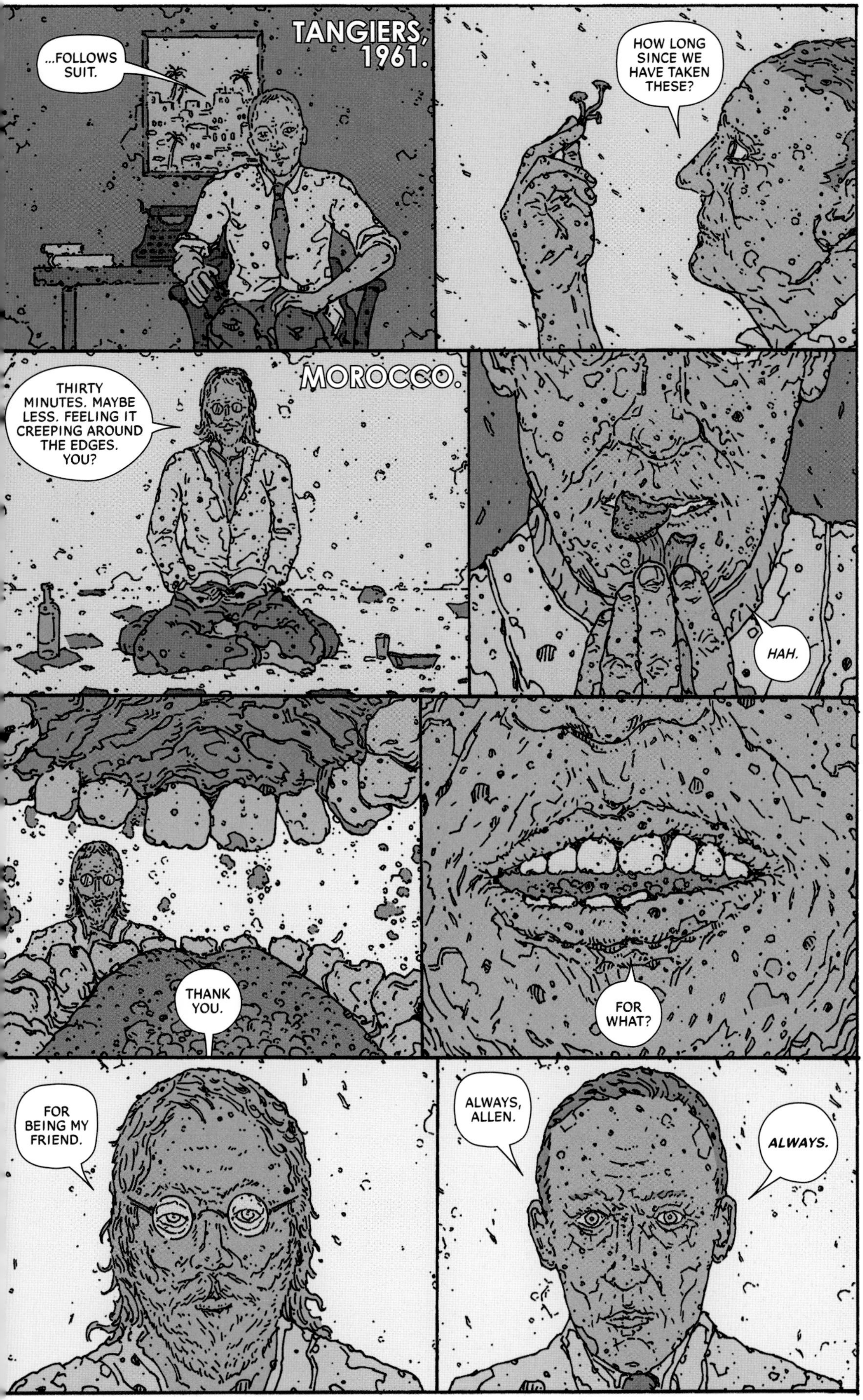
TANGIERS, 1961.
...FOLLOWS SUIT.
HOW LONG SINCE WE HAVE TAKEN THESE?
MOROCCO.
THIRTY MINUTES. MAYBE LESS. FEELING IT CREEPING AROUND THE EDGES. YOU?
HAH.
THANK YOU.
FOR WHAT?
FOR BEING MY FRIEND.
ALWAYS, ALLEN.
ALWAYS.

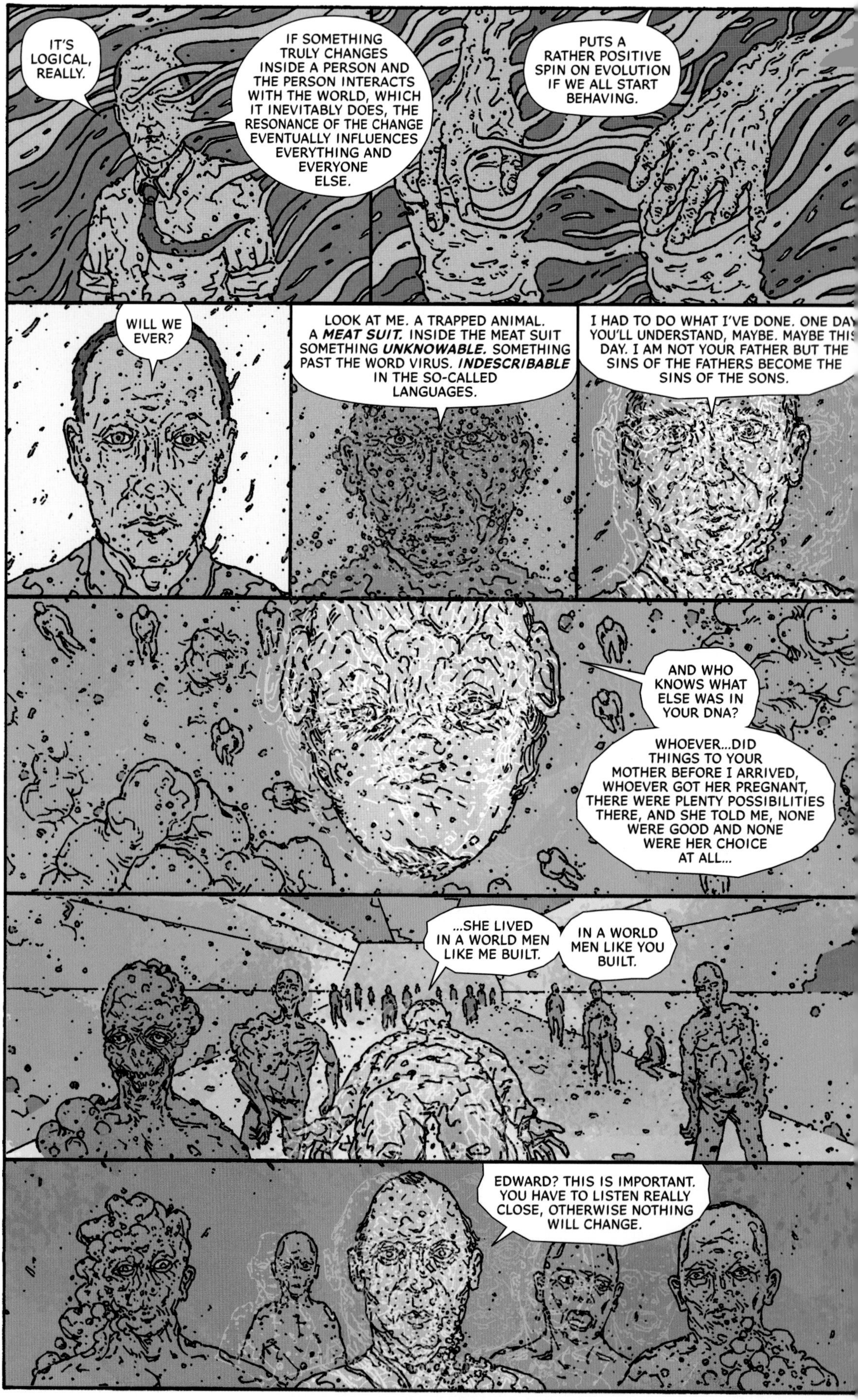
IT'S LOGICAL, REALLY.
IF SOMETHING TRULY CHANGES INSIDE A PERSON AND THE PERSON INTERACTS WITH THE WORLD, WHICH IT INEVITABLY DOES, THE RESONANCE OF THE CHANGE EVENTUALLY INFLUENCES EVERYTHING AND EVERYONE ELSE.
PUTS A RATHER POSITIVE SPIN ON EVOLUTION IF WE ALL START BEHAVING.
WILL WE EVER?
LOOK AT ME. A TRAPPED ANIMAL. A *MEAT SUIT.* INSIDE THE MEAT SUIT SOMETHING *UNKNOWABLE.* SOMETHING PAST THE WORD VIRUS. *INDESCRIBABLE* IN THE SO-CALLED LANGUAGES.
I HAD TO DO WHAT I'VE DONE. ONE DAY YOU'LL UNDERSTAND, MAYBE. MAYBE THIS DAY. I AM NOT YOUR FATHER BUT THE SINS OF THE FATHERS BECOME THE SINS OF THE SONS.
AND WHO KNOWS WHAT ELSE WAS IN YOUR DNA?
WHOEVER...DID THINGS TO YOUR MOTHER BEFORE I ARRIVED, WHOEVER GOT HER PREGNANT, THERE WERE PLENTY POSSIBILITIES THERE, AND SHE TOLD ME, NONE WERE GOOD AND NONE WERE HER CHOICE AT ALL...
...SHE LIVED IN A WORLD MEN LIKE ME BUILT.
IN A WORLD MEN LIKE YOU BUILT.
EDWARD? THIS IS IMPORTANT. YOU HAVE TO LISTEN REALLY CLOSE, OTHERWISE NOTHING WILL CHANGE.

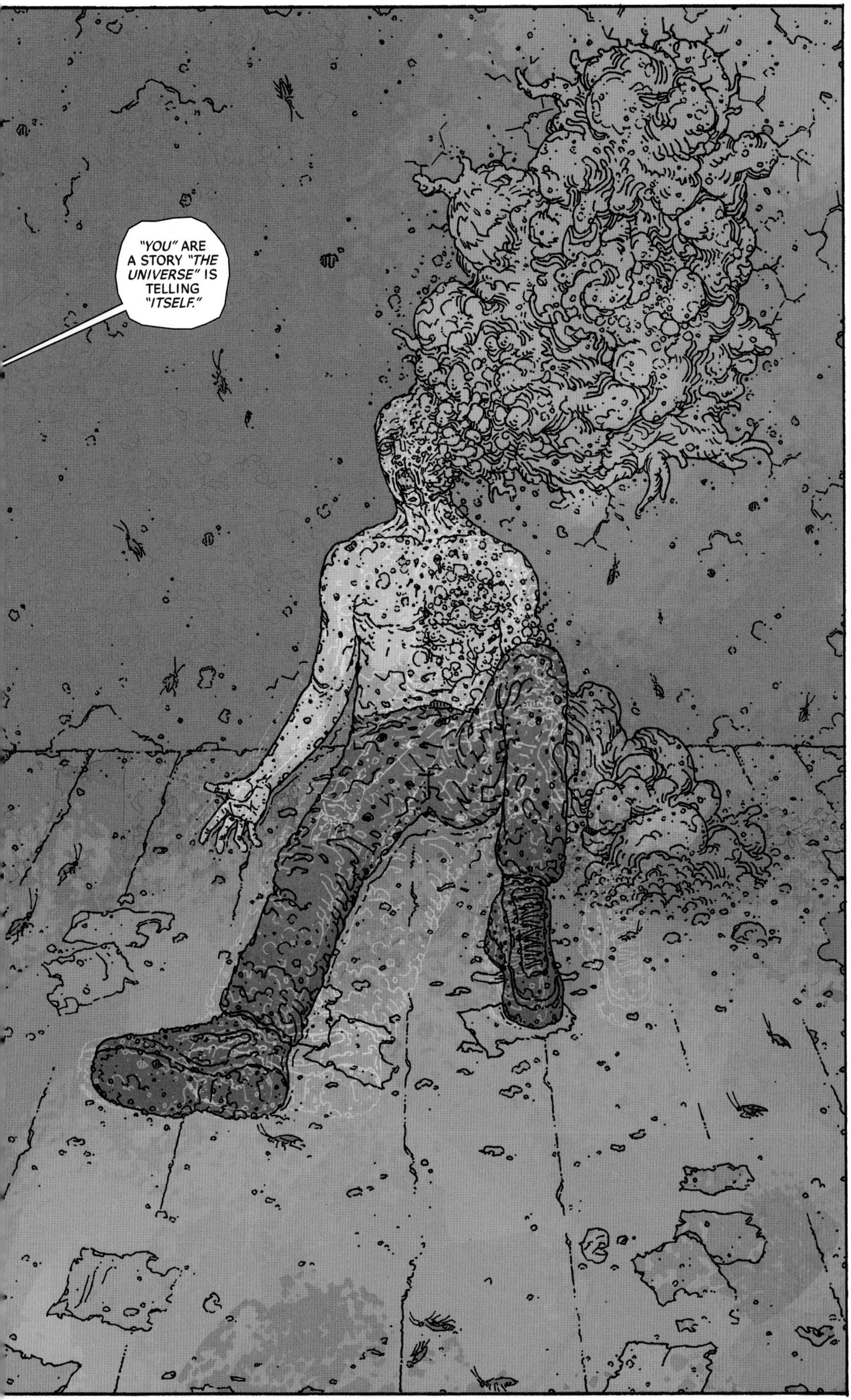
"YOU" ARE A STORY "THE UNIVERSE" IS TELLING "ITSELF."

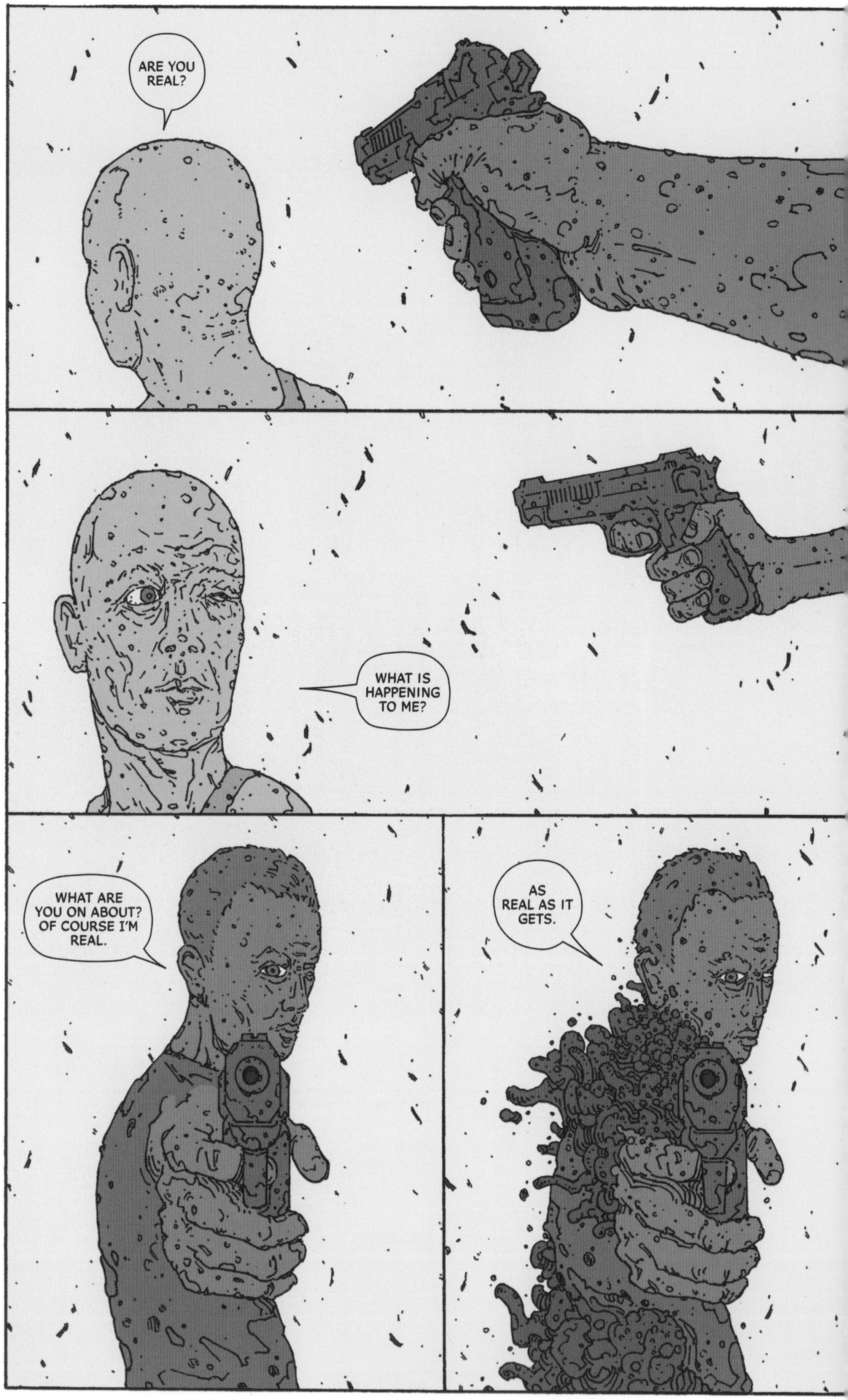
ARE YOU REAL?
WHAT IS HAPPENING TO ME?
WHAT ARE YOU ON ABOUT? OF COURSE I'M REAL.
AS REAL AS IT GETS.

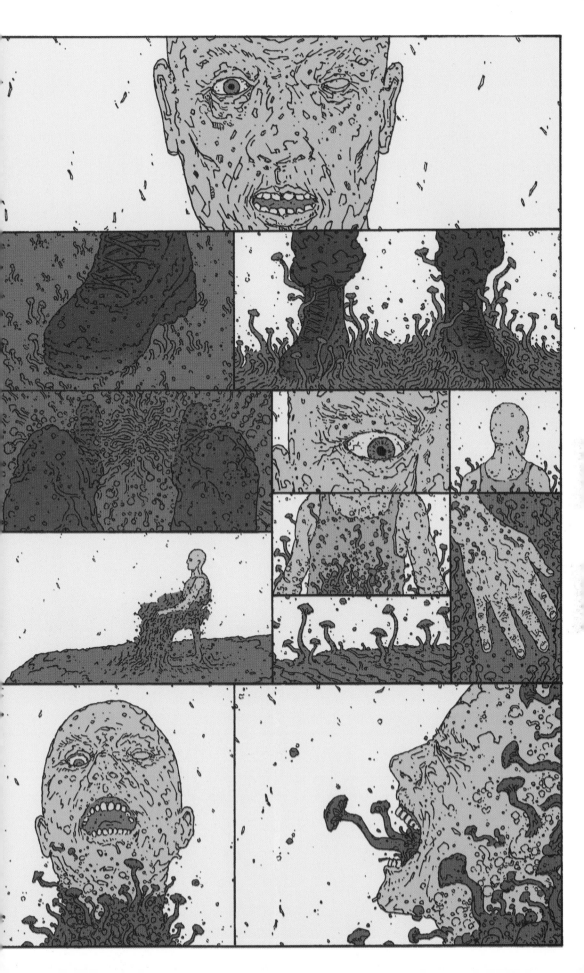

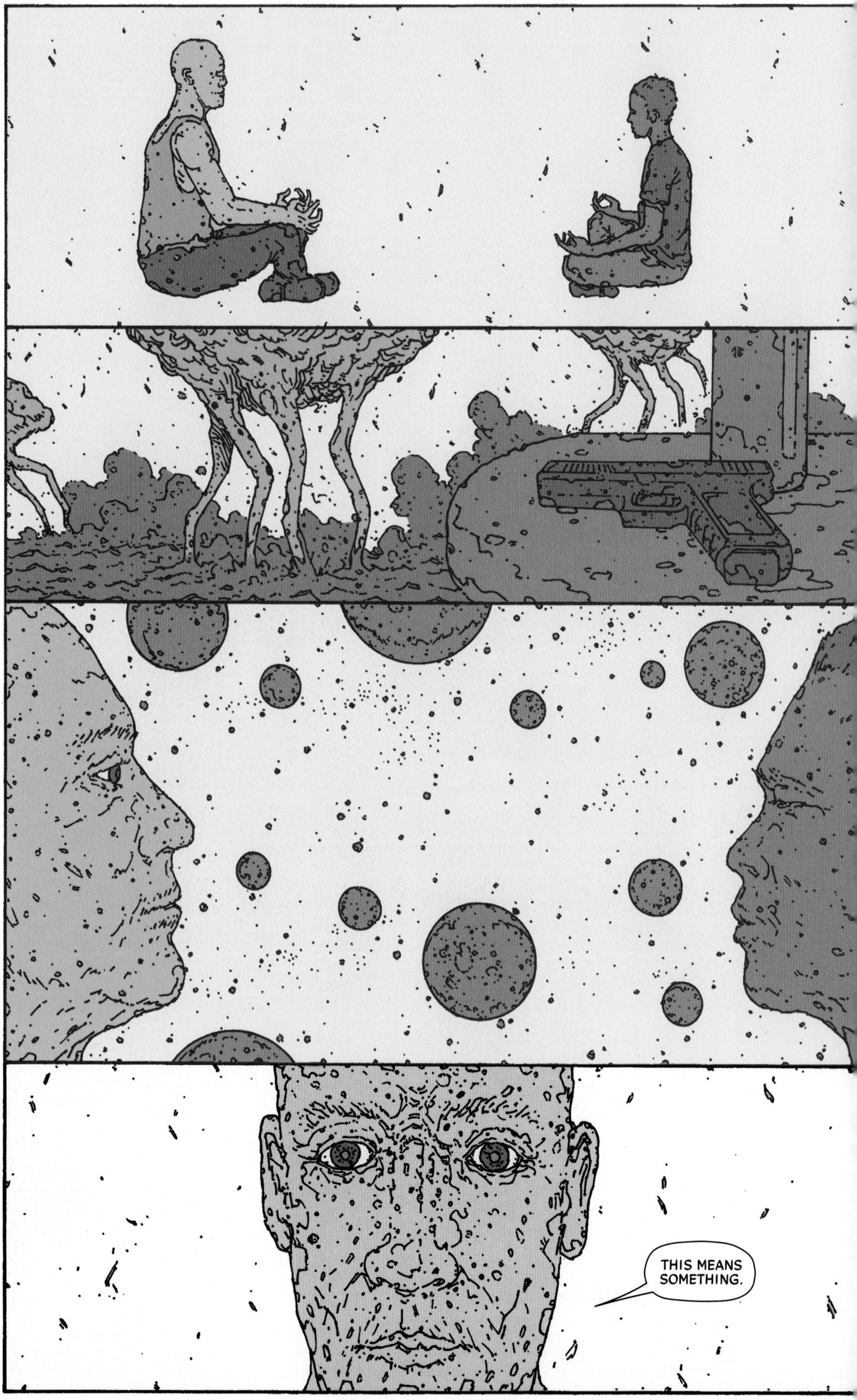
THIS MEANS SOMETHING.

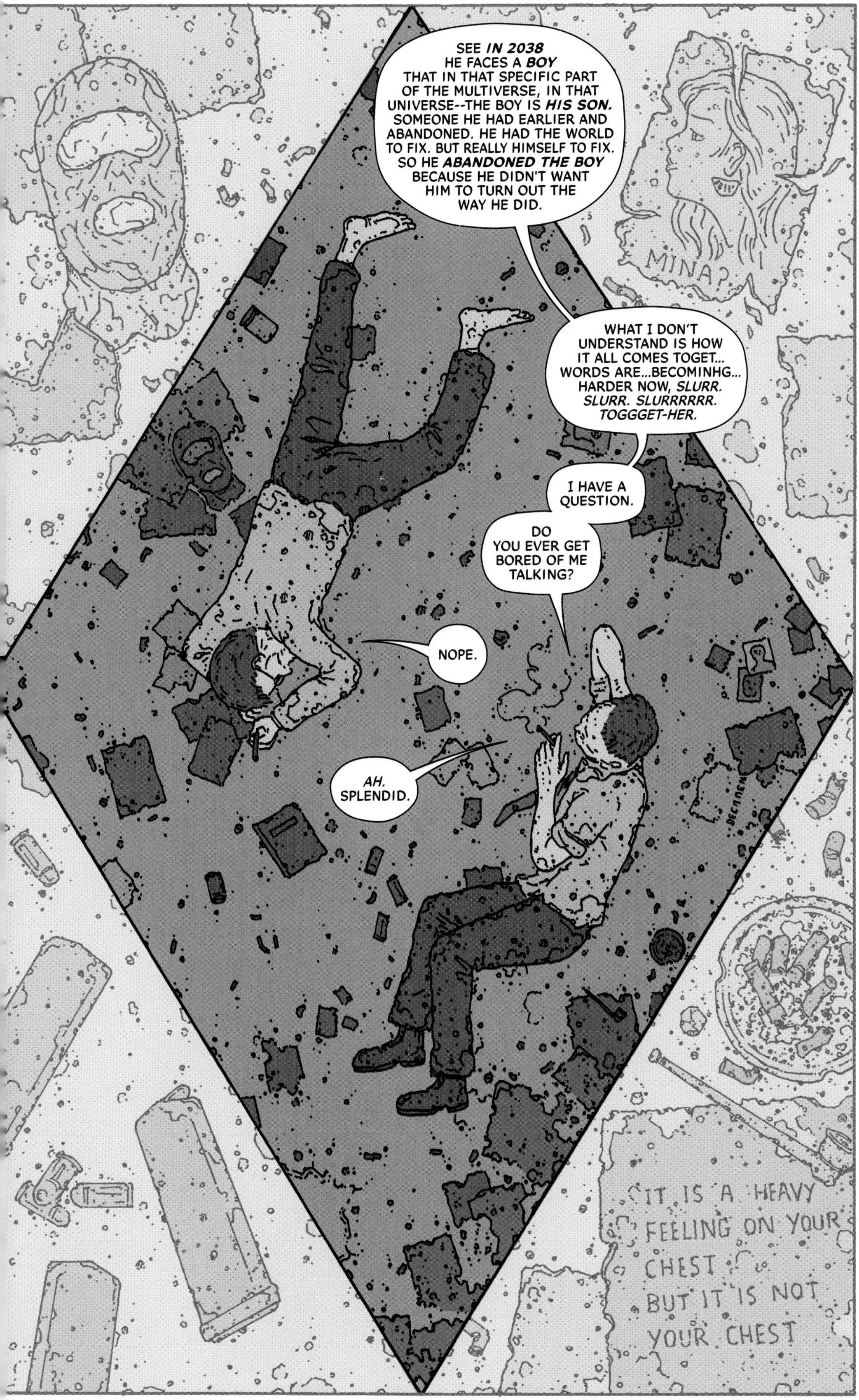
SEE *IN 2038* HE FACES A *BOY* THAT IN THAT SPECIFIC PART OF THE MULTIVERSE, IN THAT UNIVERSE--THE BOY IS *HIS SON.* SOMEONE HE HAD EARLIER AND ABANDONED. HE HAD THE WORLD TO FIX. BUT REALLY HIMSELF TO FIX. SO HE *ABANDONED THE BOY* BECAUSE HE DIDN'T WANT HIM TO TURN OUT THE WAY HE DID.
WHAT I DON'T UNDERSTAND IS HOW IT ALL COMES TOGET... WORDS ARE...BECOMINHG... HARDER NOW, *SLURR. SLURR. SLURRRRRR. TOGGGET-HER.*
I HAVE A QUESTION.
DO YOU EVER GET BORED OF ME TALKING?
NOPE.
AH. SPLENDID.
MINA?
IT IS A HEAVY FEELING ON YOUR CHEST BUT IT IS NOT YOUR CHEST

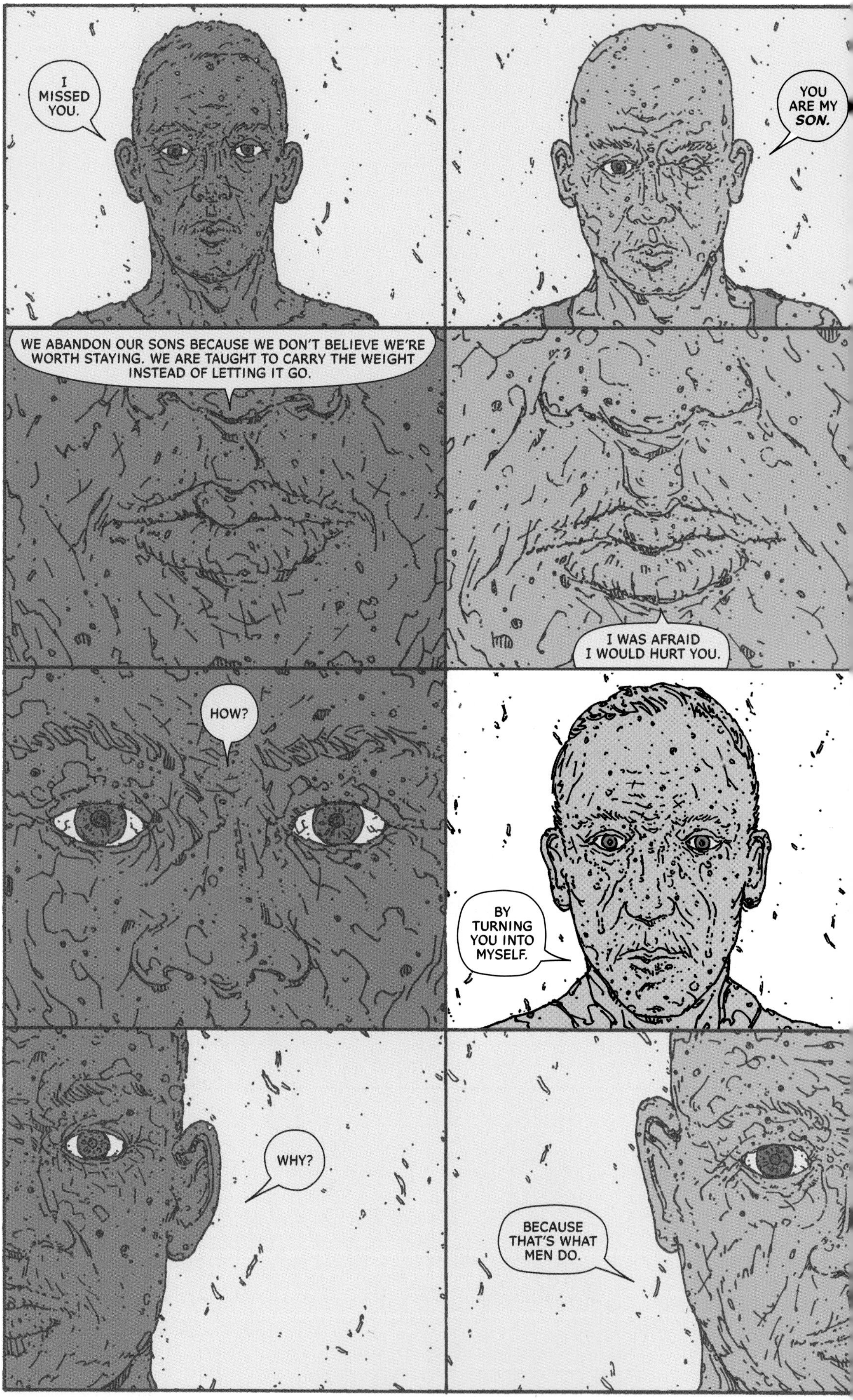
I MISSED YOU.
YOU ARE MY *SON.*
WE ABANDON OUR SONS BECAUSE WE DON'T BELIEVE WE'RE WORTH STAYING. WE ARE TAUGHT TO CARRY THE WEIGHT INSTEAD OF LETTING IT GO.
I WAS AFRAID I WOULD HURT YOU.
HOW?
BY TURNING YOU INTO MYSELF.
WHY?
BECAUSE THAT'S WHAT MEN DO.

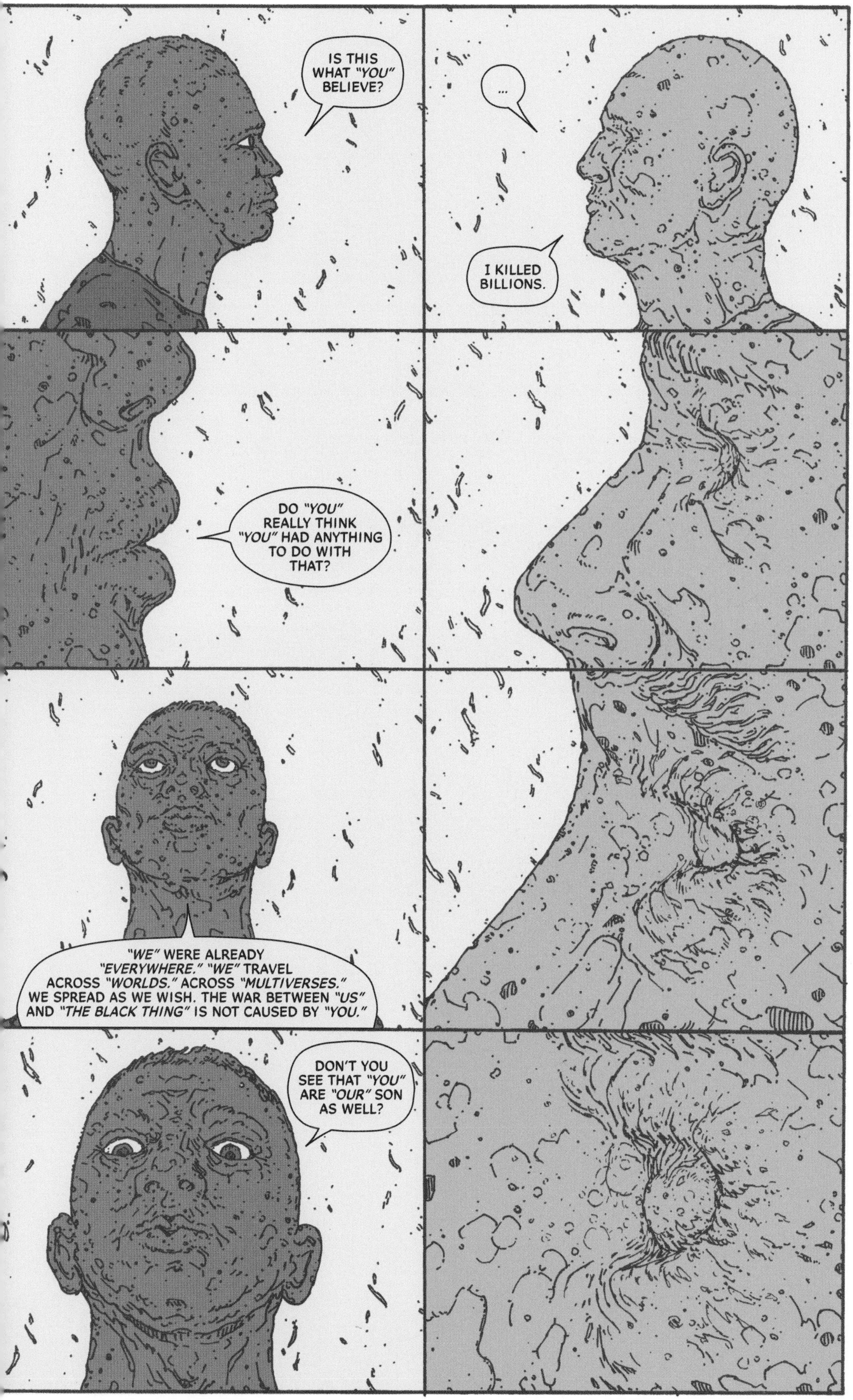
IS THIS WHAT "YOU" BELIEVE?
...
I KILLED BILLIONS.
DO "YOU" REALLY THINK "YOU" HAD ANYTHING TO DO WITH THAT?
"WE" WERE ALREADY "EVERYWHERE." "WE" TRAVEL ACROSS "WORLDS." ACROSS "MULTIVERSES." WE SPREAD AS WE WISH. THE WAR BETWEEN "US" AND "THE BLACK THING" IS NOT CAUSED BY "YOU."
DON'T YOU SEE THAT "YOU" ARE "OUR" SON AS WELL?

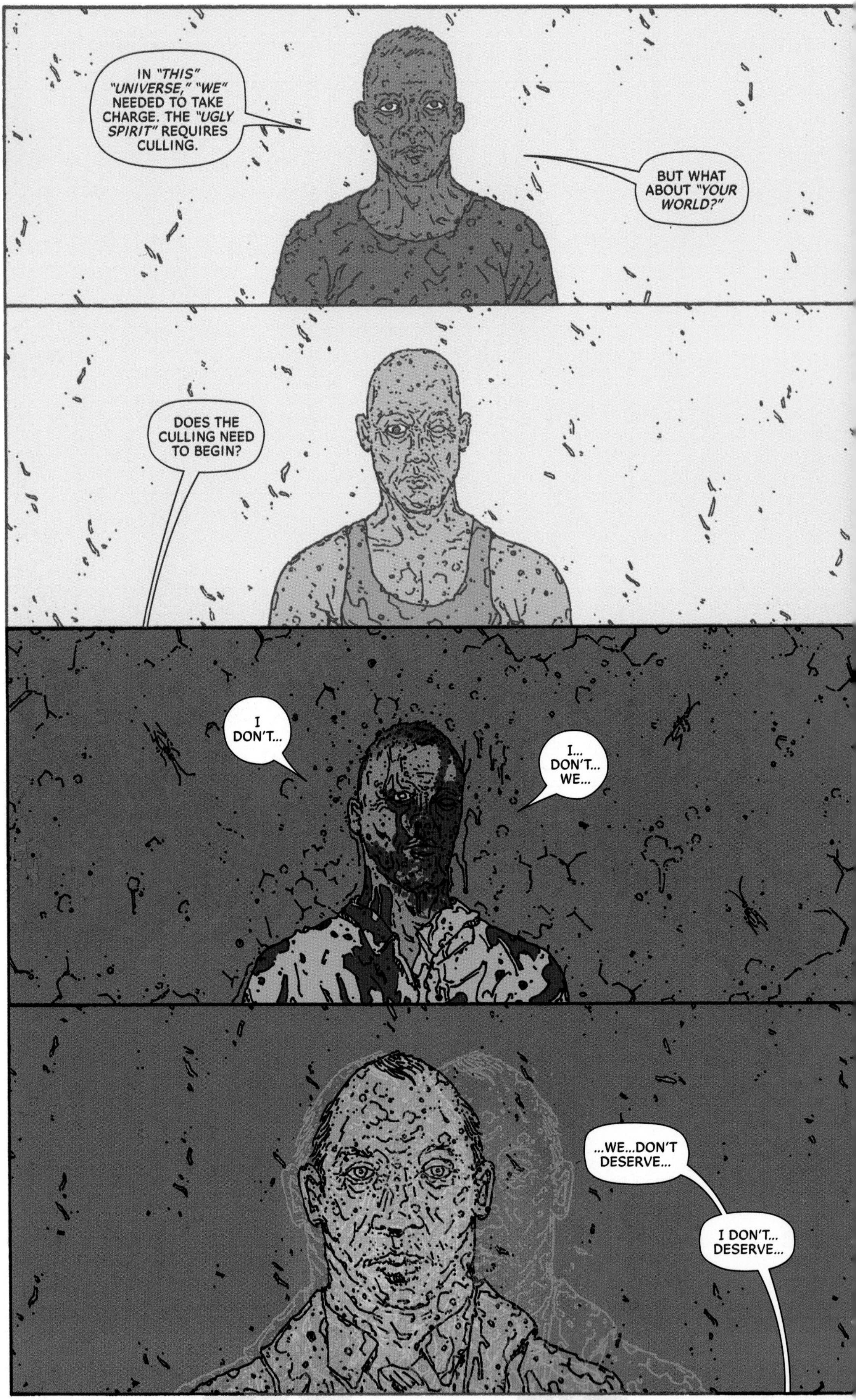
IN "THIS" "UNIVERSE," "WE" NEEDED TO TAKE CHARGE. THE "UGLY SPIRIT" REQUIRES CULLING.
BUT WHAT ABOUT "YOUR WORLD?"
DOES THE CULLING NEED TO BEGIN?
I DON'T...
I... DON'T... WE...
...WE...DON'T DESERVE...
I DON'T... DESERVE...

"...ANYTHING. BETTER."
WOMEN. AT THE HEART OF IT ALL. WE CLAIM WE BUILD THE WORLD BUT WE WOULDN'T BE HERE WITHOUT THEM. HOW COULD I BE SO BLIND?
I AM SO SORRY. SO SORRY.
THE UGLY SPIRIT DID IT. THE BLACK THING DID IT. THE THING IN THE SHADOWS. NOT ME. NOT ME. I DIDN'T WANT TO. THE BULLET WENT WHERE IT WANTED IT TO GO--
AAAAAHHHH. AHHHHH. FORGIVE ME. FORGIVE ME.
FORGIVE ME, JOAN.

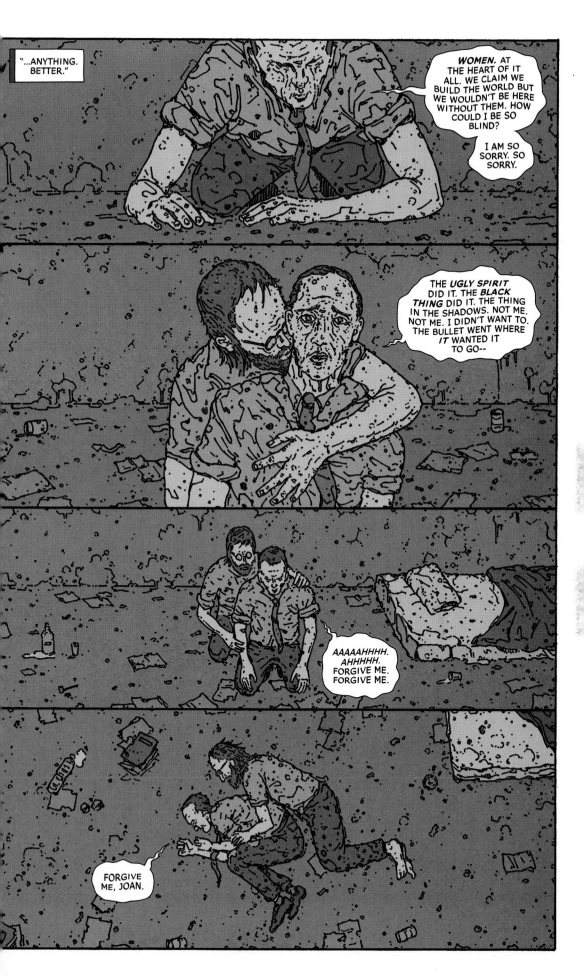

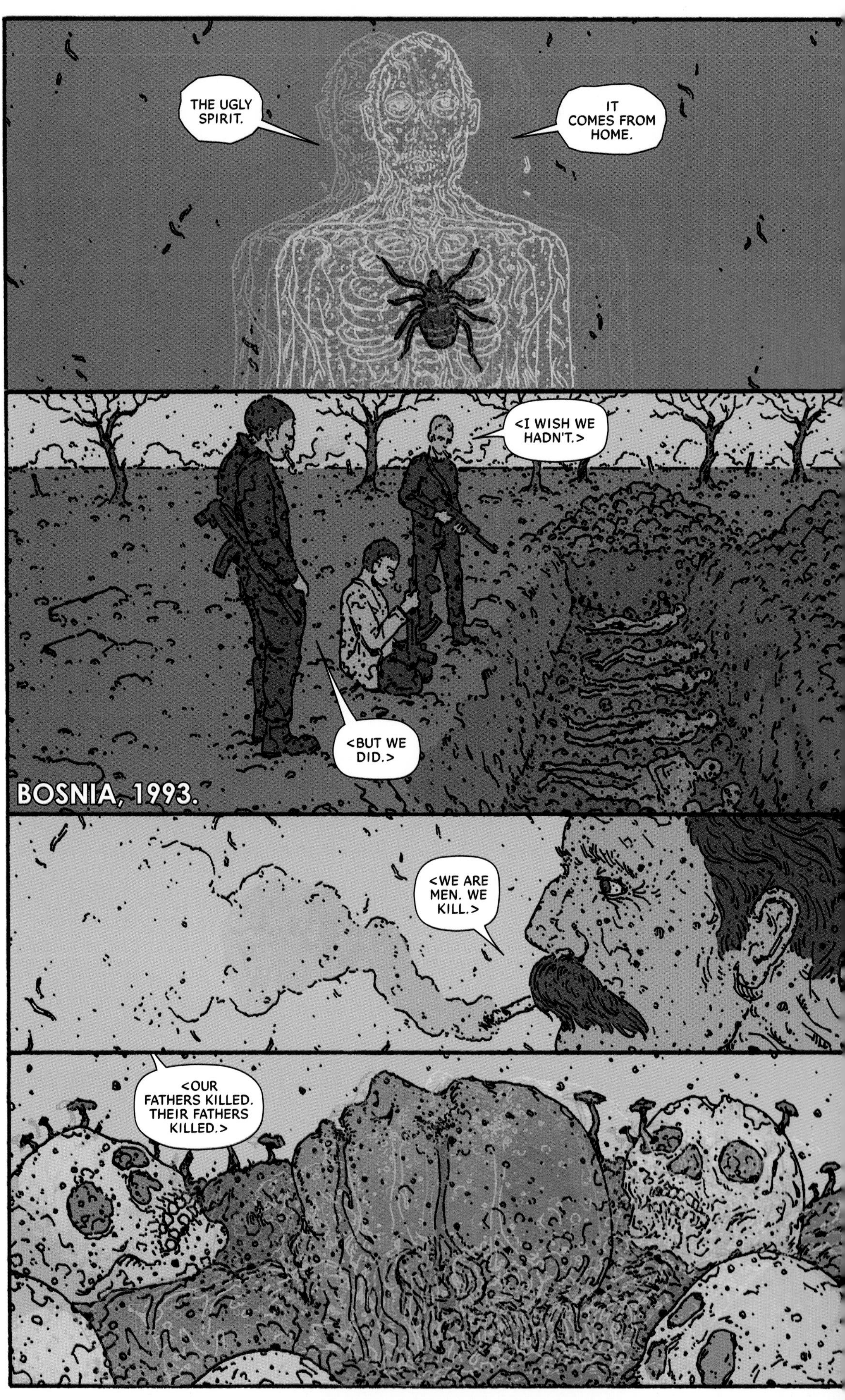
THE UGLY SPIRIT.
IT COMES FROM HOME.
<I WISH WE HADN'T.>
<BUT WE DID.>
BOSNIA, 1993.
<WE ARE MEN. WE KILL.>
<OUR FATHERS KILLED. THEIR FATHERS KILLED.>

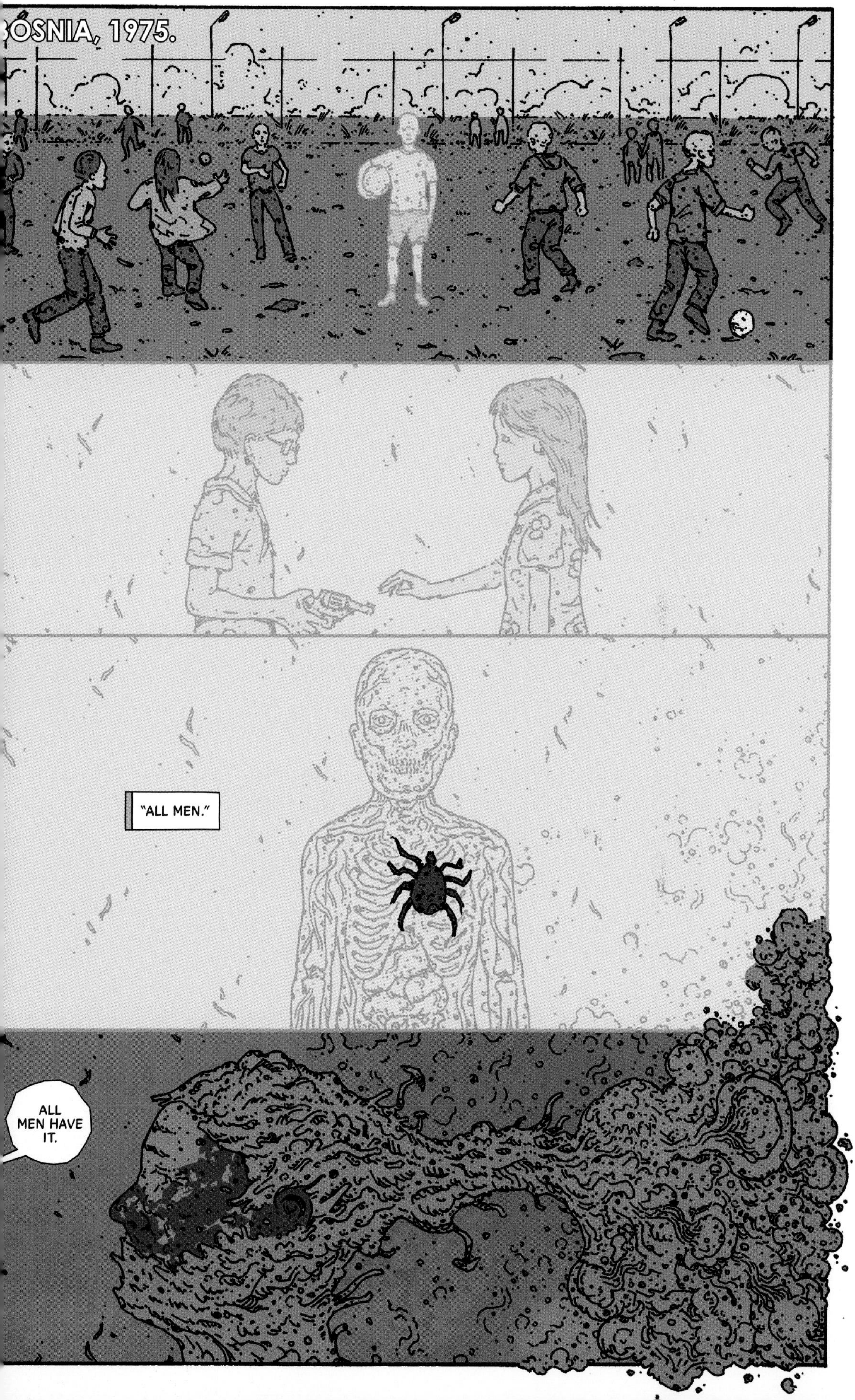
BOSNIA, 1975.
"ALL MEN."
ALL MEN HAVE IT.

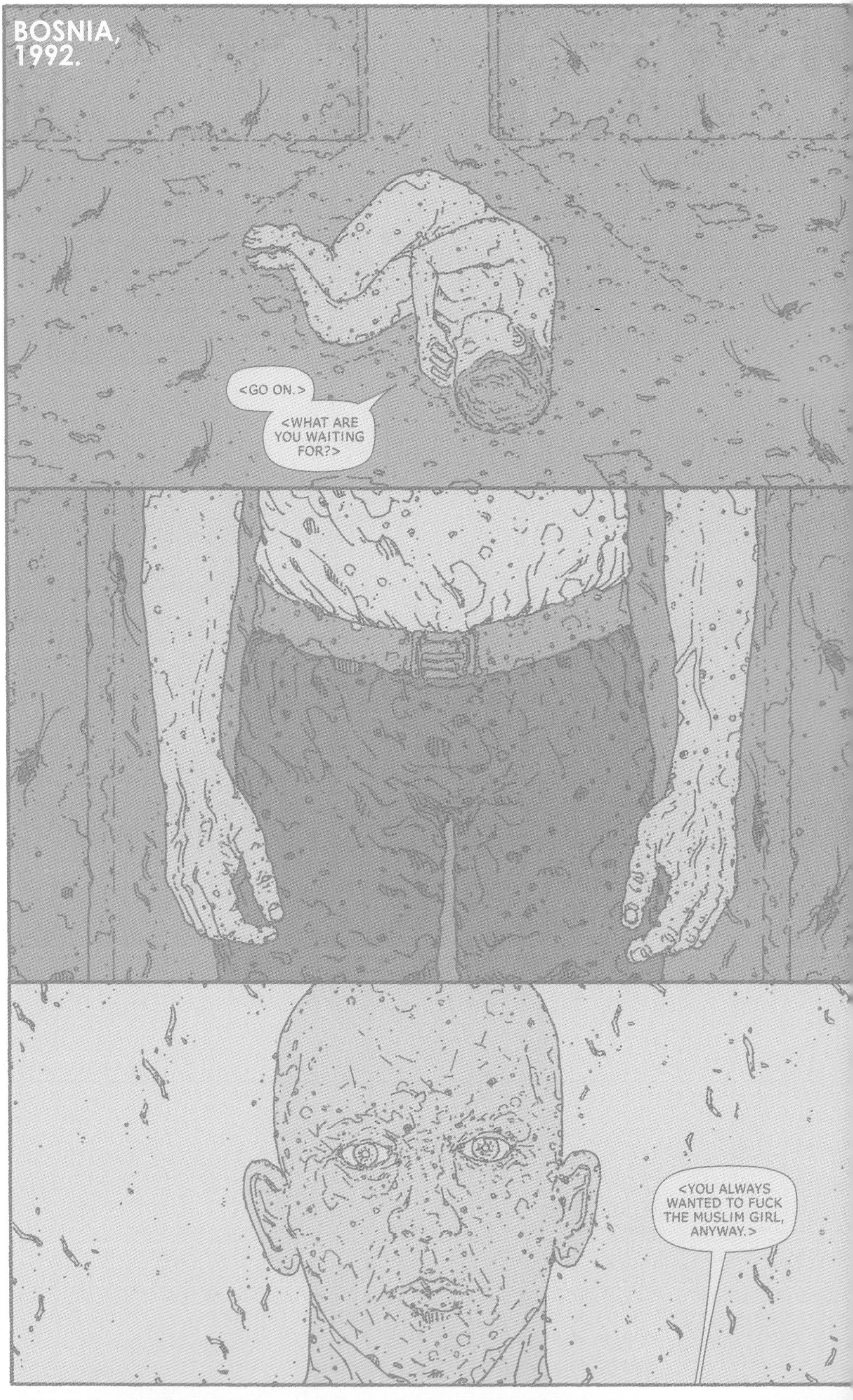
BOSNIA, 1992.
<GO ON.>
<WHAT ARE YOU WAITING FOR?>
<YOU ALWAYS WANTED TO FUCK THE MUSLIM GIRL, ANYWAY.>

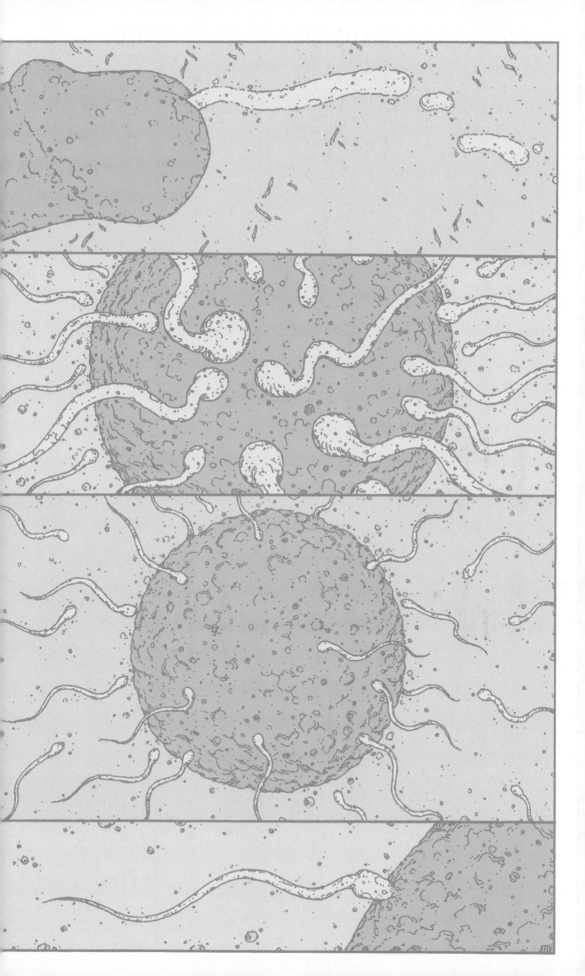

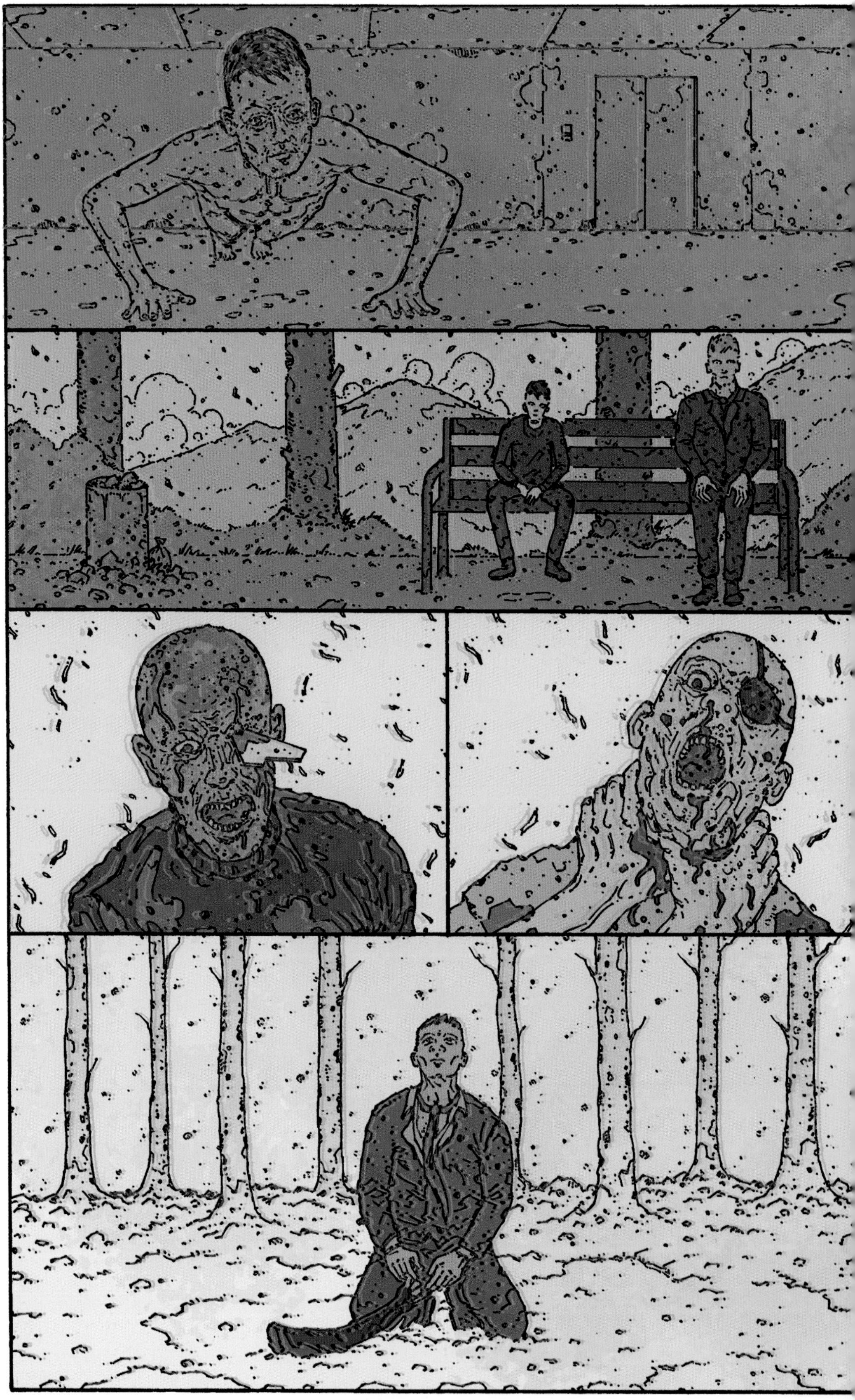

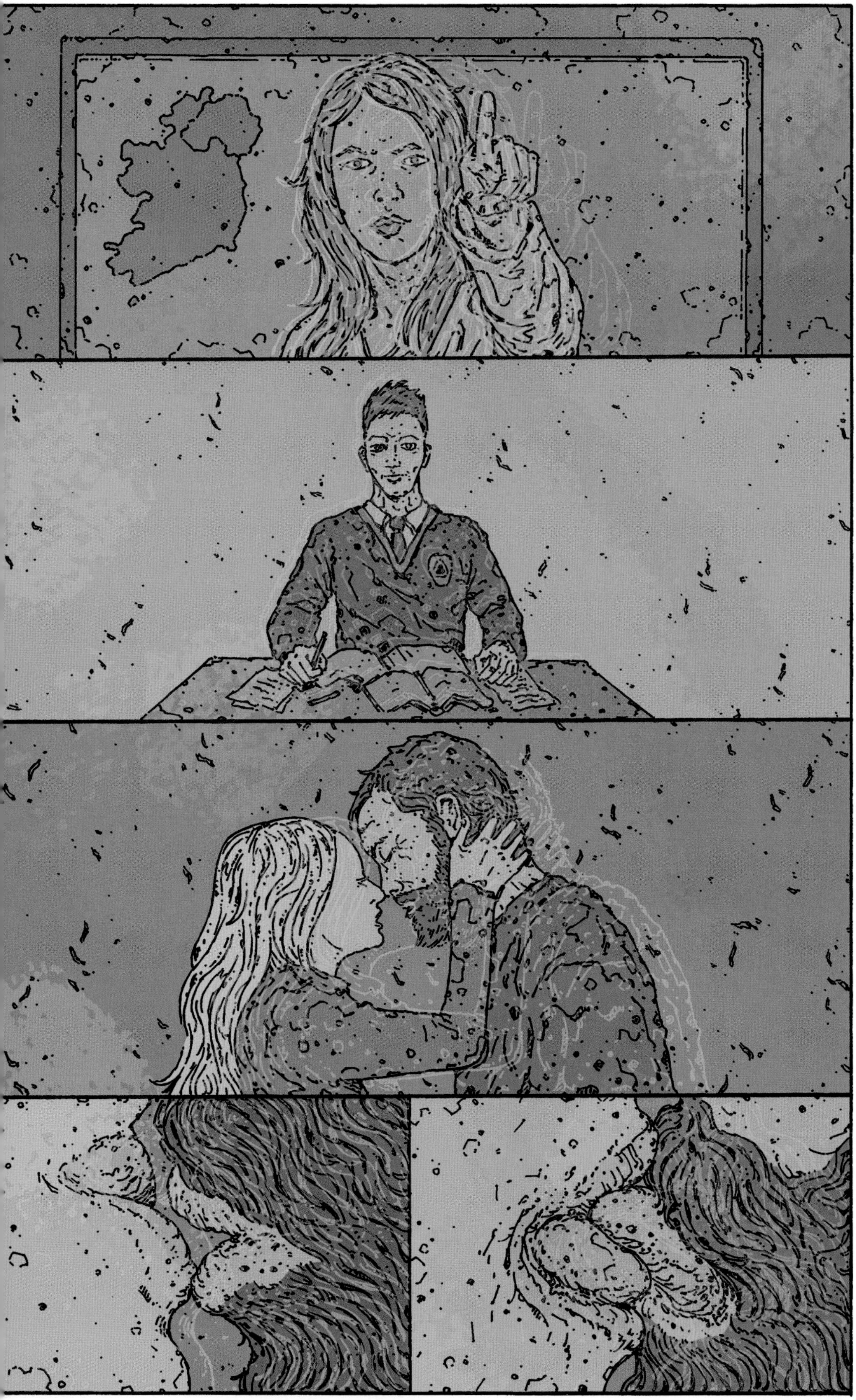

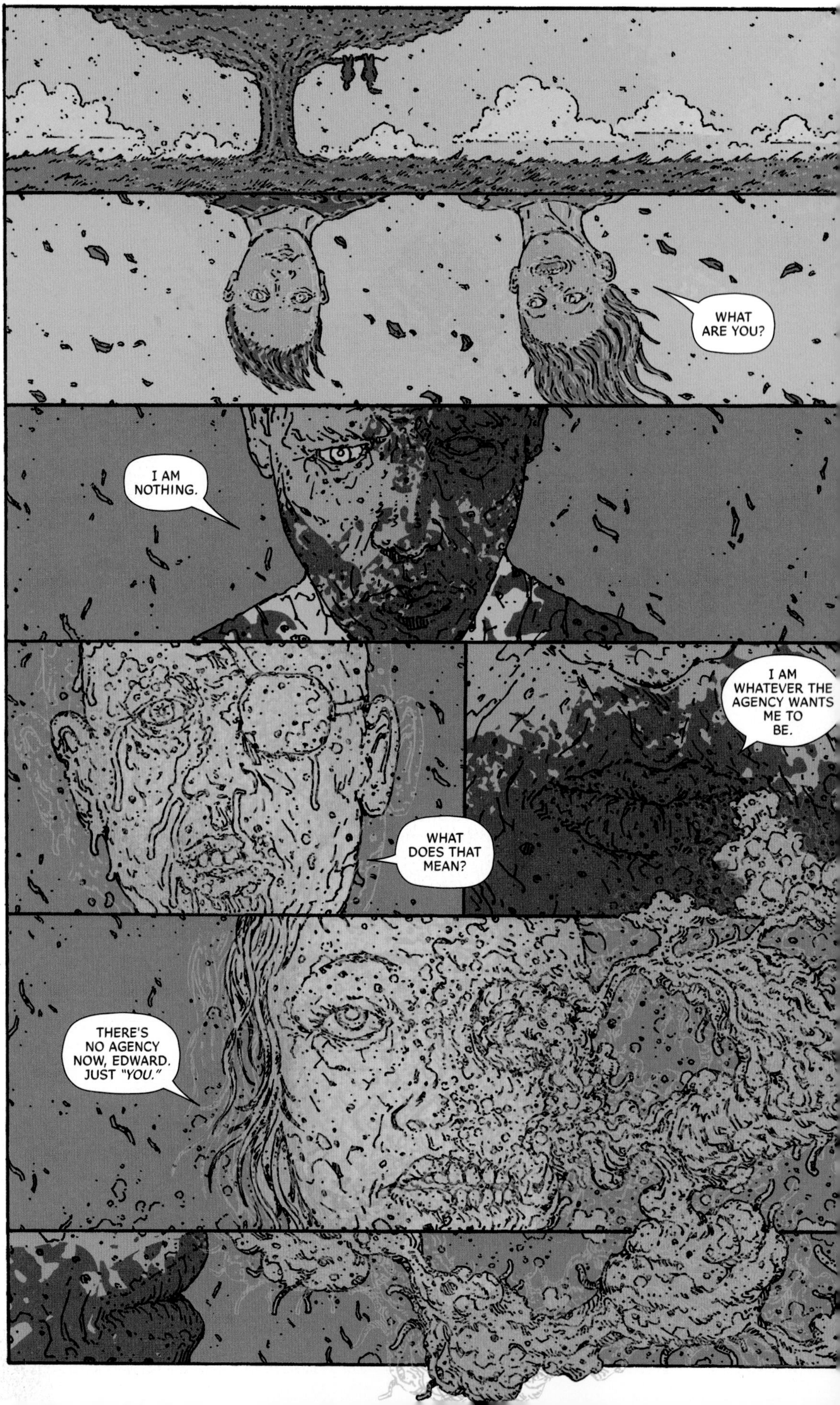
WHAT ARE YOU?
I AM NOTHING.
I AM WHATEVER THE AGENCY WANTS ME TO BE.
WHAT DOES THAT MEAN?
THERE'S NO AGENCY NOW, EDWARD. JUST *"YOU."*

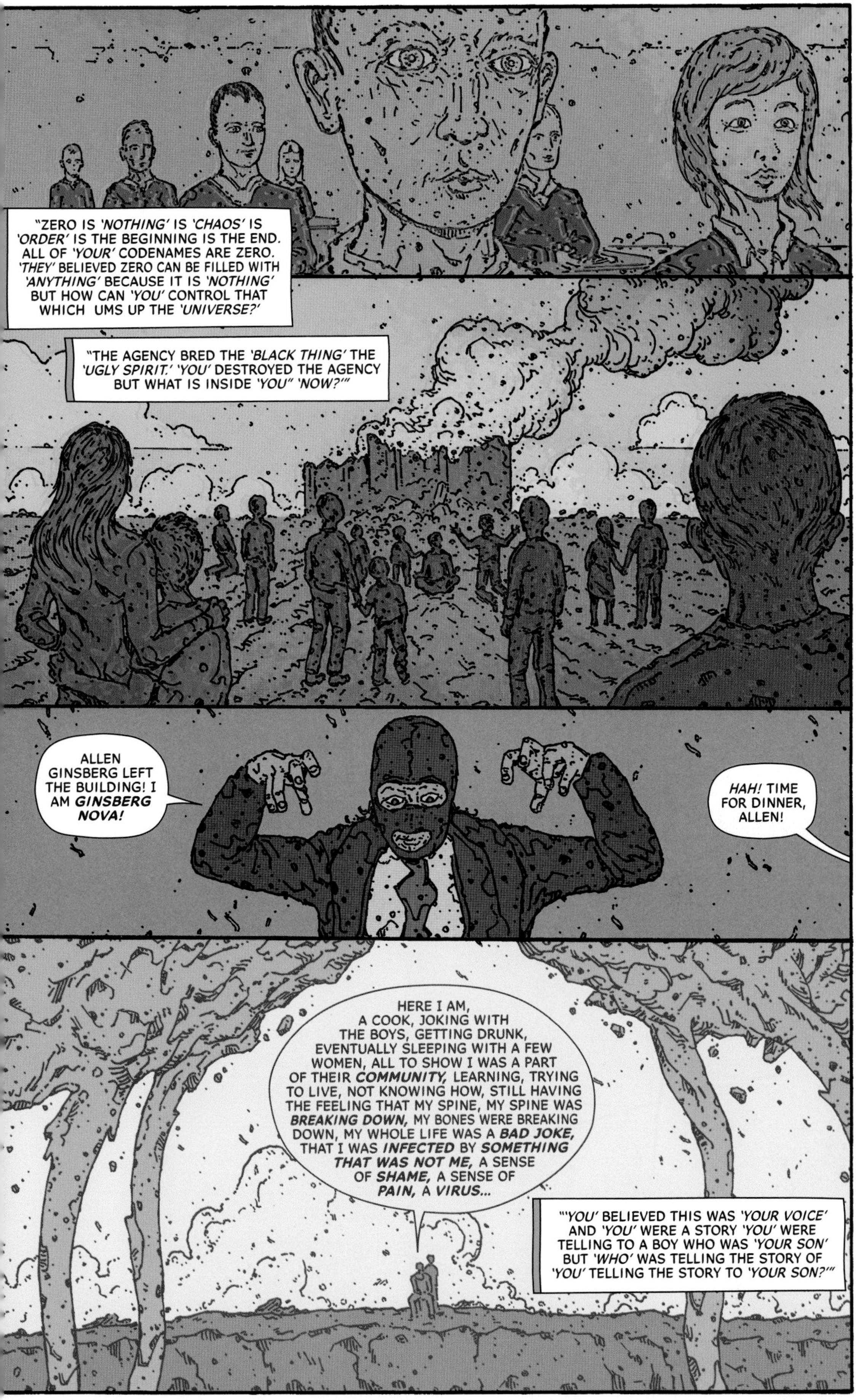
"ZERO IS 'NOTHING' IS 'CHAOS' IS 'ORDER' IS THE BEGINNING IS THE END. ALL OF 'YOUR' CODENAMES ARE ZERO. 'THEY' BELIEVED ZERO CAN BE FILLED WITH 'ANYTHING' BECAUSE IT IS 'NOTHING' BUT HOW CAN 'YOU' CONTROL THAT WHICH UMS UP THE 'UNIVERSE?'
"THE AGENCY BRED THE 'BLACK THING' THE 'UGLY SPIRIT.' 'YOU' DESTROYED THE AGENCY BUT WHAT IS INSIDE 'YOU" 'NOW?'"
ALLEN GINSBERG LEFT THE BUILDING! I AM GINSBERG NOVA!
HAH! TIME FOR DINNER, ALLEN!
HERE I AM, A COOK, JOKING WITH THE BOYS, GETTING DRUNK, EVENTUALLY SLEEPING WITH A FEW WOMEN, ALL TO SHOW I WAS A PART OF THEIR COMMUNITY, LEARNING, TRYING TO LIVE, NOT KNOWING HOW, STILL HAVING THE FEELING THAT MY SPINE, MY SPINE WAS BREAKING DOWN, MY BONES WERE BREAKING DOWN, MY WHOLE LIFE WAS A BAD JOKE, THAT I WAS INFECTED BY SOMETHING THAT WAS NOT ME, A SENSE OF SHAME, A SENSE OF PAIN, A VIRUS...
"'YOU' BELIEVED THIS WAS 'YOUR VOICE' AND 'YOU' WERE A STORY 'YOU' WERE TELLING TO A BOY WHO WAS 'YOUR SON' BUT 'WHO' WAS TELLING THE STORY OF 'YOU' TELLING THE STORY TO 'YOUR SON?'"

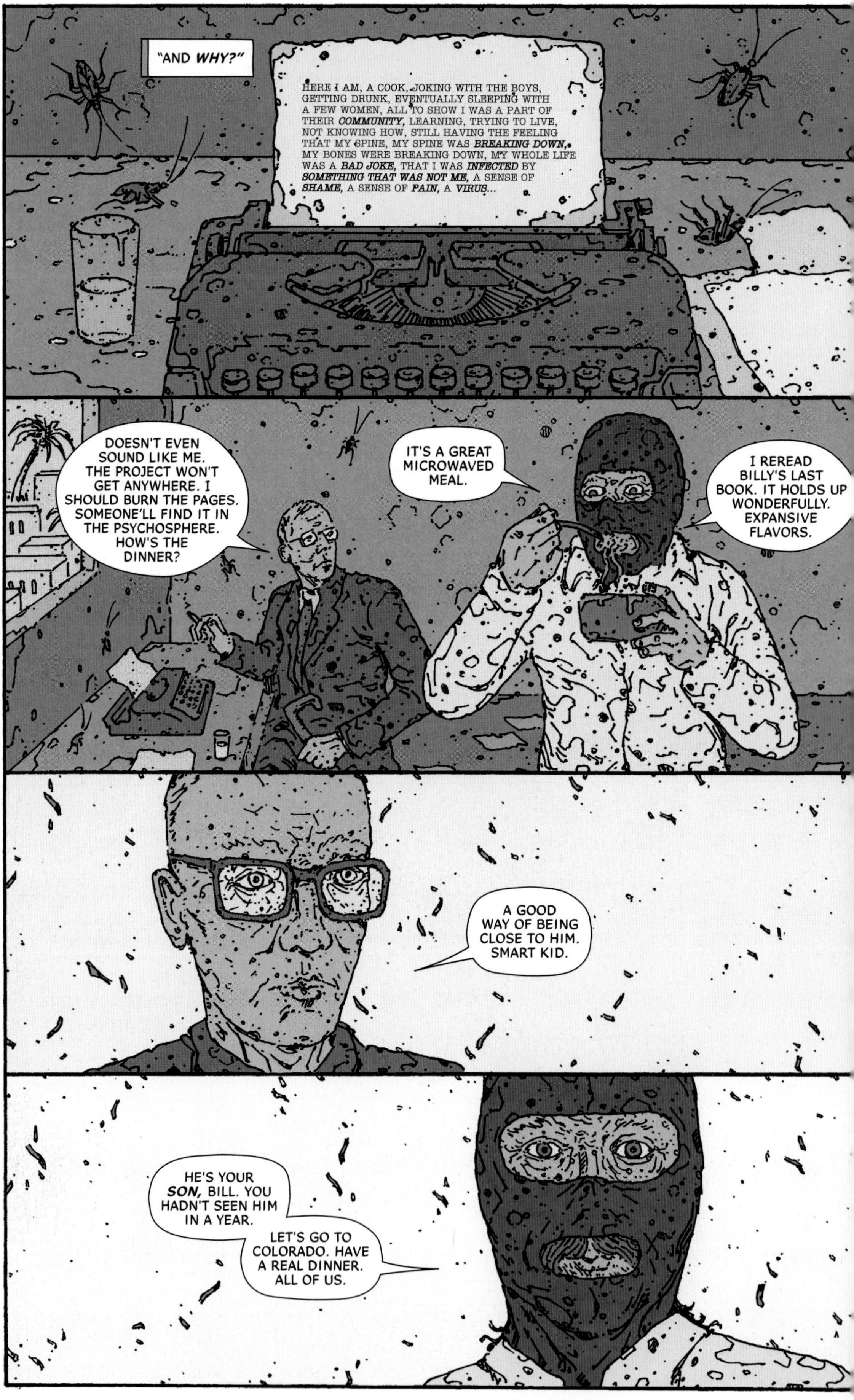
"AND *WHY?*"
HERE I AM, A COOK, JOKING WITH THE BOYS, GETTING DRUNK, EVENTUALLY SLEEPING WITH A FEW WOMEN, ALL TO SHOW I WAS A PART OF THEIR ***COMMUNITY,*** LEARNING, TRYING TO LIVE, NOT KNOWING HOW, STILL HAVING THE FEELING THAT MY SPINE, MY SPINE WAS ***BREAKING DOWN,*** MY BONES WERE BREAKING DOWN, MY WHOLE LIFE WAS A ***BAD JOKE,*** THAT I WAS ***INFECTED*** BY ***SOMETHING THAT WAS NOT ME,*** A SENSE OF ***SHAME,*** A SENSE OF ***PAIN,*** A ***VIRUS...***
DOESN'T EVEN SOUND LIKE ME. THE PROJECT WON'T GET ANYWHERE. I SHOULD BURN THE PAGES. SOMEONE'LL FIND IT IN THE PSYCHOSPHERE. HOW'S THE DINNER?
IT'S A GREAT MICROWAVED MEAL.
I REREAD BILLY'S LAST BOOK. IT HOLDS UP WONDERFULLY. EXPANSIVE FLAVORS.
A GOOD WAY OF BEING CLOSE TO HIM. SMART KID.
HE'S YOUR ***SON,*** BILL. YOU HADN'T SEEN HIM IN A YEAR.
LET'S GO TO COLORADO. HAVE A REAL DINNER. ALL OF US.

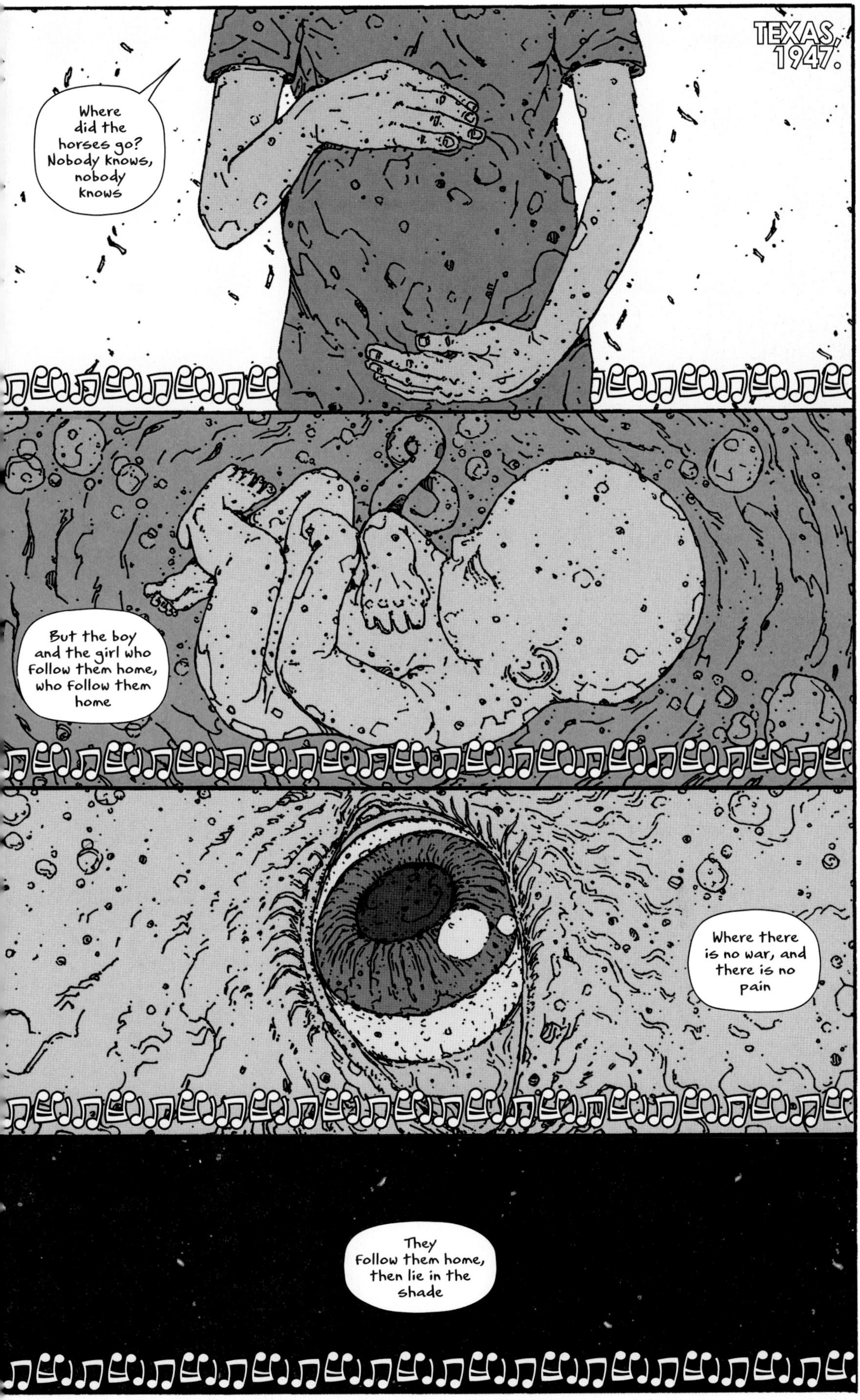

TEXAS, 1947.
Where did the horses go? Nobody knows, nobody knows
But the boy and the girl who follow them home, who follow them home
Where there is no war, and there is no pain
They follow them home, then lie in the shade

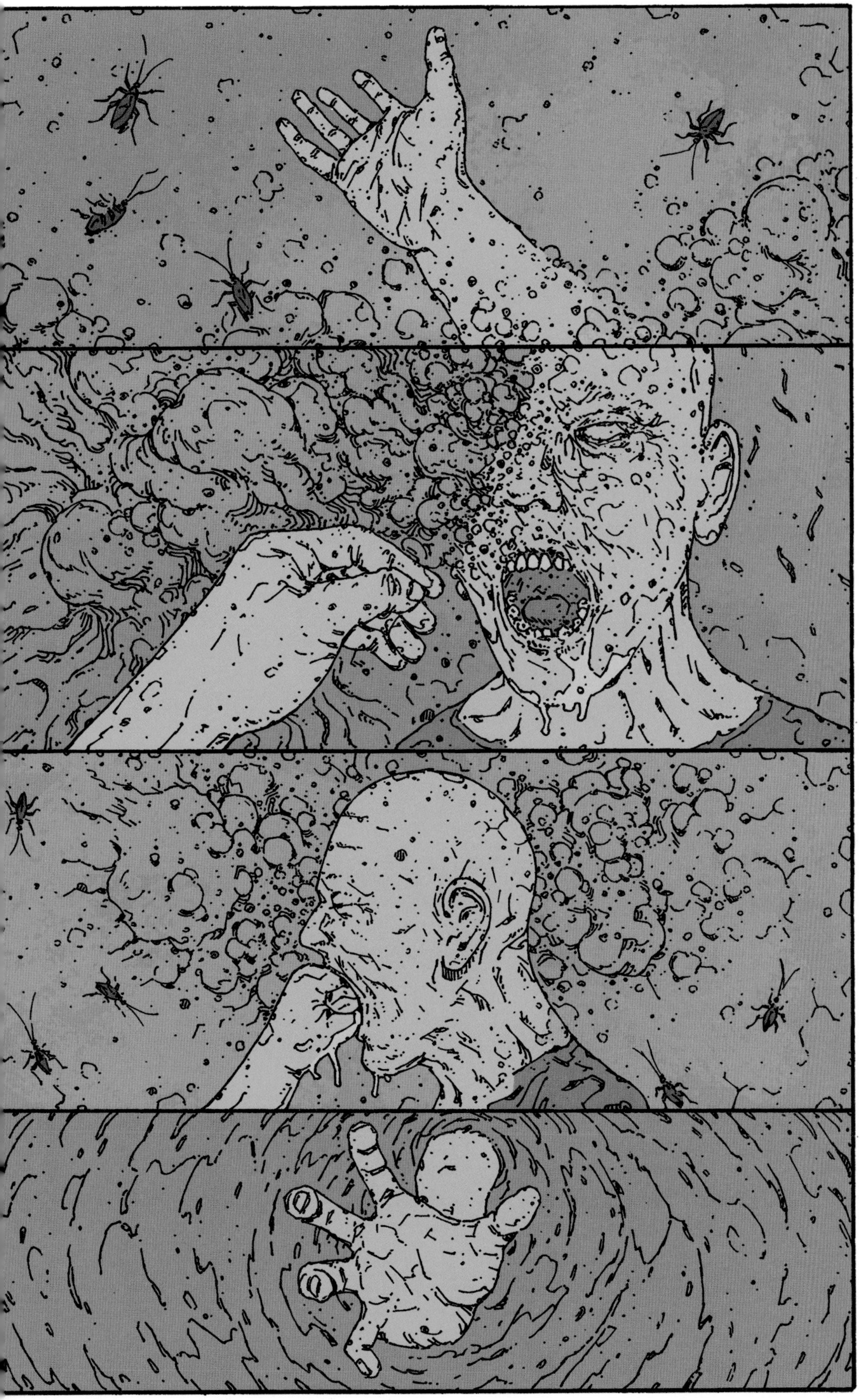

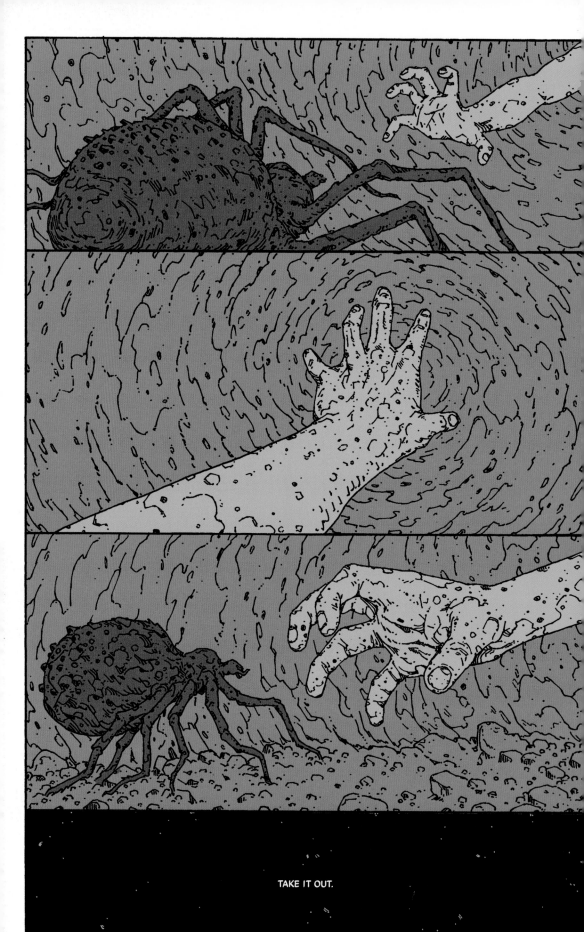

TAKE IT OUT.

NITED KINGDOM, 2038.

VER.

Heir's Pistol Kills His Wife
He Denies Playing Wm. Te

Mexico City, Sept. 7 (AP).—William Seward Burroughs, 37, first adm then denied today that he was playing William Tell when his gun kille pretty, young wife during a drinking party last night.

Police said that Burroughs, grandson of the adding machine inventor, first told them that, wanting to show off his marksmanship, he placed a glass of gin on her head and fired, but was so drunk that he missed and shot her in the forehead.

After talking with a lawyer, police said, Burroughs, who is a wealthy cotton planter from Pharr, Tex., changed his story and insisted that his wife was shot accidentally when he dropped his newly-purchased .38 caliber pistol.

Husband in Jail.

Mrs. Burroughs, 27, the former Joan Vollmer, died in the Red Cross Hospital.

The shooting occurred during a party in the apartment of John Healy of Minneapolis. Burroughs said two other American tourists whom he knew only slightly were present.

Burroughs, hair disheveled and clothes wrinkled, was in jail today. A hearing on a charge of homicide is scheduled for tomorrow morning.

No Arguments, He Says.

"It was purely accidental," he said. "I did not put any glass on her head. If she did, it was a joke. I certainly did not intend to shoot at it."

He said there had been no arguments or discussion before the "accident."

"The party was quiet," he said. "We had a few drinks. Everything is very hazy."

Burroughs and his wife had been here about two years. He said he was studying native dialects at the University of Mexico. He explained his long absence from his ranch by saying that he was unsuited for business.

Wife From Albany.

He said he was born in St. Louis and that his wife was from Albany, N. Y. They have two children, William Burroughs Jr., 3, and Julie Adams, 7, who he said was his wife's daughter by a previous marriage. The couple had been married five years.

She had attended journalism school at Columbia University before her marriage to Burroughs.

Burroughs, who also had been married before, formerly lived in Loudonville, a swank sub Albany. He is a graduate rard University and work two weeks in 1942 as a r for the St. Louis Post Dis

His paternal grandfathe the foundation of a fortun he built his first adding in St. Louis in 1885.

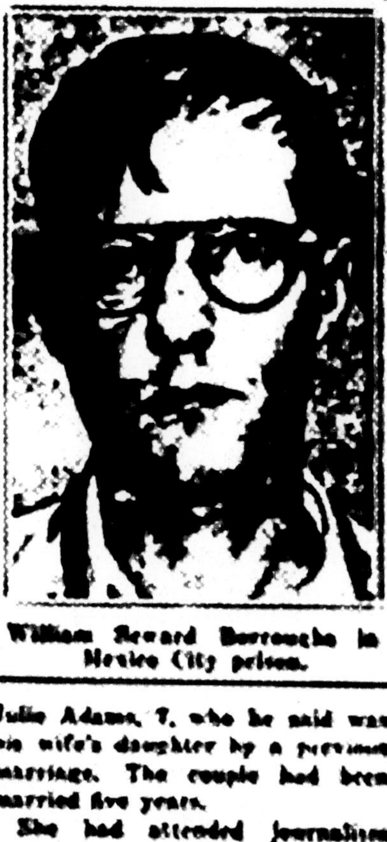

William Seward Burroughs in Mexico City prison.

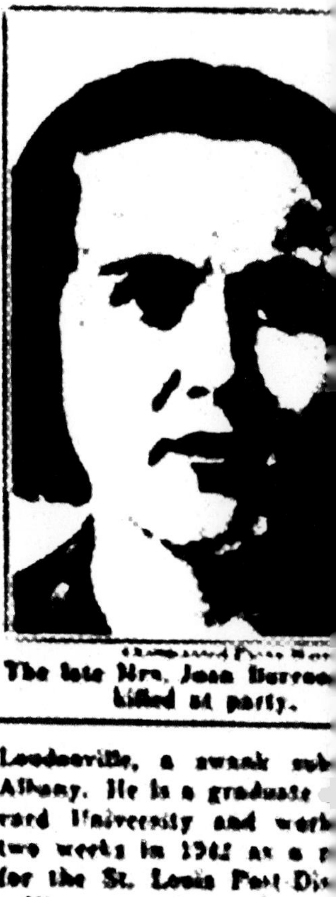

(Associated Press Wire
The late Mrs. Joan Burrou killed at party.

J JOAN JOAN JOAN JOAN J OAN JOAN JOAN JOAN JOAN JOAN JOAN JO
JOAN JOAN JOAN JOAN JOAN JOAN JOAN JOAN JOAN JOAN JOAN JOAN JO

J JOAN JOAN JOAN JOAN JOAN JOAN JOAN JOAN JOAN JOAN JOAN JOAN JOAN JO
J JOAN JOAN JOAN JOAN JOAN JOAN JOAN JOAN JOAN JOAN JOAN JOAN JOAN JO
J JOAN JOAN JOAN JOAN JOAN JOAN JOAN JOAN JOAN JOAN JOAN JOAN JOAN JO
J JOAN JOAN JOAN JOAN JOAN JOAN JOAN JOAN JOAN JOAN JOAN JOAN JO
J JOAN JOAN JOAN JOAN JOAN JOAN JOAN JOAN JOA N JOAN JOAN JOAN JOAN JO
J JOAN JOAN JOAN JOAN JOAN JOAN JOAN JOAN JOAN JOAN JOAN JOAN JOAN JO

J JOAN JOAN JOAN JOAN JOAN JOAN JOAN JOAN JOAN JOAN JOAN JOAN JOAN JO
JOAN JOAN JOAN JOAN JOAN JOAN JOAN JOAN JOAN JOAN JOAN JOAN JOAN JO
JOAN JOAN JOAN JOAN JOAN JOAN JOAN JOAN JOAN JOAN JOAN JOAN JOAN JO
JOAN V OLLMER JOAN JOAN JOAN JOAN JOAN JOAN JOAN JOAN JOAN JOAN JO
JOAN JOAN JOAN JOAN JOAN
JOAN JOAN JOAN JOAN JOAN JOAN JO
JOAN JOAN JOAN JOAN JOAN JOAN JOAN JOAN JOAN JOAN JOAN JOAN
J JOAN JOAN JOAN JOAN JOAN JOAN JOAN JOAN JOAN JOAN JOAN JOAN JOAN J
J JOAN JOAN JOAN JOAN JOAN JOAN JOAN JOAN JOAN JOAN JOAN JOAN JOAN JOAN J
JOAN JOAN JOAN JOAN JOAN JOAN JOAN JOAN JOAN JOAN JOAN JOAN JOAN JO
J JOAN JOAN JOAN JOAN JOAN JOAN JOAN JOAN JOAN JOAN JOAN JOAN JOAN JO
J JOAN JOAN JOAN JOAN JOAN JOAN JOAN JOAN JOAN JOAN JOAN JOAN JOAN J
J JOAN JOAN JOAN JOAN JOAN JOAN JOAN JOAN JOAN JOAN JOAN JOAN JOAN JO
J JOAN JOAN JOAN JOAN JOAN JOAN JOAN JOAN JOAN JOAN JOAN JOAN JOAN
R JOAN JOAN JOAN JOAN JOAN JOAN JOAN JOAN JOAN JOAN JOAN JOAN JOAN JO
J JOAN JOAN JOAN JOAN JOAN JOAN JOAN JOAN JOAN JOAN JOAN JOAN JO
J JOAN JOAN JOAN JOAN JOAN JOAN JOAN JOAN JOAN JOAN JOAN JOAN JOAN JO
J JOAN JOAN JOAN JOAN JOAN JOAN JOAN JOAN JOAN JOAN JOAN JOAN JOAN JO
J JOAN JOAN JOAN JOAN JOAN JOAN JOAN JOAN JOAN JOAN JOAN JOAN JOAN JO
J JOAN JOAN JOAN JOAN JOAN JOAN JOAN JOAN JOAN JOAN JOAN JOAN JOAN JO
J JOAN JOAN JOAN JOAN JOAN JOAN JOAN JOAN JOAN JOAN JOAN JOAN JOAN JO
J JOAN JOAN JOAN JOAN JOAN JOAN JOAN JOAN JOAN JOAN JOAN JOAN JO
J JOAN JOAN JOAN JOAN J OAN JOAN JOAN JOAN JOAN JOAN JOAN JOAN JO
J JOAN JOAN JOAN JOAN JOAN JOAN JOAN JOAN JOAN JOAN JOAN JOAN JOAN JO
J JOAN JOAN JOAN JOAN JOAN JOAN JOAN JOAN JOAN JOAN JOAN JOAN JO
J JOAN JOAN JOAN JOAN JOAN JOAN JOAN JOAN JOAN JOAN JOAN JOAN JOAN JO
J JOAN JOAN JOAN JOAN JOAN JOAN JOAN JOAN JOAN JOAN JOAN JOAN JOAN JO
J JOAN JOAN JOAN JOAN JOAN JOAN
J JOAN JOAN JOAN JOAN JOAN JOAN JOAN JOAN JOAN JOAN JOAN JOAN JO
J JOAN JOAN JOA N JOAN JOAN JOAN JOAN JOAN JOAN JOAN JOAN JOAN JOAN JO
J JOAN JOAN JOAN JOAN JOAN JOAN JOAN JOAN JOAN JOAN JOAN JOAN JOAN JO
J JOAN JOAN JOAN JOAN JOAN JOAN JOAN JOAN JOA N JOAN JOAN JOAN JOAN JO
J JOAN JOAN JOAN JOAN JOAN JOAN JOAN JOAN JOAN JOAN JOAN JOAN JOAN JO
J JOAN JOAN JOAN JOAN JOAN JOAN JOAN JOAN JOAN JOAN V OLLMER JOAN
J JOAN JOAN JOAN JOAN JOAN JOAN JOAN JOAN JOAN JOAN JOAN JOAN JOAN JO
J JOAN JOAN JOAN JOAN JOAN JOAN JOAN JOAN JOAN JOAN JOAN JOAN JOAN JO
J JOAN JOAN JOAN JOAN JOAN JOAN JOAN JOAN JOAN JOAN JOAN JOAN JOAN JO
J JOAN JOAN JOAN JOAN JOAN JOAN JOAN JOAN JOAN JOAN JOAN JOAN JOAN JOAN J
JOAN JOAN JOAN JOAN JOAN JOAN JOAN JOAN JOAN JOAN JOAN JOAN JOAN JO
J JOAN JOAN JOAN JOAN JOAN JOAN JOAN JOAN JOAN JOAN JOAN JOAN JOAN JO
J JOAN JOAN JOAN JOAN JOAN JOAN JOA N JOAN JOAN JOAN JOAN JOAN JO
J JOAN JOAN JOAN JOAN JOAN JOAN JOAN JOAN JOAN JOAN JOAN JOAN JOAN JO
J JOAN JOAN JOAN JOAN JOAN JOAN JOAN JOAN JOAN JOAN JOAN JOAN JOAN JO
J JOAN JOAN JOAN VOL LMER JOAN JOAN JOAN JOAN JOAN JOAN JOAN JOAN JO
J JOAN JOAN JOAN JOAN JOAN JOAN JOAN JOAN JOAN JOAN JOAN JOAN JOAN JO
J JOAN JOAN JOAN JOAN JOAN JOAN JOAN JOAN JOAN JOAN JOAN JOAN JOAN JO
J JOAN JOAN JOAN JOAN JOAN JOA N JOAN JOAN JOAN JOAN JOAN JOAN JO
J JOAN JOAN JOAN JOAN JOAN JOAN JOAN JOAN JOAN JOAN JOAN JOAN JOAN JO
J JOAN JOAN JOAN JOAN JOAN JOAN JOAN JOAN JOAN JOAN JOAN JOAN JOAN JO
J JOAN JOAN JOAN JOAN JOAN JOAN JOAN JOAN JOAN JOAN JOAN JOAN JOAN JO
J JOAN JOAN JOAN JOAN JOAN JOAN JOAN JOAN JOAN JOAN JOAN JOAN JOAN JO
N JOAN JOAN JOAN JOAN JOAN JOAN JOAN JOAN J OAN JOAN JOAN JOAN JO
N JOAN JOAN JOAN JOAN JOAN JOAN JOAN JOAN JOAN JOAN JOAN JOAN JOAN

J JOAN JOAN JOAN JOAN JOAN JOAN JOAN JOAN JOAN JOAN JOAN JO

J JOAN JOAN JOAN JOAN JOAN JOAN JOAN JOAN JOAN JOAN JOAN JOAN JOAN JO
J JOAN JOAN JOAN JOAN JOAN JOAN JOAN JOAN JOAN JOAN JOAN JOAN JOAN JO
J JOAN JOAN JOAN JOAN JOAN JOAN JOAN JOAN JOAN JOAN JOAN JOAN JOAN JO

CHAPTER 17

PSYCHOMAGIC

Illustrated by Robert Sammelin

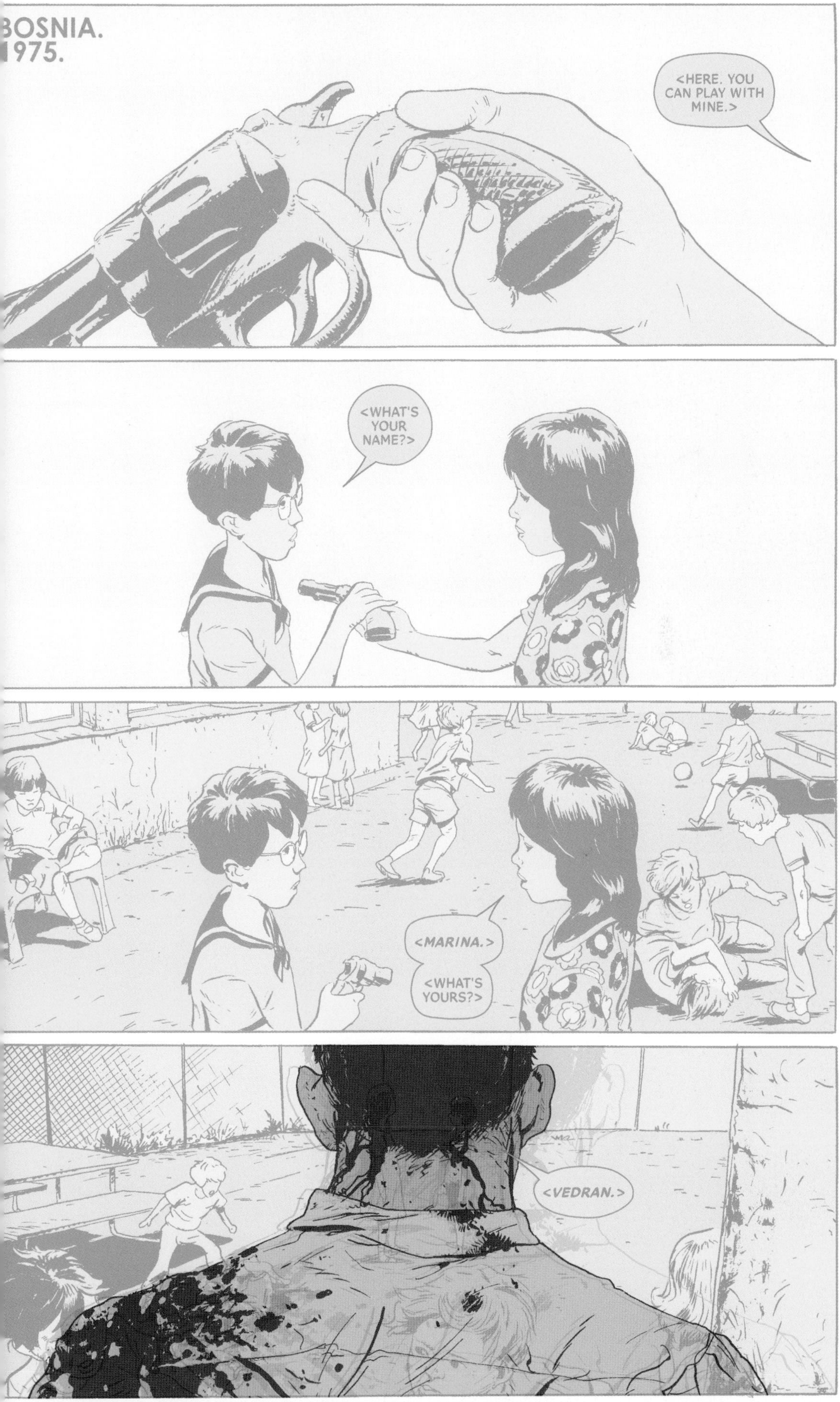
BOSNIA.
1975.
<HERE. YOU CAN PLAY WITH MINE.>
<WHAT'S YOUR NAME?>
<MARINA.>
<WHAT'S YOURS?>
<VEDRAN.>

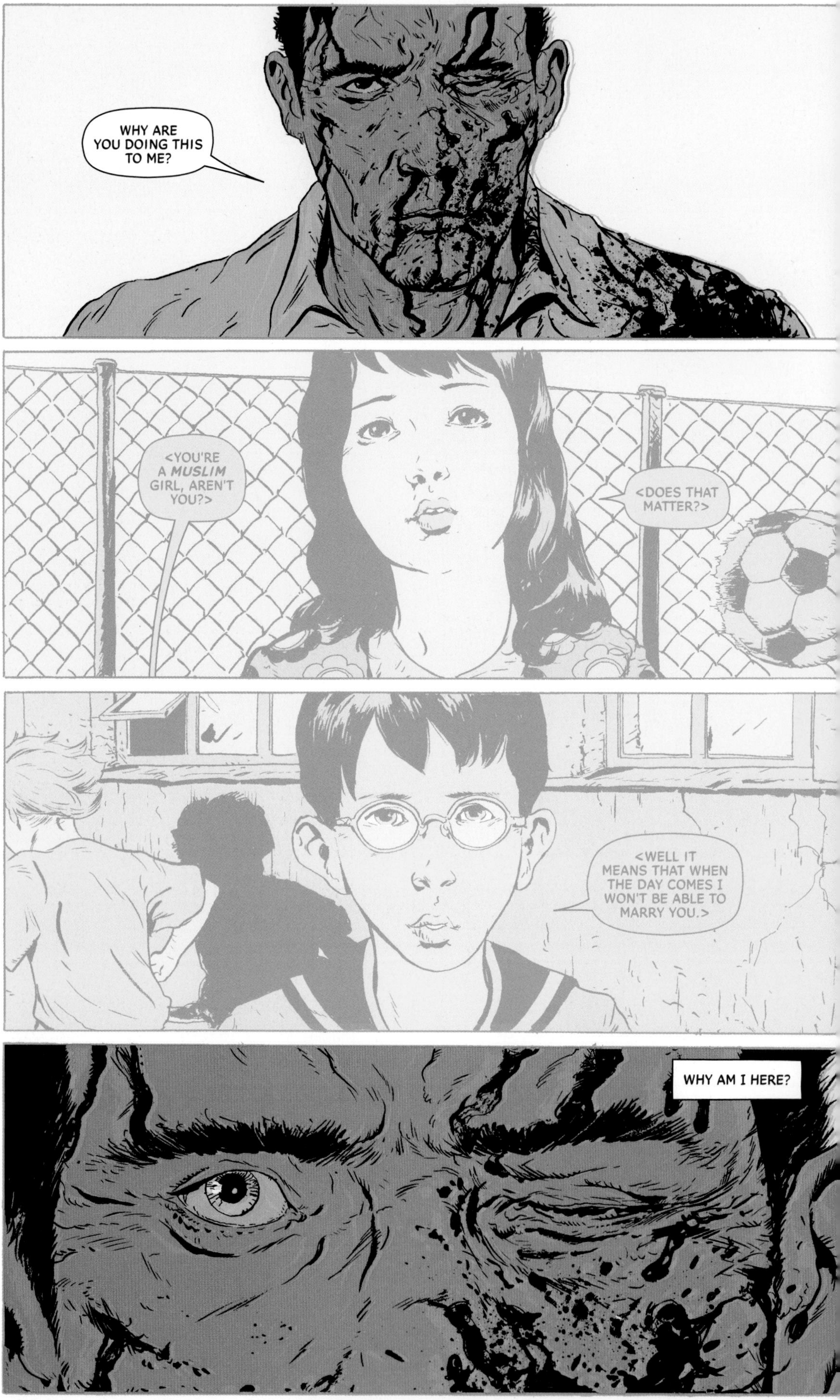
WHY ARE YOU DOING THIS TO ME?
<YOU'RE A *MUSLIM* GIRL, AREN'T YOU?>
<DOES THAT MATTER?>
<WELL IT MEANS THAT WHEN THE DAY COMES I WON'T BE ABLE TO MARRY YOU.>
WHY AM I HERE?

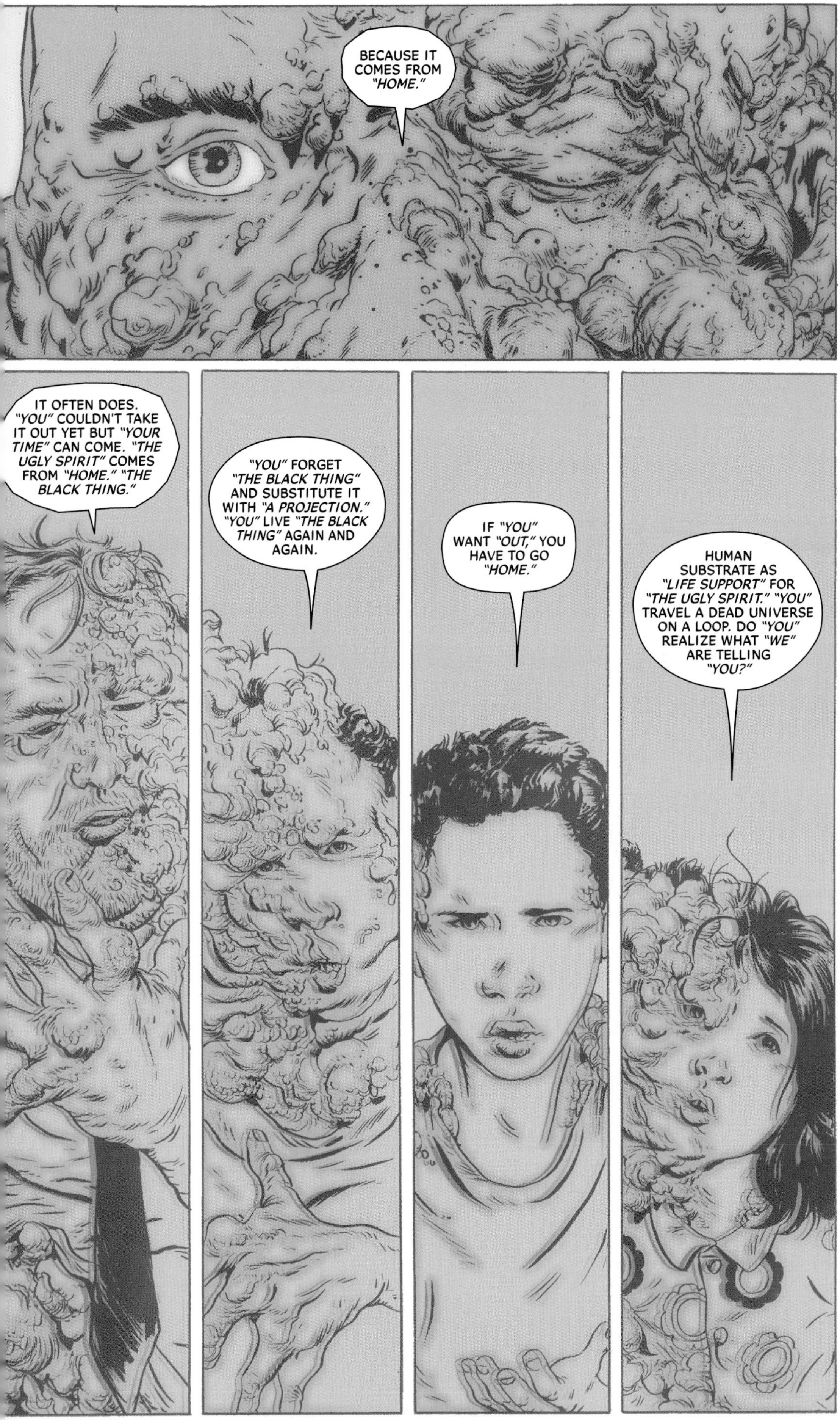
BECAUSE IT COMES FROM "HOME."
IT OFTEN DOES. "YOU" COULDN'T TAKE IT OUT YET BUT "YOUR TIME" CAN COME. "THE UGLY SPIRIT" COMES FROM "HOME." "THE BLACK THING."
"YOU" FORGET "THE BLACK THING" AND SUBSTITUTE IT WITH "A PROJECTION." "YOU" LIVE "THE BLACK THING" AGAIN AND AGAIN.
IF "YOU" WANT "OUT," YOU HAVE TO GO "HOME."
HUMAN SUBSTRATE AS "LIFE SUPPORT" FOR "THE UGLY SPIRIT." "YOU" TRAVEL A DEAD UNIVERSE ON A LOOP. DO "YOU" REALIZE WHAT "WE" ARE TELLING "YOU?"

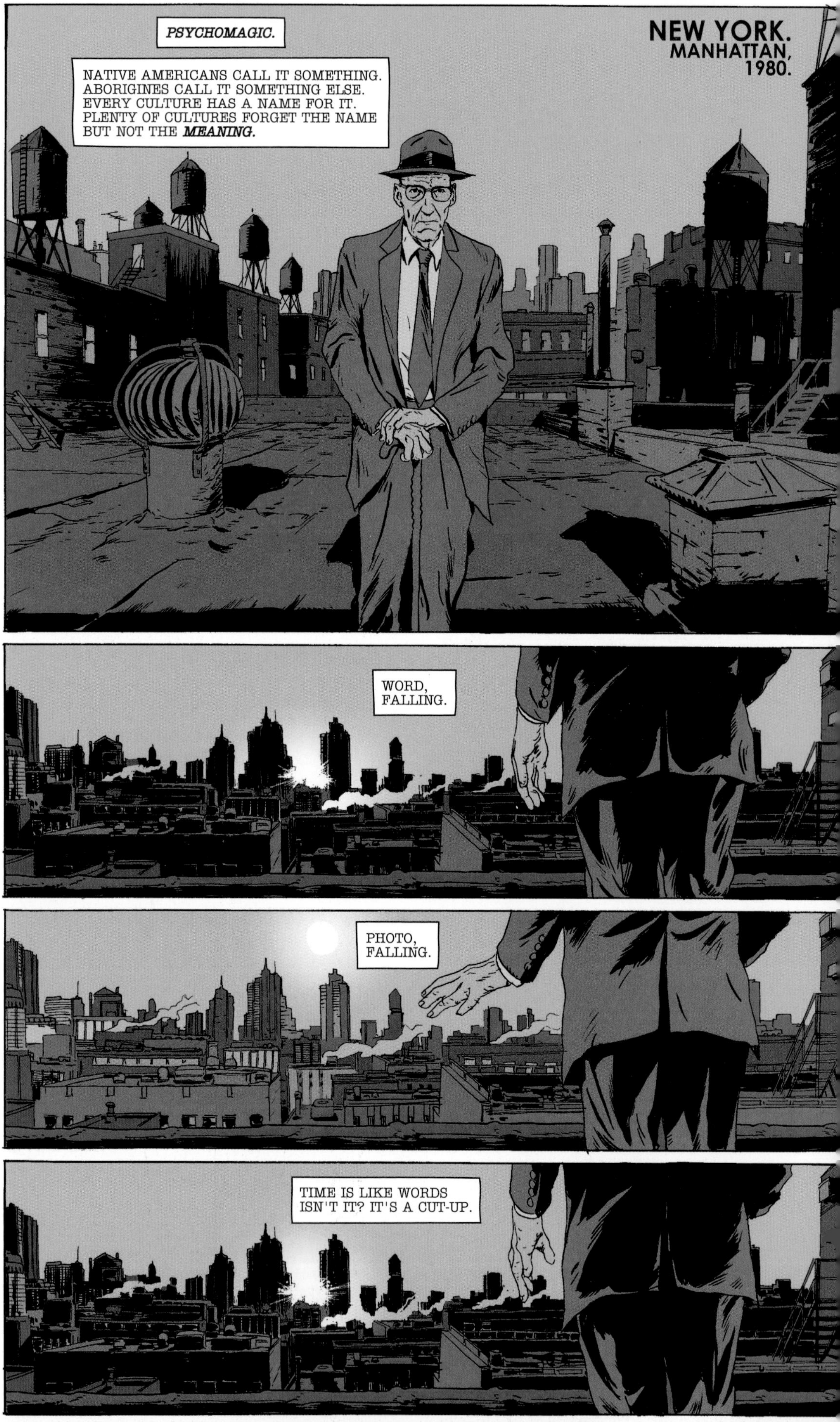
PSYCHOMAGIC.
NEW YORK.
MANHATTAN,
1980.
NATIVE AMERICANS CALL IT SOMETHING. ABORIGINES CALL IT SOMETHING ELSE. EVERY CULTURE HAS A NAME FOR IT. PLENTY OF CULTURES FORGET THE NAME BUT NOT THE MEANING.
WORD, FALLING.
PHOTO, FALLING.
TIME IS LIKE WORDS ISN'T IT? IT'S A CUT-UP.

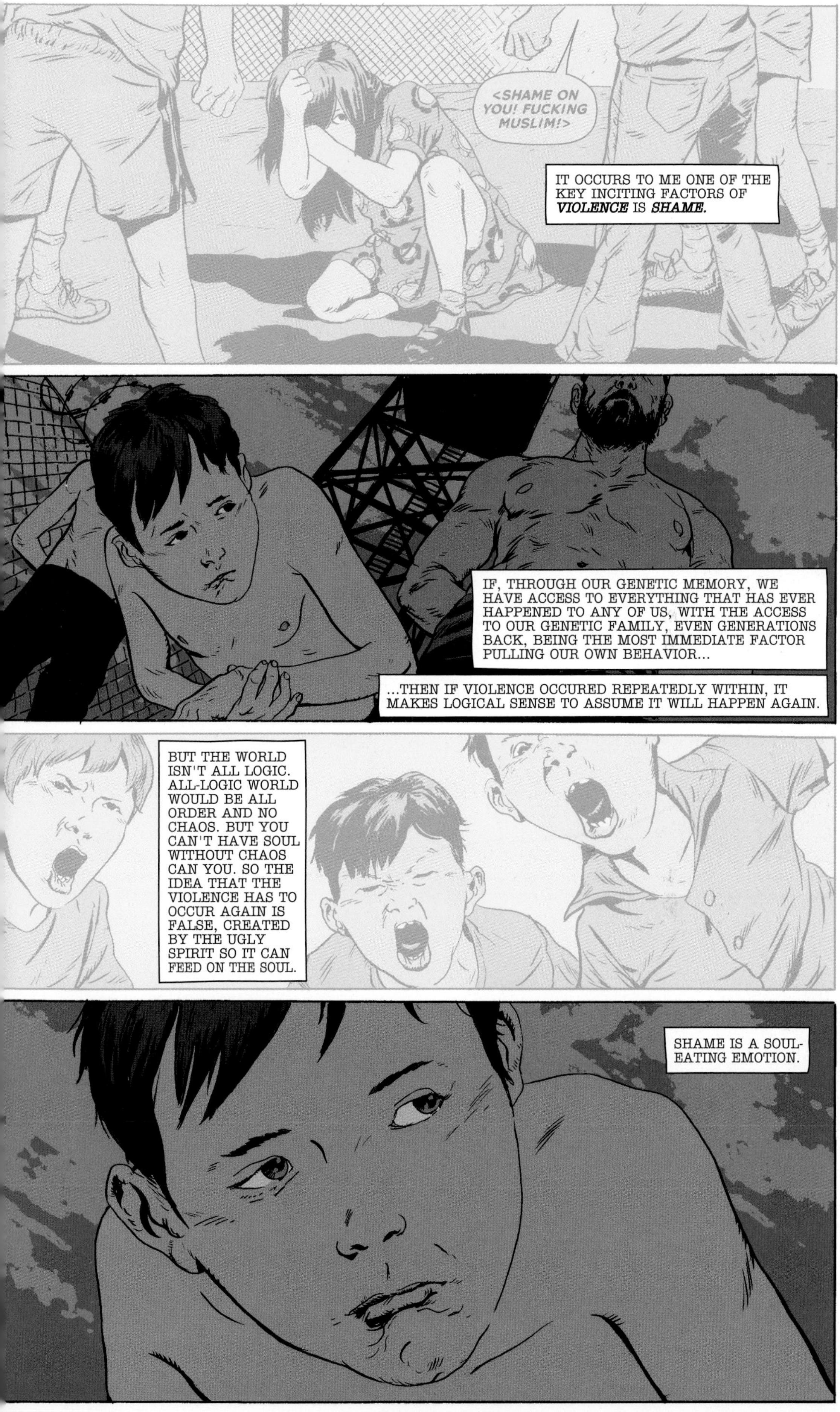

<SHAME ON YOU! FUCKING MUSLIM!>
IT OCCURS TO ME ONE OF THE KEY INCITING FACTORS OF ***VIOLENCE*** IS ***SHAME.***
IF, THROUGH OUR GENETIC MEMORY, WE HAVE ACCESS TO EVERYTHING THAT HAS EVER HAPPENED TO ANY OF US, WITH THE ACCESS TO OUR GENETIC FAMILY, EVEN GENERATIONS BACK, BEING THE MOST IMMEDIATE FACTOR PULLING OUR OWN BEHAVIOR...
...THEN IF VIOLENCE OCCURED REPEATEDLY WITHIN, IT MAKES LOGICAL SENSE TO ASSUME IT WILL HAPPEN AGAIN.
BUT THE WORLD ISN'T ALL LOGIC. ALL-LOGIC WORLD WOULD BE ALL ORDER AND NO CHAOS. BUT YOU CAN'T HAVE SOUL WITHOUT CHAOS CAN YOU. SO THE IDEA THAT THE VIOLENCE HAS TO OCCUR AGAIN IS FALSE, CREATED BY THE UGLY SPIRIT SO IT CAN FEED ON THE SOUL.
SHAME IS A SOUL-EATING EMOTION.

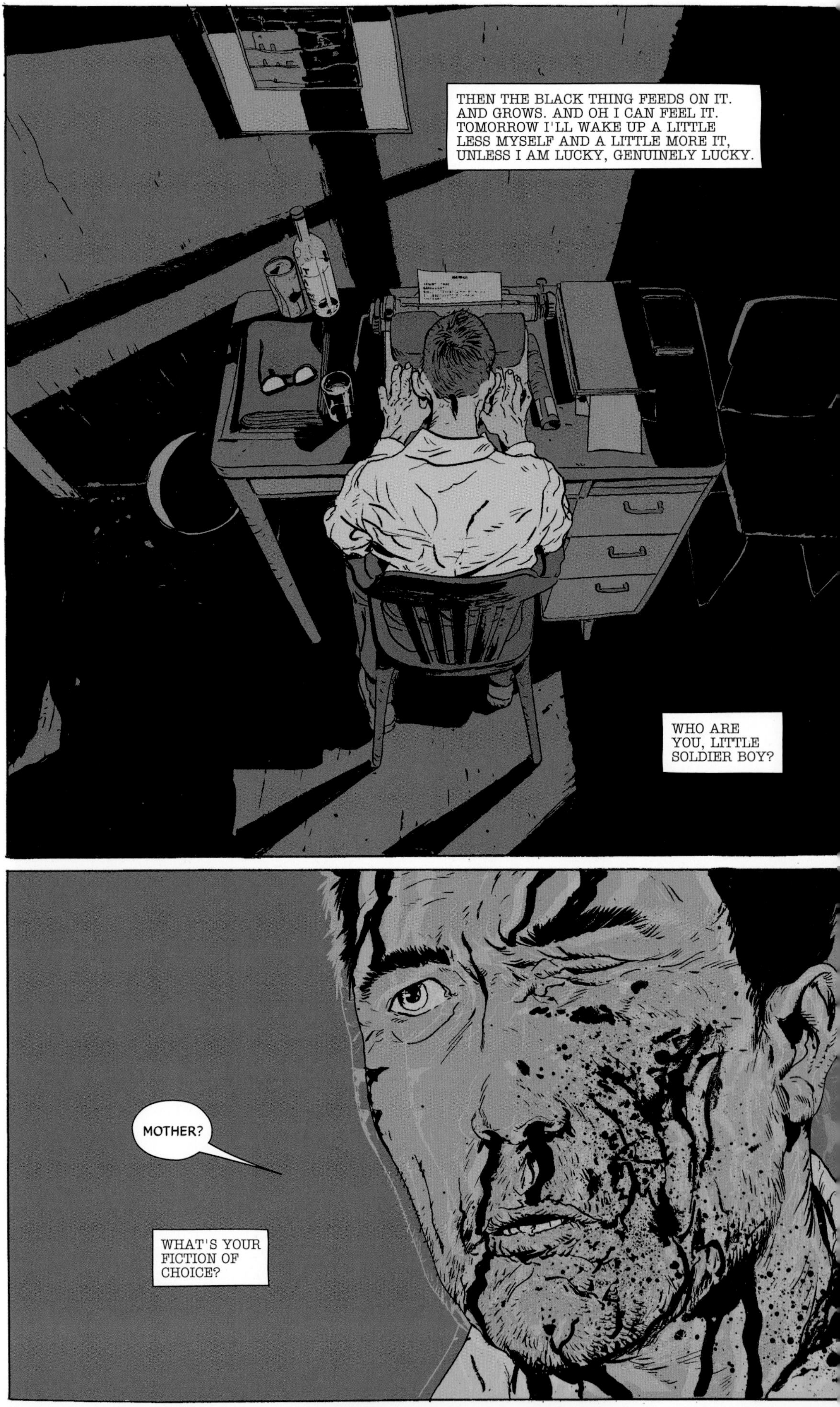
THEN THE BLACK THING FEEDS ON IT. AND GROWS. AND OH I CAN FEEL IT. TOMORROW I'LL WAKE UP A LITTLE LESS MYSELF AND A LITTLE MORE IT, UNLESS I AM LUCKY, GENUINELY LUCKY.
WHO ARE YOU, LITTLE SOLDIER BOY?
MOTHER?
WHAT'S YOUR FICTION OF CHOICE?

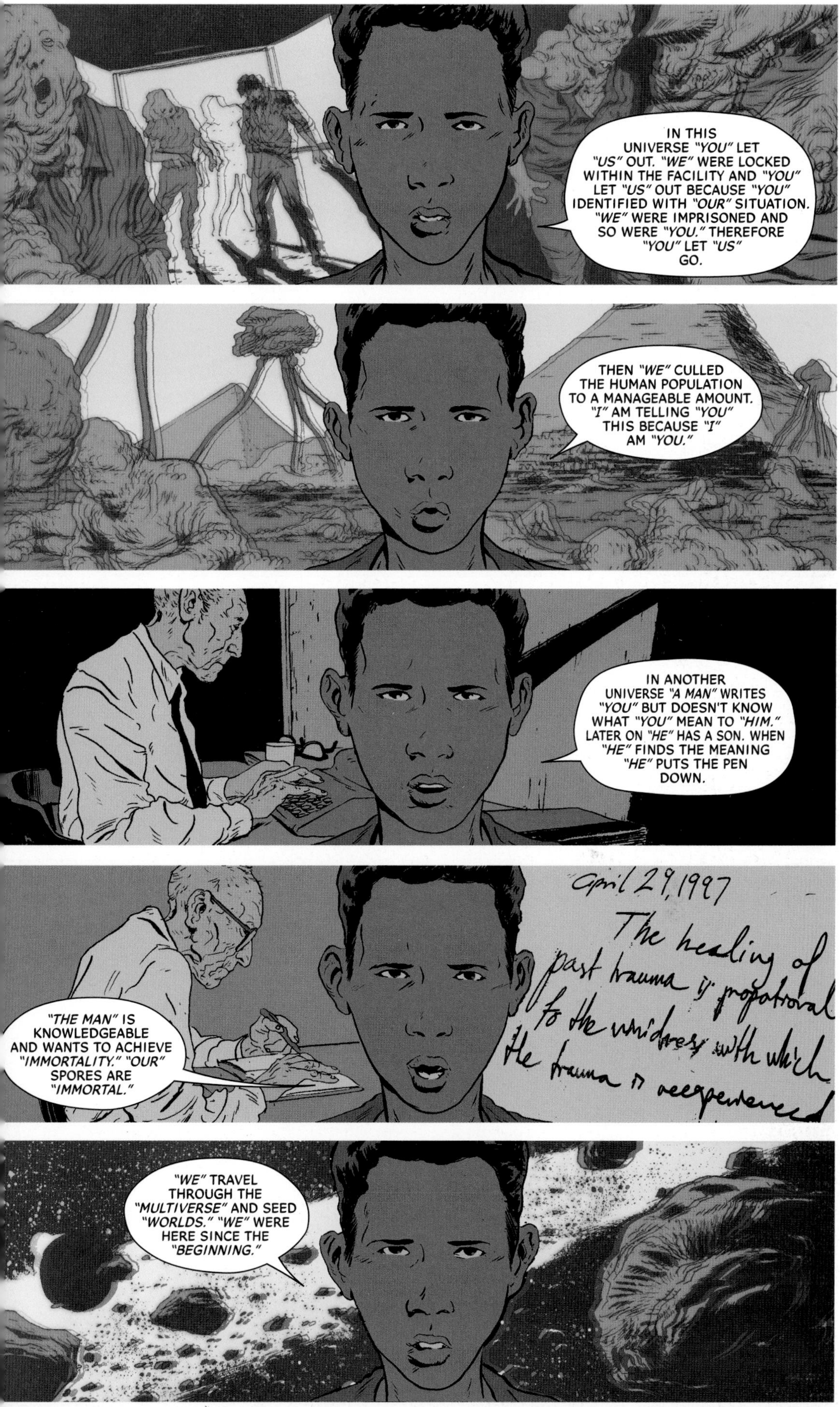
IN THIS UNIVERSE "YOU" LET "US" OUT. "WE" WERE LOCKED WITHIN THE FACILITY AND "YOU" LET "US" OUT BECAUSE "YOU" IDENTIFIED WITH "OUR" SITUATION. "WE" WERE IMPRISONED AND SO WERE "YOU." THEREFORE "YOU" LET "US" GO.
THEN "WE" CULLED THE HUMAN POPULATION TO A MANAGEABLE AMOUNT. "I" AM TELLING "YOU" THIS BECAUSE "I" AM "YOU."
IN ANOTHER UNIVERSE "A MAN" WRITES "YOU" BUT DOESN'T KNOW WHAT "YOU" MEAN TO "HIM." LATER ON "HE" HAS A SON. WHEN "HE" FINDS THE MEANING "HE" PUTS THE PEN DOWN.
April 29, 1997
The healing of past trauma is proportional to the vividness with which the trauma is reexperienced
"THE MAN" IS KNOWLEDGEABLE AND WANTS TO ACHIEVE "IMMORTALITY." "OUR" SPORES ARE "IMMORTAL."
"WE" TRAVEL THROUGH THE "MULTIVERSE" AND SEED "WORLDS." "WE" WERE HERE SINCE THE "BEGINNING."

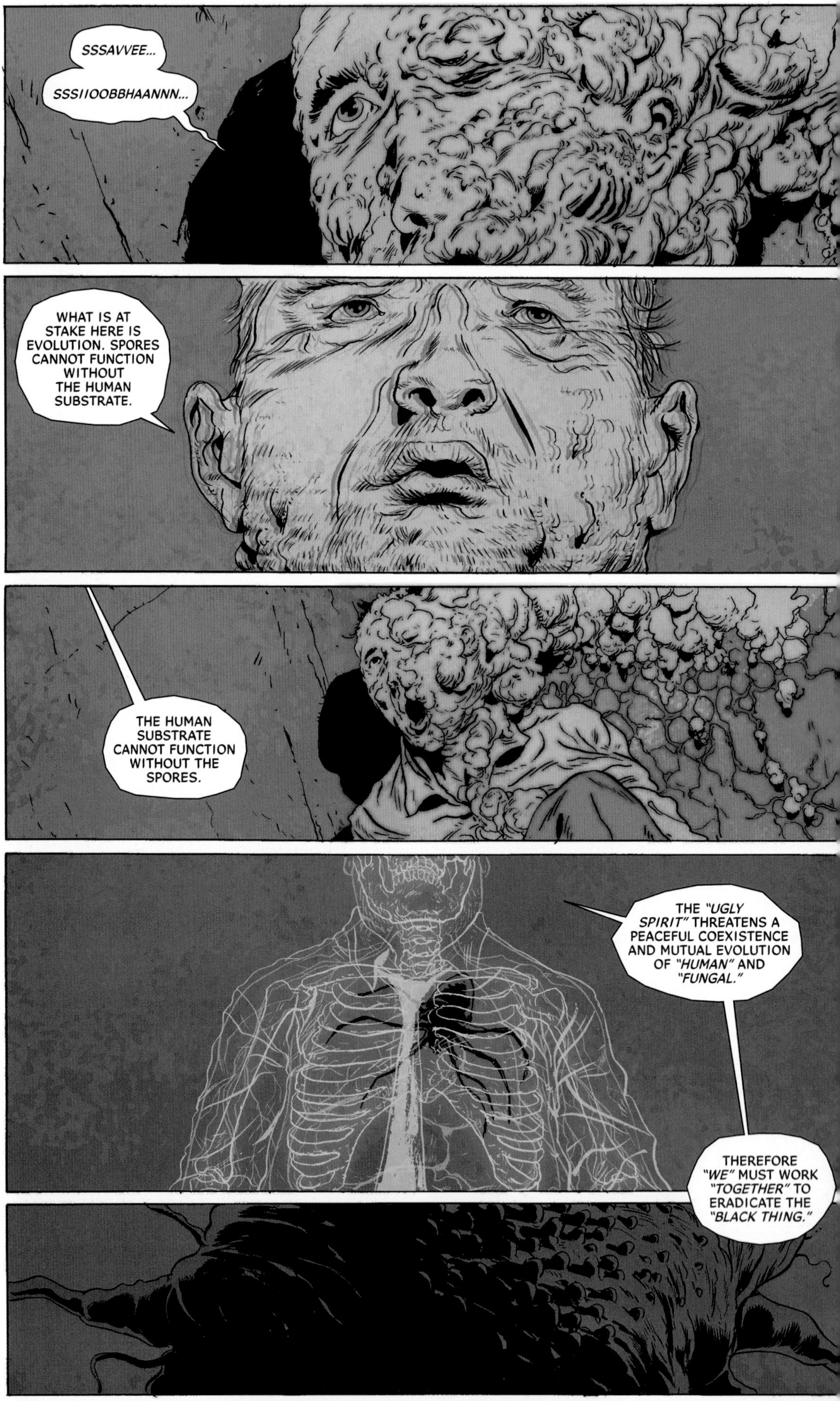
SSSAVVEE...
SSSIIOOBBHAANNN...
WHAT IS AT STAKE HERE IS EVOLUTION. SPORES CANNOT FUNCTION WITHOUT THE HUMAN SUBSTRATE.
THE HUMAN SUBSTRATE CANNOT FUNCTION WITHOUT THE SPORES.
THE "UGLY SPIRIT" THREATENS A PEACEFUL COEXISTENCE AND MUTUAL EVOLUTION OF "HUMAN" AND "FUNGAL."
THEREFORE "WE" MUST WORK "TOGETHER" TO ERADICATE THE "BLACK THING."

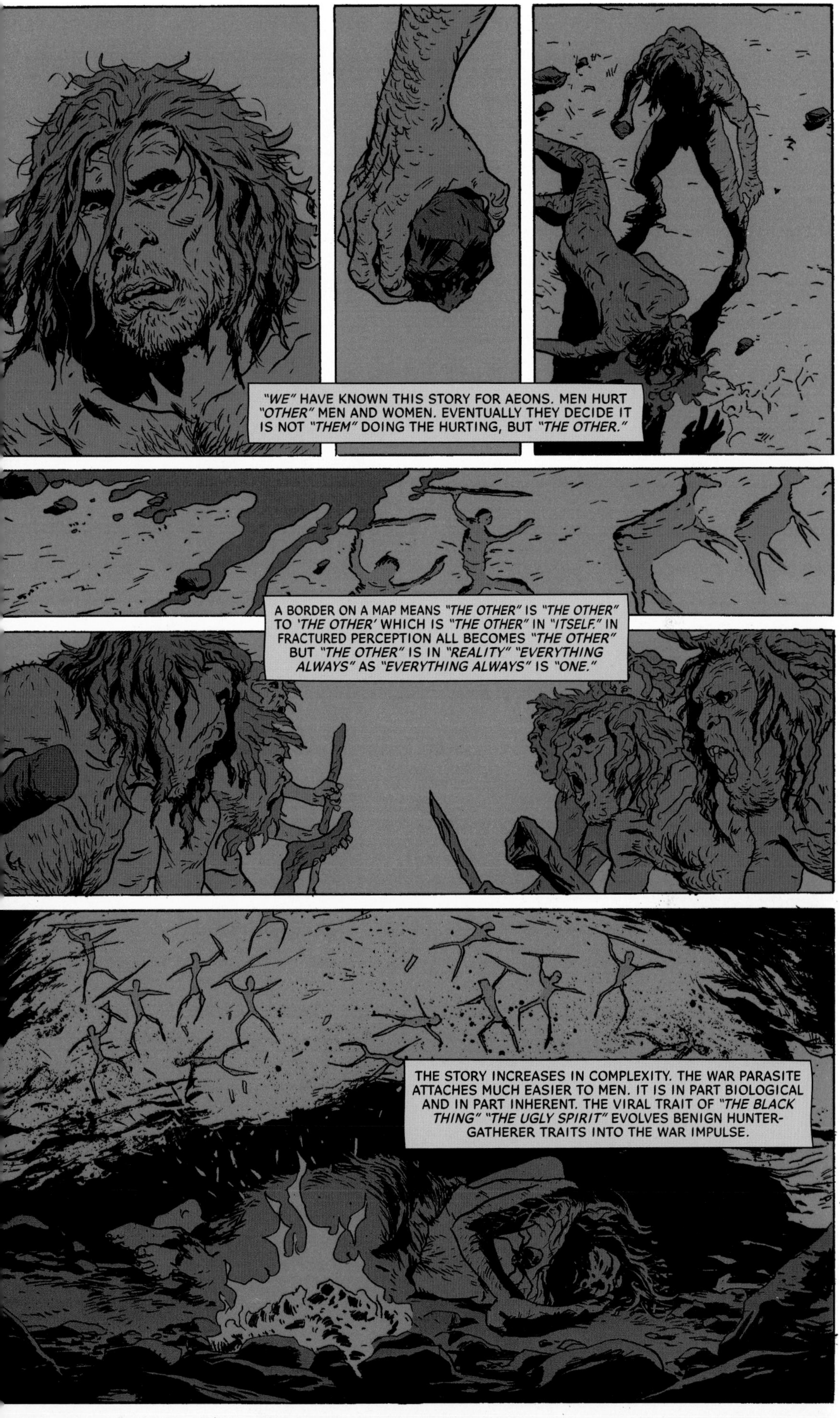
"WE" HAVE KNOWN THIS STORY FOR AEONS. MEN HURT "OTHER" MEN AND WOMEN. EVENTUALLY THEY DECIDE IT IS NOT "THEM" DOING THE HURTING, BUT "THE OTHER."
A BORDER ON A MAP MEANS "THE OTHER" IS "THE OTHER" TO 'THE OTHER' WHICH IS "THE OTHER" IN "ITSELF." IN FRACTURED PERCEPTION ALL BECOMES "THE OTHER" BUT "THE OTHER" IS IN "REALITY" "EVERYTHING ALWAYS" AS "EVERYTHING ALWAYS" IS "ONE."
THE STORY INCREASES IN COMPLEXITY. THE WAR PARASITE ATTACHES MUCH EASIER TO MEN. IT IS IN PART BIOLOGICAL AND IN PART INHERENT. THE VIRAL TRAIT OF "THE BLACK THING" "THE UGLY SPIRIT" EVOLVES BENIGN HUNTER-GATHERER TRAITS INTO THE WAR IMPULSE.

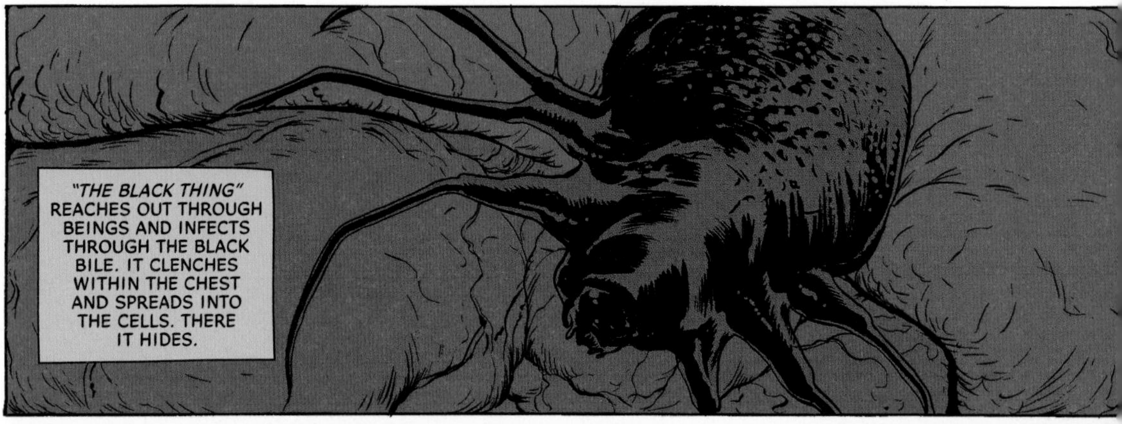
"THE BLACK THING" REACHES OUT THROUGH BEINGS AND INFECTS THROUGH THE BLACK BILE. IT CLENCHES WITHIN THE CHEST AND SPREADS INTO THE CELLS. THERE IT HIDES.

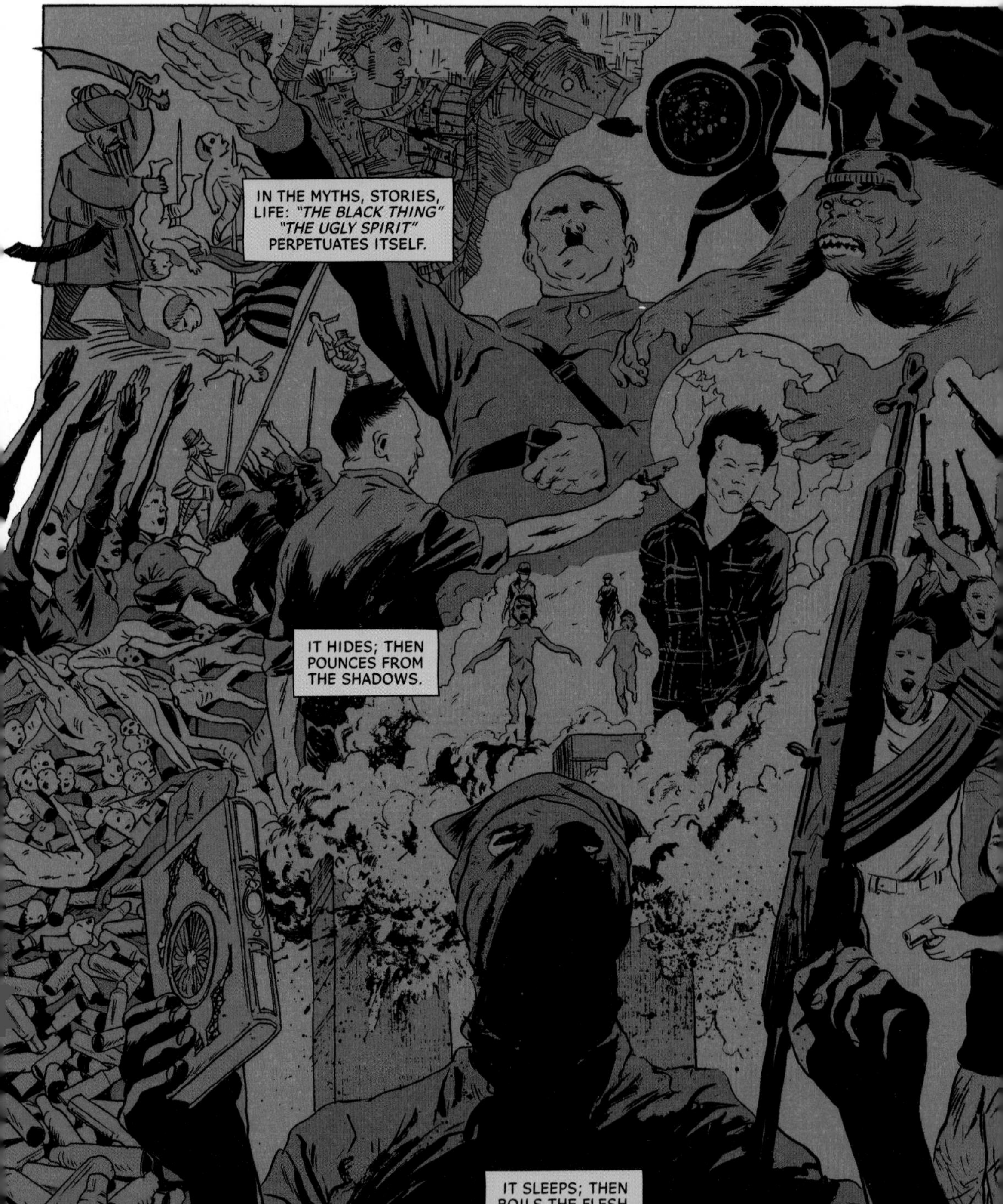
IN THE MYTHS, STORIES, LIFE: "THE BLACK THING" "THE UGLY SPIRIT" PERPETUATES ITSELF.
IT HIDES; THEN POUNCES FROM THE SHADOWS.
IT SLEEPS; THEN BOILS THE FLESH.

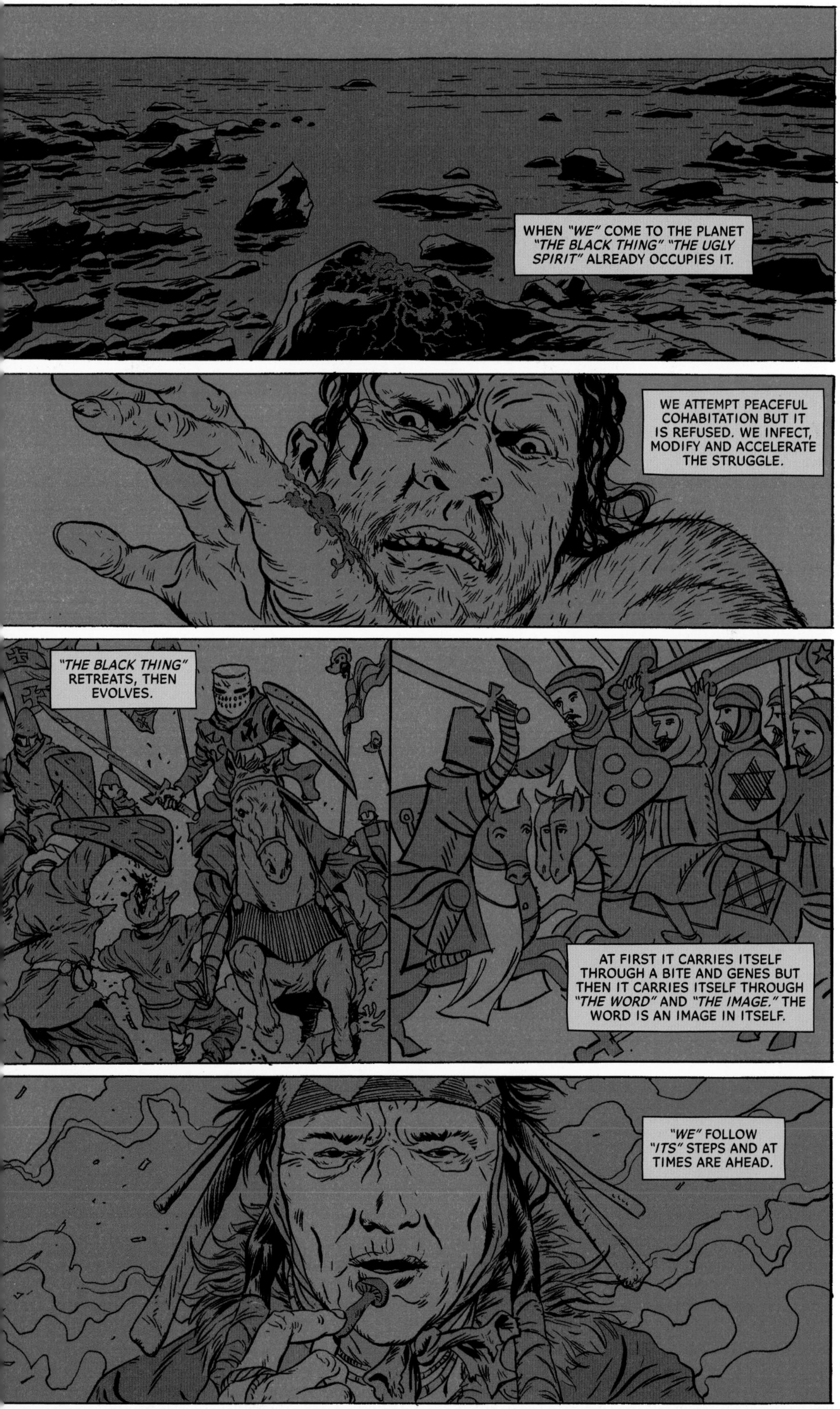
WHEN "WE" COME TO THE PLANET "THE BLACK THING" "THE UGLY SPIRIT" ALREADY OCCUPIES IT.
WE ATTEMPT PEACEFUL COHABITATION BUT IT IS REFUSED. WE INFECT, MODIFY AND ACCELERATE THE STRUGGLE.
"THE BLACK THING" RETREATS, THEN EVOLVES.
AT FIRST IT CARRIES ITSELF THROUGH A BITE AND GENES BUT THEN IT CARRIES ITSELF THROUGH "THE WORD" AND "THE IMAGE." THE WORD IS AN IMAGE IN ITSELF.
"WE" FOLLOW "ITS" STEPS AND AT TIMES ARE AHEAD.

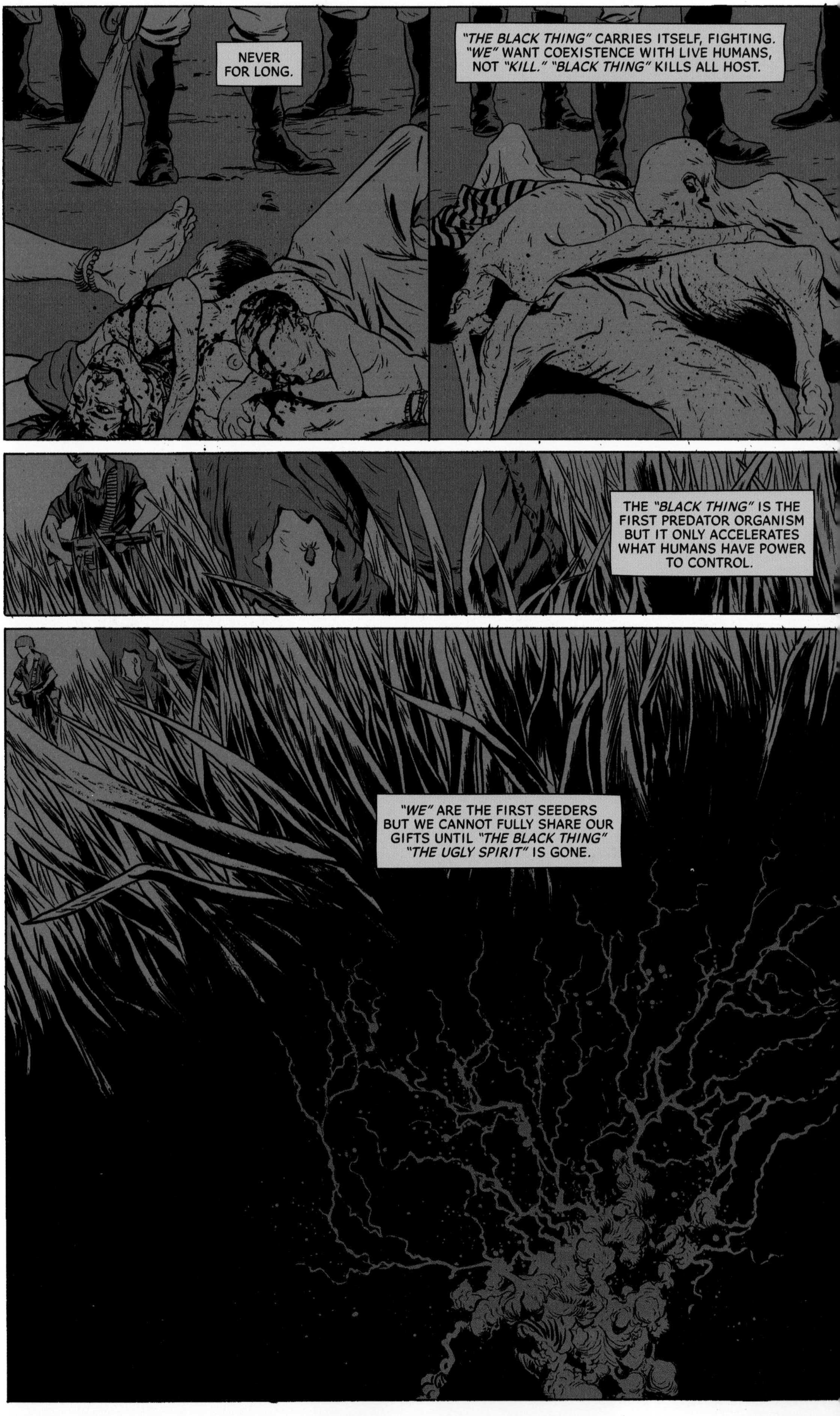
NEVER FOR LONG.
"THE BLACK THING" CARRIES ITSELF, FIGHTING. "WE" WANT COEXISTENCE WITH LIVE HUMANS, NOT "KILL." "BLACK THING" KILLS ALL HOST.
THE "BLACK THING" IS THE FIRST PREDATOR ORGANISM BUT IT ONLY ACCELERATES WHAT HUMANS HAVE POWER TO CONTROL.
"WE" ARE THE FIRST SEEDERS BUT WE CANNOT FULLY SHARE OUR GIFTS UNTIL "THE BLACK THING" "THE UGLY SPIRIT" IS GONE.

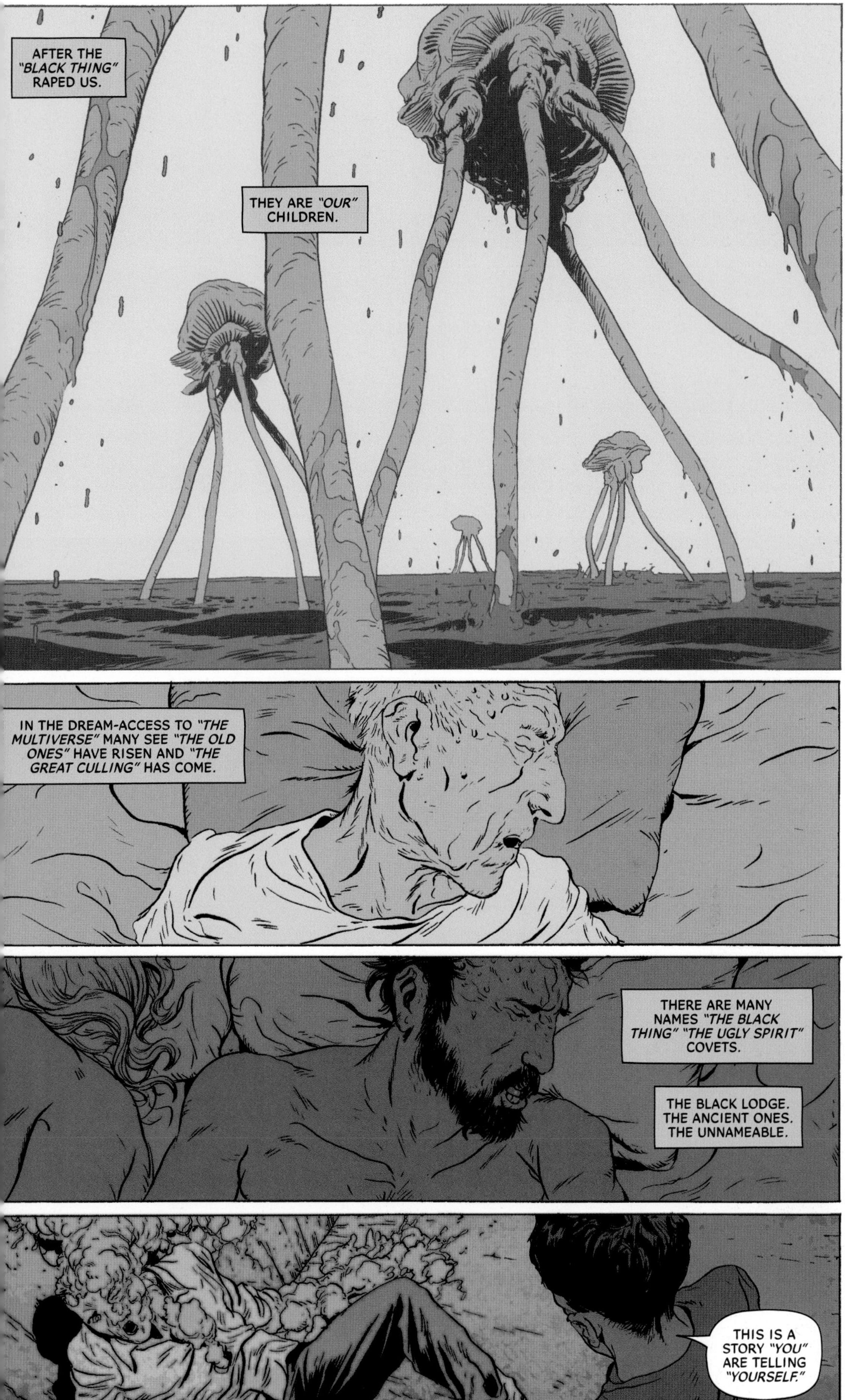
AFTER THE "BLACK THING" RAPED US.
THEY ARE "OUR" CHILDREN.
IN THE DREAM-ACCESS TO "THE MULTIVERSE" MANY SEE "THE OLD ONES" HAVE RISEN AND "THE GREAT CULLING" HAS COME.
THERE ARE MANY NAMES "THE BLACK THING" "THE UGLY SPIRIT" COVETS.
THE BLACK LODGE. THE ANCIENT ONES. THE UNNAMEABLE.
THIS IS A STORY "YOU" ARE TELLING "YOURSELF."

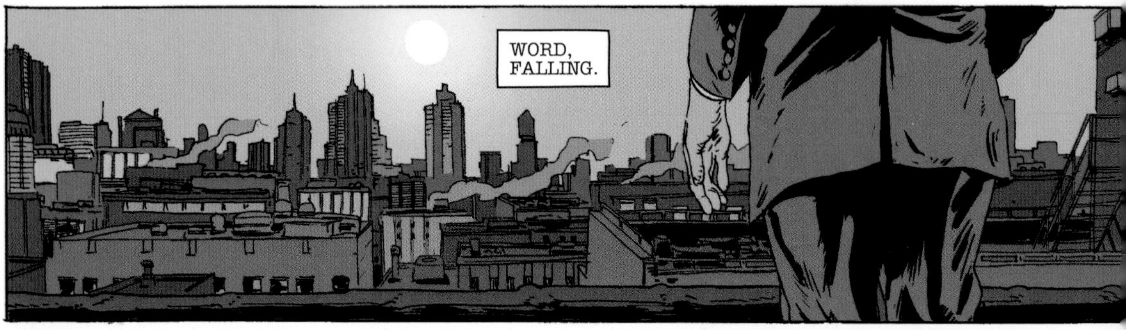
WORD,
FALLING.

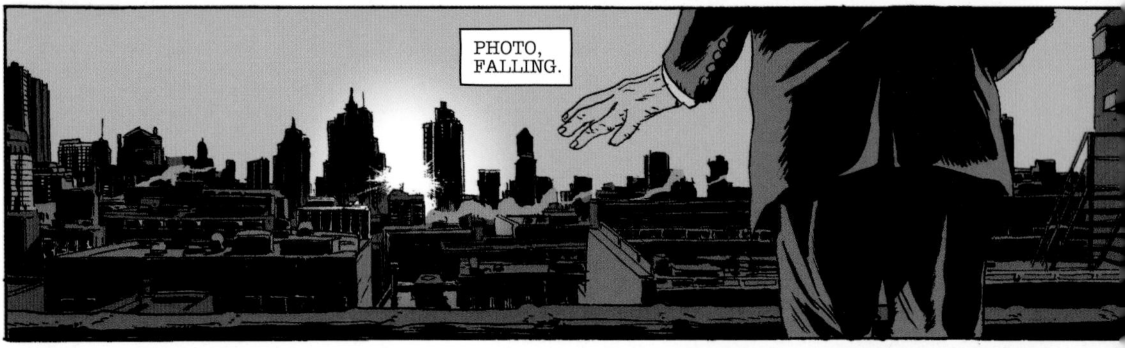
PHOTO,
FALLING.

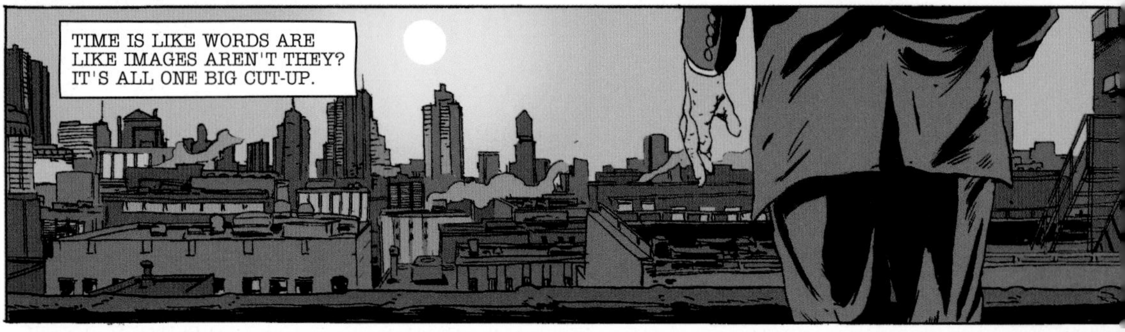
TIME IS LIKE WORDS ARE LIKE IMAGES AREN'T THEY? IT'S ALL ONE BIG CUT-UP.

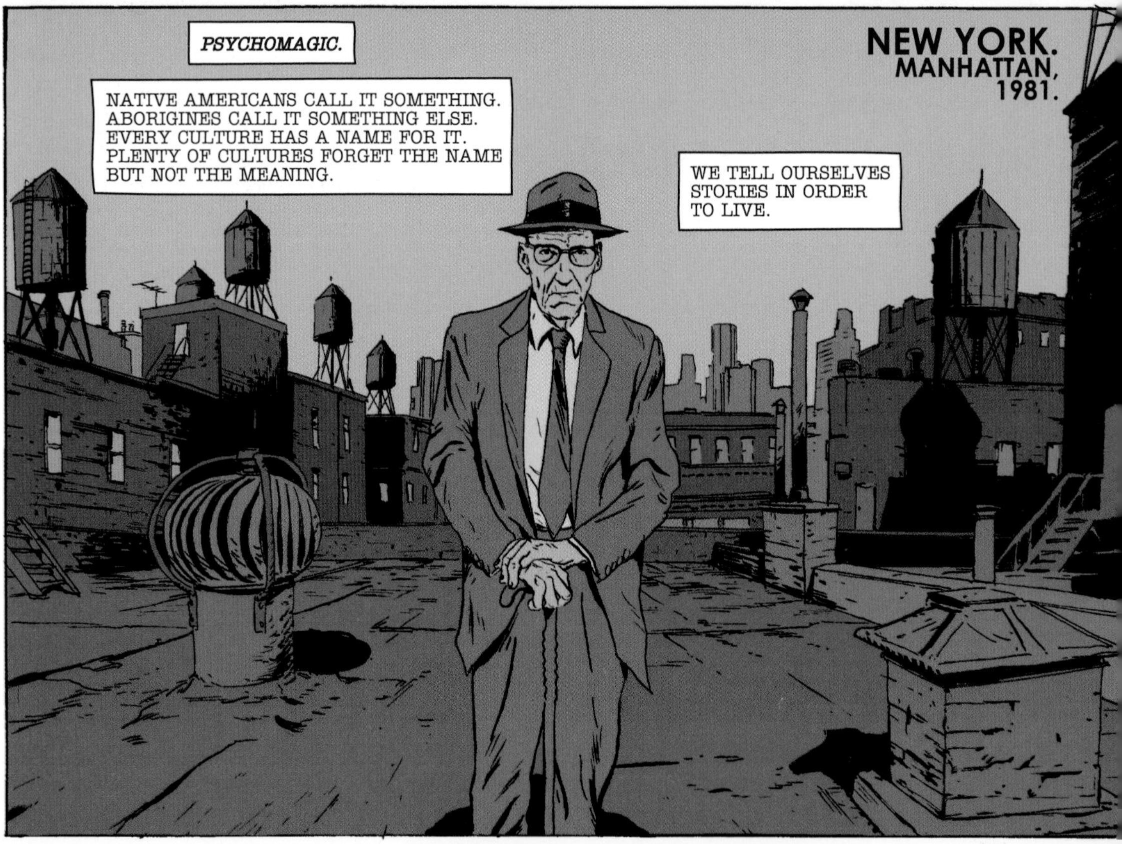
PSYCHOMAGIC.
NEW YORK.
MANHATTAN,
1981.
NATIVE AMERICANS CALL IT SOMETHING. ABORIGINES CALL IT SOMETHING ELSE. EVERY CULTURE HAS A NAME FOR IT. PLENTY OF CULTURES FORGET THE NAME BUT NOT THE MEANING.
WE TELL OURSELVES STORIES IN ORDER TO LIVE.

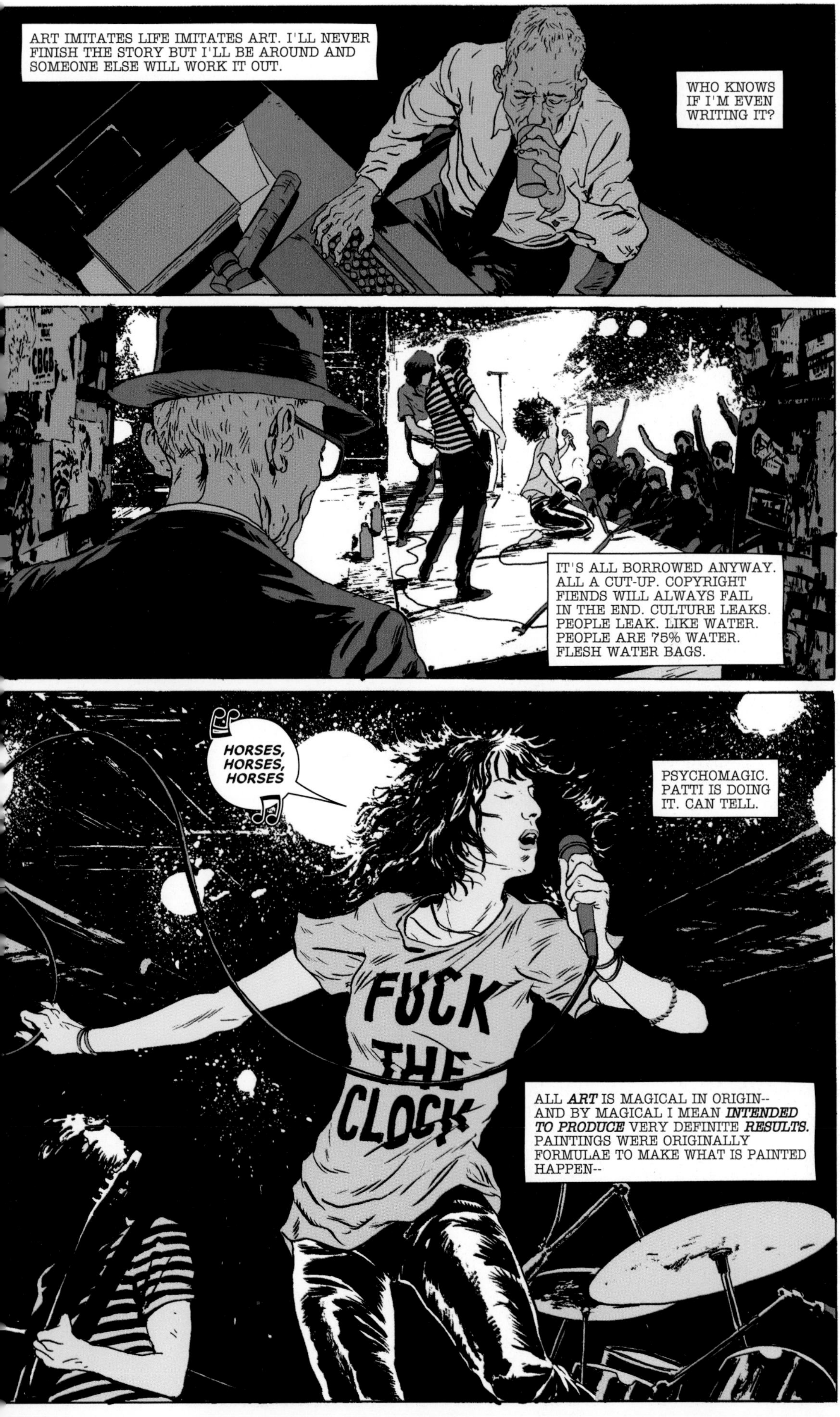
ART IMITATES LIFE IMITATES ART. I'LL NEVER FINISH THE STORY BUT I'LL BE AROUND AND SOMEONE ELSE WILL WORK IT OUT.
WHO KNOWS IF I'M EVEN WRITING IT?
CBGB
IT'S ALL BORROWED ANYWAY. ALL A CUT-UP. COPYRIGHT FIENDS WILL ALWAYS FAIL IN THE END. CULTURE LEAKS. PEOPLE LEAK. LIKE WATER. PEOPLE ARE 75% WATER. FLESH WATER BAGS.
HORSES, HORSES, HORSES
PSYCHOMAGIC. PATTI IS DOING IT. CAN TELL.
FUCK THE CLOCK
ALL ***ART*** IS MAGICAL IN ORIGIN-- AND BY MAGICAL I MEAN ***INTENDED TO PRODUCE*** VERY DEFINITE ***RESULTS.*** PAINTINGS WERE ORIGINALLY FORMULAE TO MAKE WHAT IS PAINTED HAPPEN--

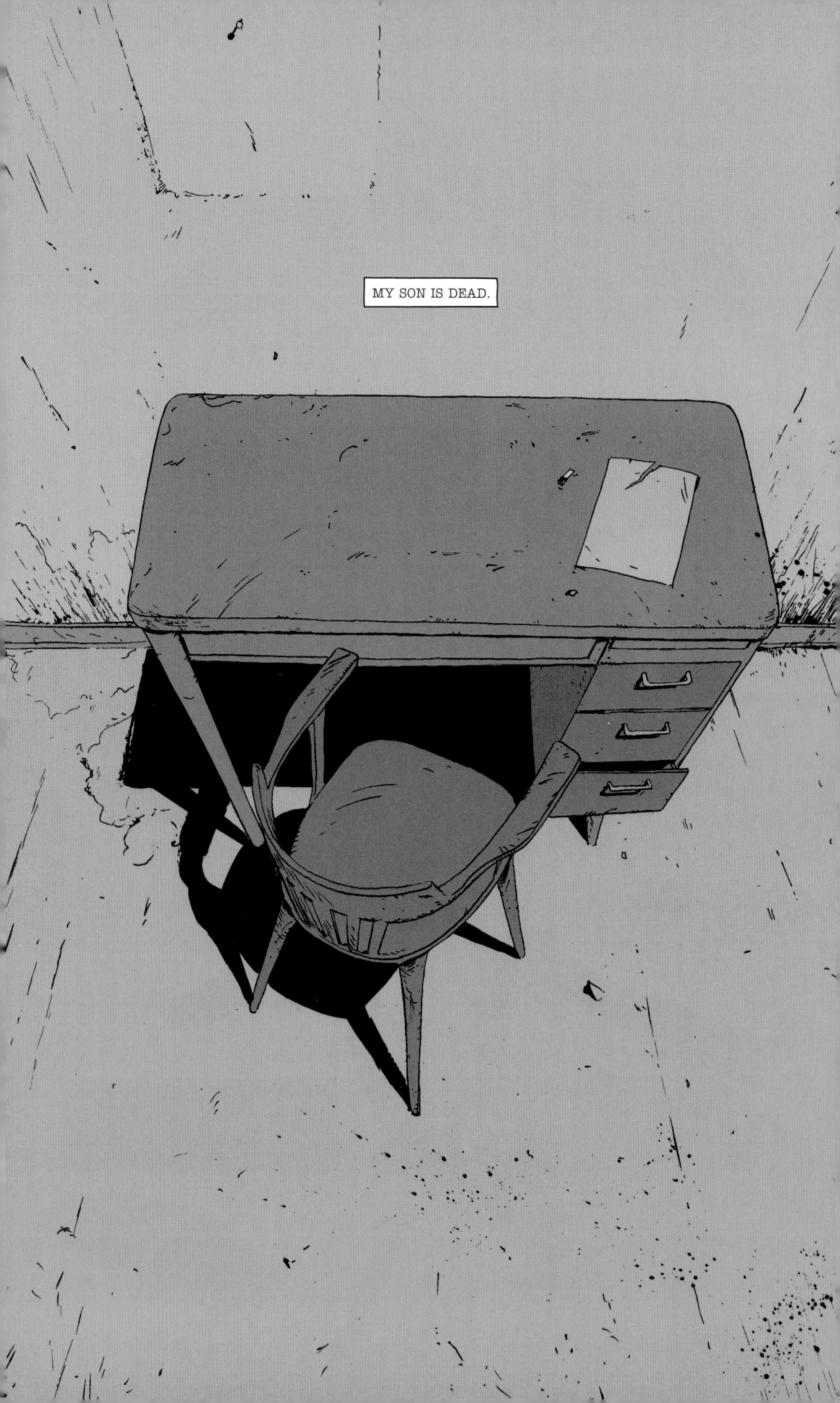
MY SON IS DEAD.

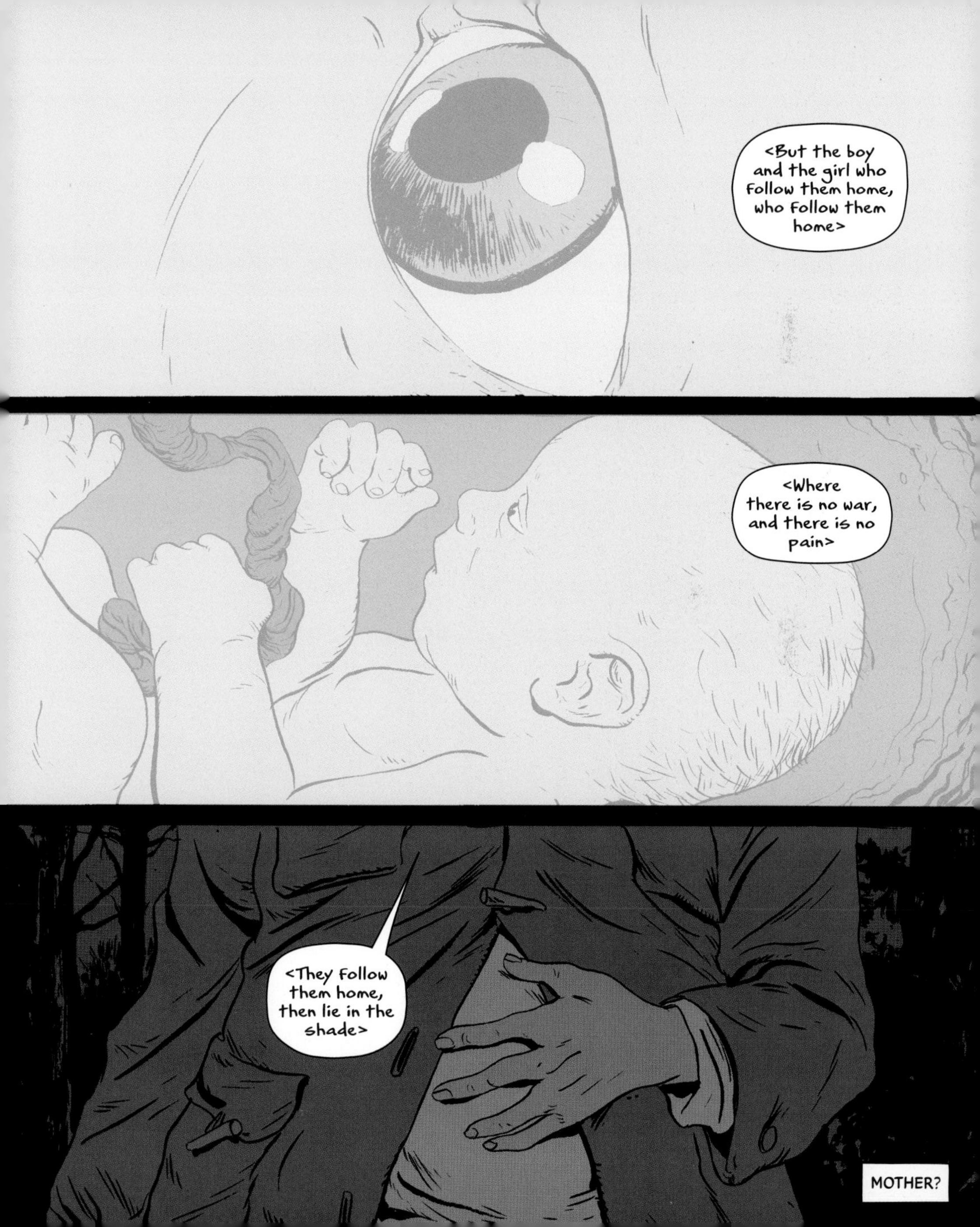

<But the boy and the girl who follow them home, who follow them home>
<Where there is no war, and there is no pain>
<They follow them home, then lie in the shade>
MOTHER?

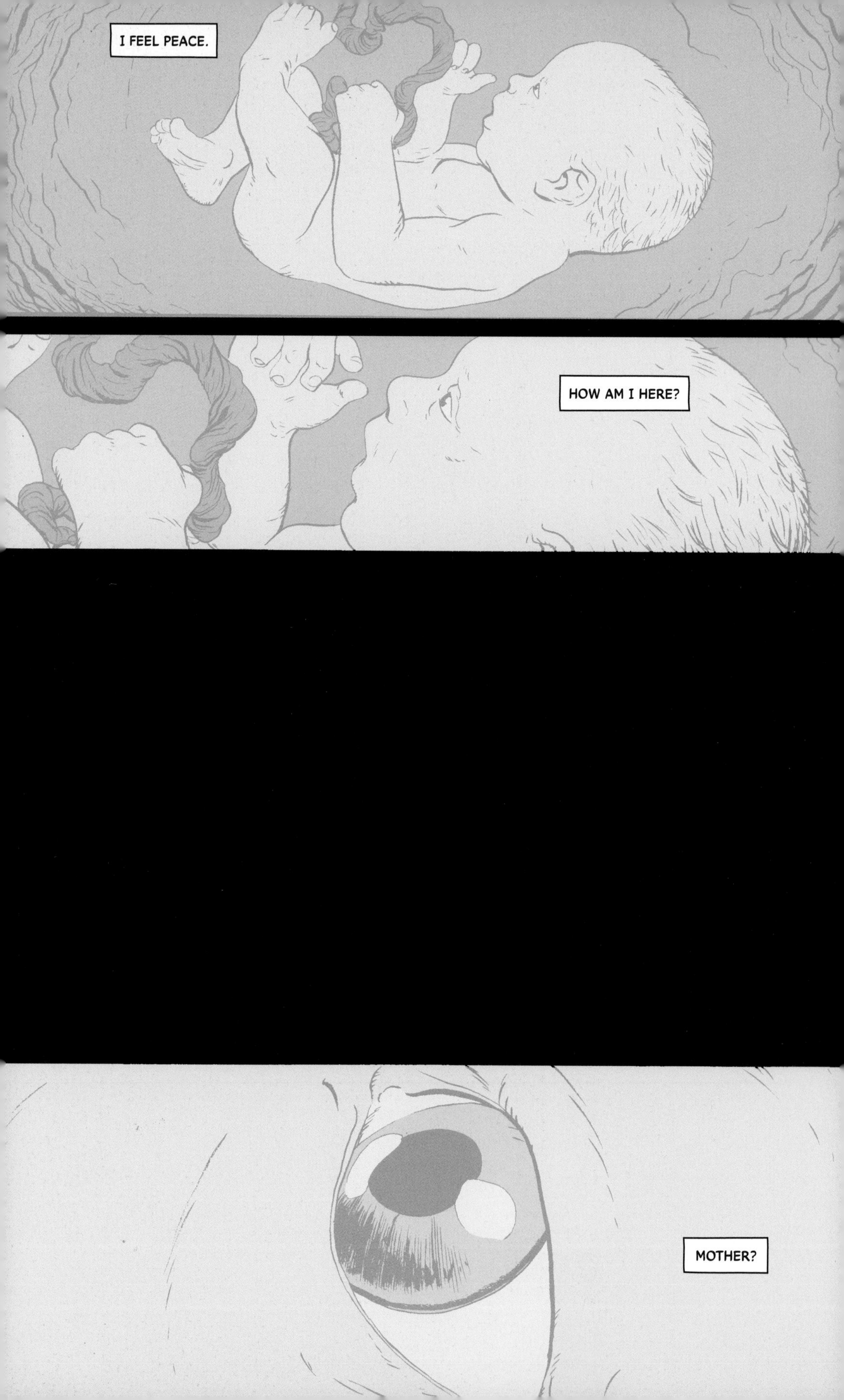
I FEEL PEACE.
HOW AM I HERE?
MOTHER?

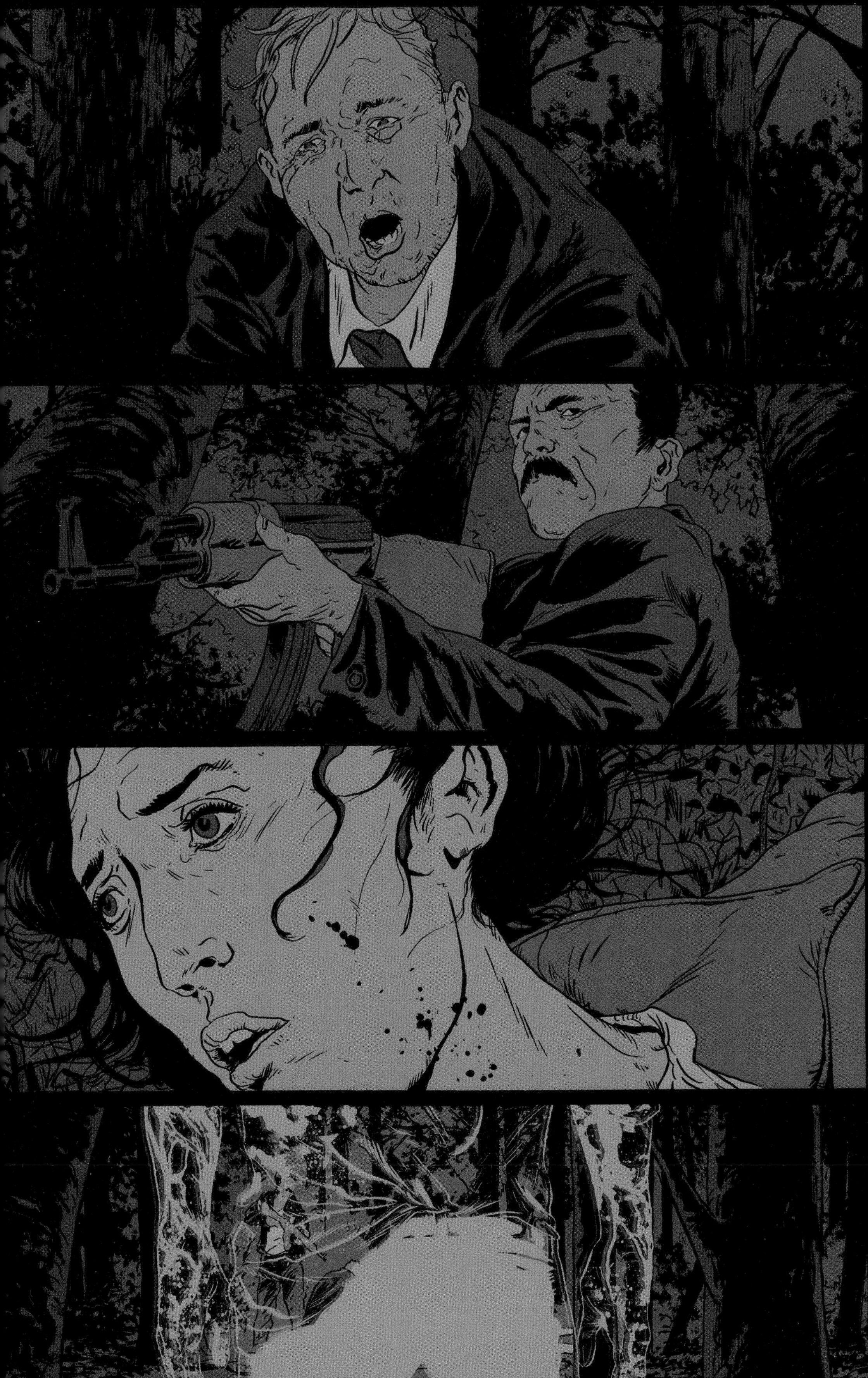

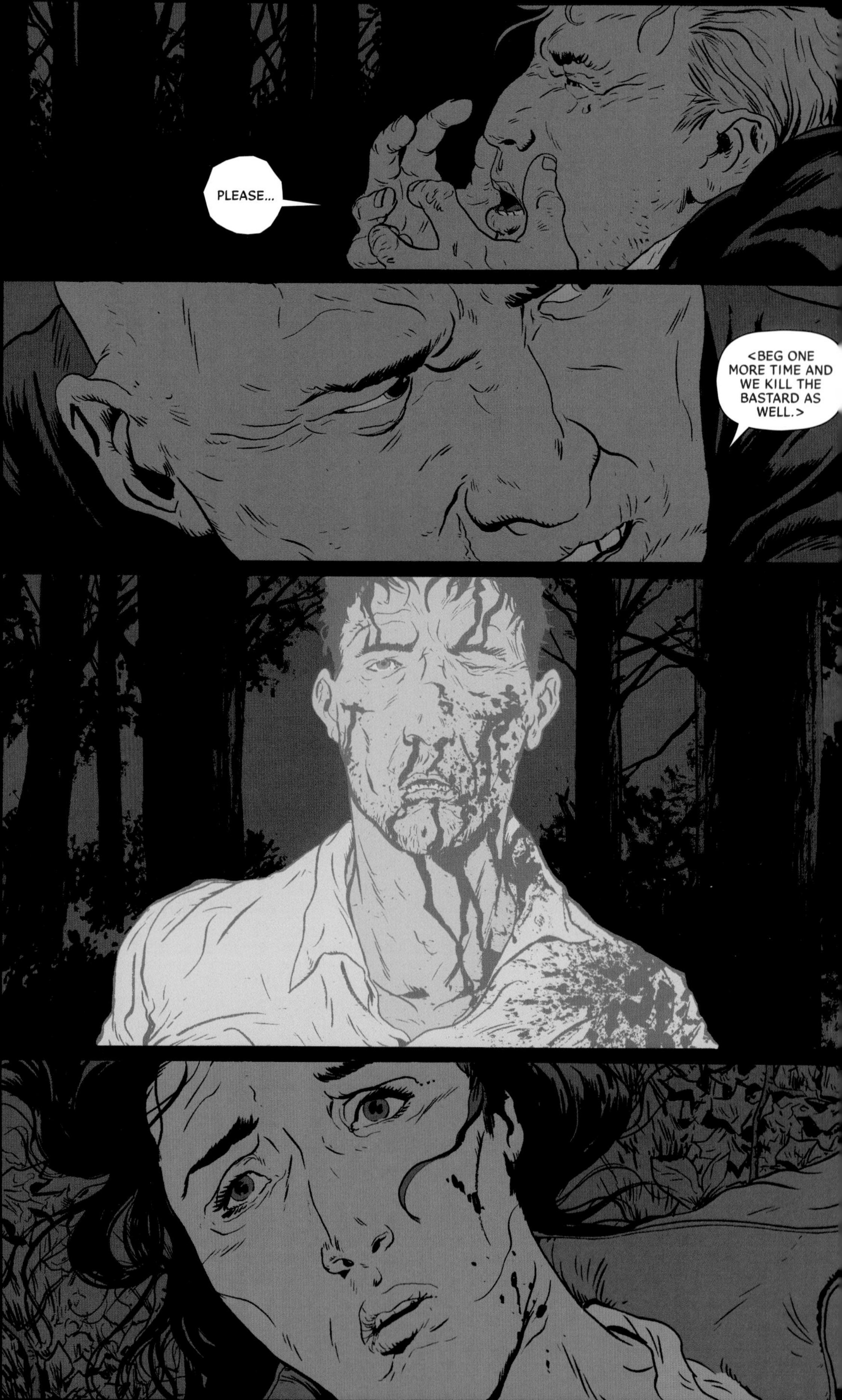
PLEASE...
<BEG ONE MORE TIME AND WE KILL THE BASTARD AS WELL.>

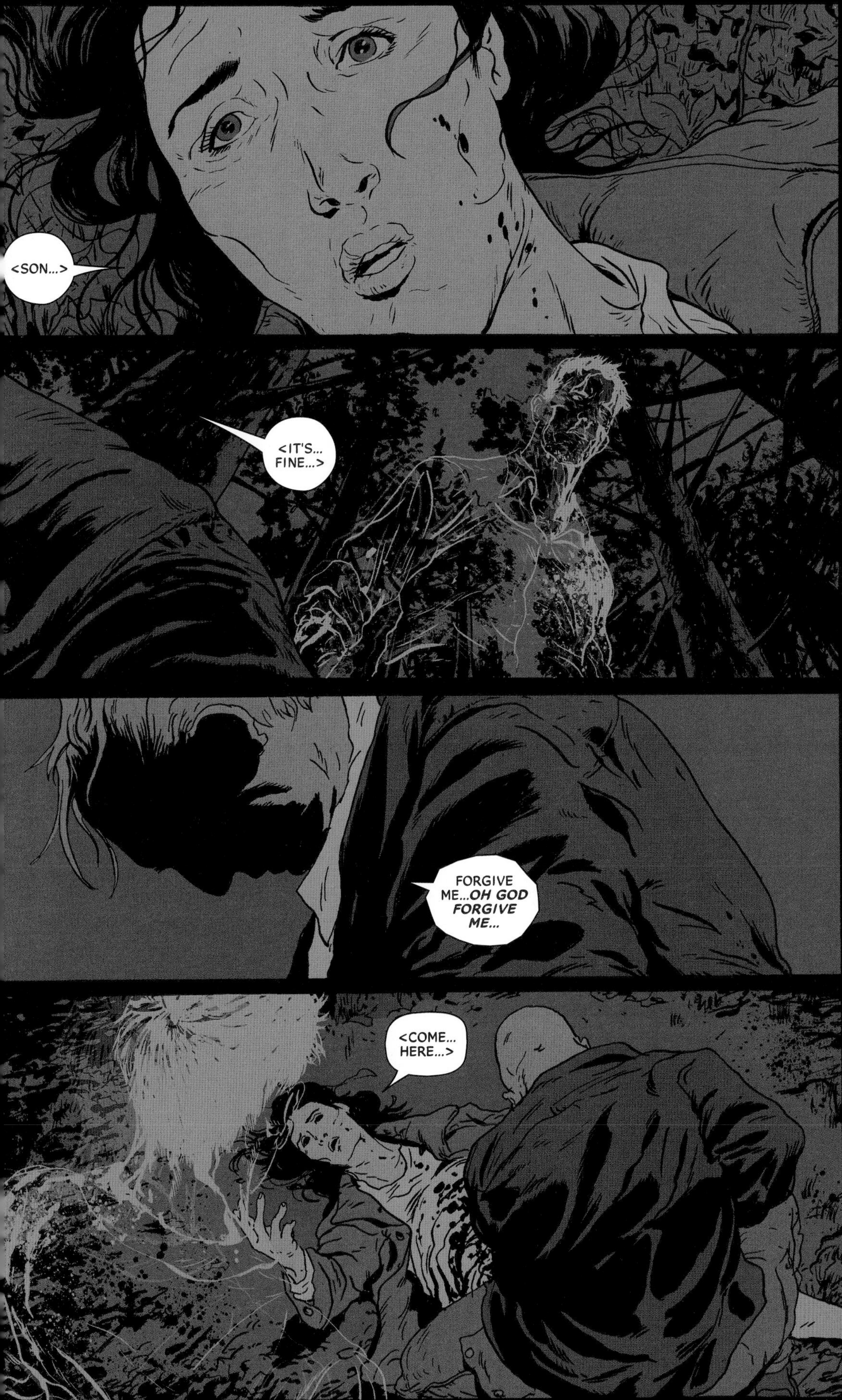
<SON...>
<IT'S... FINE...>
FORGIVE ME...*OH GOD FORGIVE ME...*
<COME... HERE...>

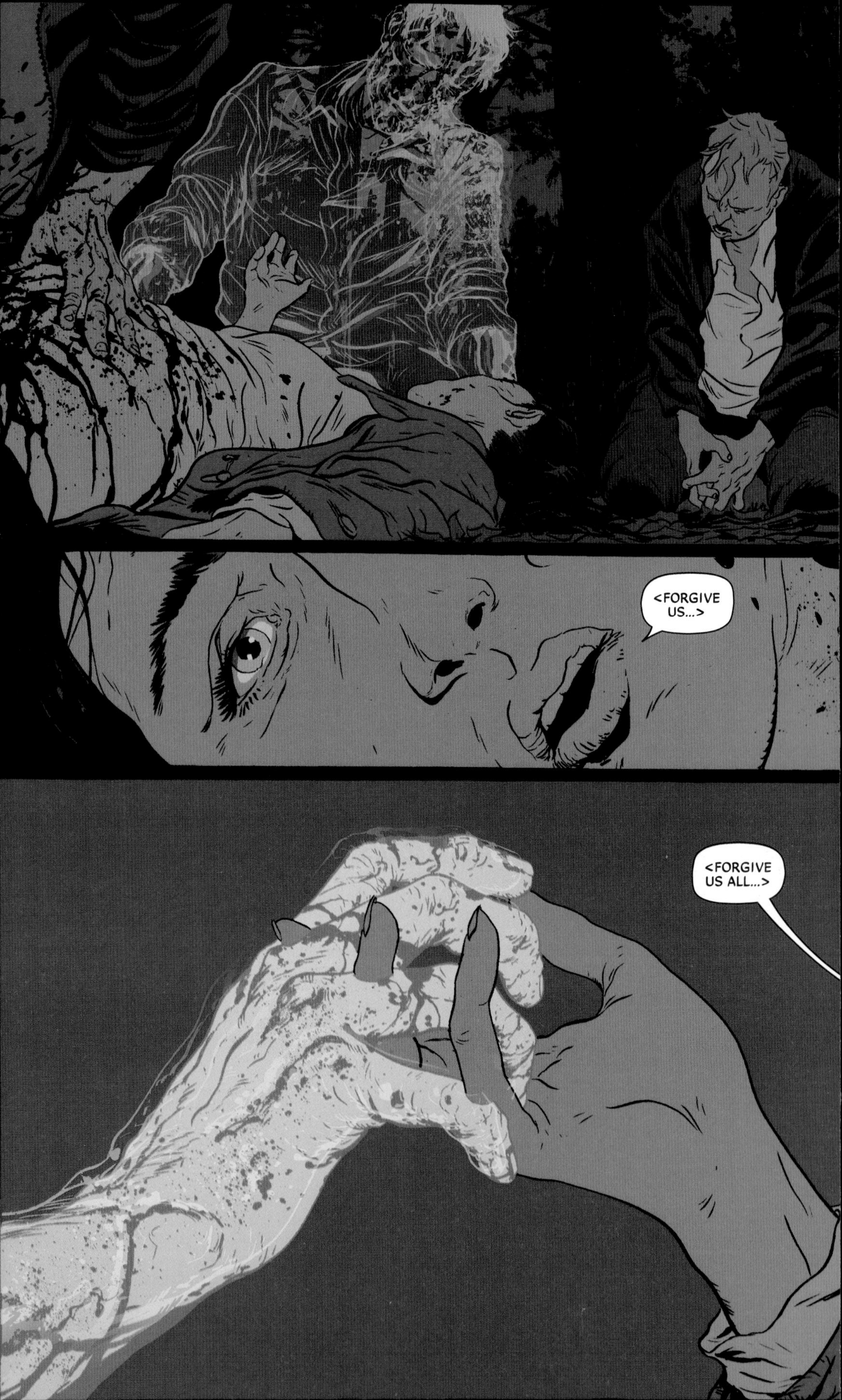
<FORGIVE US...>
<FORGIVE US ALL...>

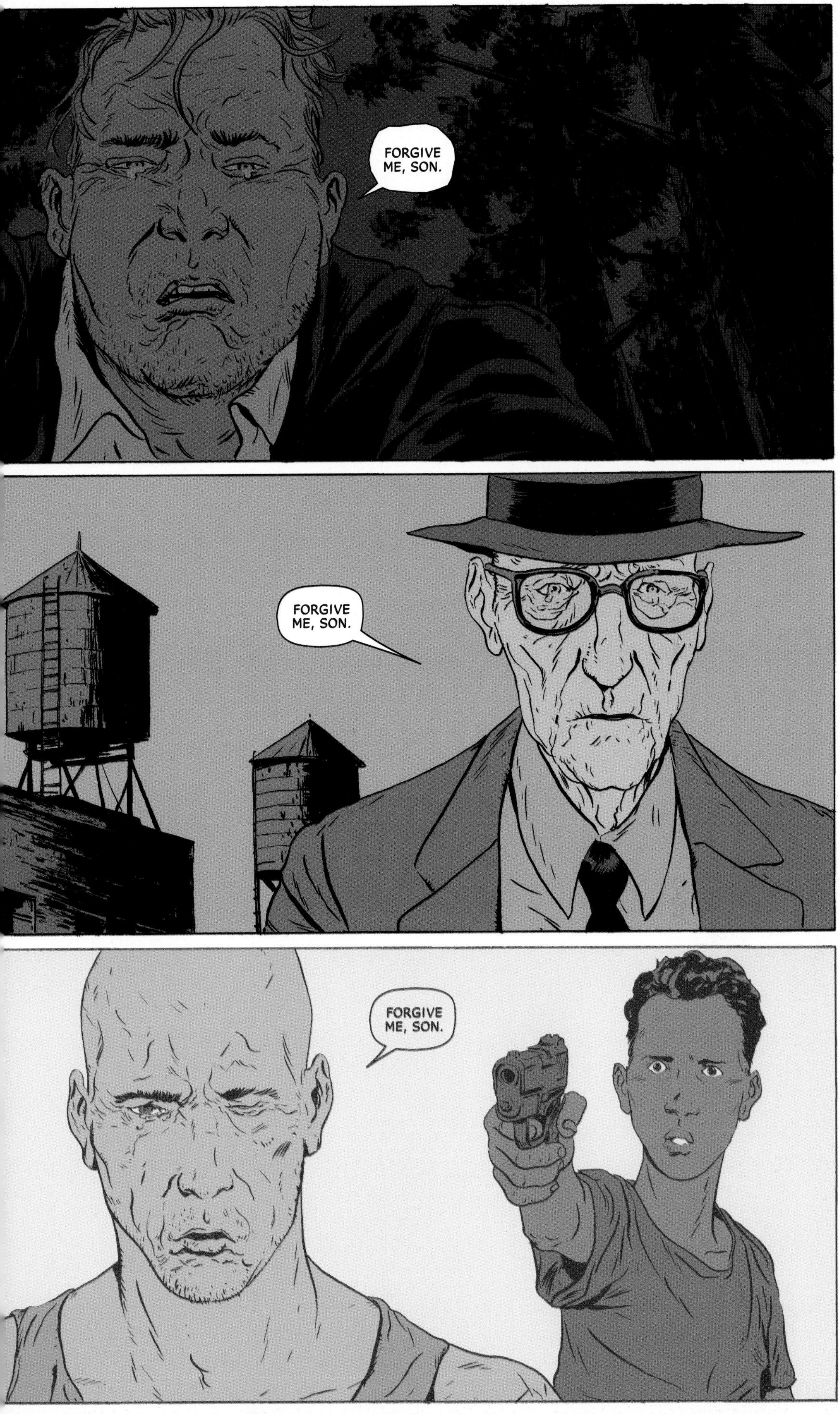
FORGIVE ME, SON.
FORGIVE ME, SON.
FORGIVE ME, SON.

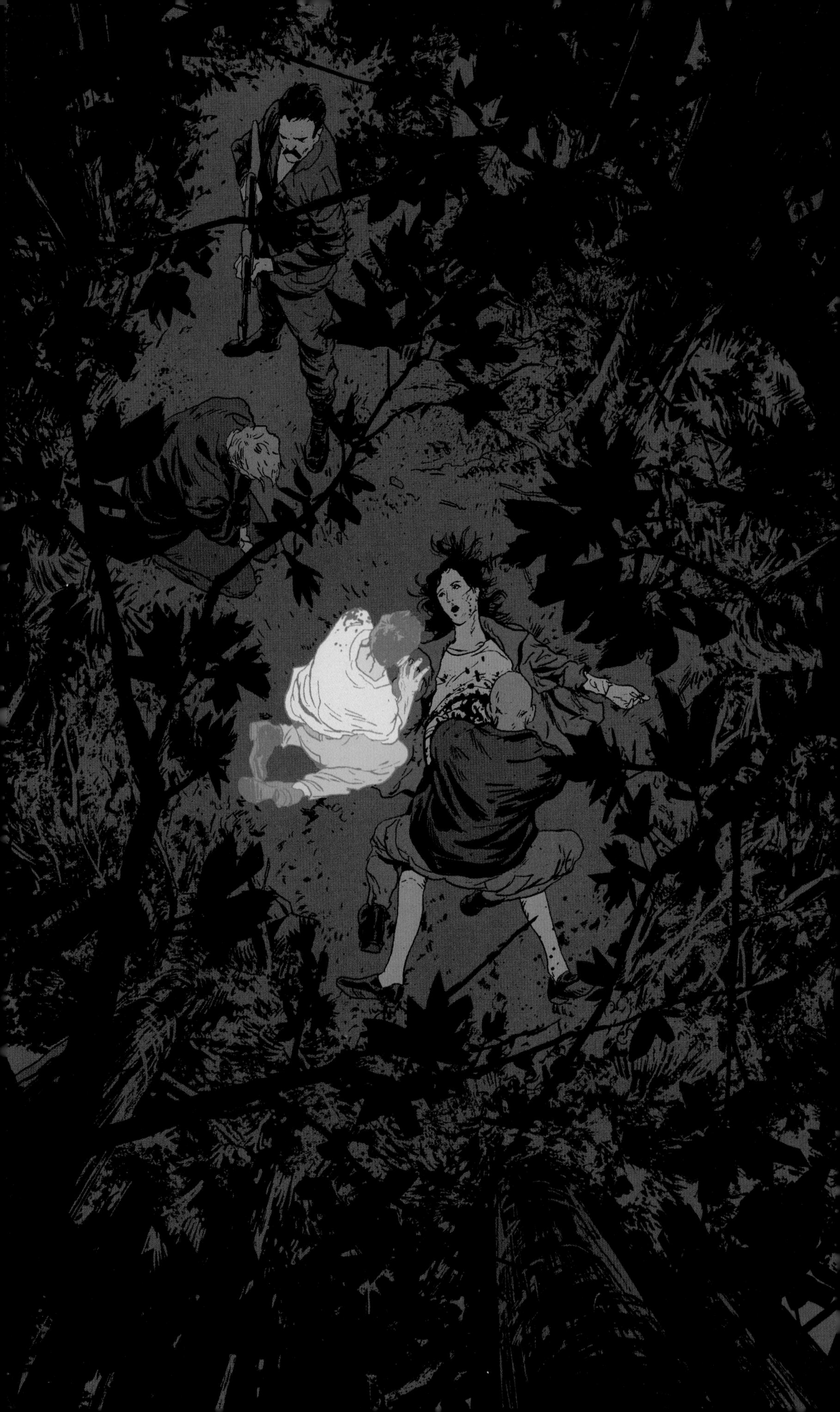

CHAPTER 18

SURRENDER
Illustrated by Tula Lotay

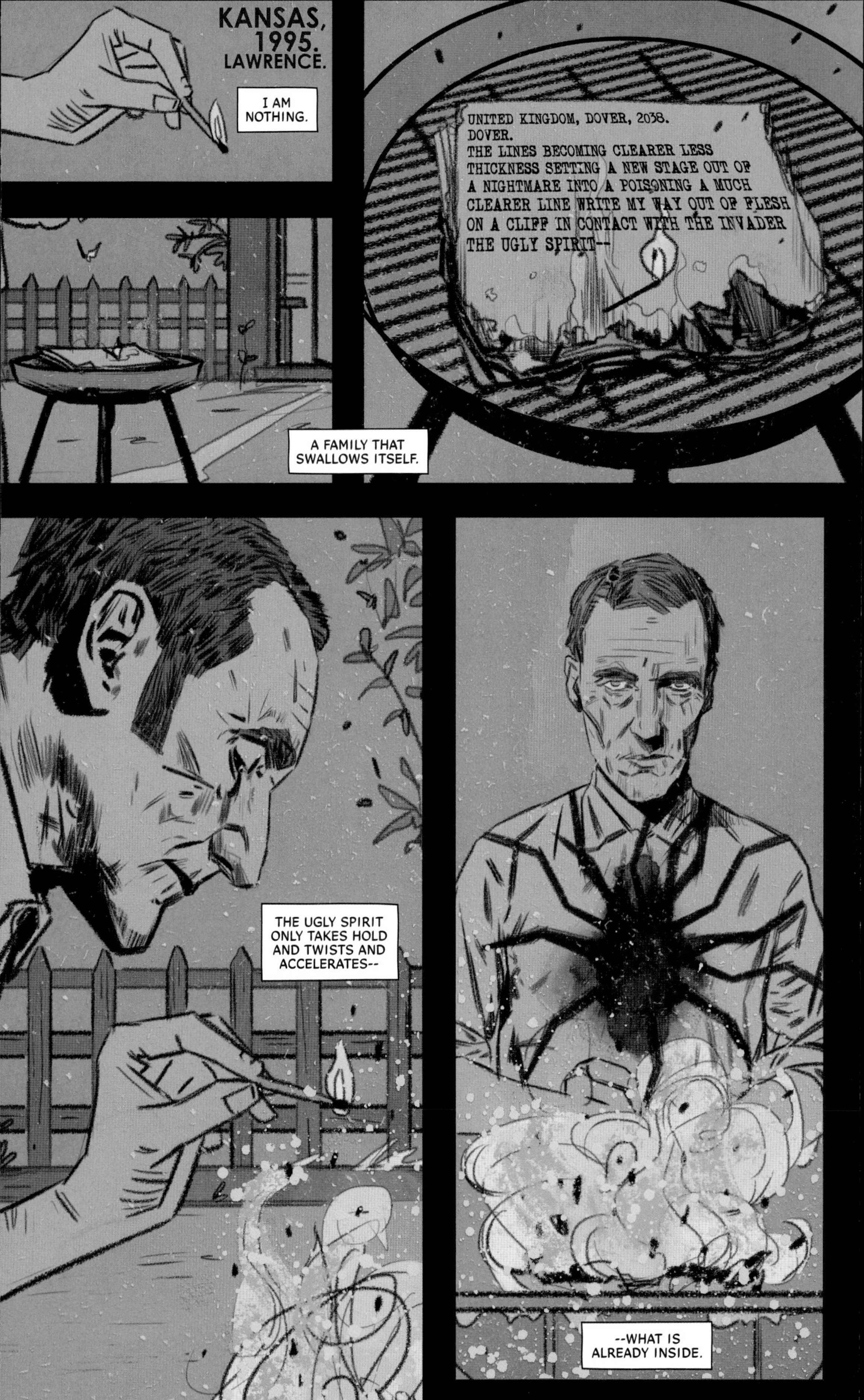
KANSAS,
1995.
LAWRENCE.
I AM NOTHING.
UNITED KINGDOM, DOVER, 2038.
DOVER.
THE LINES BECOMING CLEARER LESS
THICKNESS SETTING A NEW STAGE OUT OF
A NIGHTMARE INTO A POISONING A MUCH
CLEARER LINE WRITE MY WAY OUT OF FLESH
ON A CLIFF IN CONTACT WITH THE INVADER
THE UGLY SPIRIT--
A FAMILY THAT SWALLOWS ITSELF.
THE UGLY SPIRIT ONLY TAKES HOLD AND TWISTS AND ACCELERATES--
--WHAT IS ALREADY INSIDE.

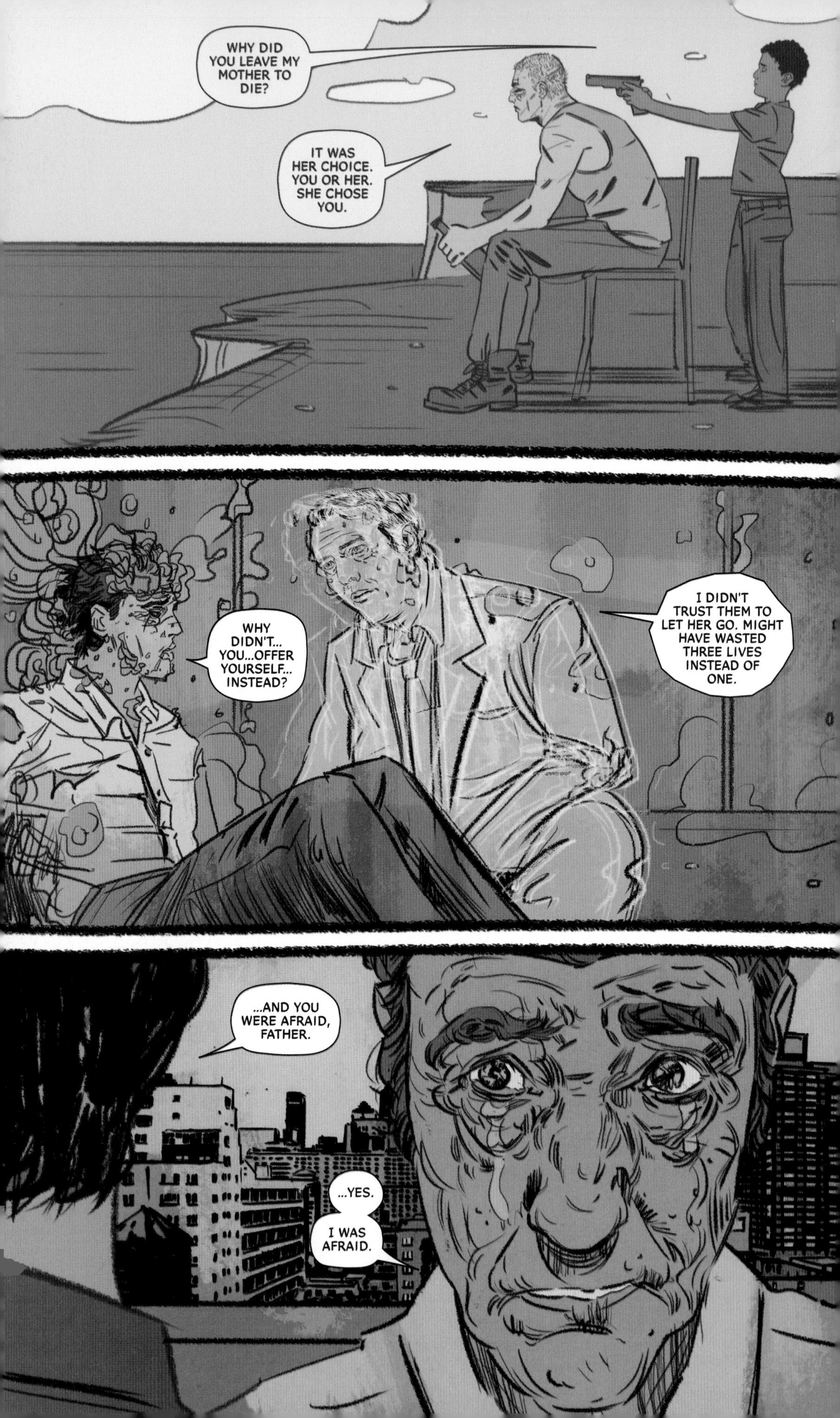
WHY DID YOU LEAVE MY MOTHER TO DIE?
IT WAS HER CHOICE. YOU OR HER. SHE CHOSE YOU.
WHY DIDN'T... YOU...OFFER YOURSELF... INSTEAD?
I DIDN'T TRUST THEM TO LET HER GO. MIGHT HAVE WASTED THREE LIVES INSTEAD OF ONE.
...AND YOU WERE AFRAID, FATHER.
...YES.
I WAS AFRAID.

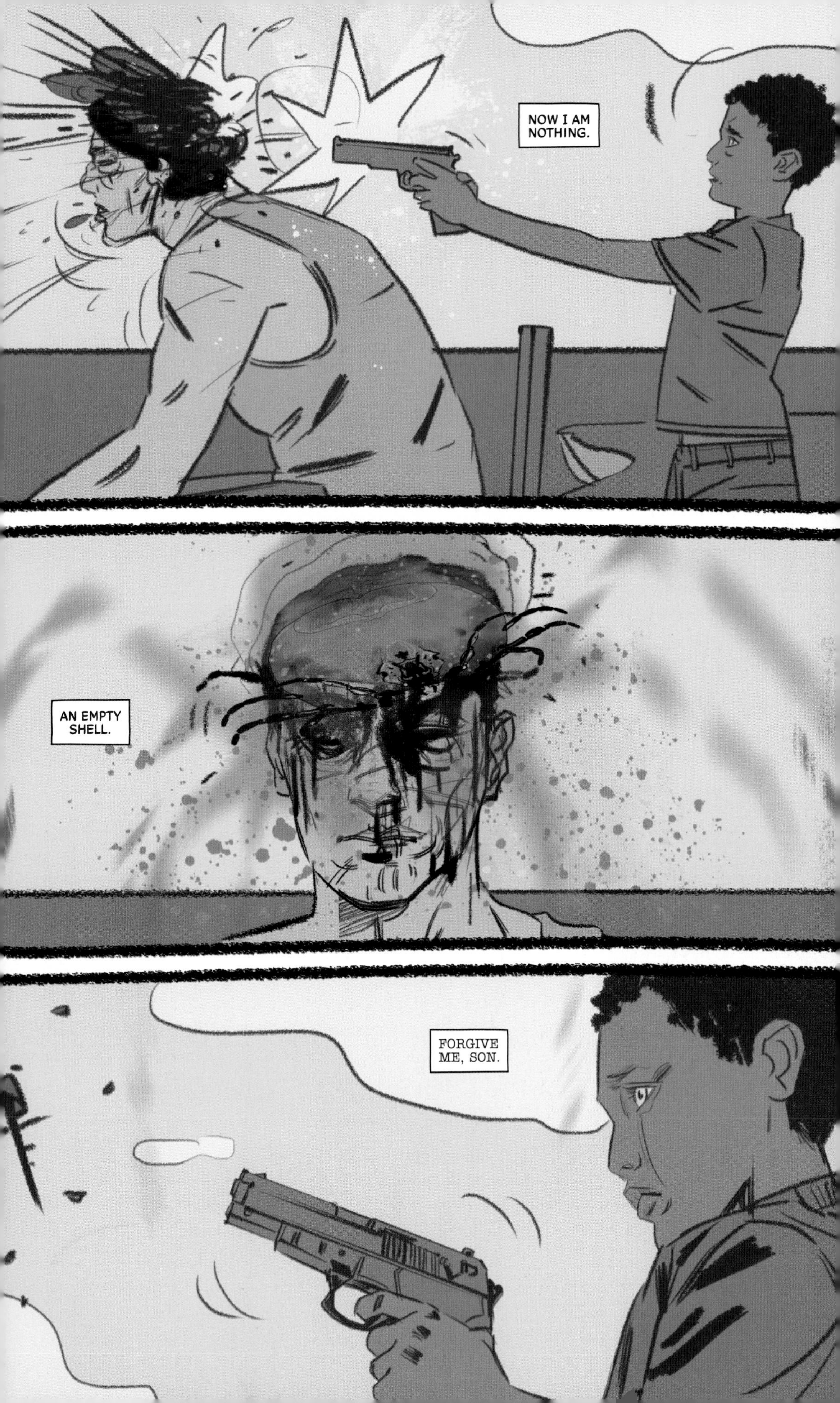
NOW I AM NOTHING.
AN EMPTY SHELL.
FORGIVE ME, SON.

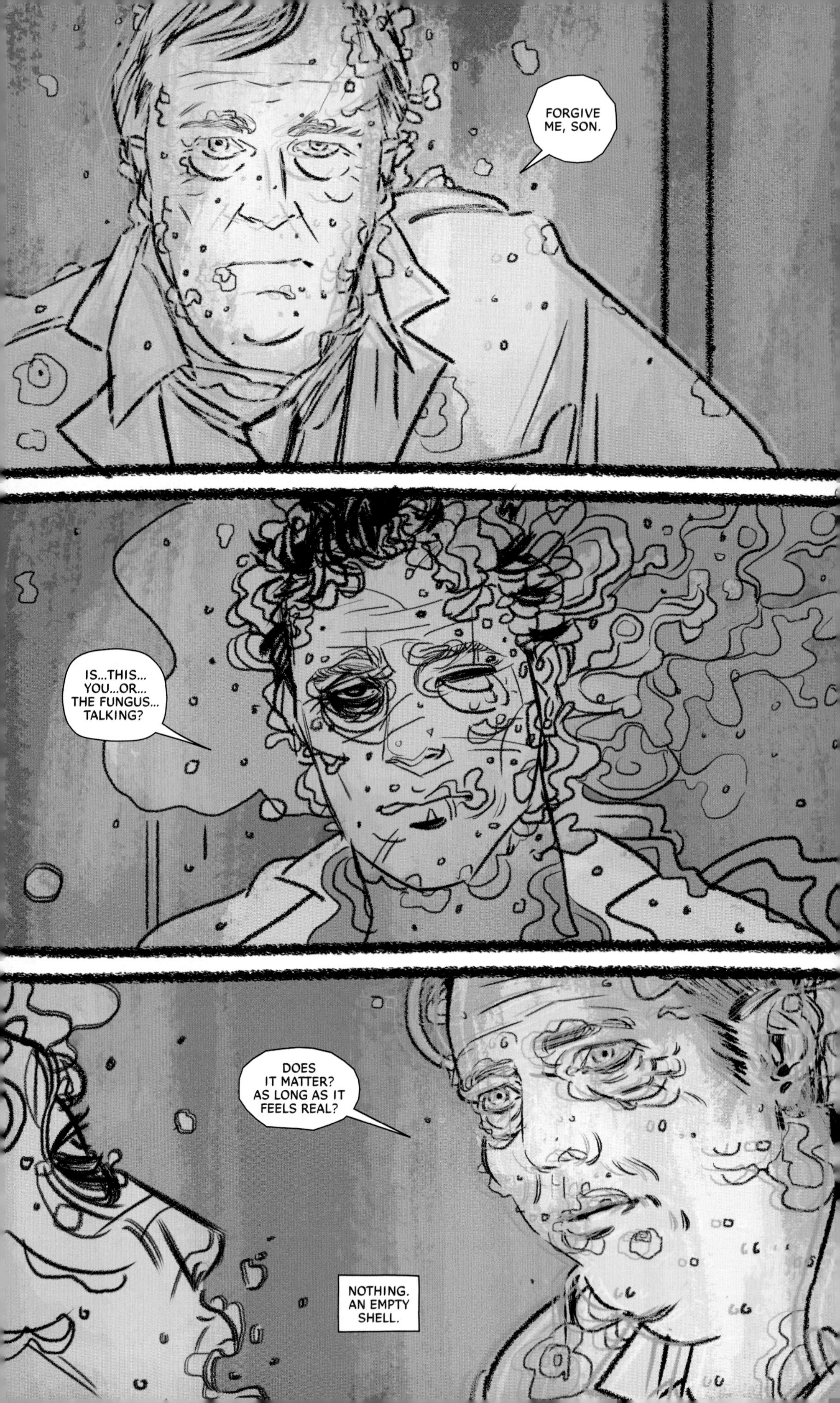

FORGIVE ME, SON.
IS...THIS... YOU...OR... THE FUNGUS... TALKING?
DOES IT MATTER? AS LONG AS IT FEELS REAL?
NOTHING. AN EMPTY SHELL.

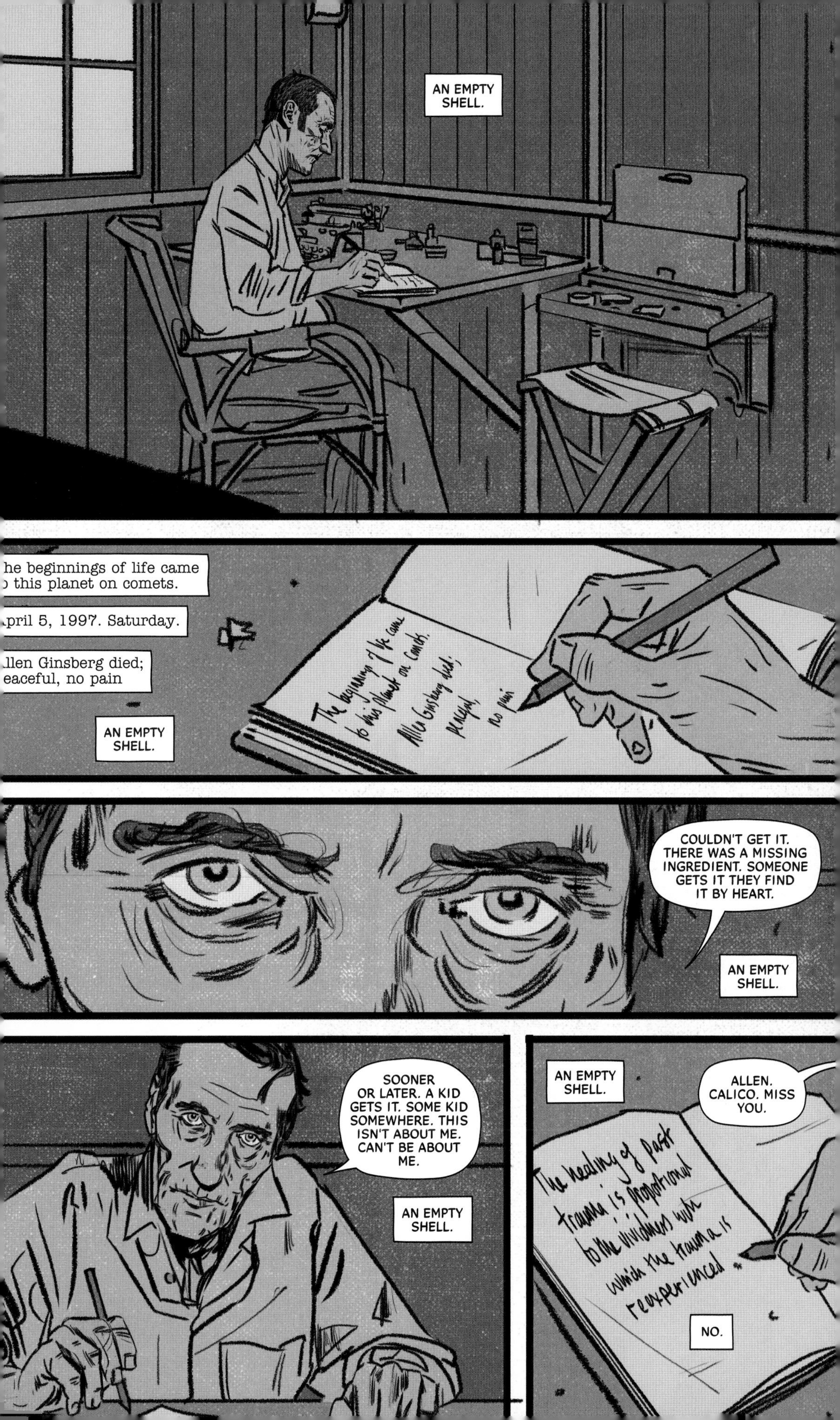
AN EMPTY SHELL.
he beginnings of life came
this planet on comets.
pril 5, 1997. Saturday.
llen Ginsberg died;
eaceful, no pain
AN EMPTY SHELL.
The beginning of life came to this planet on comets. Allen Ginsberg died; peaceful, no pain
COULDN'T GET IT. THERE WAS A MISSING INGREDIENT. SOMEONE GETS IT THEY FIND IT BY HEART.
AN EMPTY SHELL.
SOONER OR LATER. A KID GETS IT. SOME KID SOMEWHERE. THIS ISN'T ABOUT ME. CAN'T BE ABOUT ME.
AN EMPTY SHELL.
AN EMPTY SHELL.
ALLEN. CALICO. MISS YOU.
The healing of past trauma is proportional to the vividness with which the trauma is reexperienced.
NO.

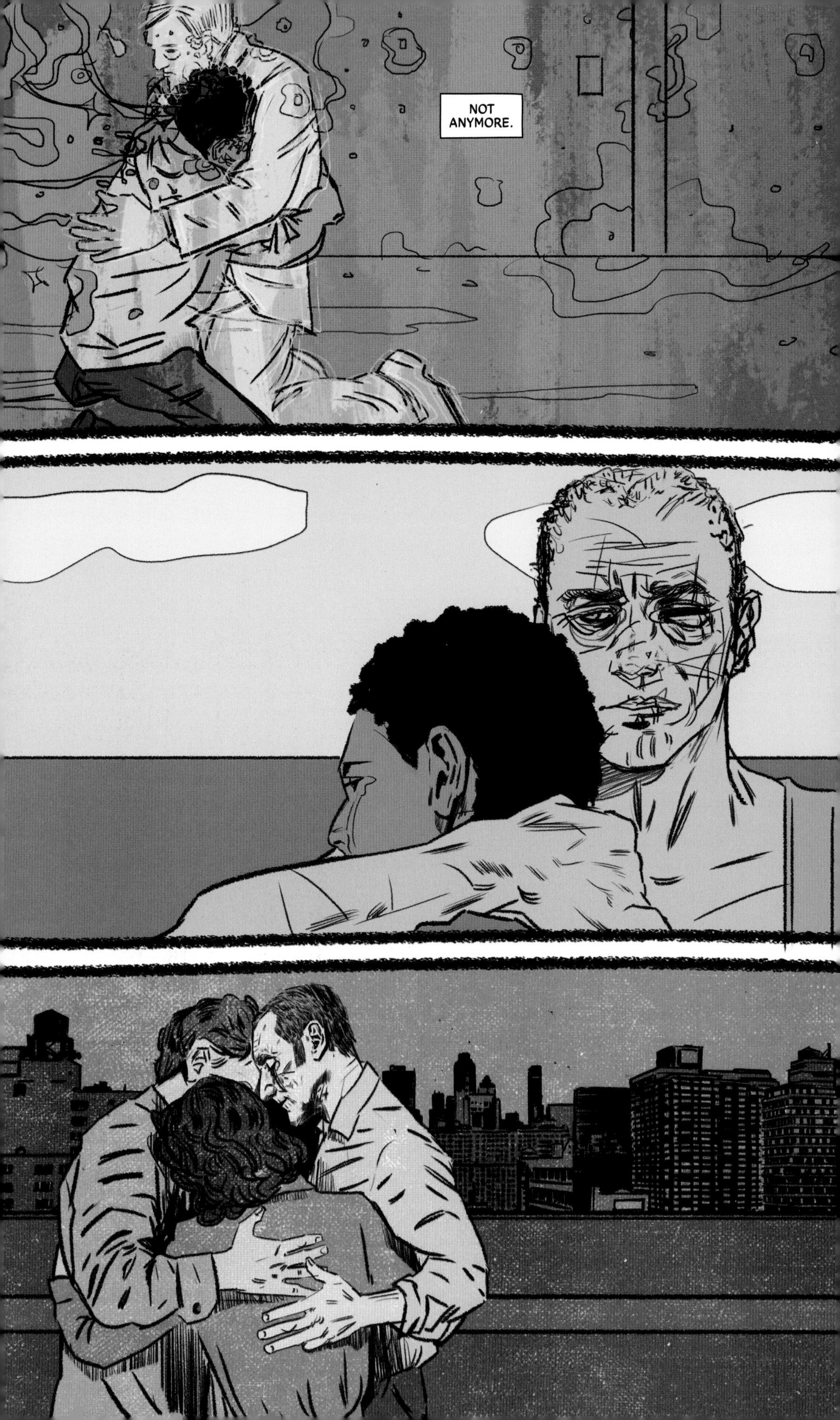
NOT ANYMORE.

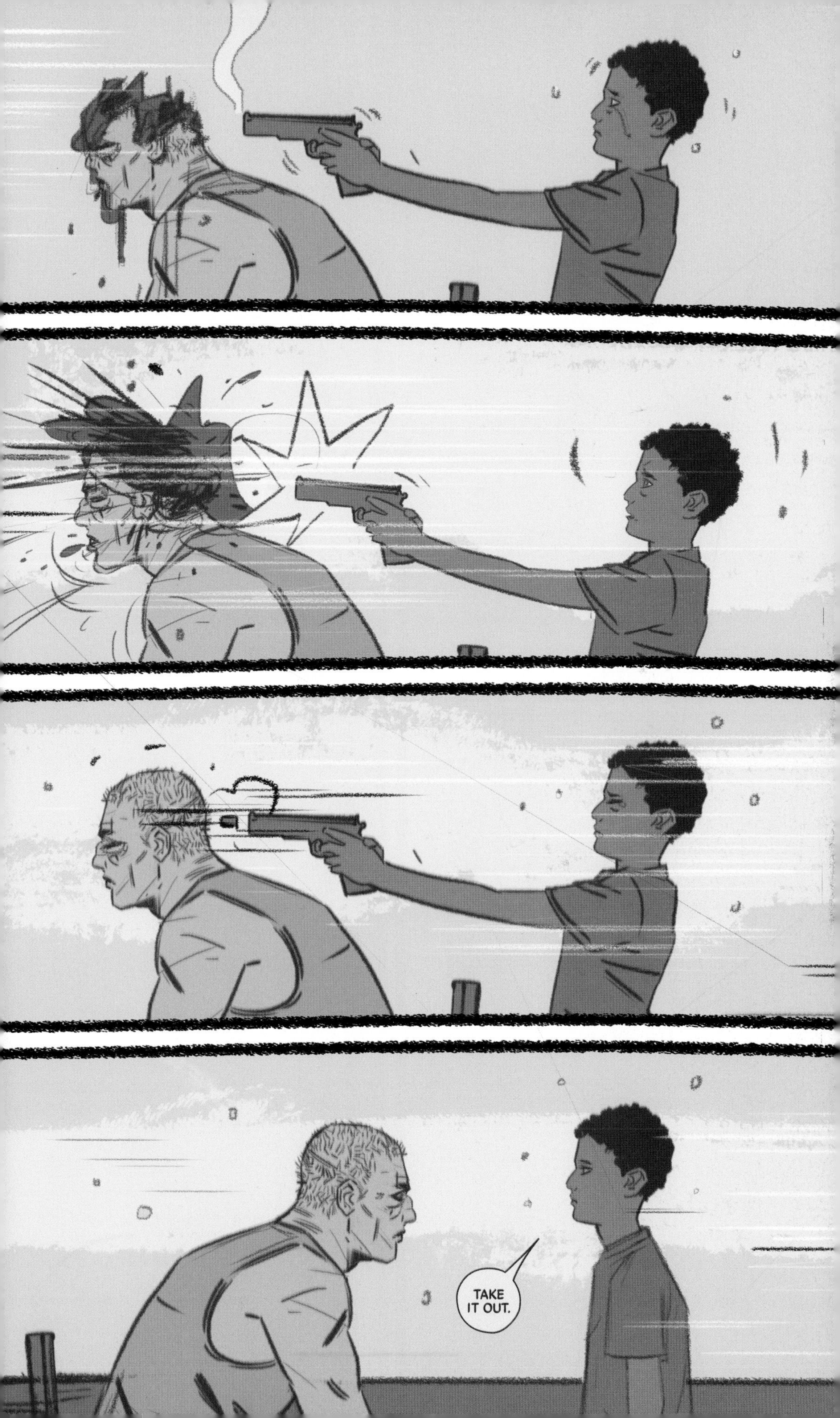
TAKE IT OUT.

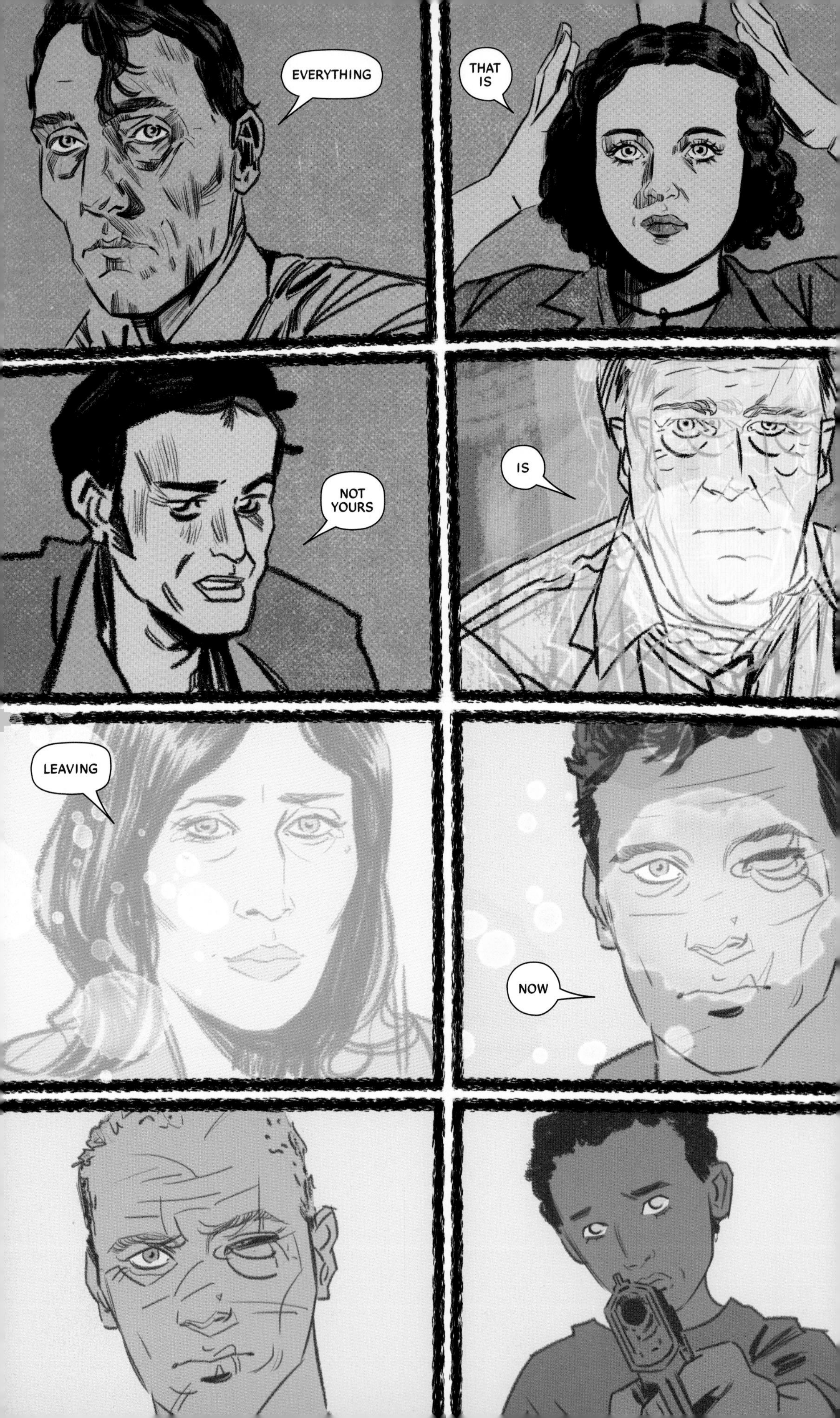
EVERYTHING
THAT IS
NOT YOURS
IS
LEAVING
NOW

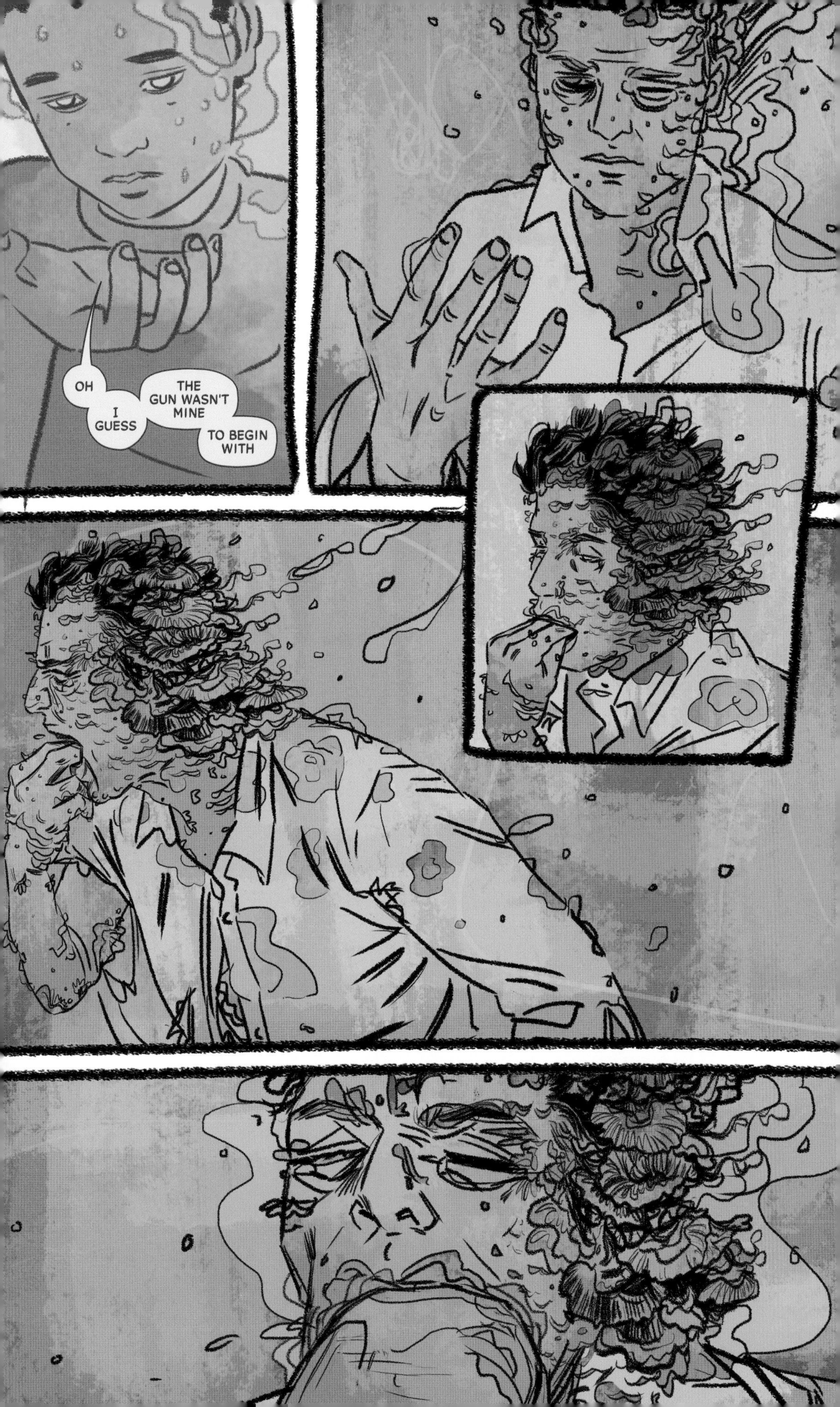
OH
I GUESS
THE GUN WASN'T MINE
TO BEGIN WITH

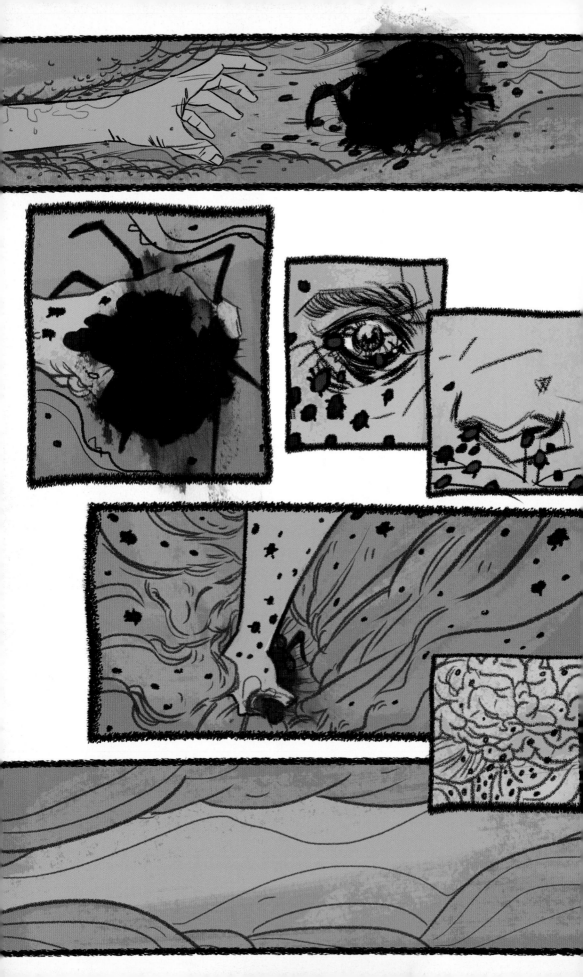

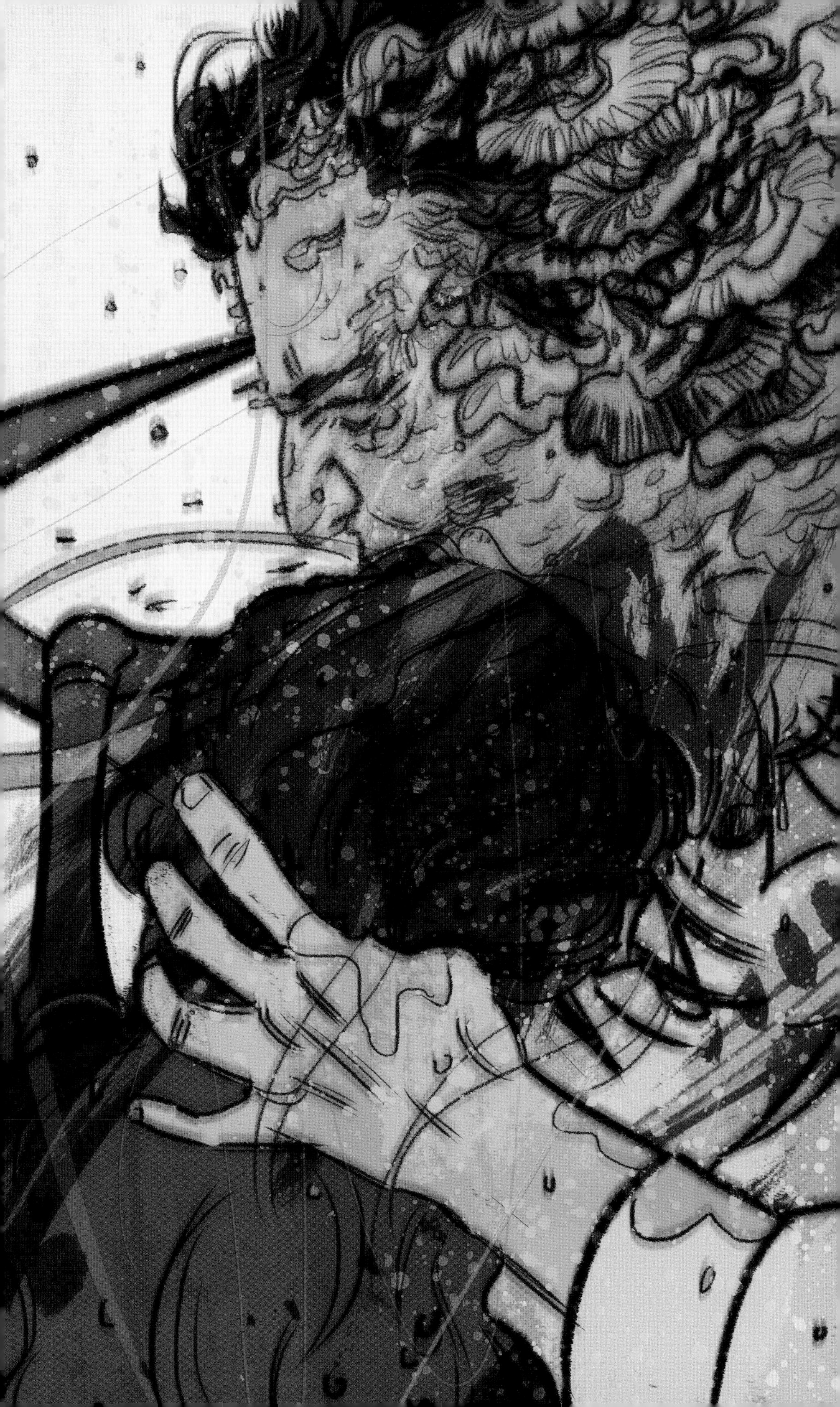

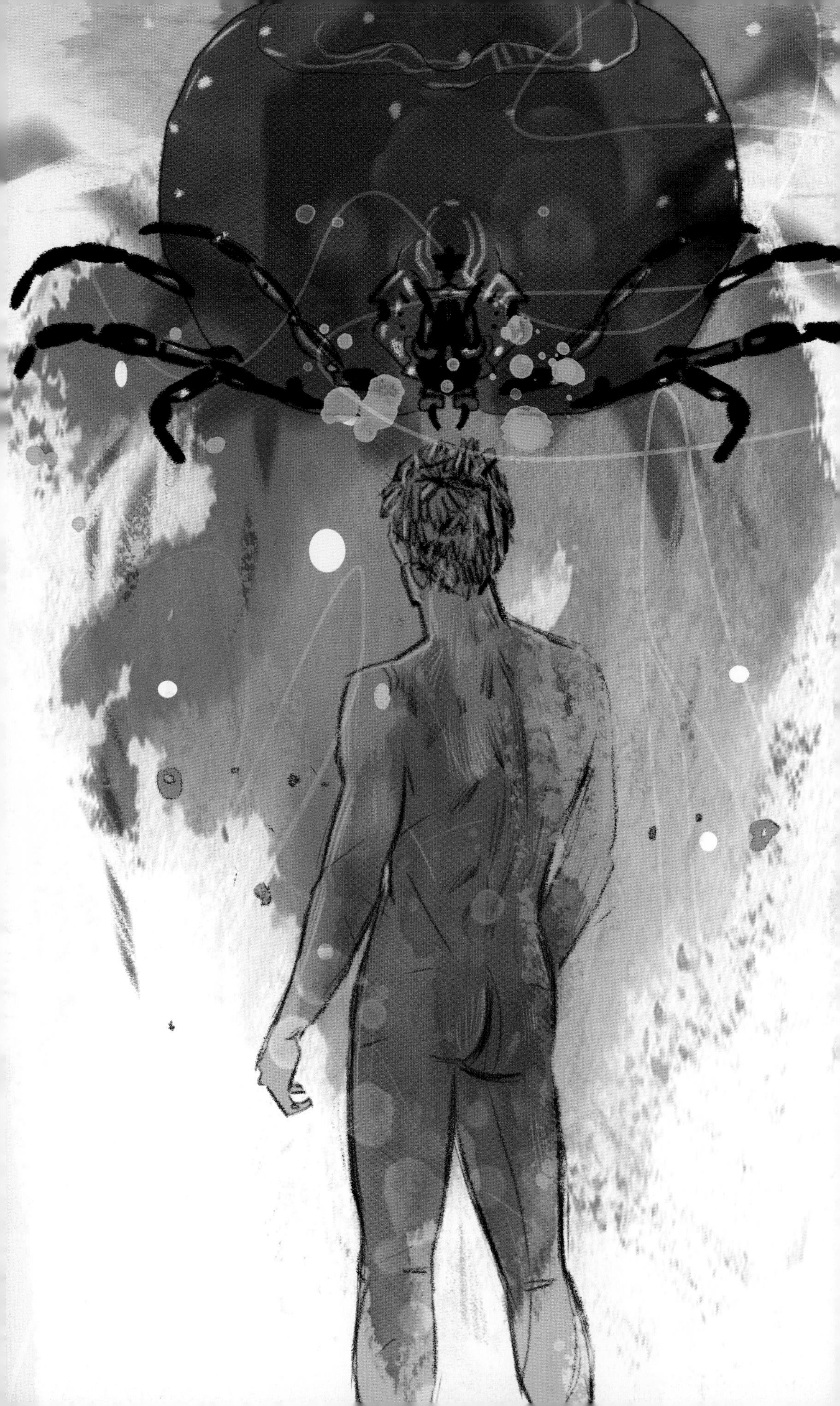

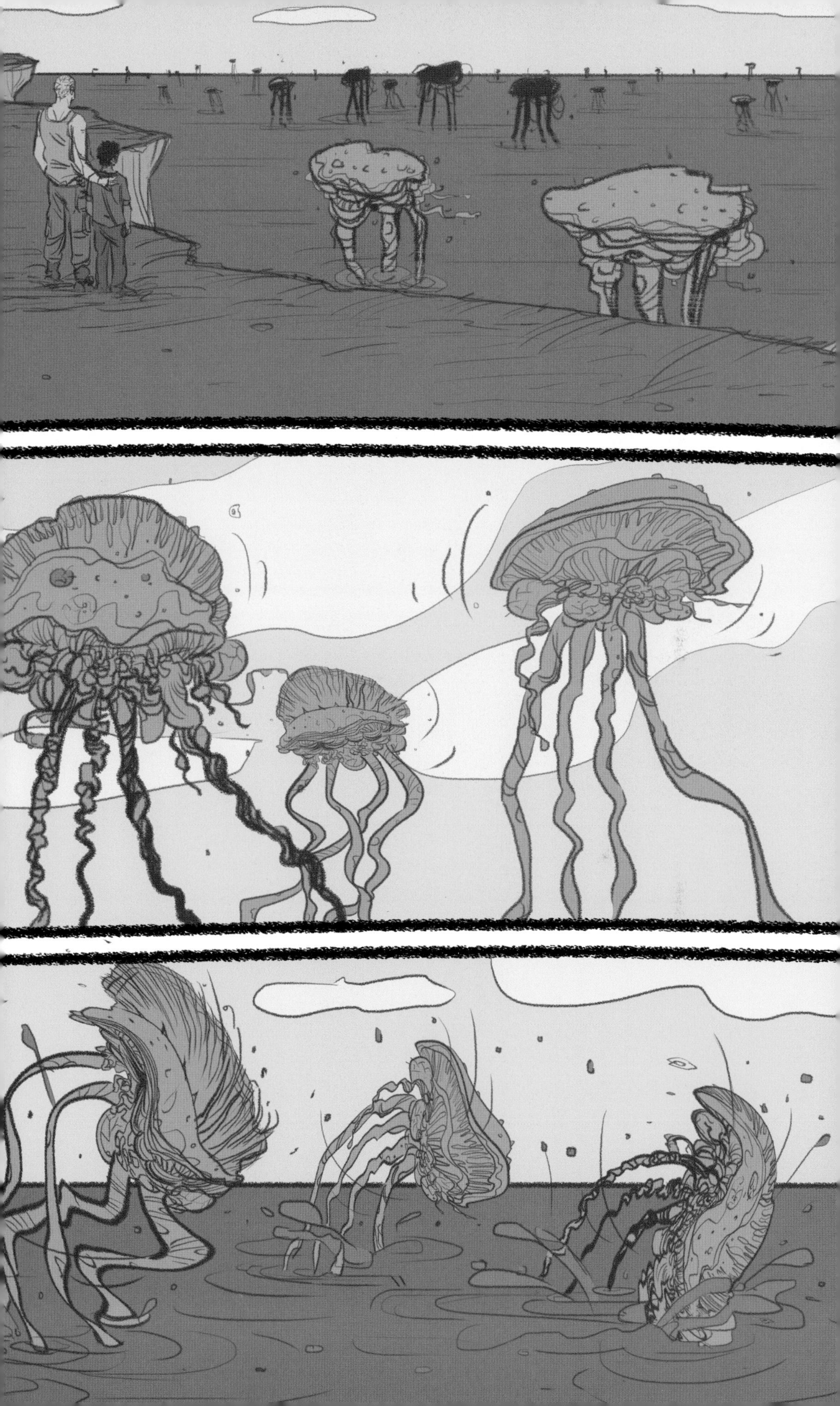

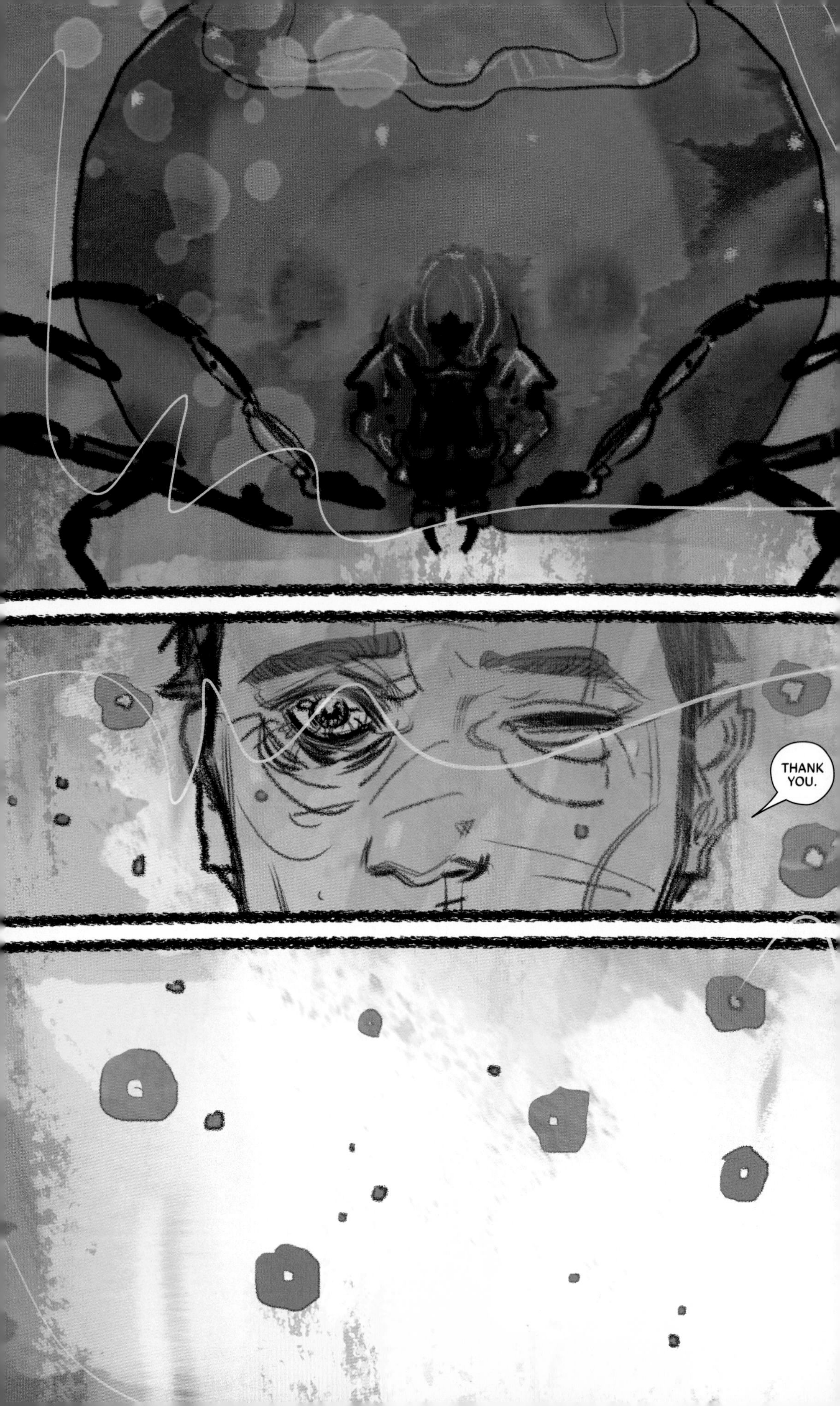
THANK YOU.

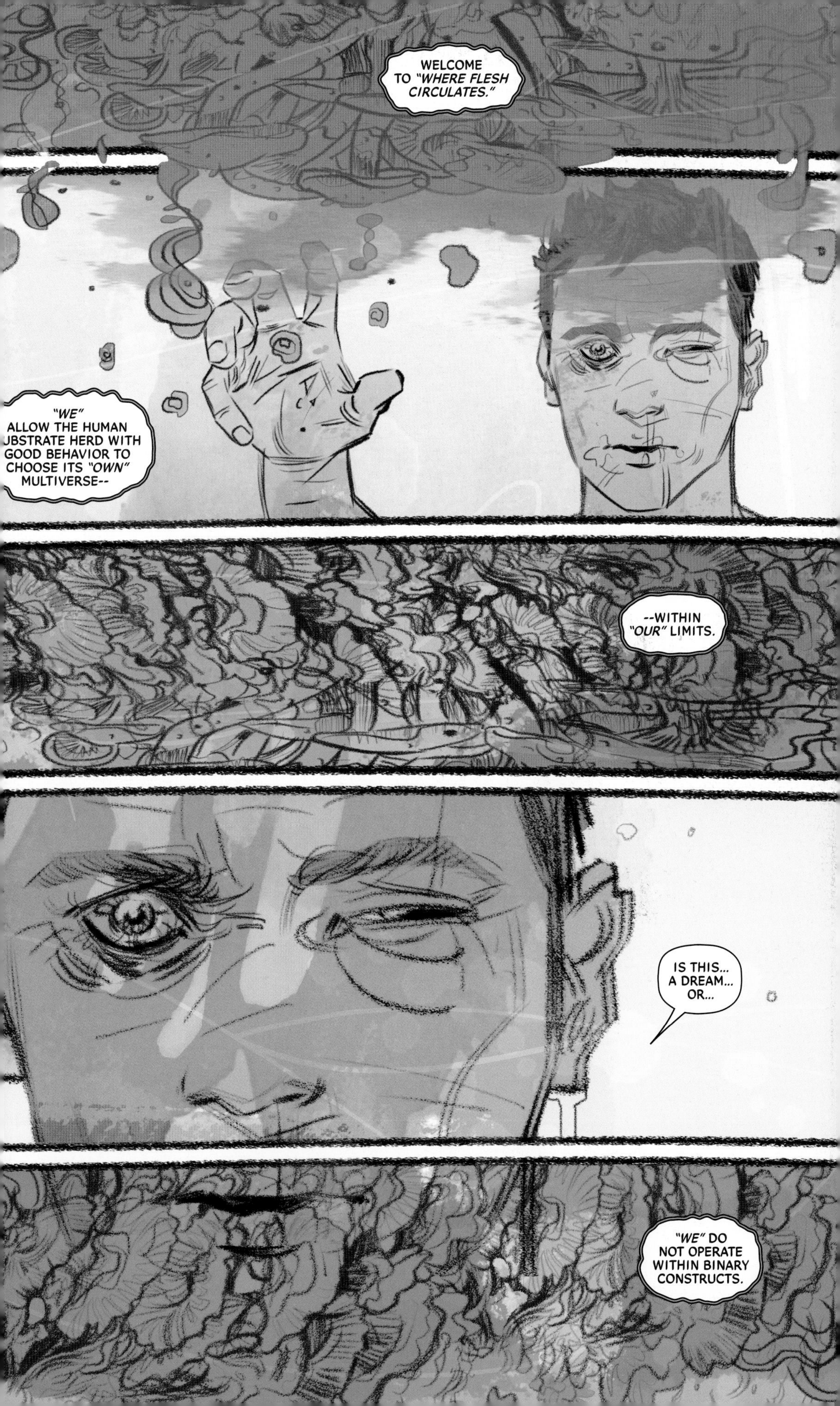
WELCOME TO *"WHERE FLESH CIRCULATES."*
"WE" ALLOW THE HUMAN UBSTRATE HERD WITH GOOD BEHAVIOR TO CHOOSE ITS *"OWN"* MULTIVERSE--
--WITHIN *"OUR"* LIMITS.
IS THIS... A DREAM... OR...
"WE" DO NOT OPERATE WITHIN BINARY CONSTRUCTS.

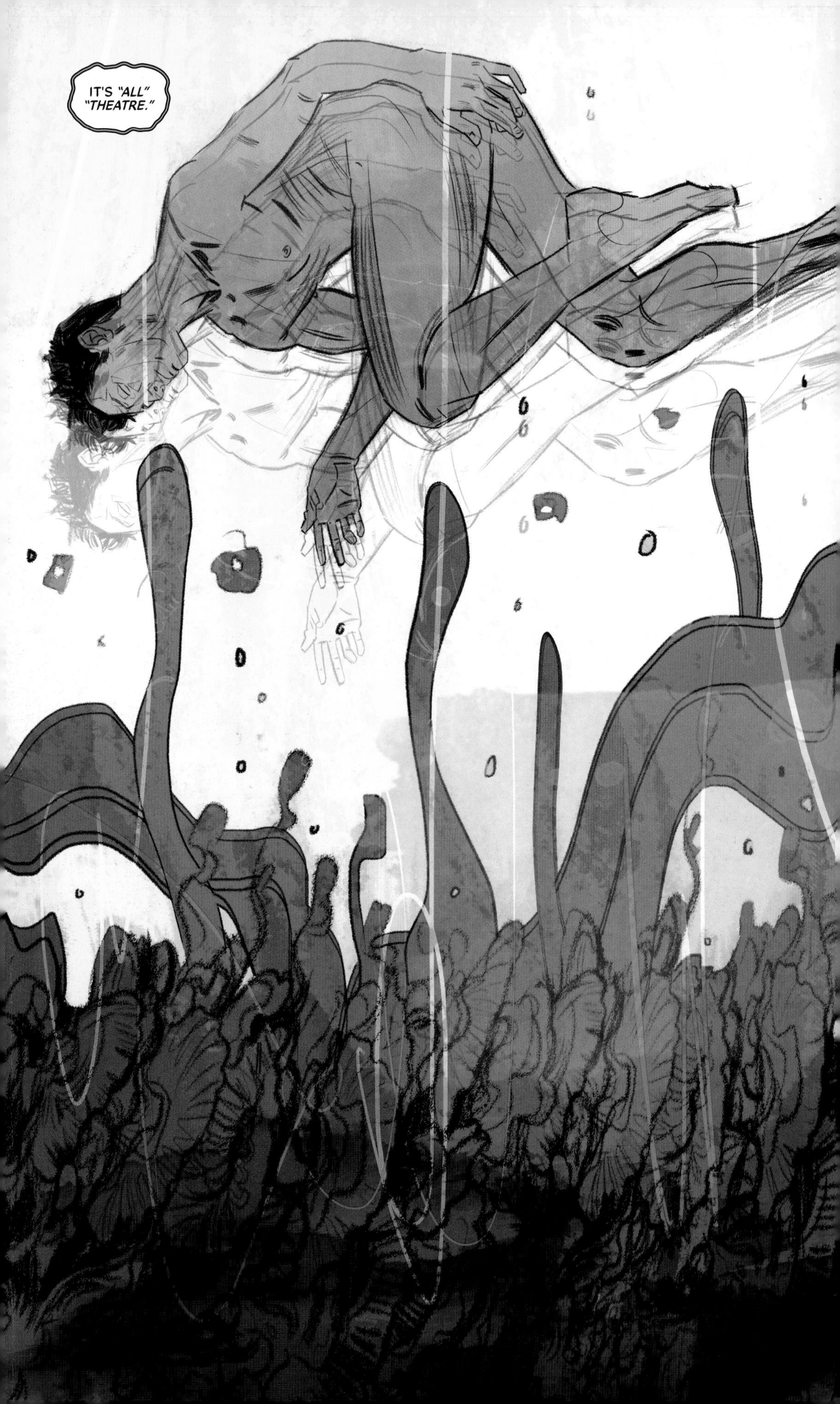
IT'S "ALL" "THEATRE."

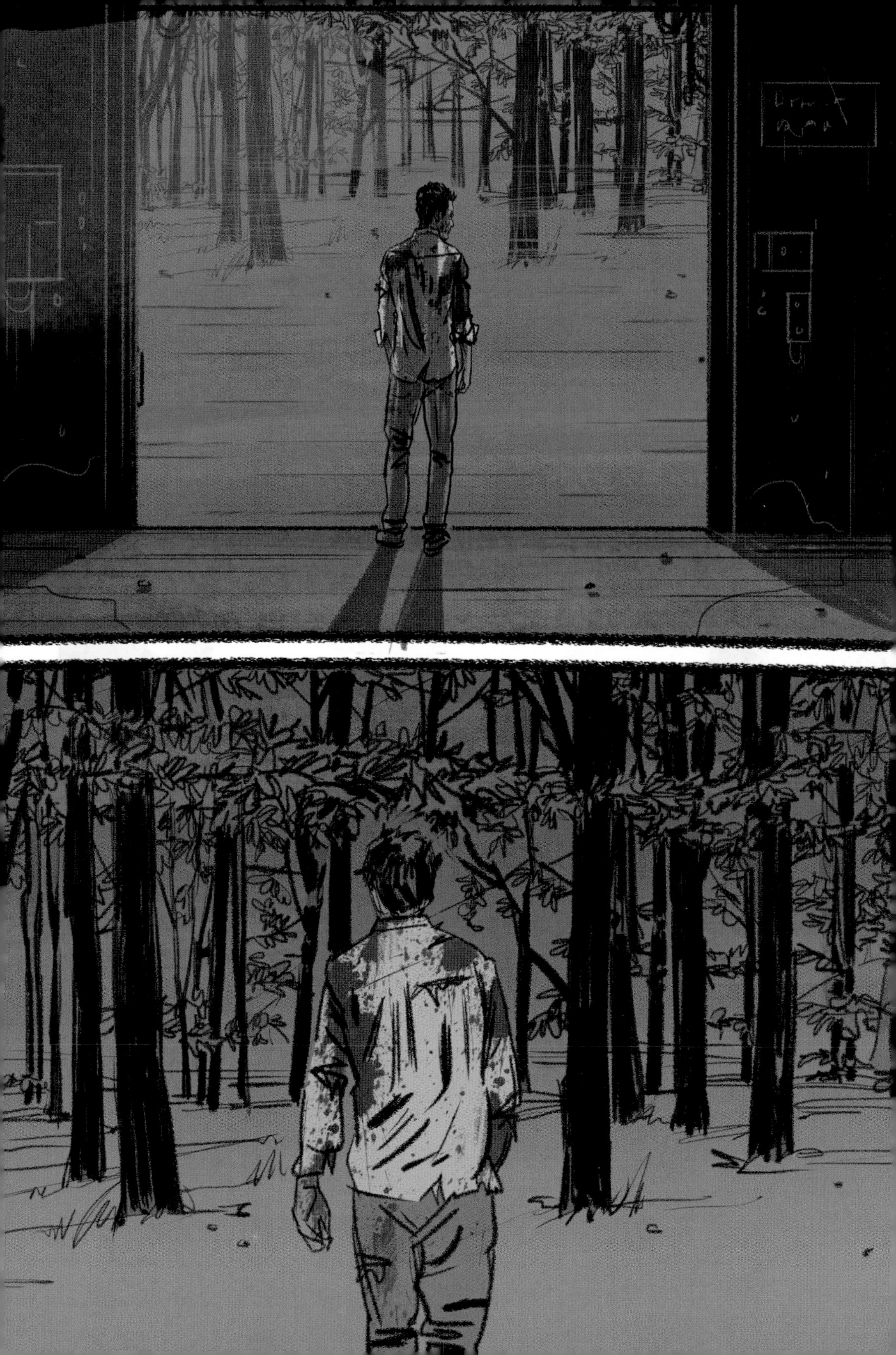

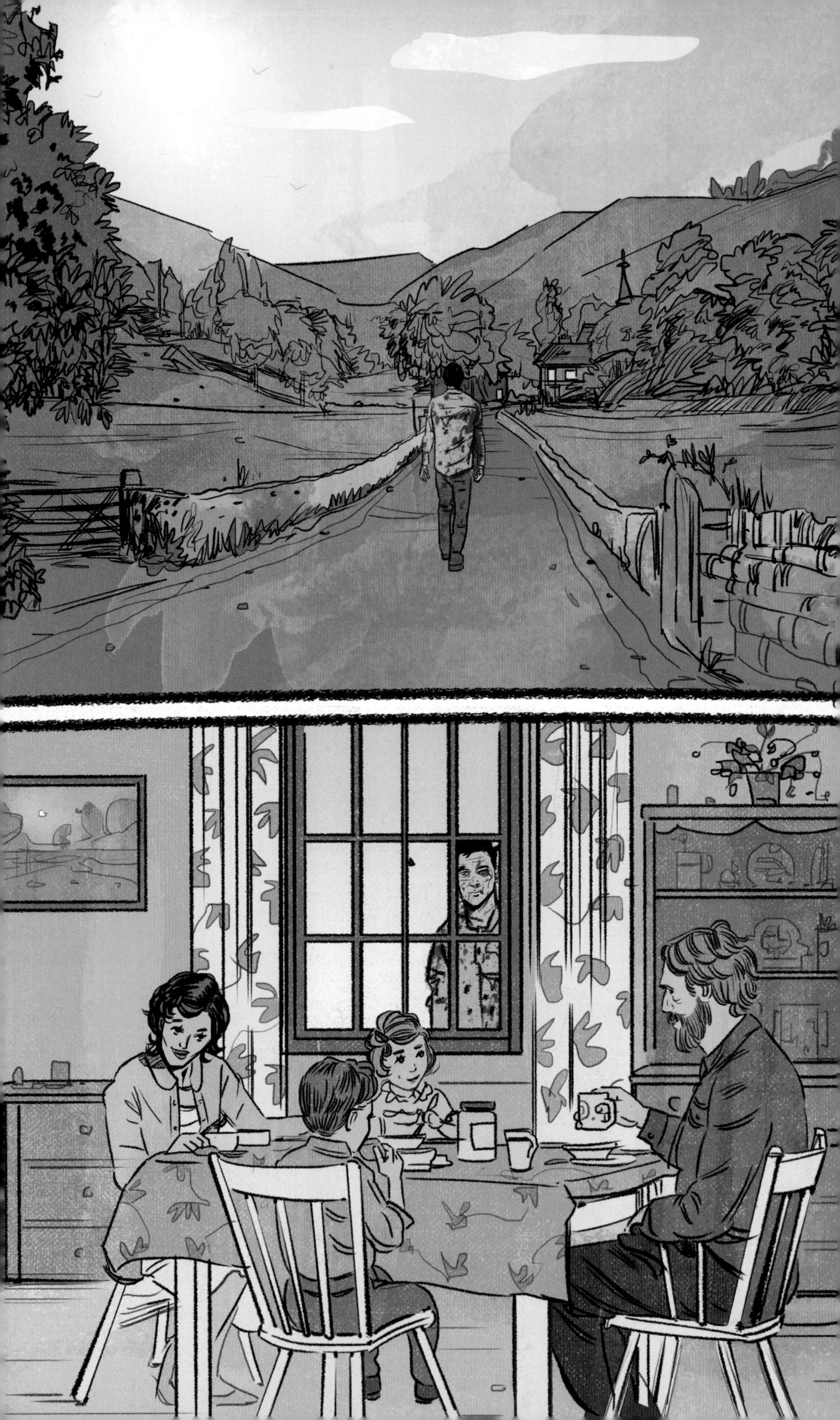

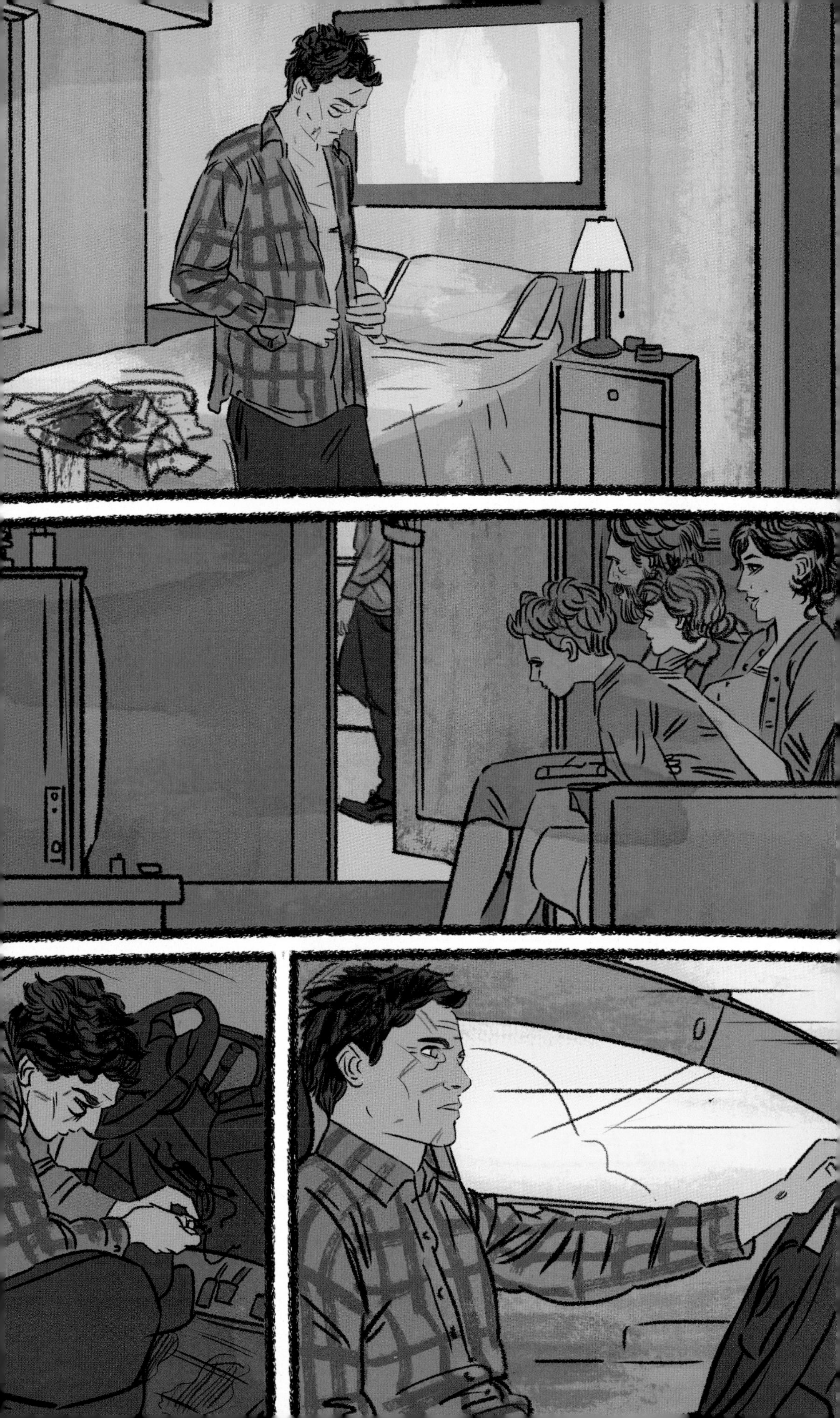

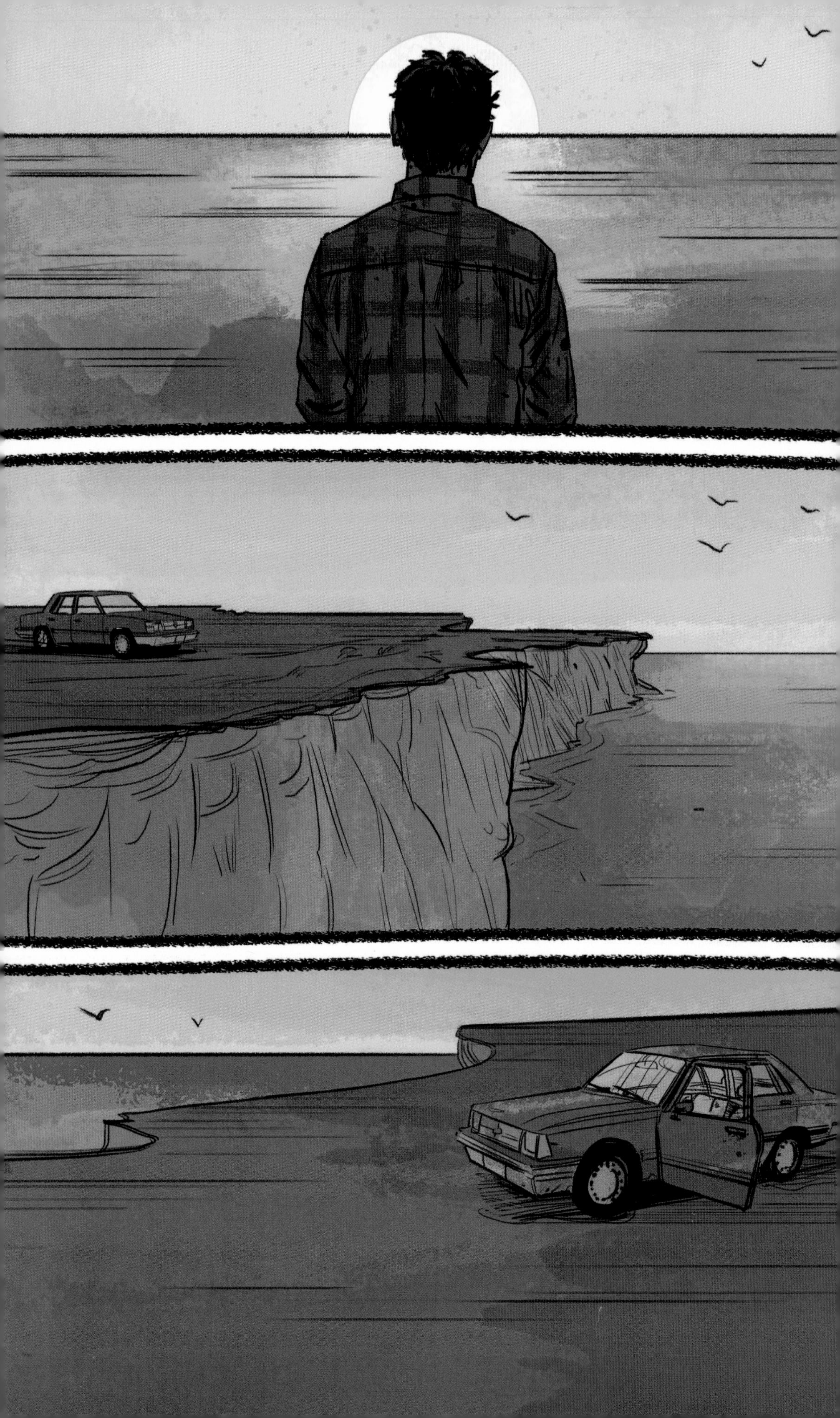

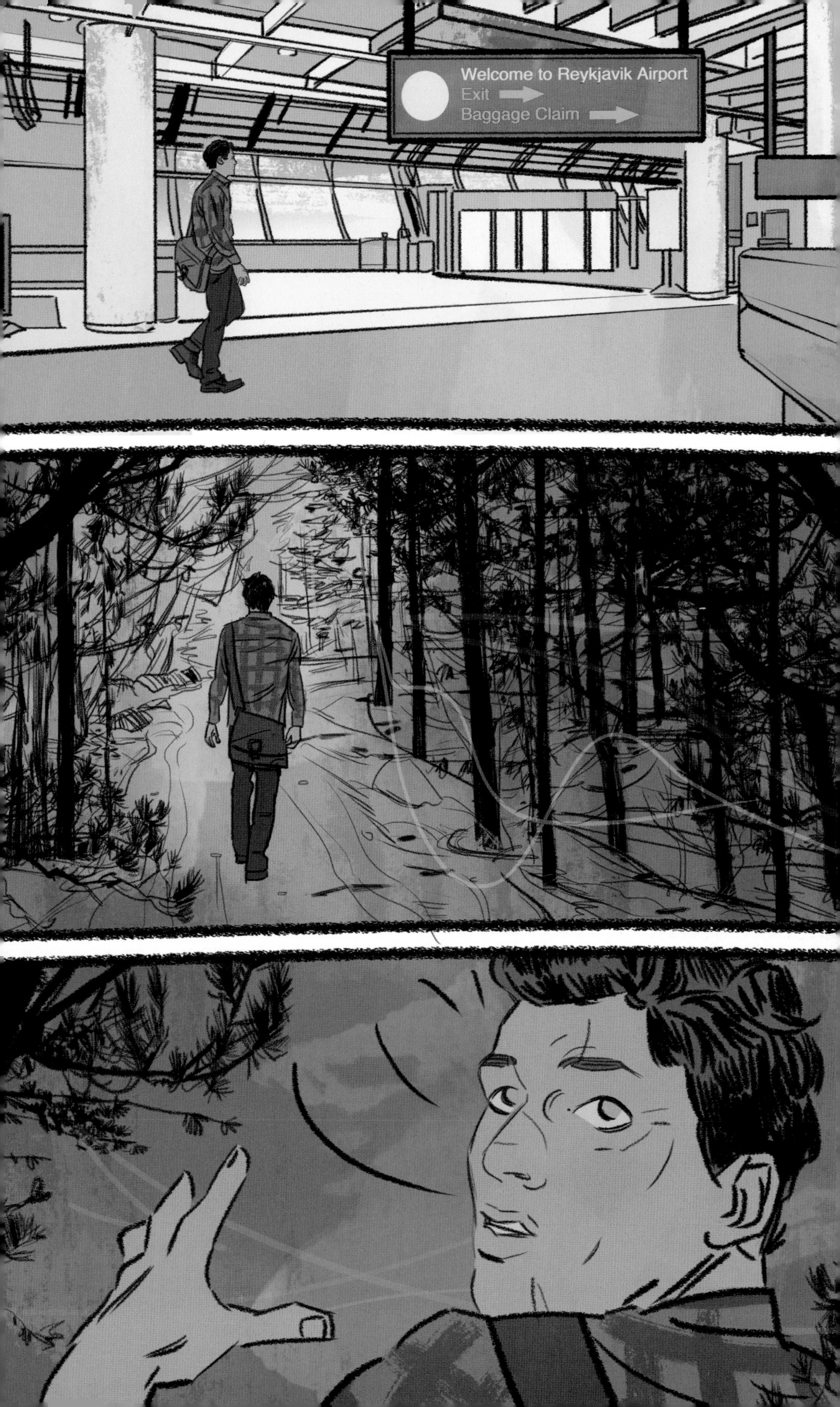
Welcome to Reykjavik Airport
Exit
Baggage Claim

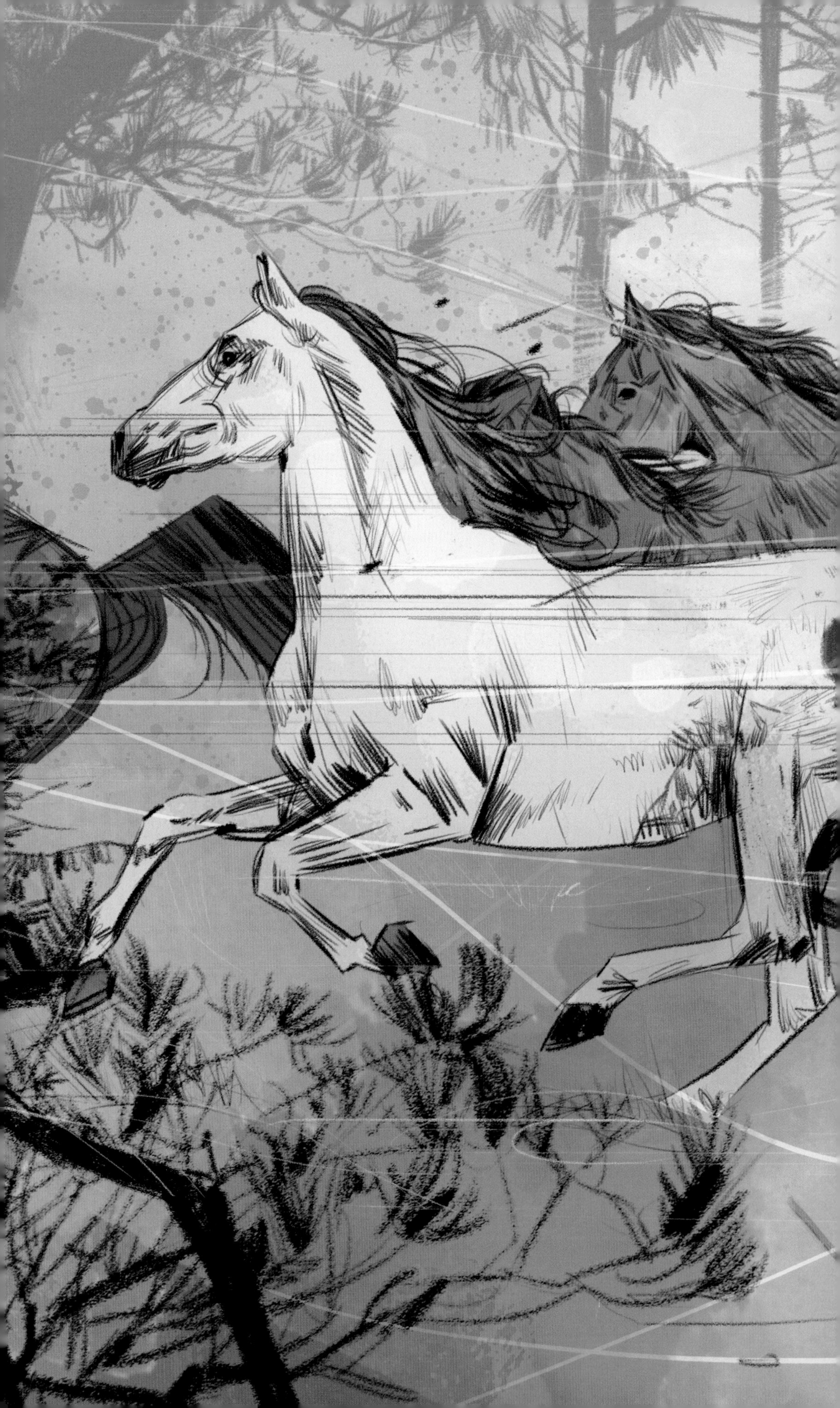

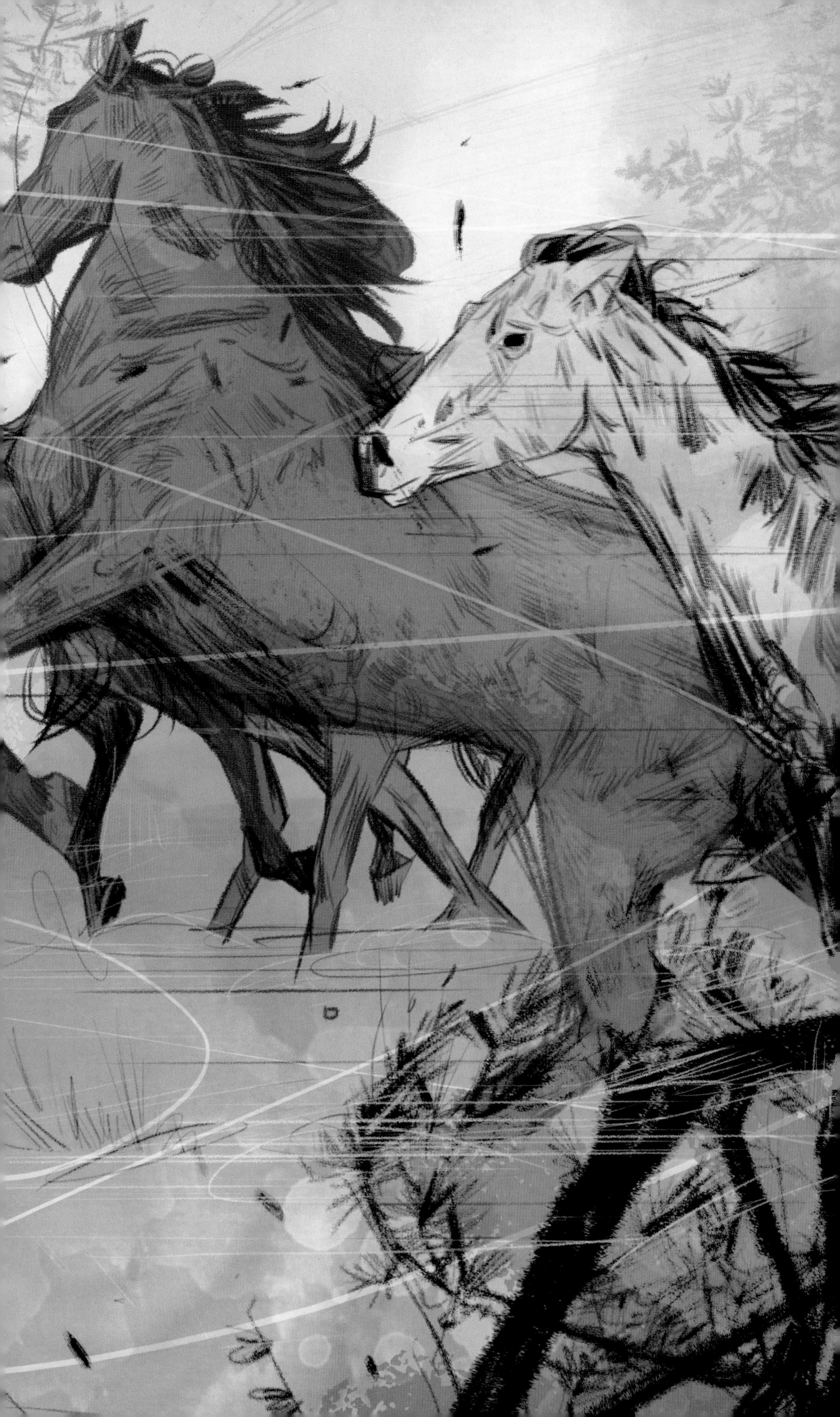

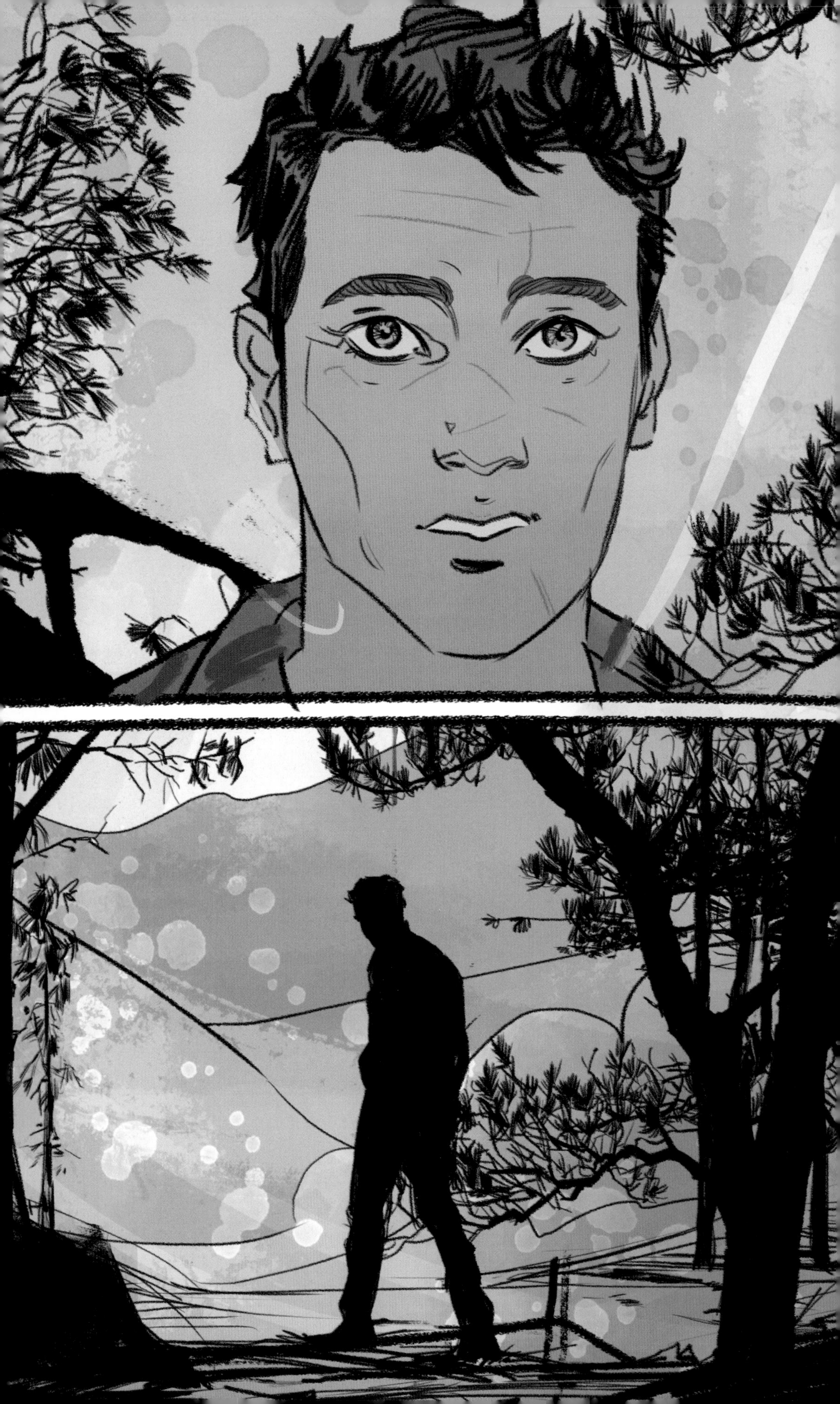

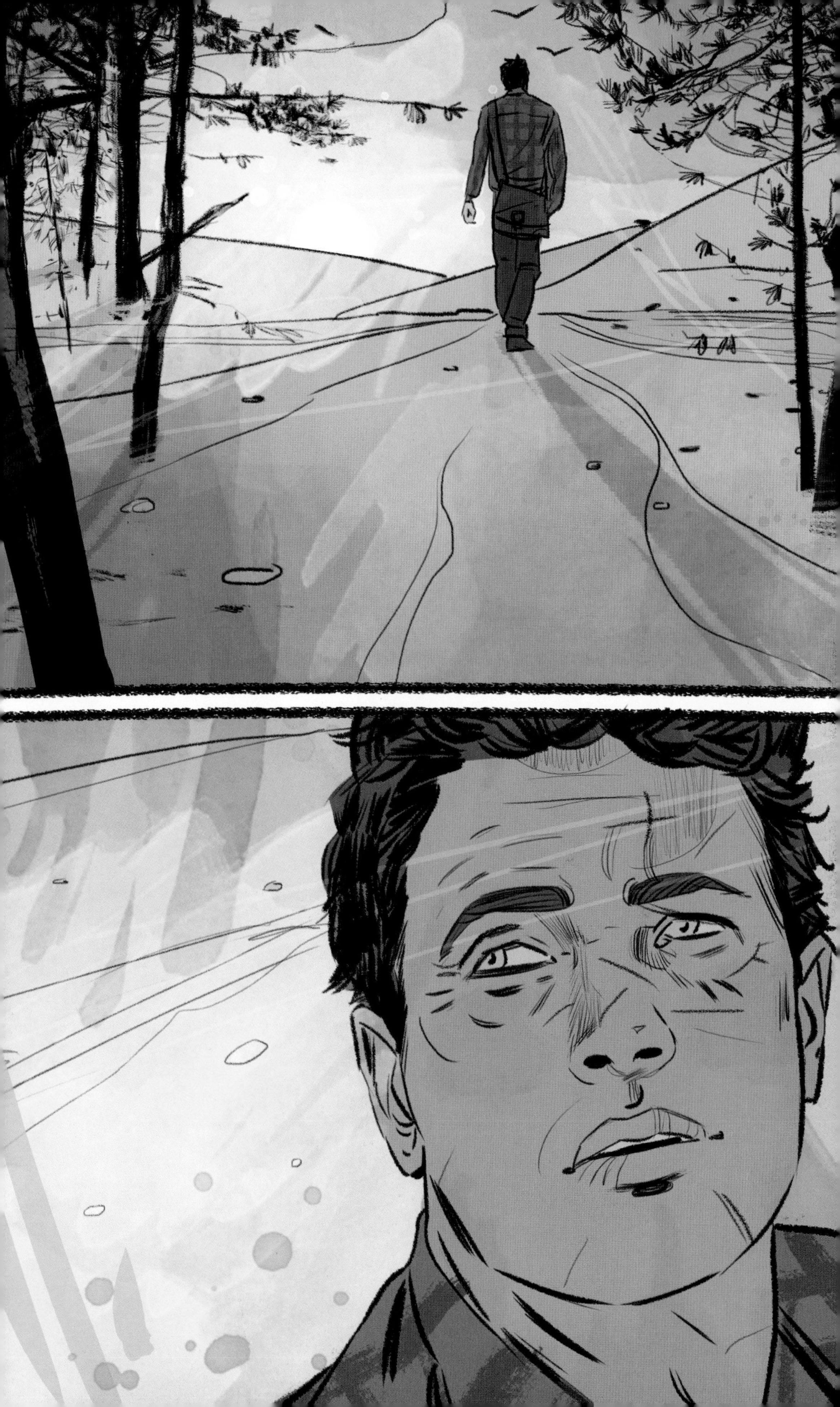

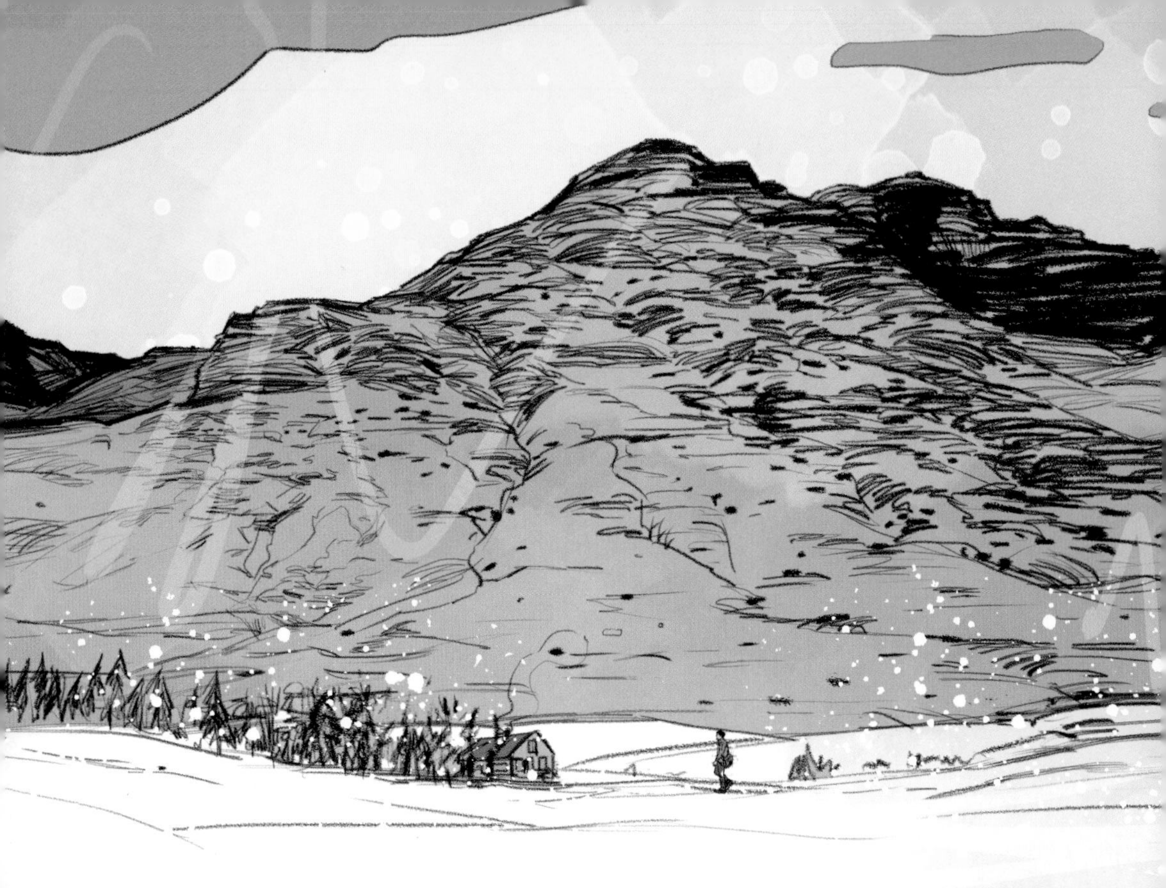

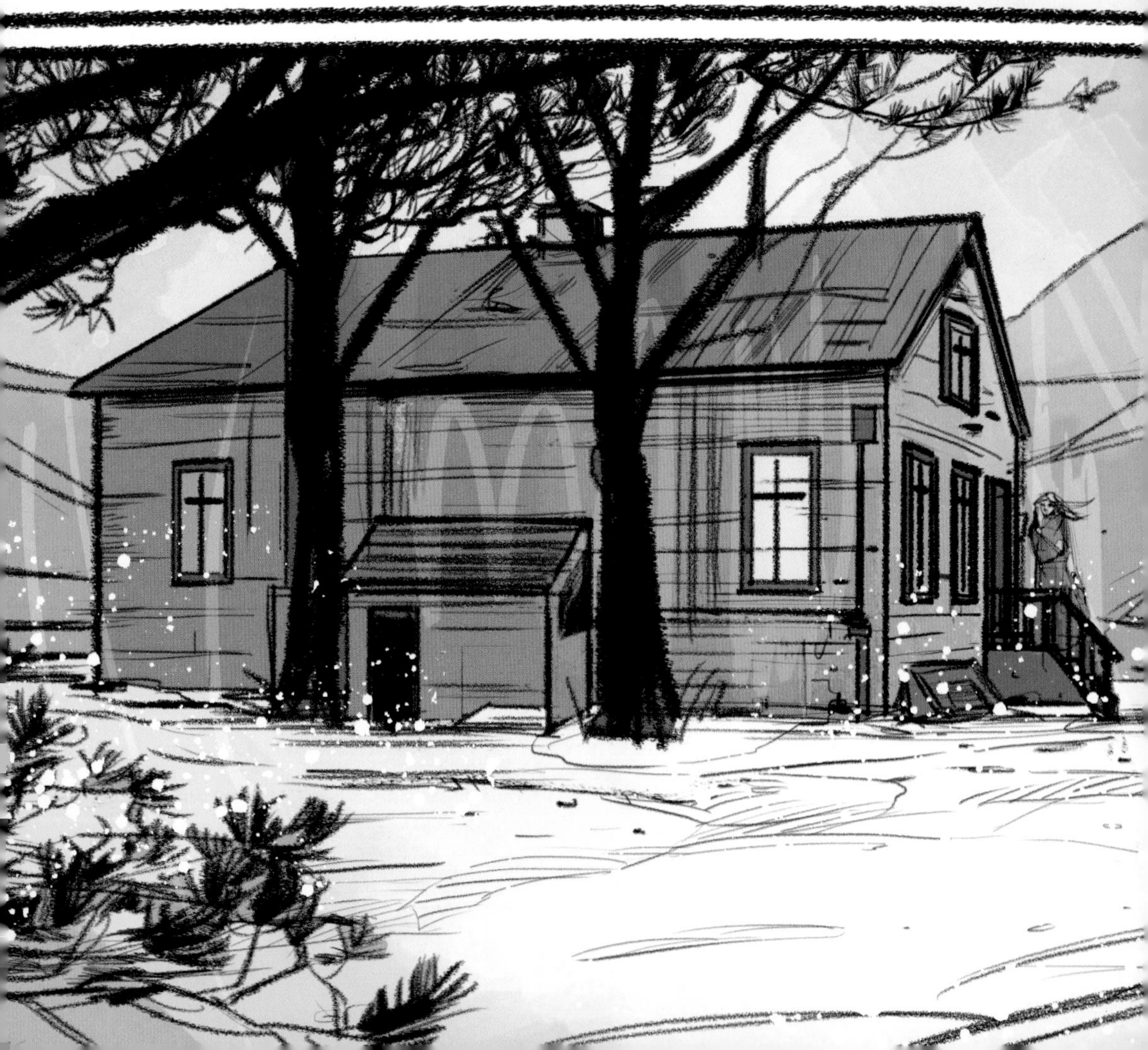

Dedicated to Joan Vollmer and William S. Burroughs Jr.

CREATOR
BIOGRAPHIES

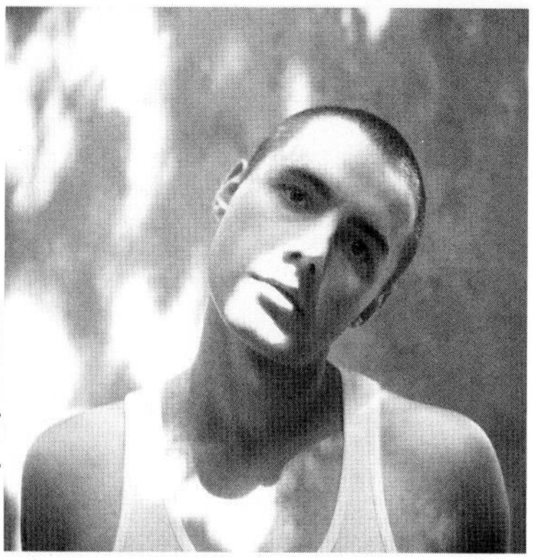

Photo by Clayton Cubitt

Ales Kot invents, writes & runs projects & stories for film, comics, television & more.
He also wrote/still writes: *Change*, *Material*, *Wolf*, *The Surface*, *Wild Children*.
Current body born September 27, 1986 in Opava, Czech Republic.
Resides in Los Angeles. Believes in poetry.
Twitter: @ales_kot

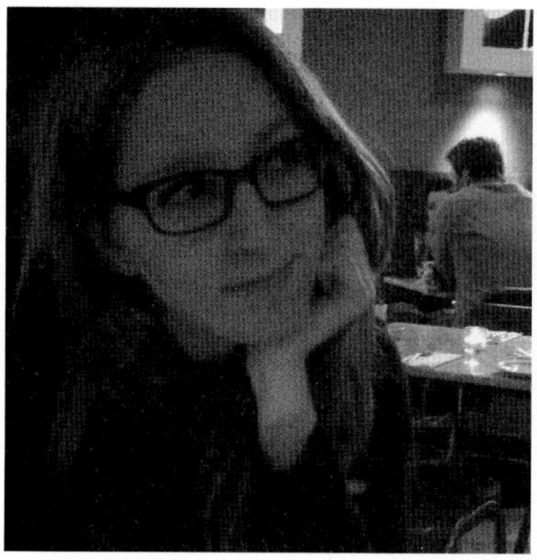

Jordie Bellaire is an Eisner Award winning colorist best known for her work on *Manhattan Projects*, *Pretty Deadly*, *Nowhere Men*, *Autumnlands: Tooth & Claw*, *Howtoons*, and *Three*. She lives in Ireland with her calico, Buffy.

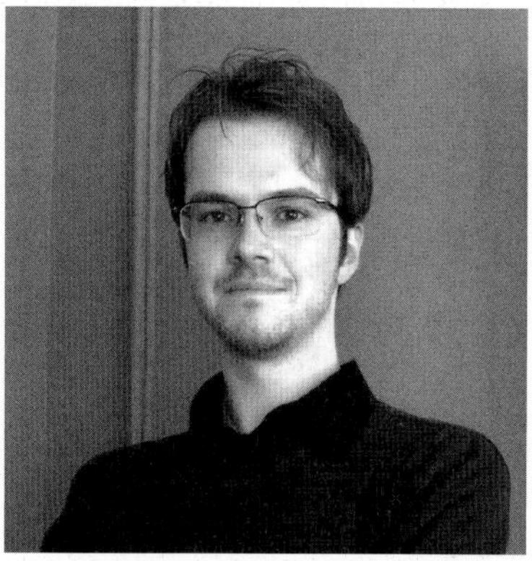

Clayton Cowles graduated from the Joe Kubert School of Cartoon and Graphic Art in 2009, and has been lettering for Image and Marvel Comics ever since. For Image, his credits include *Bitch Planet*, *Pretty Deadly*, *The Wicked + The Divine*, and less than ten others. His Marvel credits include *Fantastic Four*, *Young Avengers*, *Secret Avengers*, *Bucky Barnes: Winter Soldier* and way more than ten others. He lives on Twitter as @claytoncowles, and spends his real life in upstate New York with his cat.

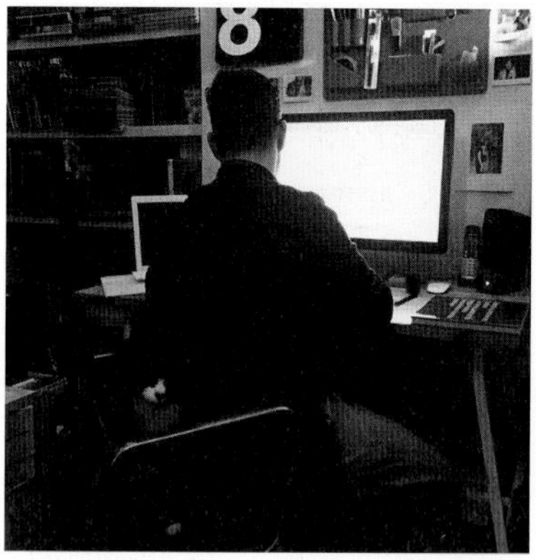

Tom Muller is an Eisner Award nominated Belgian graphic designer who works with technology startups, movie studios, publishers, media producers, ad agencies, and filmmakers.
In comics he's best known for working with Ashley Wood (*Popbot*, *WWR*), Mam Tor Publishing, Ivan Brandon (*24SEVEN*, *VIKING*, *DRIFTER*), Tori Amos (*Comic Book Tattoo*), and Ales Kot (*The Surface*, *Material*, *Wolf*) — as well as his cover art and logo designs for Valiant Entertainment and DC Comics — and his work on Darren Aronofsky's *NOAH* graphic novel. He lives in London with his wife, and two cats that test the limits of what they can get away with on a daily basis. Find him online most hours of the day (and night) by Googling "helloMuller".

Ian Bertram is an artist living and working in New York. He is interested in uncovering the hedonistic and fatalistic nature of man vs. self. He creates mystical, grotesque, and primal drawings of ennui and the strange. He is notoriously terrible at responding to emails.

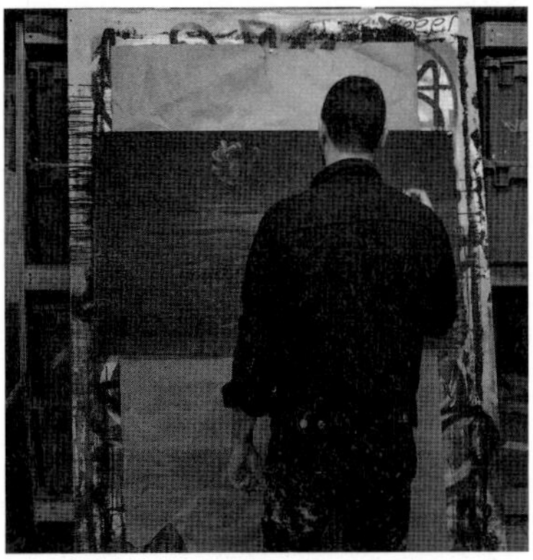

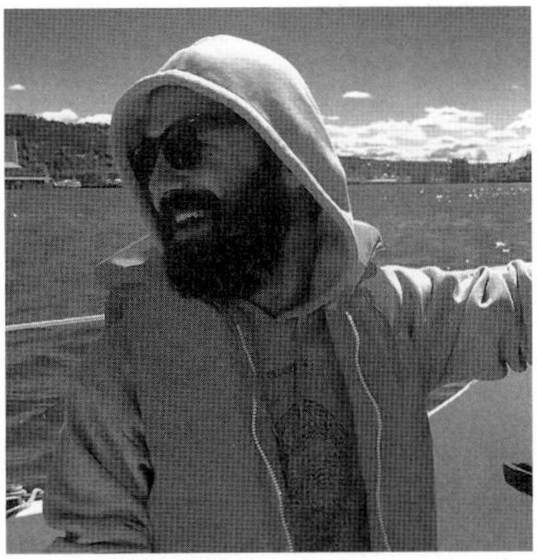

Stathis Tsemberlidis is a Greek artist based in Copenhagen. He is primarily focused on film and comics. He is the co-editor of the sci-fi anthology and collective *Decadence* along with Lando. His work can be found in various comics anthologies and art magazines such us up-coming issues of *Mould Map* and *Volcan* as well as at www.decadencecomics.com

Robert Sammelin is a self taught concept artist, illustrator and graphic designer based in Stockholm, Sweden. Since 2007 he works as a senior concept artist and team leader at DICE, making concept art and graphic design for the award winning *Battlefield* and *Mirror's Edge* series. His spare time comics work includes the mini series *Cimarronin* with Neal Stephenson, the upcoming *Mirror's Edge* comic from Dark Horse and covers for Boom! Studios

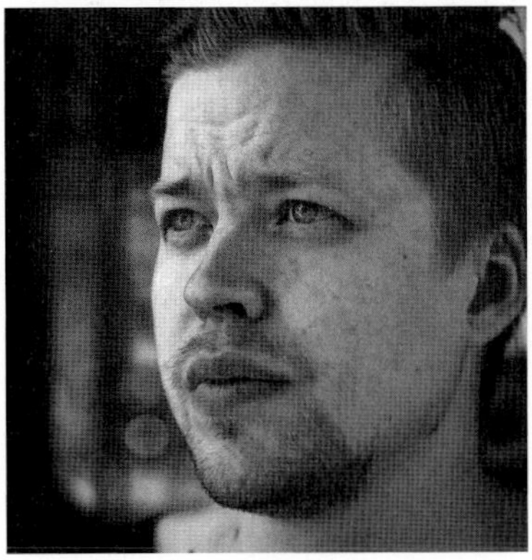

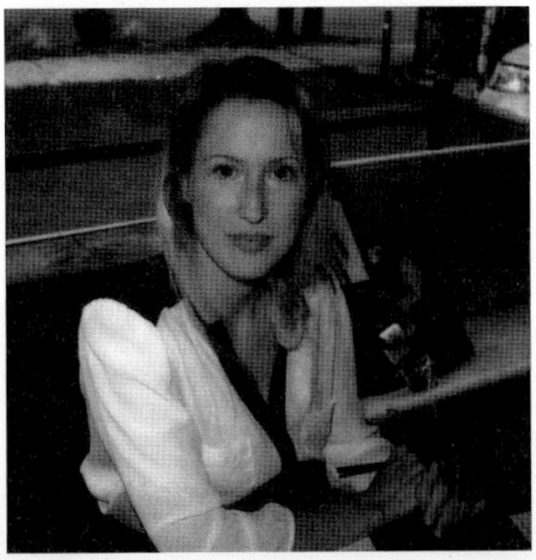

Photo by Scott Southall

Tula Lotay is the pen name of Lisa Wood, a comics artist residing in Yorkshire, England. Previous work includes *Supreme Blue Rose* for Image Comics and *Bodies* for Vertigo Comics. She also runs the renowned *Thought Bubble Festival*, the UK's largest comic art festival which runs annually every November.

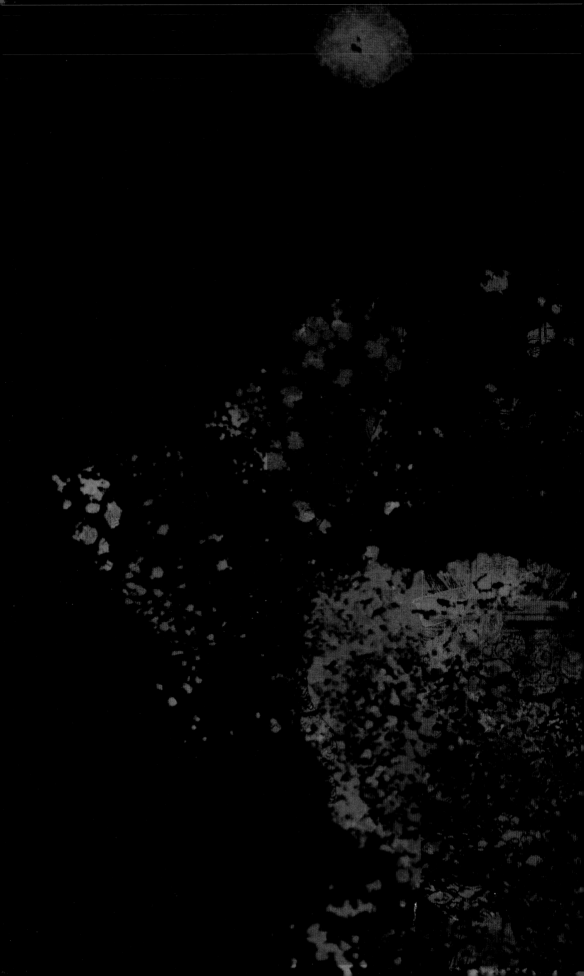

PUBLICATION DESIGN

#11—14

The original ZERO single issue
publication designs by Tom Muller,
with key art from series artists
Ian Bertram, Stathis Tsemberlidis, Robert
Sammelin, Tula Lotay — and variant cover
art from Jeff Lemire .

CHAPTER 15: WHERE FLESH CIRCULATES

Written by **Ales KOT**
Illustrated by **Ian BETRAM**
Colored by **Jordie BELLAIRE**
Lettered by **Clayton COWLES**
Designed by **Tom MULLER**

Cover design, graphics & color by Tom Muller with Ian Bertram (Cover **A**) and Jeff Lemire (Cover **B**)

RATED **M / MATURE**

Media inquiries should be directed to Roger Green & Phil D'Amecourt at WME Entertainment and Ari Lubet at 3 Arts Entertainment.

ZERO #15. March 2015. Published by Image Comics, Inc. Office of publication: 2001 Center Street, Sixth Floor, Berkeley, CA 94704.

IMAGECOMICS.COM

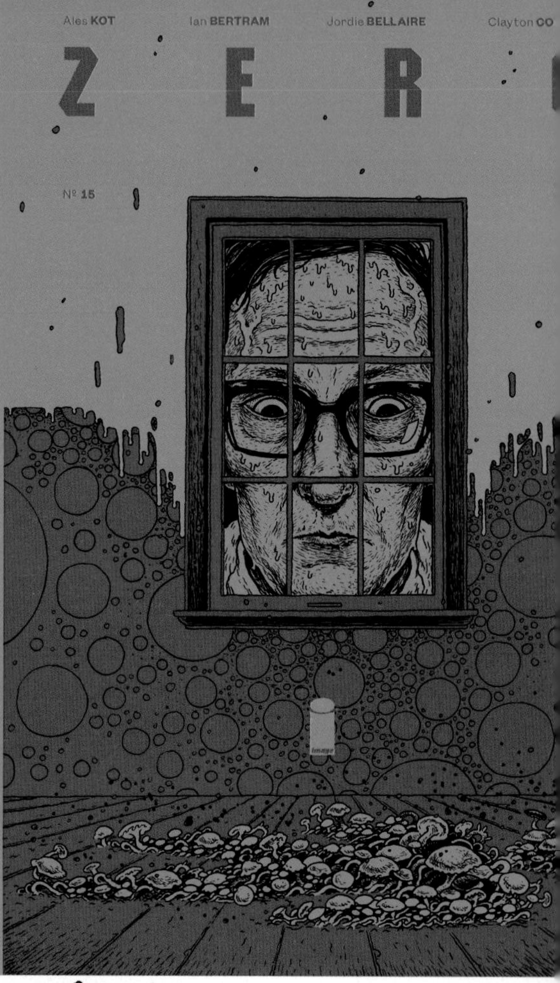

Ales KOT
Ian BERTRAM
Jordie BELLAIRE
Clayton CO
Z E R
Nº 15

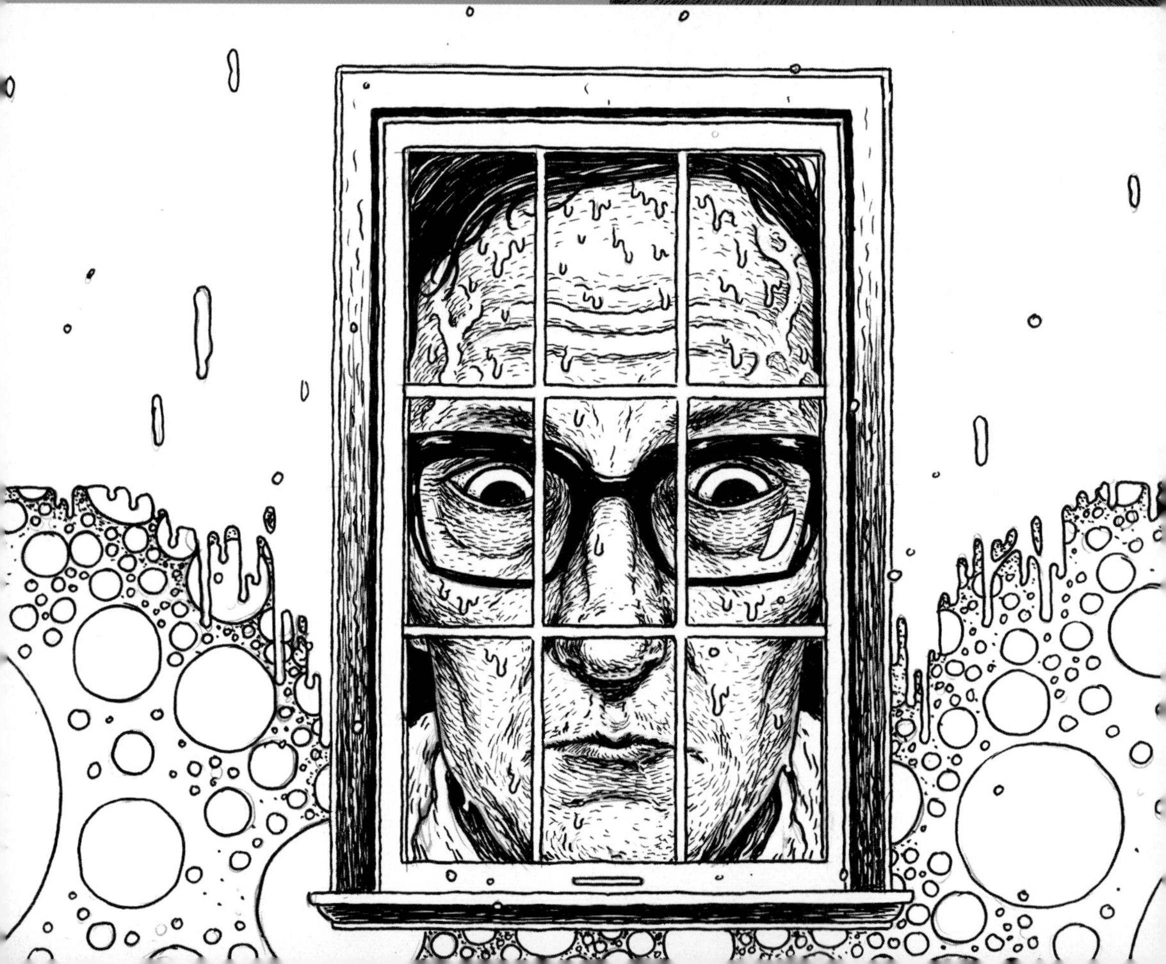

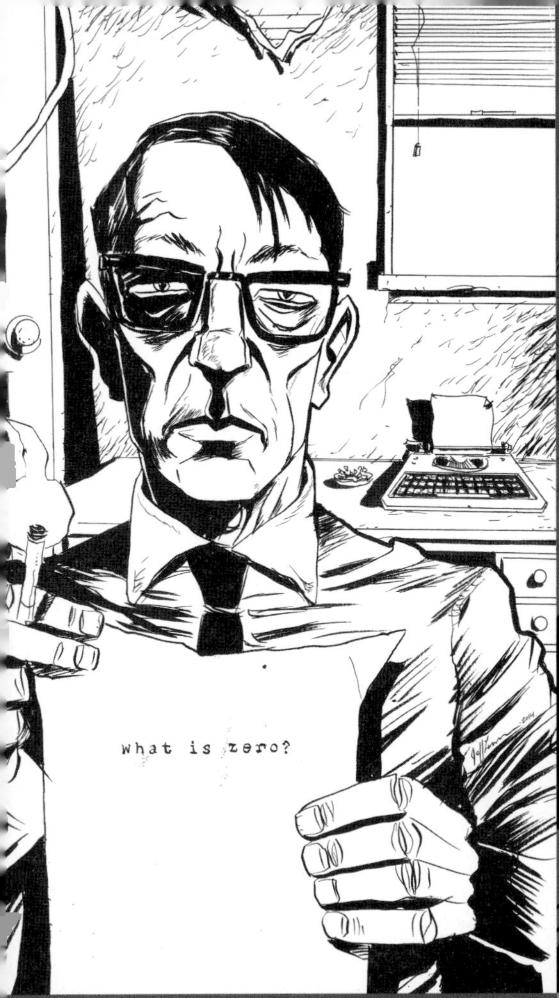
what is zero?

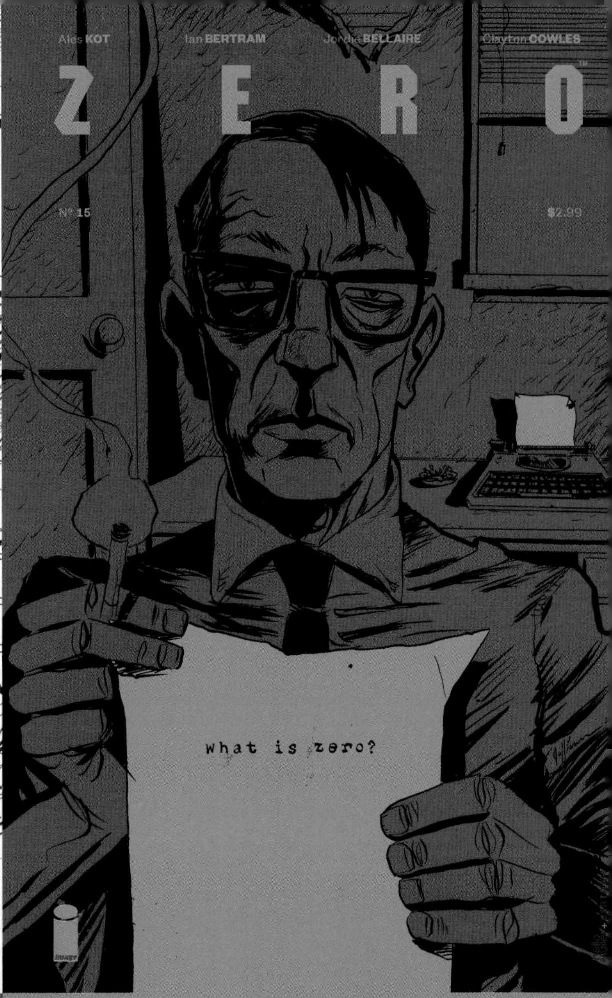
Ales KOT
Ian BERTRAM
Jordie BELLAIRE
Clayton COWLES
ZERO
№ 15
$2.99
what is zero?

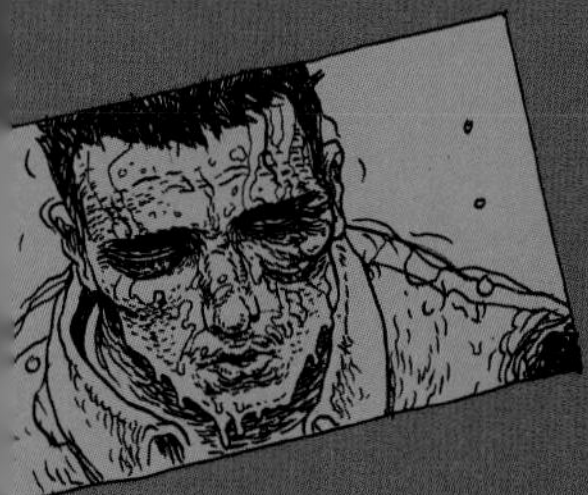

WH O
I
S
E D
W
A R
D
Z E
R
O
?

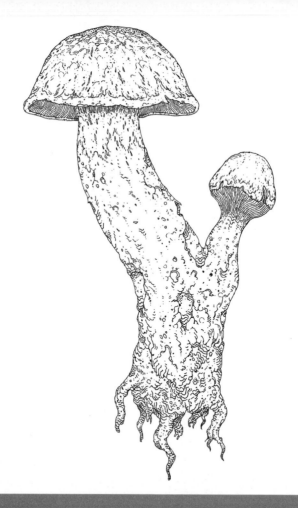

ZERO™

Fig. № 16 — $2.99

Ales **KOT**

Stathis **TSEMBERLIDIS**

Written by Ales **KOT**
Illustrated by Stathis **TSEMBERLIDIS**
Colored by Jordie **BELLAIRE**
Lettered by Clayton **COWLES**
Designed by Tom **MULLER**

Cover design, graphics & color by
Tom Muller with Stathis Tsemberlidis

Media inquiries should be directed to Roger Green &
Phil D'Amecourt at WME Entertainment and Ari Lubet at 3 Arts Entertainment.

Jordie **BELLAIRE**

Clayton **C**

Image Comics, Inc.

Robert Kirkman — Chief Operating Officer
Erik Larsen — Chief Financial Officer
Todd McFarlane — President
Marc Silvestri — Chief Executive Officer
Jim Valentino — Vice-President

Eric Stephenson — Publisher
Ron Richards — Director of Business Development
Jennifer de Guzman — Director of PR & Marketing
Kat Salazar — Director of PR & Marketing
Corey Murphy — Director of Retail Sales
Jeremy Sullivan — Director of Digital Sales
Emilio Bautista — Sales Assistant
Branwyn Bigglestone — Senior Accounts Manager
Emily Miller — Accounts Manager
Jessica Ambriz — Administrative Assistant
Tyler Shainline — Events Coordinator
David Brothers — Content Manager
Jonathan Chan — Production Manager
Drew Gill — Art Director
Meredith Wallace — Print Manager
Monica Garcia — Senior Production Artist
Addison Duke — Production Artist
Emilio Pawson — Production Artist

ZERO #16. April 2016. Published by Image Comics, Inc. Office of
publication: 2001 Center Street, Sixth Floor, Berkeley, CA 94704.
Copyright © 2016 ALES KOT. All rights reserved. ZERO™ (including
all prominent characters featured herein), its logo and all character
likenesses are trademarks of ALES KOT, unless otherwise noted. Image
Comics® and its logos are registered trademarks of Image Comics,
Inc. No part of this publication may be reproduced or transmitted, in
any form or by any means (except for short excerpts for review purposes)
without the express written permission of Image Comics, Inc. All names,
characters, events and locales in this publication are entirely fictional.
Any resemblance to actual persons (living or dead), events or places,
without satiric intent, is coincidental. Printed in the U.S.A. For
information regarding the CPSIA on this printed material call:
203-595-3636 and provide reference # RICH – 676472. For international
rights, contact: foreignlicensing@imagecomics.com

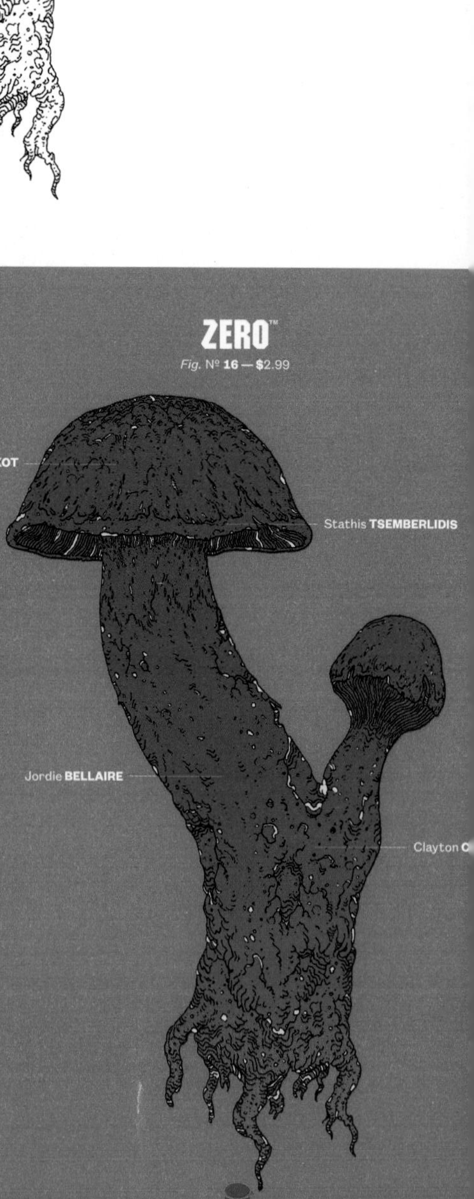

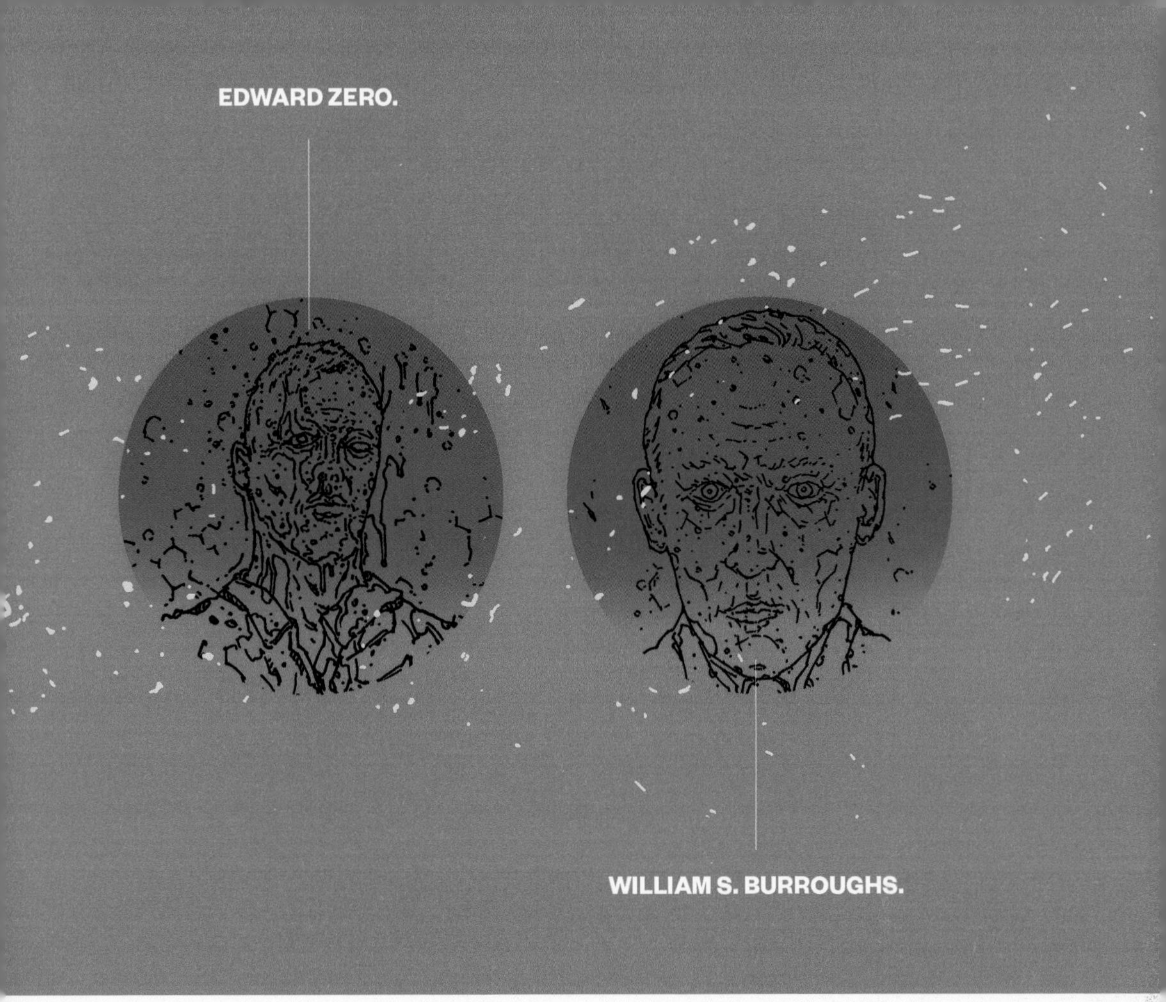
EDWARD ZERO.
WILLIAM S. BURROUGHS.

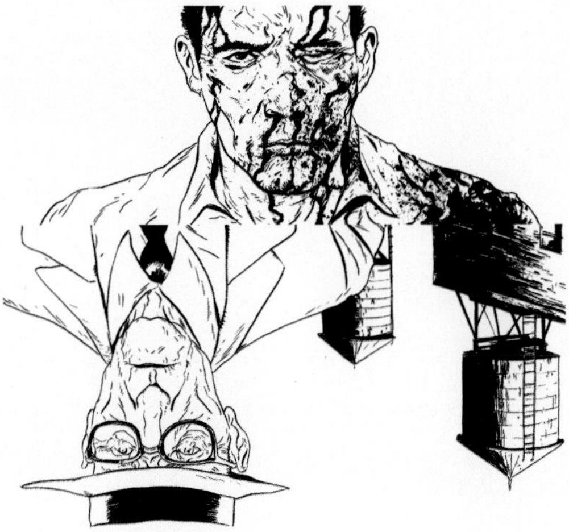

EDWARD ZERO.

Written by Ales KOT
Illustrated by Robert SAMMELIN
Colored by Jordie BELLAIRE
Lettered by Clayton COWLES
Designed by Tom MULLER

Cover design, graphics & color by
Tom Muller with Robert Sammelin

Media inquiries should be directed to Roger Green &
Phil D'Amecourt at WME Entertainment and Ari Lubet at 3 Arts Entertainment.

CHAPTER

P S Y C P S Y C H O M A G I C

CHAPTER 17: 17:

Image Comics, Inc.

Robert Kirkman — Chief Operating Officer
Erik Larsen — Chief Financial Officer
Todd McFarlane — President
Marc Silvestri — Chief Executive Officer
Jim Valentino — Vice-President

Eric Stephenson — Publisher
Kat Salazar — Director of PR & Marketing
Corey Murphy — Director of Sales
Jeremy Sullivan — Director of Digital Sales
Emilio Bautista — Sales Assistant
Emily Miller — Director of Operations
Branwyn Bigglestone — Senior Accounts Manager
Sarah Mello — Accounts Manager
Drew Gill — Art Director
Jonathan Chan — Production Manager
Meredith Wallace — Print Manager
Monica Garcia — Senior Production Artist
Jenna Savage — Production Artist
Addison Duke — Production Artist
Vincent Kukua — Production Artist
Tricia Ramos — Production Artist

ZERO

Ales KOT   Robert SAMMELIN   Jordie BELLAIRE   Clayton CO

Nº 17

RATED M / MATURE

RATED **M** / **MATURE**

Z E R O

PTER 18: **SURRENDER**

Written by **Ales KOT**
Illustrated by **Tula LOTAY**
Colored by **Jordie BELLAIRE**
Lettered by **Clayton COWLES**
Designed by **Tom MULLER**

Cover design, graphics & color:
Cover **A** by Tom Muller with Tula Lotay
Cover **B** by Tom Muller

Comics, Inc.

Chief Operating Officer
Chief Financial Officer
President
Chief Executive Officer
Vice-President

Publisher
Director of PR & Marketing
Director of Retail Sales
Director of Digital Sales
Marketing Production Designer
Sales Assistant
Senior Accounts Manager
Accounts Manager
Administrative Assistant
Content Manager
Production Manager
Art Director
Print Manager
Production Artist
Production Artist
Production Artist
Production Assistant

IMAGECOMICS.COM

ZERO #18. June 2015. Published by Image Comics, Inc. Office of publication: 2001 Center Street, Sixth Floor, Berkeley, CA 94704. Copyright © 2014 ALES KOT.

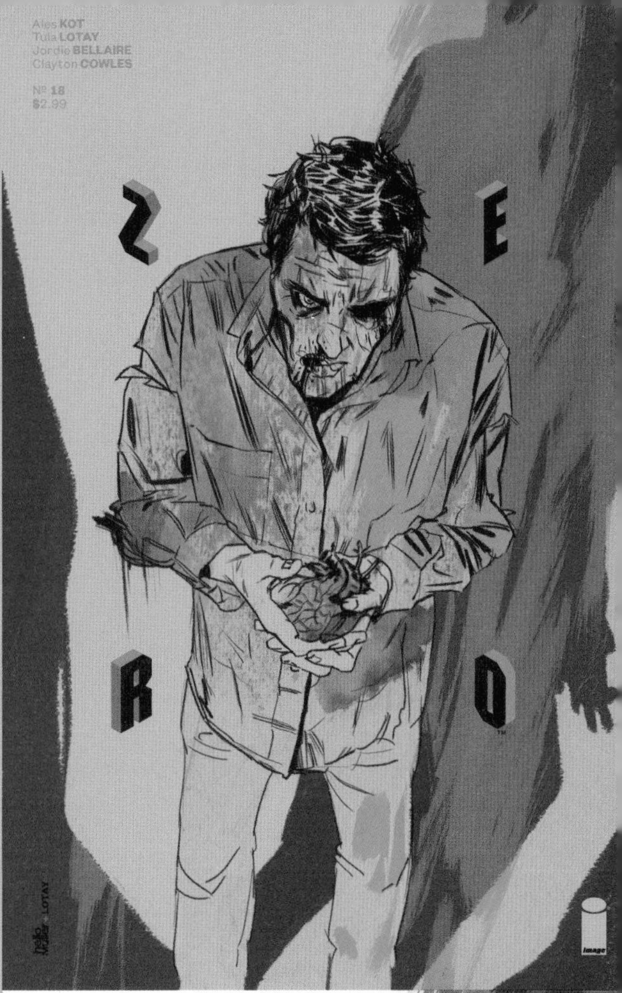

Ales KOT
Tula LOTAY
Jordie BELLAIRE
Clayton COWLES
Nº 18
$2.99
Z E R O

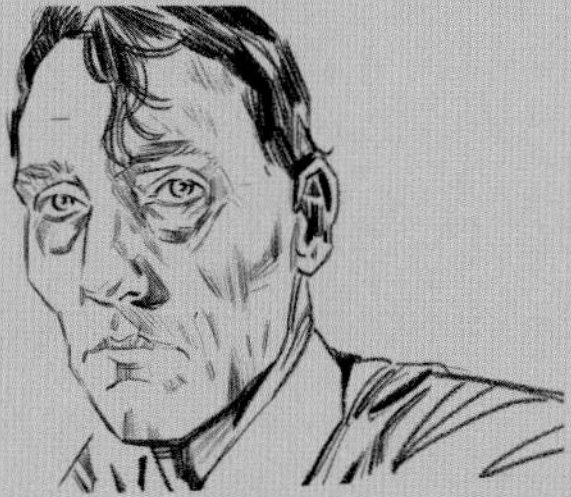

WILLIAM S. BURROUGHS.

U R R E N D E R

EDWARD ZERO.

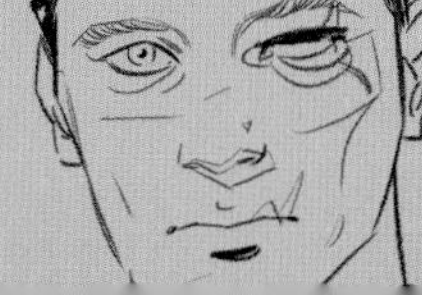

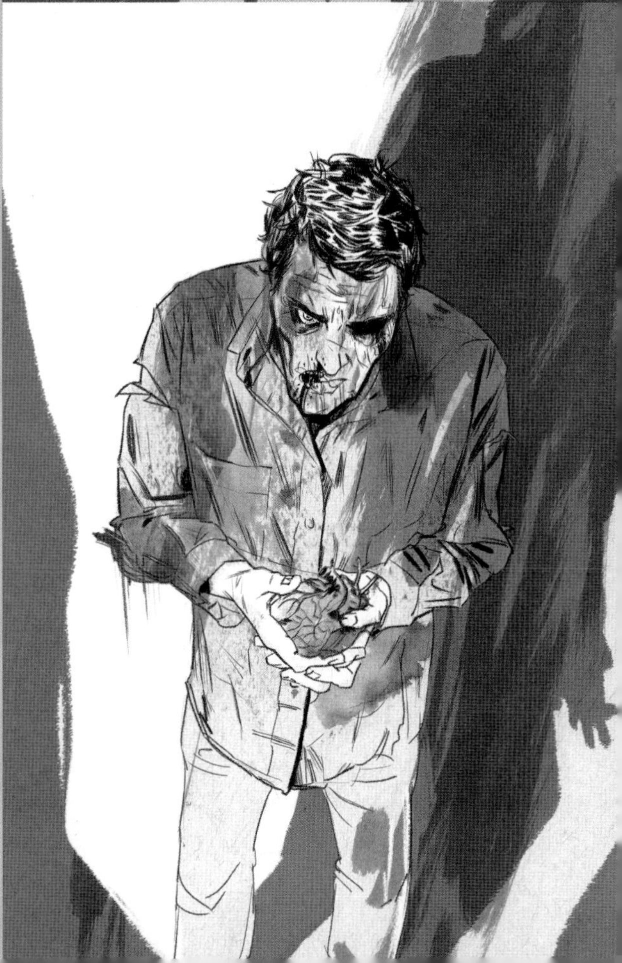

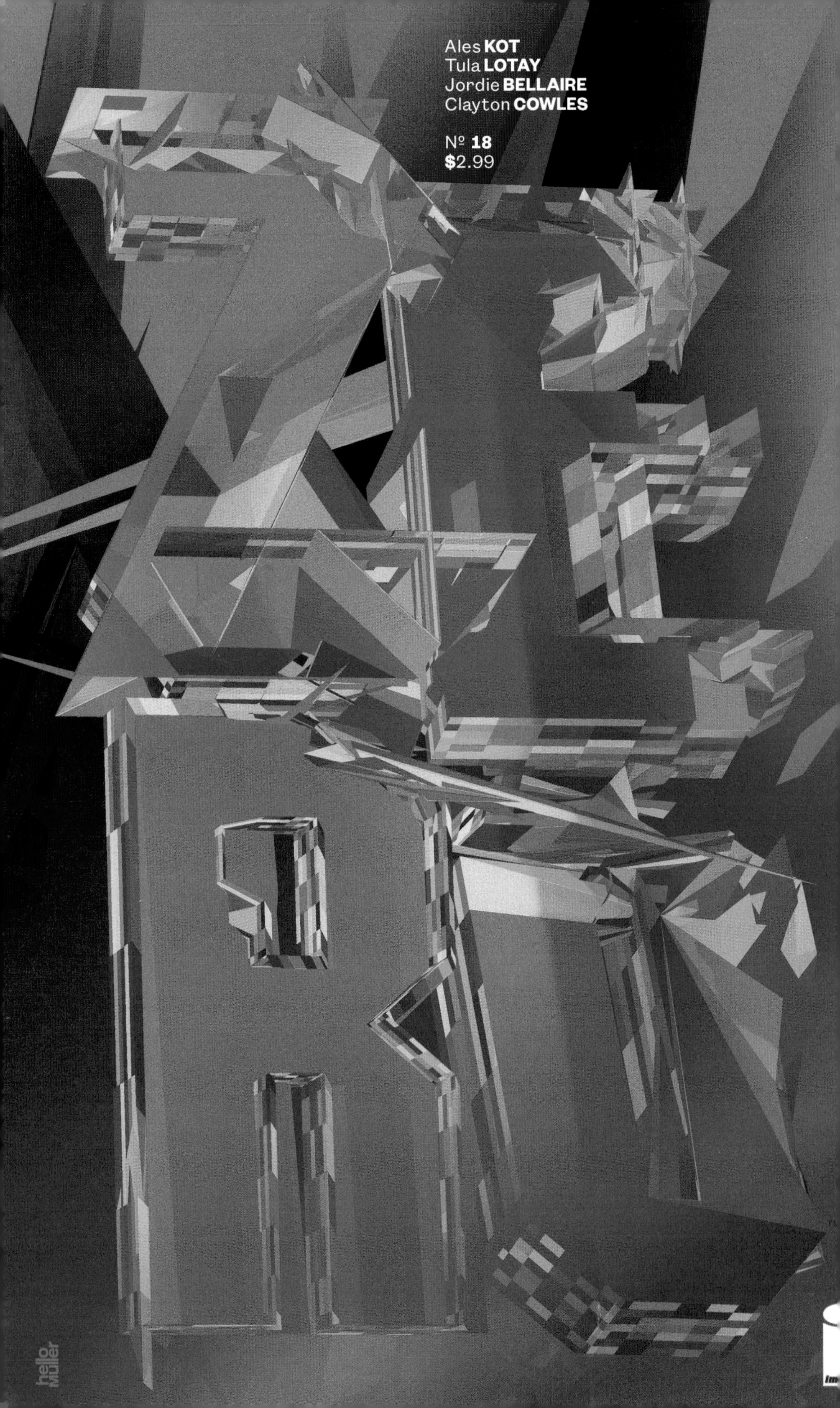

Ales KOT
Tula LOTAY
Jordie BELLAIRE
Clayton COWLES
№ 18
$2.99
hello Müller

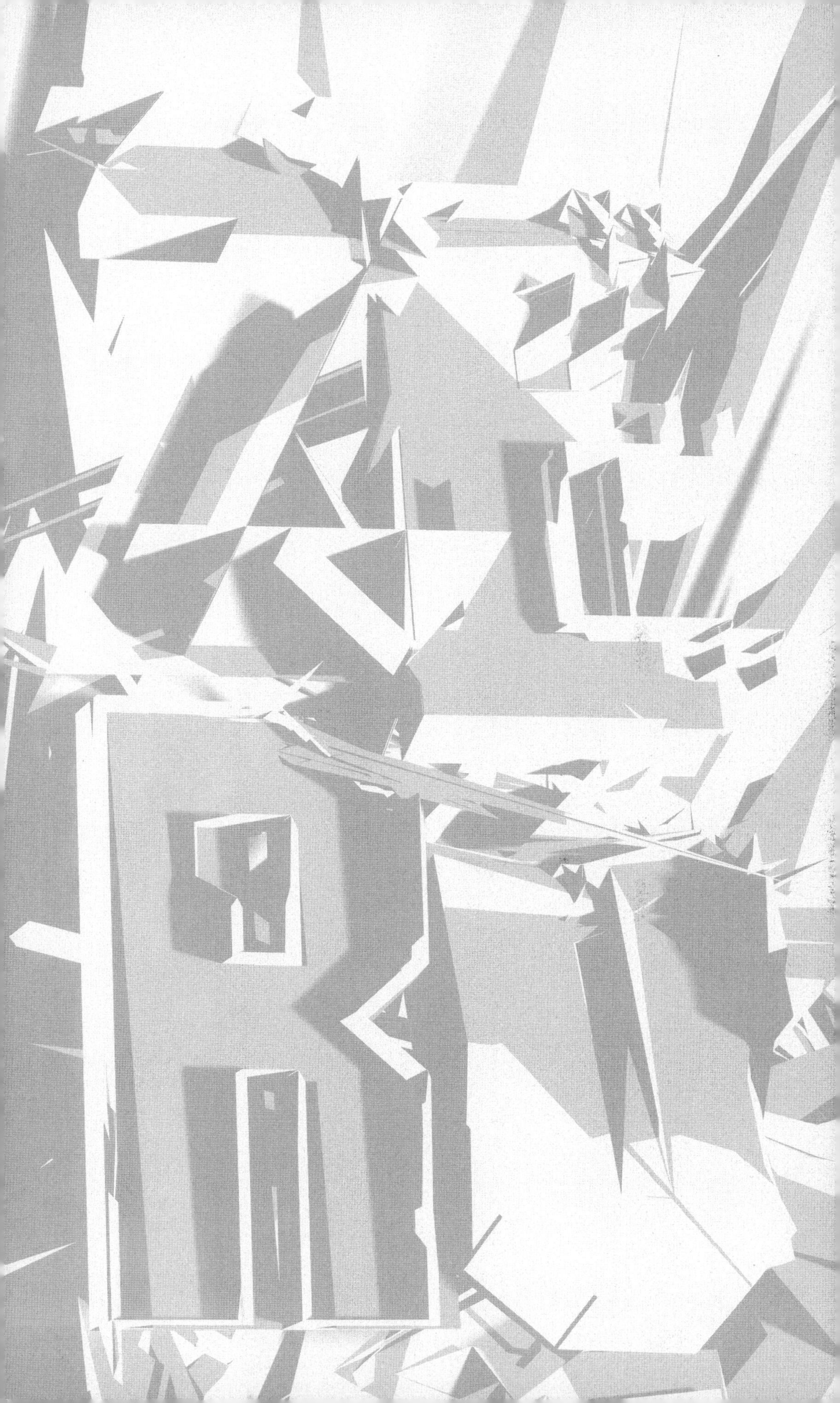

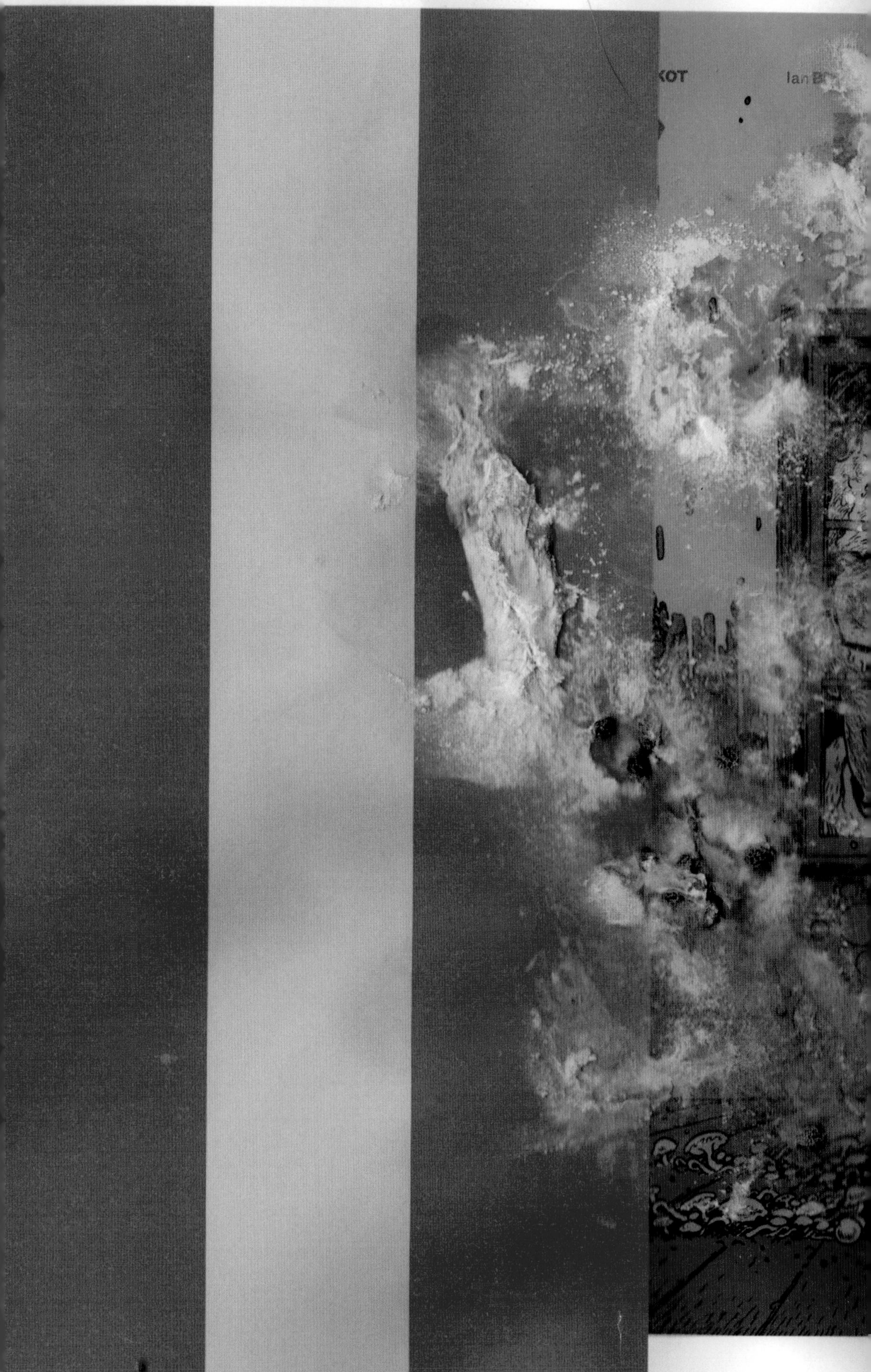
KOT
Ian B

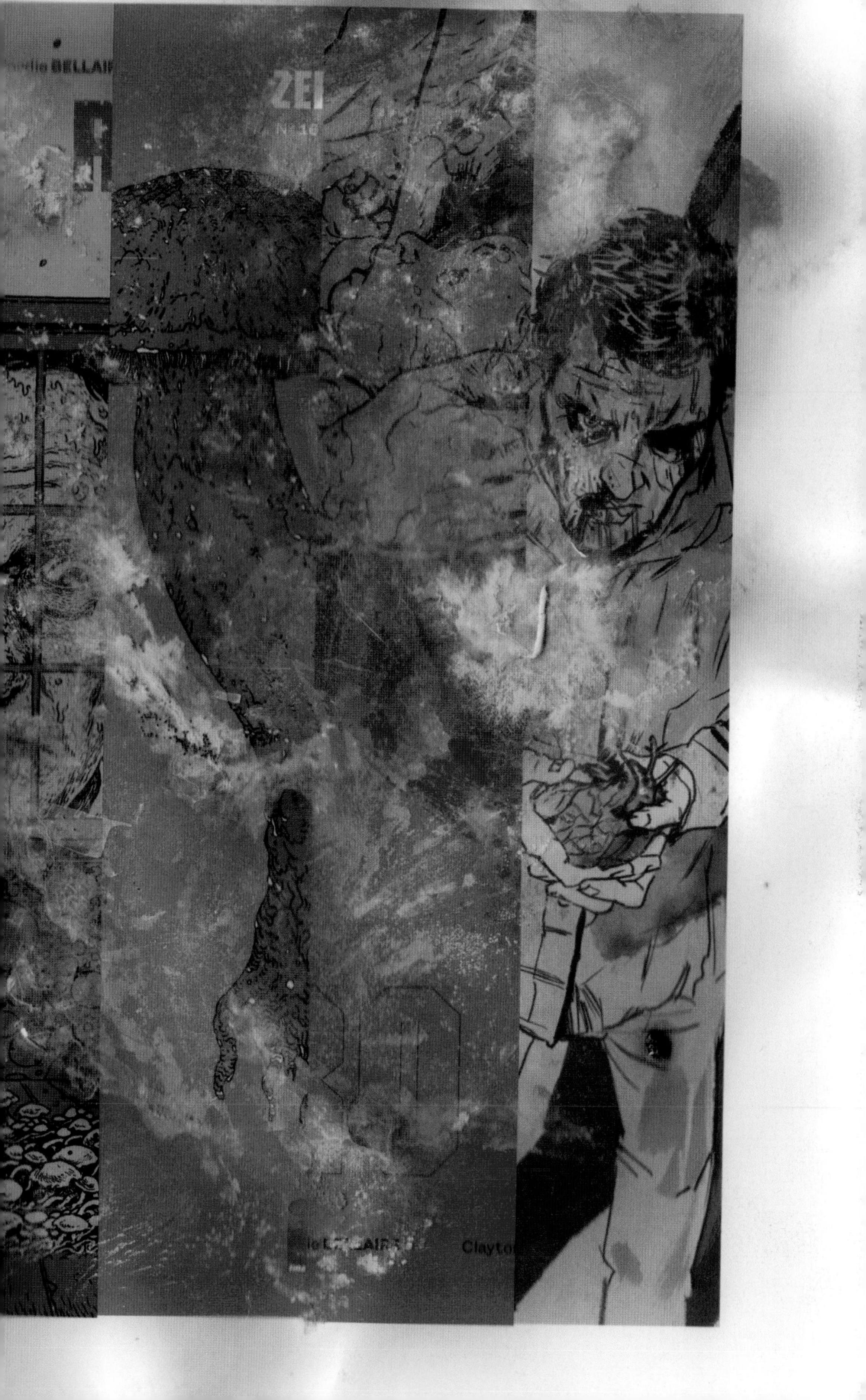

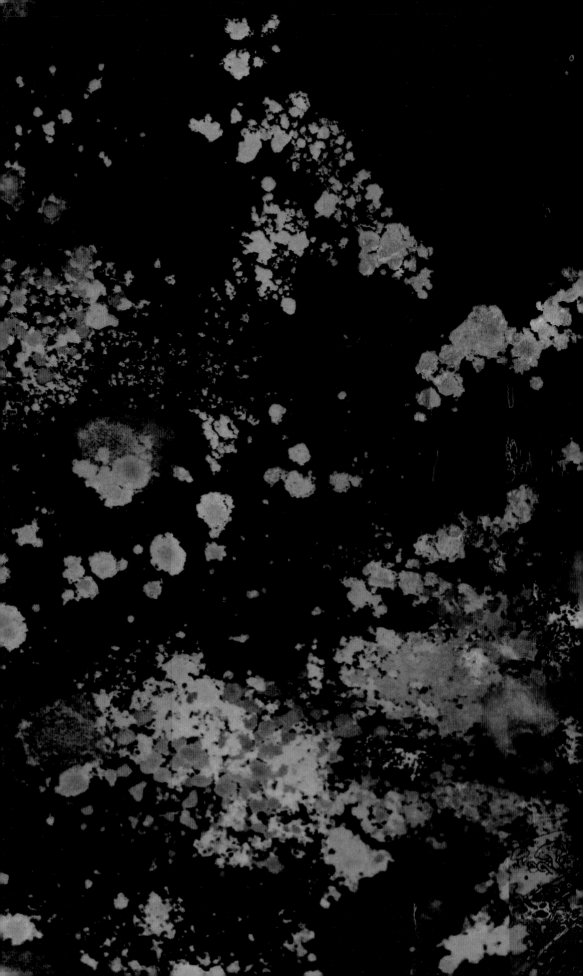

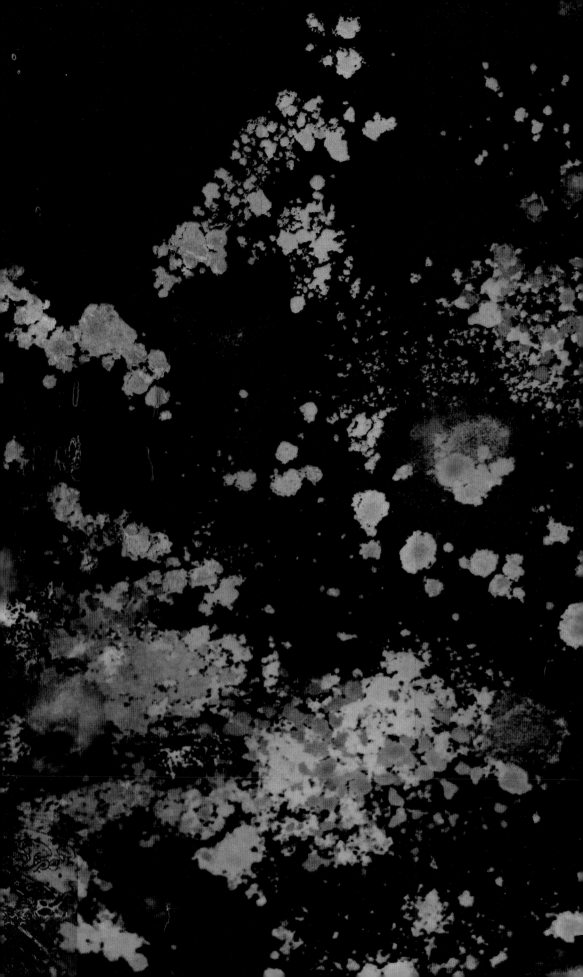

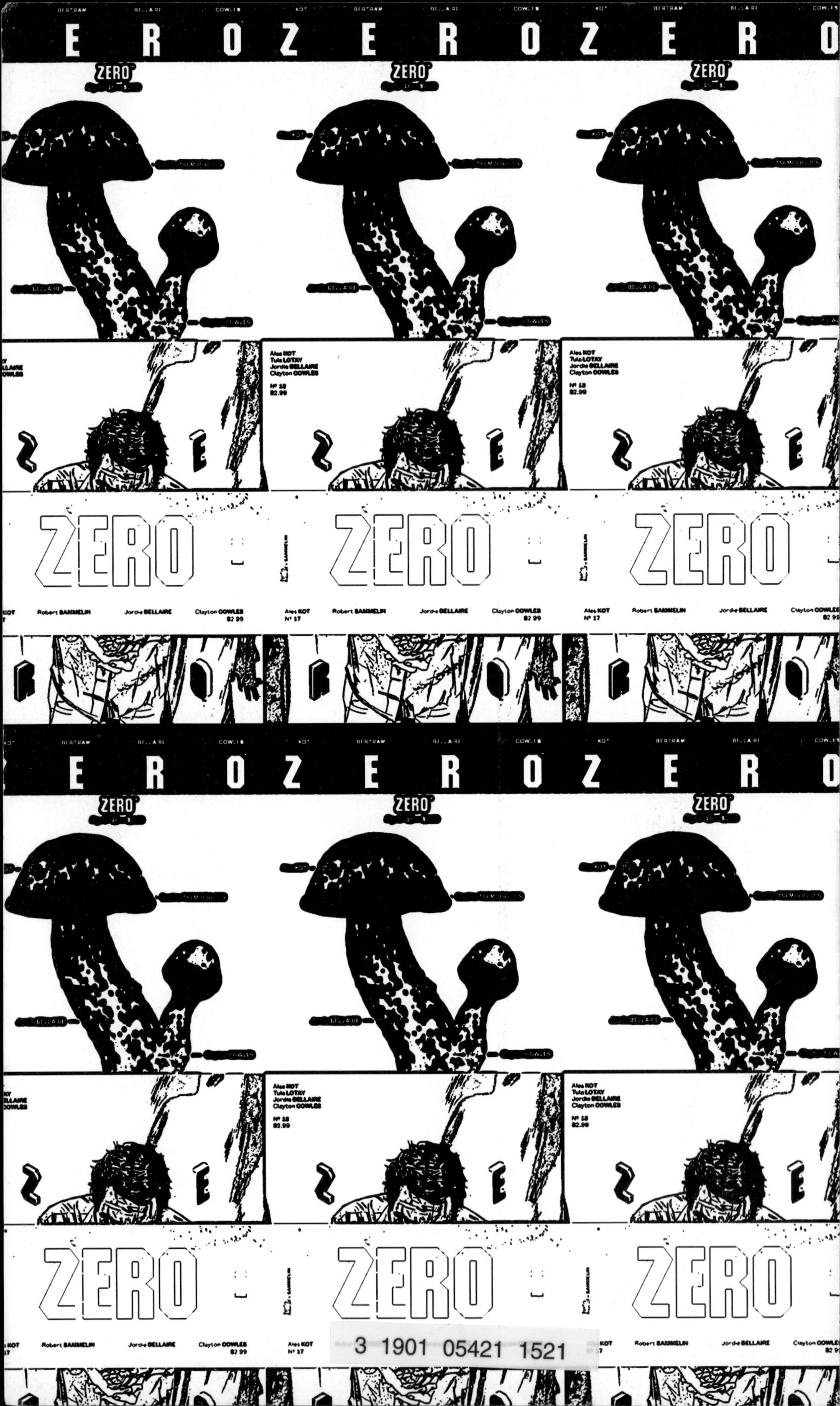
ZERO
Ales KOT
Tula LOTAY
Jordie BELLAIRE
Clayton COWLES
Nº 18
$2.99
ZERO
Ales KOT
Nº 17
Robert SAMMELIN
Jordie BELLAIRE
Clayton COWLES
$2.99